Praise for *Napole* T0281960

"Meticulous research, rich characterization, and a powerful narrative make this gripping saga of Napoleon's foray into Egypt a joy to read. Michelle Cameron is a gifted storyteller and stylist, expertly crafting a novel that allows the reader to disappear into a fully-imagined past, firmly grounded in history but never didactic. An absolute triumph!"

—Tasha Alexander, *New York Times* best-selling author of the Lady Emily mysteries, including *Secrets of the Nile*

"*Napoleon's Mirage* picks up the thread of Cameron's epic tale of the tumult, romance and volatility of the Napoleonic era. She sweeps readers from the quays of Toulon to the shimmering heat of the Egyptian desert, with a transportive narrative of assiduous research and textured, vibrant language. To be immersed in the work of Michelle Cameron is to be treated to storytelling by a skilled and masterful hand of historical fiction."

—Allison Pataki, *New York Times* bestselling author of *The Queen's Fortune* and *The Magnificent Lives of Marjorie Post*

"An epic tour de force, *Napoleon's Mirage* tells a cracking good tale of love, culture, and war during Napoleon's quixotic Egyptian Expedition of 1799. Cameron's genius lies in her expert guidance through the era's Middle Eastern morass of Jewish, Christian, and Muslim interests, laying raw the humanity and inhumanity of each faction. She deftly reveals young General Napoleon in all his tragic complexity, foreshadowing his future glory and failure. Best of all, the heart of *Napoleon's Mirage* is a charming love story (begun in *Beyond the Ghetto Gates*) that twists its way to a surprising end. Kudos for this fascinating, magnificently researched, gripping book!"

—Margaret Rodenberg, author of the award-winning *Finding Napoleon*, Secretary, Napoleonic Historical Society

"In a world…" (as epic movie trailers begin) where a cynical conqueror driven by hubris seeks to plant the French flag in the cradle of three major religions, comes Michelle Cameron's powerful, sweeping saga with a cast of thousands helmed by memorable heroes. *Napoleon's Mirage* is as timely as it is timeless; and the stakes couldn't be higher, as interfaith rivalries, deep-seated prejudices, and ties of blood continually test the hope of freedom, friendship, and the bonds of true love.

—Juliet Grey, author of the acclaimed Marie Antoinette trilogy

"Michelle Cameron's research and deep understanding of history allow her to write completely believable fiction. *Napoleon's Mirage* deals with then-General Napoleon Bonaparte's campaign in Egypt and the Holy Land. This is a Napoleonic campaign that is given less attention than it deserves, and Cameron brings it to fascinating life."

—J. David Markham, President, International Napoleonic Society, Knight, Order of the French Academic Palms

NAPOLEON'S MIRAGE

NAPOLEON'S MIRAGE

A NOVEL

MICHELLE CAMERON

SHE WRITES PRESS

Published 2024
Printed in the United States of America
Print ISBN: 978-1-64742-620-0
E-ISBN: 978-1-64742-621-7
Library of Congress Control Number: 2024913131

For information, address:
She Writes Press
1569 Solano Ave #546
Berkeley, CA 94707

Interior Design by Kiran Spees

She Writes Press is a division of SparkPoint Studio, LLC.

For my two sons—
who never had to serve in any army.

PART ONE

MAY—AUGUST 1798

1

MAY 9, 1798
TOULON, FRANCE

Excitement ballooned inside Daniel as he crossed the quay at Toulon. He paused, admiring the scene. A glorious day, the cloudless blue sky's reflection rippled in the Mediterranean's turquoise depths. Hundreds of ships of the line—frigates, sloops and more modest vessels—bobbed on the gentle swell of the waves, clustered together as far as the eye could see. Towering above them all, the French warship *L'Orient* dominated, its sheer scale a threat to any enemy fleet. A menacing quantity of naval cannons were mounted on the flagship's three decks.

Leaving the pier, Daniel twisted and turned through the mass of army tents camped on the beach, anxious to reach his artillery company and start preparing for tomorrow's inspection. The salty sea breeze helped mask the smells of smoke rising from cooking fires, horse manure, and the various odors of thousands of soldiers packed tightly together. Under the strong sun, men worked in undershirts or stood bare chested, torsos dotted with sweat, arms dripping with it, uniform jackets dropped in sandy heaps beside them. The sound of waves dashing against the beachfront and harbor rocks was nearly drowned out by a cacophony of orders, complaints, trumpet blasts, even men's voices rising in song as they used beach sand to polish swords and muskets.

As Daniel found his own company, he was pleased to find that the company sergeant, Sebastian Sarfati, had started the men scrubbing out the cannons.

"Did you hear when inspection is to be—sir?" Sebastian asked.

His hesitation in adding the word "sir" didn't go unnoticed, but Daniel decided to ignore it. Sebastian, the oldest and most experienced man in his company, had taught him everything when Daniel was an eager seventeen-year-old private. Like many in the company, the older man had not taken well to Daniel's promotion at the tender age of twenty-one, especially since it was earned not on the battlefield but in a printshop miles away from the action. Daniel had been dismissed from military printer's duty soon after being stationed in Paris, returning to the artillery a newly minted lieutenant unsure of his ability to command, but doing his best to hide his trepidation from his men.

"Tomorrow at dawn," he replied. "Will we be ready?"

"Should be," Pierre, a newly promoted sergeant, chimed in.

Daniel narrowed his eyes and glared at the man for a long, silent moment. Too often, his men refused to accord him the dignity of his rank. If he kept letting these slights go unremarked, how would they ever learn to respect him?

Sebastian, noticing his level stare, elbowed Pierre.

"Sir," Pierre added reluctantly.

"Do we know where we're headed yet? Sir?" Sebastian asked.

Daniel shook his head. "Best kept secret in the army."

Sebastian laughed. "In any army, at any time." He paused, thinking. "If it weren't that Bonaparte is in command . . ."

Daniel knew what he meant. Somehow, through some magical sleight of hand, General Bonaparte had gathered a huge force on the shores of Toulon while keeping their ultimate destination a profound mystery. Rumors circulated through camp, of course. Studying maps, the soldiers conjectured possible destinations from this vantage point of southern France. Taking Gibraltar from the British was one possibility, as was traveling down the coast to Spain or Portugal. Some even ventured to suggest that they were headed toward the impregnable capital of the Ottoman Empire, France's so-called ally. Taking Constantinople, last vanquished by the Muslim sultan Mehmet II in the 1400s, would add luster to Napoleon's rising stature as an invincible conqueror. But whenever that notion was bruited abroad, naysayers shook their heads. After all, what would be the purpose in subjugating one of the young republic's few friends, except to salve the general's seemingly relentless ambition?

And yet, despite the mystery, there wasn't a murmur of protest from the men, particularly not from the veterans of Bonaparte's victorious Army of Italy. Still, Daniel couldn't help but wonder: where could such a huge fleet, with so many thousands of soldiers, be heading?

While Bonaparte reviewed his troops the next morning, Daniel stood in formation before his men, having stayed up all night to ensure that every boot and belt buckle shone, every cannon was scoured clean. The winds had picked up overnight, and it looked like a storm was heading their way.

Watching their commanding officer stand on a platform above the ranks, the military band playing, tricolored banners hanging from the surrounding buildings flapping in the steady breeze, Daniel's chest swelled with pride. He had fought alongside the general through much of Italy, had seen him rampage from city to city, Napoleon's victories clustering like so many laurels on a conqueror's crown. At this moment, did Daniel in fact care that he had no idea where Napoleon intended to lead them? No, he told himself. He was merely one of thousands of satellites circling the general, their ever-constant star. Where Bonaparte led, his men would willingly, eagerly, follow.

Of course, Daniel couldn't help but have one regret—no matter where they were headed, it would not be back to Italy, to the harbor town of Ancona where Mirelle lived. He felt a pang, thinking of her. He remained unsure of how she felt about him, uncertain that she returned his love. He hadn't had the nerve to declare himself before leaving Italy. There was affection in the letters they exchanged, but was that merely cousinly fondness? He had been careful to mirror her tone and not say too much of his own devotion, afraid of scaring her off. He was equally afraid she might fall for another, but after all, what could he do? It was a soldier's fate, he reminded himself, to leave loved ones behind, perhaps never to meet again. But it was not easy.

Behind Napoleon were his staff officers and family, including his wife, Josephine. She had arrived just in time to bid the general bon voyage. Daniel recalled meeting her, briefly, back in Milan just over a year ago. She had been gracious to him, shielding him from the general's wrath. Now, when he would expect her to look travel-worn after days on the road from Paris—traversing nearly the whole of France—she stood straight and tall in a spotless pelisse of apricot, one hand clutching her high-crowned feathered bonnet to keep it from blowing away.

Daniel listened intently as Napoleon addressed them, his words rising above the steady wind.

"Two years ago I took command of you. At that time, you were on the Ligurian coast, in the gravest want, lacking everything, even having sold your watches to provide for your needs. I promised to end your privations. I led you into Italy. There, all was given to you in abundance. Did I not keep my word?"

Without hesitation, the troops responded, a single shout of "*Oui!*"

Daniel, lending his voice to the chorus, felt the roar reverberate, elemental in its power, like the waves crashing in the sea before them.

The general waited for the shouting to die down. Then he added, "Well, let me tell you this: you have not done enough yet for the motherland nor the motherland for you. I shall lead you now into a country where your deeds will surpass those that have already astonished your admirers, and you will render to the Republic such services as she has a right to expect from an invincible army. I promise every soldier that, upon his return to France, he shall have enough to buy himself *six arpents de terre*."

It was a dizzying thought. To be a landowner, to buy six acres of land as a hero of France, was so far-fetched an ambition for most soldiers that the phrase "*six arpets de terre*" buzzed through the ranks. Daniel was too startled by the possibility of such riches—to have such a future to offer Mirelle—to reprimand his men. But Napoleon did not seem to mind the momentary break in discipline. He grinned, watching the men's excitement mount, then dismissed them and strode off, his staff and wife at his heels.

The following afternoon, the soldiers were ordered onto their assigned ships. The seas had turned choppy, dark clouds gathering above, the wind picking up force. The men in Daniel's company struggled to shift the heavy cannon up the pitching gangplank into the frigate *le Franklin*, using thick ropes along with the weapon's clumsy wheels to haul it up. The creak of the slippery ramp as it listed from side to side deafened any attempt at conversation. A strand of rope frayed as it rubbed against the weight of a cannon. The rope split. The big gun tipped drunkenly over the ramp's edge. Daniel rushed forward. "Watch out!" A wave, more violent than others, unbalanced both soldiers and cannon.

The cannon hurtled into the sea—*splash!*—sending up a spray of salt water that drenched them all as it sank into the depths.

"How the hell are we going to pull that out?" Sebastian muttered, shaking seawater off him like a dog. He turned to Daniel and asked harshly, "Lieutenant? What are your orders?"

Daniel grimaced. "Leave it," he said, straightening his shoulders and pushing out his chest to exude authority. "If we have time, we'll fish it out later. But watch that none of the others go over."

Sebastian pursed his lips. "We can be court martialed if they learn we lost the cannon." A weighty pause, then he pushed through obvious reluctance to add, "Sir."

A pang of apprehension struck Daniel. He clamped it down. He'd lose the men's scant respect if he hesitated. "With this many men and cannons to account for? I doubt it." He was glad to see relief on the men's faces as they realized he wouldn't make them dive to retrieve the cannon.

Their uniforms soaked through, shivering in the keening wind, the men continued heaving cannons up the gangplank and stowing them below decks. Next they loaded the ammunition carts. Darkness fell before they finished, and they made the last few trips by the light of guttering torches.

Daniel dismissed them to gather their belongings and return to their new quarters aboard ship. An hour later, they marched up the ramp. Daniel, counting his men, was startled to realize that there was one more than there should be.

Halting the men, Daniel looked up and down the line. The flickering torchlight made it difficult to see clearly, but an unfamiliar, slight figure in a too-large uniform was clearly not supposed to be there. Daniel peered at the hunched body. A gust of wind rustled the soldier's cap and a curl escaped.

"Pick up your face," Daniel barked.

The head rose. A woman. Before Daniel could speak, Pierre

rushed up. "Your orderly," he gasped. "As an officer, you're entitled to a servant, you know . . . ."

Daniel remembered congratulating Pierre, who had been married during their recent leave in Paris. This must be his new wife. Once again Daniel faced a decision that could make or break him with the men. He'd heard that sailors considered having women aboard to be bad luck.

"Name?" he demanded.

"Louis Martine," she said, voice pitched in a lower register.

"My younger brother," Pierre hastened to explain. "A good boy."

"Very well." Daniel pointed at his kit bag. "Take that to my quarters, Louise, er, Louis."

Almost as one, the assembled soldiers grinned. Turning his back to face the inky black waves, Daniel let the rest tromp onboard. Staring into the depths where the lost cannon lay, he wondered: was he right to leave the cannon underwater? Right to allow Pierre's wife to stow away on ship?

What other decisions would he have to make as they sailed to their unknown destination?

2

MAY 16
ANCONA, ITALY

Mirelle was in the storeroom checking the stock of parchment and vellum when her foreman, Sabato Narduci, stuck his head around the door.

"A message for you," he said, handing her a folded piece of paper.

She nodded, thanking him, and opened it. The unfamiliar handwriting slanted upward, looking as though it were written in haste.

> *Cousin Mirelle,*
>
> *Unexpectedly, I find myself at the docks in Ancona, awaiting passage to Venice. My ship sails in about an hour. I would enjoy meeting you, having heard so much about you from our mutual cousin, Daniel. Is it possible for you to join me here?*
>
> *Your servant, Cousin Ethan ben Dovid*

Ethan ben Dovid—the famous writer of essays about how the French Revolution had affected that country's Jews. Her father had been proud of his young relation, had read out passages of his published articles to the family. It would be an honor to meet him. Since Papa's passing, she had heard little of him, except for the death of his wife—and unborn child.

And besides, could he have news of Daniel?

She went out of the storeroom, enjoying, as ever, the manufactory's quiet hum as the men bent over their painstaking work, the stinging smell of the oil paints, the scratch of the pen on parchment or vellum. Narducci called her over to look at a completed ketubah, a Jewish marriage document brilliantly illuminated with Biblical motifs. She congratulated the artist, receiving a startled look from the customer, who, she'd been told earlier in the day, had come all the way from Milan to bring the sacred document home with him.

"What is this woman doing here?" he whispered to Narducci, in a mutter Mirelle couldn't help but overhear.

"Mirelle d'Ancona, I'd like you to meet Abramo Tedeschi, the father of the groom," Narducci said rather than replying to his question. "Signor Tedeschi, Senorina d'Ancona is the owner of the workshop—as well as our manager."

The man took a step back. "Ah, yes," he said, his voice laced with scorn. "I've heard of you."

Mirelle flushed. She could only imagine what he'd heard. That she was a loose woman who had slept with a French Catholic soldier. That she'd jilted her betrothed, the wealthy David Morpurgo, who despite being even older than her father, had been considered a suitable match—a matrimonial prize, in fact. That she had insisted on working here at the ketubah manufactory, despite the protests of both her mother and the town rabbi, managing the accounts, scheduling and matching the right craftsman with the right assignment, making the entire enterprise run smoothly.

"Your son is lucky to have had our young Elazar illuminate his ketubah," she said now, ignoring the man's insulting tone. "He's one of our most talented artists. I'm sure you understand the allusion intended by the Biblical couples"—she pointed at the figures, making Tedeschi wince—"Abraham and Sarah, Jacob and Rachel, Moses and

Zipporah. How delicately he drew them—the joy of marriage caught on those small faces!"

Tedeschi nodded curtly, turning away from her. Shrugging, she left to get her hat from the office, tying the ribbons under an upthrust chin. *Let Narducci deal with him.*

But the workshop was tiny, and Tedeschi no longer bothered to lower his voice. "The men don't mind her being here? A woman? Surely it's unusual. Wrong."

"Don't mind?" Narducci sounded weary. He often fielded these questions about her. "You don't know what she does here, do you?"

Tedeschi grunted.

"I said she was our manager—she's a pure genius when it comes to balancing our accounts, to anything that has to do with numbers. She understands our work as no one else possibly could—practically grew up in the shop. And then, of course, there is what all of us here owe her."

"Owe her?" Teduschi sounded incredulous.

"None of us would be here today if it weren't for her."

"But the stories I've heard . . ."

Not wanting to hear any more, Mirelle came out of the office. "Sabato, I'm headed to the docks. We have some ketubot that are bound for Venice, do we not?"

One of the men gathered them up and handed her the bound packages, touching his forelock in a deliberate gesture of respect.

Tedeschi had walked off, almost as if he did not want to be contaminated by her proximity. She was used to it.

Narducci looked at the customer's retreating back. "Mirelle," he said. "Let Matteo take them."

Mirelle flinched, then glared at the foreman. "Sabato, when will you learn? I know you mean well. But I refuse to let the tittle-tattle of wagging tongues dictate what I do."

Narducci raised his hands as if in surrender.

"Signor Tedeschi," Mirelle called out defiantly. "I wish your son joy in his marriage."

Astonished, the man half turned, his mouth screwed up, raising a reluctant hand in acknowledgement.

Mirelle left the workshop, making her way quickly through the Jewish Quarter. As always, she paused before passing through the archway at the end of Via Astaga which led to the harbor, where the gates that had secured the Jewish population of Ancona had long stood, before Napoleon's soldiers—including her cousin Daniel and his friend Christophe—had demolished them. She put a hand out to touch the rough stones before hurrying on.

She spied the stranger on the quay, a man perhaps in his midthirties, his hair the color of straw, his face turned toward the steep mountain slopes that rose out of the harbor. She glanced in the same direction, trying to see her city through his eyes. For a moment, she savored the cool sea breeze lifting from the lapping waves of the Adriatic Sea, the sight of the pink and orange-toned buildings climbing the steep hills, glowing in the sunset. As she walked toward the man, Mirelle waved at a couple of French soldiers she knew, who were patrolling along the harbor. While the non-Jews of Ancona were still bitter that the French controlled their city—and much of Italy—the Jews hailed their continuing presence as a guarantee of safety. Memories of attacks in the ghetto were all too fresh.

"Ethan ben Dovid?" she asked, drawing nearer.

He turned, and she was surprised at the drawn look on his face, the harsh light in his green eyes as he studied her. "Mirelle d'Ancona?"

"I'm pleased to meet you, cousin," she said. "My father was a great admirer of yours. He used to read passages of your essays to my younger brother and me." A pause, then she added, "When they were both alive, of course."

"I was sorry to hear of your loss," Ethan said stiffly, then added the Hebrew phrase of condolence, "*Baruch dayan emet.*"

Mirelle still found it hard to talk about her brother, killed in the riots before General Bonaparte had taken the city a year past, or about her father, who had died unexpectedly of a chill, leaving both her and her mother bereft. "I was sorry to hear about your wife's passing," she told her cousin.

His face froze. "Yes, thank you," he muttered.

She shrugged, surprised that a man so elegant on the page was so tongue-tied in real life. Perhaps, she thought, it was always that way with writers. "You said this visit to Ancona was unexpected," she said. "What brought you here?"

"I needed to make a stop at Agence d'Ancône. Before traveling on."

"At where?"

"Agence d'Ancône," he repeated.

"I've lived in Ancona my entire life and never knew such an agency existed. It's French, isn't it?"

"It is. The French Directory established it when we took Ancona. A commercial concern. Your city's port makes it a practical location for trade."

"Are you in trade? Are you no longer writing?"

"In a way. And, no, I don't write any longer—I lost my taste for it after Adara died."

"But isn't that a shame?"

His lips compressed. "What was there left to write about, anyway? My essays were about the Jews attaining citizenship during the Revolution. We have that, now. My other essays, about becoming more French in our attitudes were not—shall we say—well received by the Jewish community in much of France. So, it's better that I turn my talents elsewhere."

"To trade?" She couldn't help her note of censure and hoped he didn't notice.

But he must have, for he hunched his shoulders. "As you say."

She waved them into seats at one of the cafés lining the quay. "Have you come from Paris? Have you—have you seen Daniel recently?"

He glanced at her, eyebrows raised. "A month ago. If I'd known I was coming here, I'm sure he would have sent a letter with me. I know you're corresponding."

"Was he well when you saw him?"

"Yes. Very. Proud to be serving Napoleon. He told me all about how Bonaparte ordered his soldiers to destroy the ghetto gates here. How he and his friend considered it one of the high points of their military service."

"His friend? You mean Christophe?"

Ethan's face, which had never fully relaxed, tightened even more. "Yes."

"How—how is he? Christophe, I mean?"

Ethan's eyes narrowed. "As brash as ever. I never understood their friendship—as boys, Christophe bullied Daniel, and his mother was the most virulent Jew hater I've ever met. And then, in the army . . ." His voice trailed off as he looked down at the tabletop.

Mirelle felt the heat rising into her cheeks. *What did Daniel tell him?*

But she was not destined to find out, for the call to board the ship rang out, along with the purser's bell. "I must go," Ethan said, rising.

She handed him the wrapped tubes containing the ketubot. "Please give these to the purser—he'll make sure they reach their destination. It was a pleasure meeting you, Ethan."

"The pleasure was entirely mine," he said, bowing.

He made his way onto the gangway, clutching the ketubot to his chest, a small portmanteau hanging over one arm. She stared after him, wondering—had it indeed been a pleasure? For either of them? She found her cousin Ethan to be a complete mystery.

3

After watching the boat nose out of the dock into the thickening twilight, Mirelle turned to head back to the workshop. While it was late and the workers were undoubtedly gone for the day, she still had work to complete. Before she could turn onto Via Astagna, someone blocked her path.

"I know you," the hulking stranger said. "You're the little Jewess who sleeps with French soldiers."

Mirelle peered at the shadowy figure, heart quickening. A nauseating odor of sweat and dirt rose off him. "Let me pass," she demanded.

"Should I?" The man looked her up and down, running his tongue over thick lips. "Or should I have a closer look at you? See why the French army is so enamored?"

Mirelle winced as fumes of liquor wafted over her. If he weren't drunk, he was well on his way to it. "Leave me be!" she cried, trying to push past.

"I've never had a Jewess before." The man grabbed her arm in an iron grip, his hand rough, calloused. "Plenty of strumpets, even a gypsy once, but never a Jewess."

Frantic, Mirelle tried to wrench her arm free. "Let go!"

He pulled her into the light of a torch affixed to the side of a warehouse and stared her up and down, making her flesh creep. "You're a tasty bit, I grant you."

Now that he was fully illuminated, Mirelle grew light-headed with desperation. He had the look of a dock worker: broad-chested, with muscular arms and a drooping black moustache. She couldn't twist out of the grasp of his meaty fingers.

Someone rounded the corner and stopped short at the sight of them. "Stefano! What are you doing?"

Mirelle recognized the woman with profound relief. She exhaled, feeling the tension drain from her body. "Francesca Marotti! Help!"

Without letting go of her arm, Stefano swerved to confront Francesca. "What's it to you?"

"Let her go, Stefano," Francesca said. "What are you thinking?"

"What am I thinking?" he blustered. "That I want to get a good look at this Jew *puttana*."

Mirelle gasped at the slur. She tried again to wrench herself free from his powerful clasp. "Tell him, Francesca," she gasped, feeling the bruises of his fingers start on her forearm. "He's no business grabbing me like this. Leering at me."

Their raised voices caused a curious crowd to head out of a nearby café, joined by others from the tavern next door. Several men, a few women with children in tow despite the evening hour, even a couple of nuns, all jostled their way into a tight circle around them.

Stefano glared at Francesca. "Helping Jews again, are you? For shame! And especially this one. She's slept with half the French army, I hear. Why shouldn't an honest Italian get a chance with her?"

Mortification seared through Mirelle as salacious grins spread widely over several of the men's faces. His grasp finally slackened, she wrenched her arm free.

"Think you're a big, brave man, imposing upon an innocent girl?" Francesca demanded of Stefano, arms locked across her chest. "If you want a whore, take yourself off to the bordello."

"Francesca Marotti!" chided one of the nuns, while several mothers covered their children's ears.

Stefano spit. "Innocent? *Porca Madonna!*" Then, as the shocked nuns gasped, he added, "But I've lost my taste for her Jew *culo.* Just you be careful not to be tainted by her, Francesca."

He stalked off. Mirelle, trembling, nearly stumbled, but Francesca wrapped an arm about her shoulders. "I'd better take you home," she said in calming tones. "You'll never make it on your own."

"I'm fine," Mirelle insisted. Home was a small, dank room rented from a widow. Mirelle didn't want Francesca to see how reduced her circumstances had become. "I'm headed to the workshop."

Francesca pulled back, scrutinizing her face. "You're not fine," she said coolly. "I'll walk you to this workshop of yours. *Andiamo.*" She pushed past the chattering bystanders, Mirelle wincing as they passed through.

As they walked by another torch, Mirelle, to shake off her shock and alarm, cast a curious glance at the Catholic woman. They hadn't met since Daniel, who had befriended Francesca, had left Ancona—why should they, after all? But while Francesca's face was as worn as Mirelle remembered, her shoulders stooped from farming her tiny parcel of land, she looked calmer than a year since. As if life were treating her more kindly. Mirelle had always admired the woman's devout Catholic faith, misguided though she thought it. Now Francesca wore her devotion like a halo—stepping with a sure stride, her features composed in serene lines.

"How are your children?" Mirelle asked. Anything to distract them both.

Francesca smiled sweetly, and Mirelle thought that she must resemble the infamous Madonna portrait in the cathedral—so much tender mother love crossed her face. "They are well, I thank you," she said. "Barbara is still a handful but Mario is a good boy."

They walked the narrow main street of the ghetto's remnants.

Several Jewish families had left its crowded quarters after Bonaparte had liberated them from its confines, but many felt more comfortable remaining in the homes where their families had lived for generations. Before his death, Mirelle's father had idly wondered if they should move the workshop to new, more spacious quarters. But the idea of placing such a Jewish enterprise so prominently among Catholics felt threatening, and Simone had always been a timid man.

Mirelle hoped the workshop would be empty, but candlelight glowed through its windows. Peering inside, her heart sank. Sitting in earnest conference were Narducci and David Morpurgo—the last people she wanted to see. But there was no help for it. David, who held a significant stake in the workshop, often dropped in to discuss business with her—their broken betrothal not forgotten, but rarely mentioned. She turned to thank Francesca, hoping she'd take the hint and leave, but the Catholic woman led her inexorably instead into the large workroom. The two men rose as they entered, mouths agape.

"Mirelle," David Morpurgo said, "what happened? Why are you here so late? And who . . . ?"

Mirelle turned to Francesca. "Thank you again," she said. "Surely your children are waiting for you. *Addio!*"

Francesca ignored her. "She was accosted at the harbor by one of the dock workers," she told the two men, her voice suddenly stern—even accusing. "Why do you allow her to walk alone after dark? Why isn't her family taking better care of her?"

"Accosted?" Sabato took a step forward, raising a candle so he could study Mirelle's face. "What do you mean? Mirelle, are you all right?"

"I'm fine," Mirelle said, scowling at Francesca. "It was nothing." Involuntarily, she rubbed the arm the dockworker had seized, wincing at the pain of the bruise.

"Nothing?" Francesca shook her head, all her kindness wiped

away in confusion, quickly followed by a look of disgust. "You call his pawing you nothing? Is it true then?"

Mirelle felt heat rise to envelop her neck and cheeks. "Is what true?"

"That you sleep with the French soldiers?"

Dear lord, Mirelle thought, *will I never be free of this disgrace?* "I do not," she said in measured tones. "I was in love—thought I was in love. With one soldier." Then, remembering how Christophe had killed Francesca's husband, she stopped short of volunteering his name. "Just one," she mumbled, hanging her head so she wouldn't see David's face. She had shamed him in front of the entire Jewish community by her intimacy with another man. She hated that he had to listen to this.

"Is that not a sin in your religion?" the Catholic woman persisted, her tone now a mixture of curiosity and distaste.

"It is," Morpurgo interjected between clenched teeth, "most definitely a sin. Signora, we will restore Mirelle to the protection of her family and thank you for bringing her back to us." He turned to Mirelle, his mouth curled sardonically. "Unscathed, I assume?"

Francesca's forehead wrinkled in embarrassment. "Do you ask, did he manage to force her? He did not."

"*Baruch HaShem*," Sabato murmured, then translated for Francesca's benefit, "Praise the Lord."

"I will go now," Francesca told them. "Mirelle, take better care in the future, heh?"

Mirelle nodded, eyes downcast. "Thank you again, Francesca."

The Catholic woman left. Morpurgo and Narducci stared at Mirelle.

"This can't continue," David said. "You can't live alone, walk alone. Not if this is what happens."

"I'll just be more careful," Mirelle protested.

"No," David retorted. "I know you, Mirelle. This streak of independence, of recklessness, has landed you in trouble before. If you insist on it going unchecked, it's inevitable it will again."

"Signor Morpurgo—"

"You will come home with me. Your mother needs to have a care for you."

Mirelle shook her head. "Home—with you? You must be joking!"

"It's truly the best thing." Sabato's voice was gentle but firm. "Mirelle, you must see that."

She was close to tears, holding her flushed cheeks in ice-cold hands. "After all I've put you through, Signor Morpurgo, the disgrace and shame I brought upon you, you would shelter me? The gossip will kill us both."

"You have been heedless of the gossip thus far," David said harshly before his voice softened. "And it is long past time you were reconciled with your mother. Come now."

Knowing she would regret this, Mirelle shut her eyes for an anguished moment, then followed him with dragging footsteps.

"What's she doing here?" Dolce demanded, staring at her father. She stood blocking Mirelle's path to the library, arms crossed on her chest, lips compressed.

Mirelle flinched at her erstwhile best friend's scathing stare, at her vibrant blue eyes turned dark and stormy.

"Where's Pinina?" David asked, seemingly oblivious to the waves of hatred that made Mirelle take a step back.

"Pinina? You mean, your *housekeeper*?" Dolce's voice filled with derision. "She's retired to her room, Papa. I really don't think she wants to see Mirelle. After all . . ."

The footman who had opened the door stood to one side, face averted, as if trying to pretend he wasn't listening to Dolce's barbs. David, jaw set, turned to him. "Antonio, will you fetch Signora d'Ancona? Now please?"

The whip of command made the servant spin on his heel, hurrying from the room.

"I should go," Mirelle murmured, feeling wretched. "Signor Morpurgo, Dolce is right. Neither she nor my mama want me here."

David ignored that as well. He swiveled to face his daughter. "Dolce, I don't want to hear another word from you unless you can be civil. Is that understood?"

The clock's ticking on the mantlepiece was the only sound for a few strained minutes before Mirelle's mother hurried into the room, hair disheveled, a few grey strands, having escaped hasty pins, tumbling untidily down her neck. She stopped short at the sight of her daughter. "Mirelle!"

Mirelle swallowed hard, hearing the mixture of surprise and shame in her mother's voice. It had been more than a year since she had refused to see Mirelle, had refused any attempts at reconciliation.

"Pinina, I want you to put Mirelle back in her old room. She's going to stay with us," David said.

"Stay here?" Dolce chimed in, eyes wide and voice icy. "Here? We're housing sluts, now?"

Mirelle and her mother both gasped.

"Dolce!" David roared.

Mirelle's mother spun on her. "My daughter is no slut!"

Mirelle wondered if Mama had defended her this fiercely all these months in the face of the Jewish Quarter's gossips. Poor Mama. Mirelle's ignominy reflected as much on her mother as it did on her. A sharp pang of guilt smote her.

"Call it what you will," Dolce persisted, two spots of red appearing on the pale skin of her cheeks. "She bedded a man, and he refused to marry her."

We agreed not to marry, Mirelle thought but didn't say. *We both agreed it was a mistake.* Her legs trembled beneath her, but she stiffened her spine. She refused to give Dolce the satisfaction of showing how deeply her words cut.

"Pinina, take Mirelle upstairs, please. I want a word with my daughter," David said.

Soundlessly, her mother led Mirelle upstairs and into the room that she'd occupied for months after her father's death. Mama turned to leave.

"Mama!" Mirelle cried. "Please talk to me."

Mama stood in the doorway, her back to her daughter. "What is left to say?" she asked, letting the door click softly shut behind her.

4

JUNE 14
MALTA

Daniel perched on the lower battlements of the Maltese Fort Tigné overlooking the ocean. He was trying to finish his letter to Mirelle before he had to board ship again. The small skiff that carried the diplomatic packet back to France would depart soon, and he'd already paid one of the sailors to extract the letter once they landed so it could be sent via post overland to Ancona.

Daniel wondered how much to include of the last few days, which had reminded him all too strongly of the fear a pitched battle could evoke. He had not seen warfare personally for more than a year—and never before from the sea. As they approached Malta three days earlier, a twisting helplessness took hold of him. He could do nothing but watch as *le Franklin*'s cannon fired upon the stone fort. Somehow, the ship miraculously avoided being hit by the return fire that boomed out of the small fort's narrow embrasures.

The next day Daniel and his men were loaded into a chaloupe and put ashore to overpower the knight defenders. As always, action steadied him. He hid his relief as he commanded his men for the first time in battle, realizing he did know what orders to give.

One moment in particular stayed with him—making him flush

with pride as he recalled it. He positioned the light cannon they'd brought with them in a small dip in the rockface of the shore.

Pierre had protested the order. "Surely we'd be better off moving to higher ground, sir," he'd said. "Where we can aim straight ahead at the fort."

But Daniel shook his head. He had a particular target in mind—the cannon the knights had placed at the top of the tower, which was raining grapeshot down at the French forces, causing them to shy back.

"Tilt up," was all Daniel said, pointing.

Sebastian, looking in the direction of his outstretched arm, nodded. And a few seconds later, they had destroyed the enemy cannon, allowing their forces to surge forward.

The Maltese surrendered on the third day, abandoning the fort to the French.

Would Mirelle be interested in any of that? Would any noncombatant?

"What are you writing with such fervor, young man?" came a voice from behind him.

Daniel glanced up, recognizing Dominque-Vivant Denon, whom Daniel had met back in Toulon. At forty-three, Denon was the elder statesman of the more than one hundred civilians taking part in the military expedition. An aristocrat who had barely escaped the guillotine, Denon was known to be the smoothly spoken favorite of Josephine Bonaparte and other society ladies of Paris. While many of the savants were housed in *L'Orient* with Napoleon, Denon had been assigned a berth on *le Franklin*. Rumor had it that General Bonaparte was none too pleased at the artist's close friendship with his wife.

Rather than answer his question, Daniel said, "For a civilian, you were particularly cool headed in the face of gunfire. I noticed you standing in the thick of the battle, sketching our victory." Daniel had been amazed at Denon's ice-cold calm during the sea battle, standing at the ship's bow to capture the skirmish despite bullets whizzing about his head and cannon balls throwing up wave after wave of drenching sea water as they landed right beneath him. Say what you might about him, Daniel reflected: a flirt and a gossip, his long lace sleeves and preoccupation with his art making him a figure of fun for many of the soldiers. But despite these idiosyncrasies, he was clearly a brave man.

"Surely you soldiers cannot claim all the glory of this expedition." Denon ran a hand carelessly through his tangled black curls. "Curious, is it not? That so many men have trusted that wherever Napoleon leads them, it will be toward glory? For the sake of science for some—to be touched by art's grandeur for dabblers like me?"

Daniel surveyed the artist for a long, thoughtful moment. Was there truth buried in his pomposity? Deciding Denon sounded sincere, Daniel said, "Yes, but as a soldier, I wonder why the general is burdening us with so many civilians."

"So many savants," Denon corrected him. "We're not mere civilians."

Savants. The word stirred something in Daniel's memory. In his mind's eye, he saw a tract, its ink still damp, hanging to dry on a clothesline. It had been an unusually quiet night at the Parisian print shop and Daniel—had he been fourteen or fifteen then?—had lingered under the page, intrigued by the legend it described. "I once read," he murmured, "that a large group of savants had accompanied Alexander the Great on his military campaigns. I wonder . . ."

Denon turned to peer at him, eyebrows raised. "You have unexpected depths, young lieutenant. Are you a scholar?"

"A printer," Daniel replied. "In Paris as an apprentice, and then in Italy, working for General Bonaparte."

"Ah! That explains your erudition. I'm impressed."

Daniel shrugged off the compliment. "I've seen the general in action and heard him speak of his destiny. It doesn't shock me that he wishes to model himself after Alexander the Great. But even so, to drag so many civilians—savants—along with us on a military campaign is simply asking for trouble. You should hear my men grumbling on the matter!"

Now it was Denon's turn to shrug. "Don't you trust your general?"

"With my life!" Daniel meant it.

"Well said!" Then, after a pause, Denon repeated: "So who are you writing to?" The artist gestured toward the piece of foolscap clutched in Daniel's hand.

"My cousin," Daniel responded.

"A cousin! A particularly charming relation, I'd wager. Describe her for me." Denon leaned on the stone parapet, restlessly pushing his curly hair back from a broad forehead. Living as they did in such close quarters, Daniel had been amused to see Denon style it in a small pocket glass every morning, brushing the curls forward to disguise a thinning pate. It took the former aristocrat almost as much time as it did to meticulously arrange his cravat.

"I didn't say my cousin was a woman," Daniel replied.

"But she is, no?"

At Daniel's embarrassed nod, Denon's sharp eyes twinkled under bushy brows. "I thought so—you were writing with such fervor. Describe her." He flipped to an empty page in his sketchpad, pulling a stick of charcoal from a pocket and settling himself on the ground.

Daniel wanted to refuse, but Denon, head perched to one side like an inquisitive bird, was somehow irresistible.

"Go on," the artist urged.

So Daniel closed his eyes and thought of Mirelle—her long chestnut hair, penetrating green eyes, slender curves, the challenging tilt of her sharp chin, her long, graceful fingers. Words emerged, awkwardly at first, but then picking up speed and fluency.

When he was done, he opened his eyes just as Denon tore a sheet of paper from his sketchpad. The artist rose, brushing off his pant legs, and extended the page to Daniel. "A small souvenir," he said, before turning away, laughing, and loping toward the beach.

Daniel nearly dropped the paper in shock. Denon had drawn Mirelle brilliantly—it was her eyes that stared back at him, her upthrust chin, her long, curly hair splayed over shoulders, partially covering her face. He recognized her in the lines. But that was not all. She wore no clothes and was twisted upward, as if caught in the act of love, her beautiful body arched, her legs akimbo, her most private parts . . .

"Daniel! What's so fascinating?"

Daniel tore his eyes from the page. Christophe stood before him, leaning nonchalantly against the wall. His childhood friend, the two had met as young apprentices in the printshop Christophe's uncle owned and had joined the army together. Daniel always considered himself lacking in comparison. Where he plodded, Christophe swaggered. Where he felt uncertain in command, Christophe led his calvary unit with sheer bravado. And then, with Mirelle . . .

Quickly, Daniel crumpled the drawing into a ball, thrusting it behind his back.

Christophe laughed. "Oh, no, my friend—now you must show me." Taking two quick steps, he snatched the paper from Daniel's grasp.

Daniel, wretched, watched him uncrinkle the page and smooth out its creases. Christophe was the only man in the world who would know how accurate the drawing was—the only man who had seen Mirelle in the throes of passion.

"What in the . . . ?" Christophe stared at the picture, at first unbelieving, then indignant. "Where did you get this?"

"Denon. He asked me to describe . . . but I never . . ."

Christophe grimaced. "Vivant Denon? That artist who numbers pornography among his so-called talents? And you allowed him?"

"All I did was describe her. Her hair, her eyes. I had no idea he was a pornographer. And I didn't ask him to draw her!" The impulse to ask Christophe if the portrait resembled the real-life woman was strong. Daniel pushed it away.

"That must have been some description!" Christophe stared first at Daniel, then back at the portrait, the stern expression on his face softening as he lingered on her image.

Daniel resisted an urge to tear it out of his hands. "Give it back."

Christophe's eyes widened. "Give it back? What are you going to do with it?" He laughed, the mocking, guttural sound from deep in his throat making Daniel flinch. "I should keep it, just to protect your innocence."

Daniel wished, more than anything, that Mirelle's innocence still needed protection. But she had surrendered her virtue to the man who was now staring at her picture. The thought of the woman he loved in bed with his friend was a sharp thrust to heart and head. With a swift motion, he yanked the portrait out of Christophe's hand, tearing it in two, then four. "You gave up your rights to her, remember? Decided not to wed despite having—having . . ."

"Bedded her?" Christophe sighed. "I do regret that. You know I do. But we were in love."

Daniel, ripping the paper into smaller and smaller pieces, tamped down the fury he felt, but the words forced themselves out of his mouth. "You *were* in love. It didn't last, though, did it?"

Christophe reached out a hand. "Give those to me," he demanded. "If anyone should have them, it should be me."

Instead, Daniel flung the pieces off the ramparts and into the ocean, watching them soak through, charcoal lines spreading and blurring until the form was no longer recognizable. "No one should have them."

Christophe shrugged and walked off. Daniel kept his eyes on the wet and ruined pages until they were hurled by a wave into the depths of the sea.

5

JUNE 15

A day later, Denon strode up to where *le Franklin* was docked in Marsamxett Harbor and called out to Daniel. Daniel, leaning on the railing at the ship's bow, waved and turned away. He was still unsettled after seeing Mirelle's nude portrait, yearning for her, almost wishing he had kept the drawing as a private treasure. He had decided to avoid its artist—which generally shouldn't be a difficult task, not with the thousands of men accompanying Napoleon. But Denon, for some indiscernible reason, kept seeking him out.

"I could use your help, young man," he called. "Have you time to accompany me?"

As much as he wanted to say no, Daniel was bored. They had been ordered to remain on the ship except for a couple of hours a day—and then were limited to the fort or close to the harbor. The frigate was overcrowded, soldiers packed into tight quarters. Quarrels broke out over the men edging into one another's space, over middle of the night snoring, as well as fiery accusations of cheating over the endless games of chance played to while away the time. Tiring of the arguments he was asked to arbitrate and of the tight quarters, Daniel had climbed to the deck for a breath of fresh air.

"What do you want?" he called back.

"I have been asked to make some sketches of the general as he meets with Maltese officials. I could use someone to help me carry my easel and paraphernalia."

"I'm a lieutenant, not an orderly, Denon. Do you want me to loan you one of my men?"

"Come down, won't you? I don't want to keep shouting at you."

Reluctantly, Daniel made his way down the gangplank.

"These are delicate negotiations," Denon told him. "The general will be more comfortable if an officer accompanies me. And besides— aren't you curious about what's happening behind those closed doors?"

Daniel had to admit that he was. Exiled from working on General Bonaparte's military press, he was no longer privy to the news of the day. And from everything he'd heard, Bonaparte was completely reshaping the laws of the Maltese archipelago. It would be fascinating to catch a glimpse of the process.

On the other hand, it was hard to trust Denon's intentions after his sketch of Mirelle.

"I'm ordered to stay on the ship with my men," Daniel replied.

"Will someone actually miss you?"

Probably not. But it was a good excuse. "Orders are orders."

"Who would have the gall to countermand General Bonaparte's wishes?"

Daniel had to admit that Denon had a point. "Very well," he said, sighing. "When do we go?"

"Right now." Denon pointed at the easel and cabinet of oils. "If you manage those, I'll take my sketchpad and charcoals."

A few feet down the docks, a brightly colored fishing boat was waiting for them, its vibrant blue-, red-, and yellow-painted hull brilliant in the morning sunlight. Denon handed the fisherman some coins, and the man grinned, revealing broken, blackened teeth. Daniel loaded the easel and oils, and then, before climbing in himself, demurred. "You really don't need me, do you?"

Denon put a hand on his arm. "I've taken an odd liking to you, young lieutenant. Besides, don't you want to see more of Malta while you're here?"

Better than being cooped up in the stink and clamor of *le Franklin*, Daniel thought, and perched himself uncomfortably on a bench in the boat's stern. They traversed the Marsamxett Harbor with difficulty, dotted as it was with hundreds of French vessels. The fisherman muttered under his breath as he maneuvered around the ships, growing increasingly more vocal as he sailed deeper into the water and found himself almost trapped between the various warships.

"*Ostja!*" he cried, as he had to turn the rudder sharply around a frigate, and then, "*F'oxx ruhek,*" followed rapidly by, "*F'oxx il maxtura t'alla!*"

"What in the world is he saying?" Denon asked, clinging to the side of the rowboat.

Daniel shrugged, but then curiosity got the better of him. Leaning forward, he tried to talk to the man in French, which drew a blank stare. He tried Italian, which made the fisherman nod rapidly.

"*Fanculo la culla di Dio,*" he responded.

Daniel flushed, stunned by the unexpectedly vibrant obscenity despite his years in the military.

Denon looked at Daniel, eyebrows raised. "Well?" he asked.

"He said, 'Fuck God's cradle,'" Daniel said. "I'm not asking him about the others."

Denon laughed. "Well, since he understands you, ask him about the eye."

"Eye?"

"Didn't you notice it when we boarded the boat? There's an eye painted on the hull."

Daniel leaned over, catching sight of the odd symbol. He waited until they were out in open water, then posed the question. The fisherman jabbered in broken Italian and Daniel struggled to keep up.

Finally, after the Maltese man subsided, Daniel turned to Denon. "He says it's the Eye of Horus. An evil eye symbol if I've understood him correctly."

"Ah, so Dutertre was right. He told me the fishing boats here were inherited from father to son all the way back to the Phoenicians. Horus was the Phoenician God who protected these fishermen from evil."

While the savants might be a nuisance in the heat of battle, Daniel thought, they were certainly making this expedition more interesting. Perhaps Napoleon was right to bring them, after all.

The trip across the harbor took about an hour. As they approached Valletta, the cluster of French vessels around St. Elmo Bay made the fisherman swear with even greater ferocity. As they climbed out of the boat, he stuck out a hand. "*Perché è stato così difficile.*"

"He says we owe him more money because the trip was so difficult," Daniel translated.

"Tell him to wait for us for the return trip—I'll pay more then." Denon patted Daniel's back. "I knew bringing you along was a good idea! I could never have understood him without you."

Daniel translated. The fisherman nodded and settled down to wait, pulling a pipe out of his pocket and a snarl of knotted rope from beneath one of the seats. Before Daniel and Denon had finished pulling the art supplies out of the boat, he was already repairing a rip in his fishing net.

Since the trip by foot would take more than an hour, Denon gave a coin to a stripling lounging idly in a donkey cart, engaging him to take them to the Palazzo Pariso. As they drove through the city, Daniel was struck by the beauty of the golden limestone buildings, many embellished with enclosed wooden balconies protruding from the upper stories, painted in vibrant primary or pastel colors. The streets were narrow but didn't twist and turn like so many of the other cities Daniel had marched into in the general's wake.

When Daniel commented on it, Denon responded in his best pro-fessorial tones, "An astute observation, young man! During my time in Italy, I of course studied not only the works, but also the history of our great classical and medieval artists. When I was summoned to Malta's capital, I recalled a passage I'd once read."

"A passage?"

"That Pope Pius IV sent a Florentine architect, Laparelli, one of the revered Michelangelo's assistants, to lay out Valletta in a grid so the island would be easier to defend."

The garrulous artist, with his rich and varied knowledge, was beginning to endear himself to Daniel, despite his misstep in draw-ing Mirelle in that lascivious pose.

The cool sea breeze rifled Daniel's hair as they arrived at the palazzo. Throwing the youth another coin, Denon led the way into the lobby of the stately mansion where Bonaparte had established his headquarters. Denon, craning his neck as he took in the palazzo's opulence, whistled sharply. But Daniel, who had visited the general's lodgings twice before, in Ancona and Milan, was unimpressed by the villa's grandeur.

They mounted a shallow step between two pillars into a square lobby dotted with marble statuary, overhung by a balcony on the second floor. A guard pointed to the broad staircase, and they found themselves in a narrow hallway crowded with men, many wearing dour expressions. A few looked downright belligerent, grumbling in undertones to one another. They wore long cassocks, tunics, or vests emblazoned with massive crosses, or else heavy chains with the bejeweled symbol of Christ sparkling prominently on their chests.

Sidling past them, Daniel followed Denon through a yellow door at the end of the corridor. In a spacious room, the general sat at a table under an elaborate frieze of greyish blue, festooned with flowers and mythological renderings. A large Greek god—most likely Zeus—was depicted in the center. Bonaparte was poring over the papers neatly stacked before him, a quill in his hand, an inkhorn at his elbow.

At the other end of the table was a face familiar to Daniel—Louis Antoine Fauvelet de Bourrienne, Napoleon's secretary. His bulbous nose and intense eyes were likewise buried in parchment, but he looked up as the two men walked in. "Daniel Isidore?" he exclaimed in surprise.

Daniel bowed. The general glanced at him impatiently, then stared. "I know you."

Snapping to attention, Daniel saluted. "Yes, Citizen General. We met several times during your Italian campaign. Most recently in Milan, but before that in Ancona. And at the bridge in Lodi."

Napoleon wrinkled his brow, then nodded briskly. "Ah, yes. That ridiculous miracle portrait. They tell me the painted Virgin Mother no longer smiles or cries upon the pious of Ancona. In the end, it was all just hysteria and superstition."

"So I understand, Citizen General." Daniel was taken aback by the general's off-hand tone. He recalled the day Napoleon had admitted that he'd been deeply disturbed by something he'd spied in the portrait, something that had rocked his belief in his own sense of destiny. Perhaps his denying its importance simply meant he didn't want to admit to weakness. At least not now, when the episode was long past.

"And so, you are once again one of my soldiers—having been promoted, I see. But what are you doing here?"

Daniel waved a hand toward Denon. "Citizen Denon, here to sketch the day's events, asked me to accompany him. We are berthed on the same ship and he requested my assistance."

But the general had already lost interest, ignoring Denon's bow and turning back to the mass of papers piled high on the brilliantly polished table. Bourrienne indicated with a wave of his arm where Denon was to set up his easel, then returned to the task at hand.

"I didn't realize you were so well liked in these rarified military circles," Denon muttered as Daniel helped him adjust the height of the easel and lay out his paints and charcoals. "It seems I made a good choice in soliciting your friendship."

"Don't be absurd," Daniel retorted.

As Denon drew preliminary charcoal sketches, Napoleon dictated several orders in quick succession. Daniel listened as the general abolished slavery, ordered the inhabitants of Malta to wear the tricolor cockade, forbade the title of Knight, sent the sons of the wealthiest Maltese to study in France, established hospitals, banished any nuns or priests who were not originally from Malta . . . . The general's voice droned on and Daniel's head began to nod.

But then one order made him perk up. Napoleon gave the country's Jews permission to build a synagogue.

Daniel had heard how the Maltese knights, when attacking Ottoman ships and coastal towns, seized the Jews they discovered onboard, holding them hostage. They ransomed some, enslaved the others. Just as Napoleon had liberated the Jews from the ghettos in Italy, he was now spreading the mantle of his protection over the poor, misery-stricken Jews of Malta. Daniel couldn't smother his gasp of delight as Bourrienne's pen scratched out the directive.

The general glanced toward him, surprised. "You approve, lieutenant?"

He straightened. "Yes, sir."

"Why precisely?" Bonaparte's piercing eyes raked his face.

Daniel swallowed hard. "I'm proud that you're continuing to ease the burdens of my people, Citizen General. I was one of the men who demolished the ghetto gates at Ancona. It was a historic day for me and for my fellow Jewish soldiers."

The general's expression softened. "I see. Then I'm glad you are here to witness this directive too, young man."

"Thank you, sir."

Bonaparte turned back to work and Denon elbowed Daniel in the ribs. "See," the artist said. "Aren't you glad I insisted you come with me? Wasn't it worth it?"

But as the day crawled on, the massive number of orders seemed to meld one into another. While Daniel couldn't help but admire Napoleon's enormous capacity for detail, he fidgeted in the back of the room, wishing he had something to do aside from watching Denon sketch portrait after portrait, littering the floor with his discards. Of course, army life should have inured him to long periods of inactivity. But even while kicking his heels in camp or on ship, Daniel would try to keep himself and his men busy. His company grumbled that he held more inspections and battery practices than other artillery commanders. He ordered them because he was still somewhat unsure of his command. Yet Sebastian, the most experienced of his soldiers, offered him grudging respect for it. "I hate to admit it, young sir, but you're right to keep the men on the hop," he'd once said.

A sudden commotion outside the door—shouting and banging— made Daniel shake off his lethargy. The door burst open. A well-appointed gentleman in yellow pantaloons and a long red jacket worn open over a gold-embroidered vest, a huge Maltese cross hung about his neck, dragged a young woman into the room. She was covered, head to foot, in a capacious blue cape, her face shadowed by an enormous hood trimmed in fur. A panic-stricken guard followed.

"What is the meaning of this?" Napoleon roared, head jerking up from his papers.

Denon instantly abandoned the half-drawn portrait and turned to a new page, quickly sketching the scene before him.

The soldier pushed his shoulders back in attention. "Citizen General, this man—"

"Knight!" the man snapped. "I am Ramón Martínez de Aragon, a Knight of Malta, and I wish to lodge a complaint!"

Napoleon sent a scathing glare toward the guard. "You let him through? You couldn't stop him?"

Daniel pitied the soldier, whose shaking legs could barely hold him upright. He opened his mouth a few times, but no sound emerged. "Answer the general, corporal," Daniel said gently.

"Sir, I—I—he pushed through and refused—"

"Enough!" Bonaparte turned from the quaking guard to confront the knight. "You are interrupting serious business. State your complaint and be gone!"

"One of your officers, general, wickedly tried to seduce my innocent niece. Rianne, remove your hood and let the general see purity threatened!"

Rianne lifted a white hand and the hood dropped back. Daniel, standing behind Denon, heard his soft gasp as he tore off yet another page from the sketchpad and swiftly drew the girl's figure. She could not have been more than sixteen or seventeen. Her face was a perfect oval, with high cheekbones and luminous dark eyes. Her hair fell in inky rippling waves down her back. There was a sensual quality to the way she carried herself that belied de Aragon's claim of innocence, a hint of bedroom delights in the swan-like neck that she tilted suggestively toward the general.

Daniel, tearing his gaze from the girl to gauge Napoleon's reaction, saw that the general was struck by her beauty. Was that de Aragon's intention? To beguile the island's conqueror and distract him? Perhaps somehow to sway him?

"Your niece?" Napoleon's eyebrows rose in disbelief. "Surely not."

The knight's mouth thinned. "What can you possibly be implying?"

"One has heard of the many *nieces* you knights have entertained. Do I need to be more explicit?"

"Sir—you insult me!"

Napoleon laughed sourly. "If I do, you and your licentious fellow knights are to blame. You claim one of my officers attempted to seduce this niece of yours, but where's your proof? And what precisely do you expect me to do about it?"

"One of your calvary officers! He should be whipped! Demoted!"

The general shrugged. "I cannot act without evidence."

De Aragon straightened and stuck out his chest. "My word should be more than enough. I am of aristocratic blood, tracing my roots back to the nobles of Aragon. And I am a knight of Malta, sworn to Christ's service. Question my word and you impugn my honor!"

Bonaparte turned to his secretary, smirking. "A noble and a knight, Bourrienne! Imagine! Do you remember what we did to aristocrats during the Terror?" He swiveled toward the guard. "Remove him. I've no time for this nonsense." He waved at Daniel. "Assist the guard, would you, lieutenant?"

Daniel put a hand on his sword hilt and stepped toward the knight. "Sir, if you please."

"Am I to have no satisfaction?" de Aragon cried, affronted.

"You're lucky to be leaving with your head," Bonaparte told him coldly.

Daniel ushered Rianne and the knight out of the room. Rianne let her eyes linger on the general before leaving, but he had already returned to his papers. The knight muttered protests as Daniel shut the yellow door behind them.

"I have never been so insulted!" the knight persisted as Daniel led them down the staircase and into the street.

Rianne flipped the roomy hood over her hair and told him, her voice melodious and deep, "Oh, do calm yourself, Ramón. I told you, it meant nothing. There was no need for this. The boy was charming, that's all."

De Aragon was beet red with fury, a vein pulsing in his forehead. "Charming, was he? Charming? I've told you, Rianne . . ."

She laid the tips of her long fingers on his arm. "Please, you're going to make yourself ill. Go home. I'll see you there."

The knight stalked off. Clearly his so-called niece held considerable sway over him. She watched him disappear around a corner before turning to Daniel. "He's a fool, but a dear fool. And he's been good to me."

Daniel knew better than to ask, but he couldn't contain his curiosity. "What actually happened, signorina?"

"I was in the market and this young officer offered to carry my basket. He bought me a flower to wear and told me all about his favorite horse."

"His horse?"

"Yes, a steed called Étoile Noire."

Daniel's eyes widened. Étoile Noire was the name of Christophe's horse. *I should have known.*

Rianne continued blithely, "I love riding and so we sat on a bench by the sea and chatted about horses for a while. Which is where Ramón found us. He's terribly jealous of me, you understand."

Daniel, having seen Rianne's beauty, was not in the least surprised that his childhood friend had stopped whatever he was doing to flirt with her. "So there was no seduction? Why didn't you explain that to your—uncle?"

Rianne laughed, a sound like cathedral bells. "We both know he's not my uncle, Lieutenant."

"Then why accompany him to the general and make such a scene?"

"I was curious to see this mighty general of the French. That's why I let Ramón make his complaint."

Daniel watched her stroll languidly down the street. He was glad to know that Christophe's crime—this time—amounted to no more than stopping to talk with a beautiful woman. As he made his way back to the Palazzo Parisdo, Daniel wondered when Christophe's predilection for beautiful women would lead him too far.

6

JUNE 15
CONSTANTINOPLE, TURKEY

Ethan sat cross-legged on a cushion, watching the stream of thick coffee being poured from the long-handed *ibrik*. The servant, kneeling before them, wielded the copper coffee pot with artistic flair, raising it almost shoulder level before tipping the aromatic liquid into two tiny porcelain cups. Ethan, unused to the *jubba*, the long shift he wore over baggy trousers called *şalvar*, and the fez tilted awkwardly on his head, kept himself still with an effort, to avoid jostling the low mother-of-pearl tray the cups and small sticky cakes rested on.

"Tell me," his host Tubias Çelebi asked, after the servant had risen to his feet, bowed, and backed out of one of the wide archways surrounding the cool, spacious room. "Why dress as a Turk?"

"It's allowed me to walk the marketplace unobserved," Ethan said. "To eavesdrop. You never know what gems of knowledge you might glean." He knew, if questioned about his light complexion, wheat-colored hair and green eyes, to claim he was from the Caucasus, where his coloring was common.

"So you speak Turkish?" Çelebi looked impressed.

"I speak several languages," Ethan replied.

"Several? How many?"

"Twelve. No, thirteen."

"Thirteen?" His eyebrows rose.

"Languages come easily to me."

"All fluently?"

"Not all—I have only a little ancient Greek, for instance, and my Hungarian is rusty. But I recently learned Turkish and Arabic and a smattering of Persian. At the *ecole publique*, studying under Sylvestre de Sacy."

Çelebi's nose wrinkled in confusion. "Sylvestre de . . . ?" he asked.

Ethan nodded. "De Sacy. You don't know who he is. Why should you? But if you want to learn Oriental languages—and the history of the East—he's the man to study with."

"Impressive. And what have you learned during your eavesdropping?" Çelebi's eyes crinkled as if amused.

"It's more what I haven't heard," Ethan said. "No one has mentioned the French. Or Talleyrand."

"Should they?"

"If an important French minister had arrived in Constantinople, one assumes there would be gossip about it in the marketplace."

Çelebi looked at him quizzically. A Jewish Turk whose family had lived in Constantinople for decades, he looked completely at home in his own *jubba* and *şalvar*, an ensemble he complemented with a fringed gold sash looped with beads at his waist. "I didn't hear that there were any French dignitaries visiting the Grand Porte."

"No?" Ethan shrugged. "Perhaps he arrived incognito. No matter—I'll just call on him."

His host shook his head. "You can't simply call on someone staying in Topkapı Palace. It isn't permitted."

Ethan cursed his mistake. He had taken painstaking care to master the rules governing the palace and knew this to be true. And if someone at the palace suspected that he was a spy, it could mean a death sentence, not only for him but for Çelebi as well. He hurried to correct himself before Çelebi could doubt his shrewdness. "I realize that. But I must see him on a matter of urgency. I have orders for him from the general—and Bonaparte needs to know how Talleyrand's diplomatic mission here has prospered."

"I'm sure those are your orders. But it can't be done."

Ethan thought for a minute, ticking through the possibilities that Turkish protocol afforded him. "But if I approach a noble who lives in the palace, he can approve my visit. If I pretend to be a spice merchant, which noble should that be?"

"Ah, that's a cunning approach," his host said, rubbing his ample stomach. "As a trader, you'll need permission to export large quantities of spice, and the best person to obtain that from would be one of the pashas. And if you want someone who has the authority to allow you to call upon the French minister, that had better be the Grand Vizier."

"Koca Yusuf Pasha himself, then. Can you secure me an audience?"

Çelebi nodded, before reaching over for a piece of baklava, popping it into his mouth and sipping his coffee. "You realize I'm taking a risk, bringing you into the court," he said, his face suddenly serious. "If they learned you were a spy and I had given you aid . . ."

"What's the worst that could happen?" Ethan asked. "You're an advisor to Sultan Selim III. Surely your position is secure."

But Çelebi sliced a forefinger swiftly across his throat. "You have to understand, young man," he said, "my father was physician to Selim's father, among several other Jewish doctors. But it is whispered that our young, impressionable sultan has less affection for Jews. Many in his court want to keep the inner circle pure of non-Islamic influence."

Ethan's eyebrows rose. "Why, then, are you willing . . . ?"

One corner of Çelebi's mouth twisted upward. "I've heard much about this French general that you serve," he said. "One likes to be on the right side of history. It's just impossible to know what that side will be. So one hedges their bets." With a fluid motion, he stood. "Come, you must be weary, and I must head to the palace to request your audience." Reaching down, he extended a hand to Ethan, who pulled himself to his feet.

In the solitude of his spacious quarters the next morning, Ethan wondered just how loyal his host would be if his guest's identity were uncovered at the palace. Steeling himself for the business at hand, he dressed in European clothing—knee-length socks, pantaloons, an elaborately embroidered vest worn over a linen shirt, a cutaway coat. In the guise of a wealthy merchant, supplied with funds from Napoleon's discretionary fund, Ethan added a quizzing glass, a watch and fob and took care with his elaborately tied cravat. He powdered his fair hair and tied it back with a ribbon at the nape of his neck, topping it with a tricorne hat.

As he dressed, Ethan could not help his feelings of amazement. Who could ever have dreamed he would be here, in Constantinople? Or that he would be on a mission for the most famous general in all of France? His sense of wonder almost crowded out the perpetual cloud that had shadowed him after the agony of losing both wife and son in childbirth. His beloved wife lost so suddenly, so unexpectedly, had incapacitated him for months, drying the ink on his quill's nib as he hunkered over blank sheets of foolscap. Consumed with fury at the fate that had robbed him of years of happiness, of the ability to write, with guilt in his own role in his wife's death, he had fled his home in Bischheim for Paris and cast about for a life completely unrelated to anything he'd known before. He'd found it in an unexpected quarter—an offer by Sylvestre de Sacy to become one of Napoleon's many Jewish agents.

As a mark of favor by the previous sultan, Çelebi's father had been granted a spacious house on the fringes of the heavily wooded Gülhane Park. The trip to the palace could have been accomplished on foot. But when Ethan suggested it, Çelebi looked at him in horror. "One approaches the palace in state or not at all," he chided, as a turbaned servant brought an open-sided carriage led by a matched pair of dappled horses up to the mansion's front steps.

Brushing aside the fringed curtain that hung from the rooftop, Ethan sat on a cushioned bench. He was soon grateful for the padding, as the carriage—called an *araba*, Çelebi told him—had no springs and bounced uncomfortably along the hard-packed dirt roadway. Ethan clung tight to the gift he'd brought from Paris, delicately wrapped in jasmine-scented silk.

As they bowled past, Çelebi pointed out various landmarks, including the jaw-dropping Hagia Sophia, a Byzantine church now converted into a mosque. "I'm told the Byzantine mosaics were exquisite," he said. "But they are covered up now. Muslim worship prohibits images of figures. They've whitewashed over them, especially the ones that face Mecca. This stems from a prohibition of idolatry—very similar to our own Jewish creed—as well as a fervent belief that creating living forms is purely God's prerogative."

The entrance to Topkapı Palace, the Gate of Salutation, made Ethan draw in a startled breath. It towered above, its two turrets piercing the blue sky. They drove through, heading to the audience chamber.

"I've secured the audience with the Grand Vizier," Çelebi said. "An interpreter will be on hand, as you requested."

Ethan nodded. He did not plan to reveal that he was fluent in Turkish, figuring the vizier might reveal more if he thought Ethan ignorant of their language. At the entrance to the audience chamber, he deposited the traditional bribe or *bakshish*—an enameled snuff box—by sliding it through the large gift window by the fountain of Suleiman I. He was frankly glad to be rid of the too-valuable item. He'd carried it with him on the long journey, constantly on the lookout for pickpockets. But the inducement of an expensive gift was the only way to ensure entrance to the inner reaches of the palace.

They waited for nearly an hour with other suitors for the Grand Vizier's attention in a tiled antechamber surrounded by dizzying blue mosaics of contrasting design: florals, Arabic script, patterned

squares and diamonds. A servant offered refreshment. Ethan and
Çelebi refused, but several of the others nodded. The servant snapped
his fingers into the hallway. A servant girl padded through, carrying
a coffee pot and cups on a silver tray that would have seemed too
heavy for her if not for her grace in balancing it. Placing it on a low
table, she lowered her eyes, effacing herself by bowing almost to the
ground as she backed silently out of the room.

Something about her stirred a memory of Adara. Ethan couldn't
understand why—his wife had been outspoken and her bearing
proud, certainly nothing like this silent, doe-eyed creature. And yet,
there Adara was, dancing in his head, bewitching him, at a ball held
by her father back in Strasbourg before they'd wed. The two women
were united by their innate beauty and their fluidity of movement,
Ethan realized. His grief rose again and he squelched it, irritated by
the too-familiar pang. He had moved on, he told himself. He forced
himself out of the memory by noticing the details of the foreign surroundings: the colorful low divans, the ornate blue-hued tiles, the
arched doorways. His dead wife had no place here.

Finally, the Grand Vizier's servant announced them. Ethan bowed
low as Çelebi presented him to Koca Yusuf Pasha, reassuring himself
that the slight tremor in his limbs would be construed as simple ner-
vousness. The right-hand man to the Sultan wore an ankle-length
white robe with green and gold trim and a headpiece that marked
him as chief among the Sultan's circle of advisors—a towering tri-
angular turban bisected in a diagonal slash by a gold band. His long,
white beard reached the middle of his chest and frizzled on all sides.
"You are the envoy from the French spice confederation," he said. It
wasn't a question.

As Ethan waited for the interpreter to repeat the words, he let his
eyes wander. Several Turkish nobles were lounging on low settees
in the back of the room, all looking bored. When the interpreter
finally broke off, having inserted several additional poetic phrases

of welcome, Ethan responded, "I am, Effendi. It is gracious of you to receive me."

"I don't have much time," the Grand Vizier replied, attention fixed on a scroll he held in his lap. "How can I serve you?"

Once again the interpreter translated—this time simply and to the point.

"I beg your permission to negotiate with the merchants in the bazaar," Ethan said. "I've been informed your approval is necessary to purchase large quantities of spice to ship back to France."

Koca Yusuf Pasha nodded, still focused on the scroll. But as a servant entered, carrying the wrapped gift on a silver salver, he rolled the parchment up and extended a hand. The servant unwrapped it and gently placed the snuff box in his palm before bowing himself out.

"A pretty trifle," the Grand Vizier said, turning it from side to side and upside down.

"Fashioned by one of the most renowned artists in Paris," Ethan told him through the agency of the translator.

Placing it on a table, the Turkish noble nodded coolly. "I'll arrange for the appropriate permission. Tell me, what spices are you most interested in?"

Ethan listed them: various types of pepper, cumin, cardamom, aniseed, and oregano. As the translator relayed his list, Ethan could tell that the Vizier was barely attending. It was when he deliberately mentioned saffron that the Turk's eyebrows quirked upward in surprise.

"Saffron? No. Saffron is worth its weight in gold, young man," he said. "And as such, only suitable for the Sultan's table."

"Indeed?" Ethan injected some surprise into his voice. He was arriving at the purpose of the entire masquerade. "I was told differently by Citizen Minister Talleyrand."

"You were told wrong, then." The Grand Vizier turned to one of

the nobles lounging in the back of the Audience Chamber and commented, "He clearly wants to steal from us. Do these French fools
think they can outwit us by pretending in this way?"

"I am sorry to hear it," Ethan said deferentially, taking care to
show that he hadn't understood the insult. "There is great demand
for saffron in France. I will ask Minister Talleyrand why he misled
me when I meet him next. I can do so tomorrow if you permit me to
see him. He is staying at the palace, correct?"

"Tomorrow? At the palace? You mean here?" The Vizier looked
shocked. Again, he turned to the courtier, speaking in rapid Turkish.
"Talleyrand is in Paris, is he not? Why does this man think he's here
in Constantinople? Here at the palace?"

Ethan again controlled his expression, waiting for the translator
to tell him that the minister was not in Turkey. "I beg your pardon,"
he replied smoothly, as though this were no great matter. "I must be
misinformed once more. I was told Minister Talleyrand would be in
Constantinople now. In fact, I have important messages to relay to
him from the Directory." That last was nearly true—but the message
was from Bonaparte, not the ministers back in Paris.

Another rapid exchange in Turkish. Ethan kept his face blank,
listening intently.

"Is the Frenchman here or not?" demanded the Vizier.

"Is it likely—or even possible—that he'd come into the country
without our knowing, blessed Vizier?" one of the courtiers responded.

"Is he on his way here? Perhaps he was delayed en route?"

Now a babble broke out among the nobles. Fixing his eyes on the
spacious domed ceiling, Ethan coolly followed their discussion. One
of the nobles claimed that he had heard from their spies in France
that Talleyrand was in Paris, immersed in a morass of naval strug-
gles against the newly formed United States.

"If he is planning on coming here," this most informed noble concluded, "he couldn't possibly arrive for at least a month."

Finally, the Vizier turned to Ethan. "You are mistaken, sir. I will arrange for the permission you need to deal with the spice merchants. But no saffron, is that clear?"

Ethan bowed when the interpreter finished his translation, his brain racing as he backed out of the room. It was critical to the success of Bonaparte's plans that Talleyrand inform the sultan of what the general intended. It was obvious that the minister had not done so, and time was now of the essence. Ethan had to find a passage—or an overland route—to rendezvous with the French fleet immediately.

7

JUNE 16
ANCONA

As long as Mirelle left the mansion early and returned late at night, avoiding both Dolce and her mother, living at the Morpurgo villa was just about bearable.

When she did meet Dolce, she was painstakingly polite. Dolce was too—in a poisonously sweet voice that shot innumerable barbs under her old friend's skin. Mama spoke as little as possible, asking only about such mundane things as laundry and meals. The kitchen staff grew used to packing Mirelle a basket of food every day so that she could eat her afternoon and evening meals at the workshop. But they had picked up on the strained atmosphere and clearly had their own opinion of her, so Mirelle often had to toss sour and ill-prepared food and purchase something edible. She refused to complain.

The one day Mirelle could not escape the mansion was Shabbat. She wouldn't dare go to the workshop and felt uncomfortable walking in town now. Occasionally she escaped to stroll along the beach, but this particular Saturday was scorching hot, and even the cool ocean breeze couldn't tempt her to leave her room.

A knock on her door startled her from a half doze. "Come in," she called, dreading whomever the visitor might be.

It was David, who looked concerned when he saw her in the chair drawn up to the window, hoping for a breath of fresh air. He was holding a newspaper in his hand.

"Why do you confine yourself like this, *piccola*?" he asked, making her blink at the use of his old nickname for her. "Come downstairs and join us."

"Thank you, Signor Morpurgo, but no," Mirelle replied. "I already disturb your household too much."

"That's nonsense," he told her. "If I want you to join us, who would dare tell me nay?"

Your daughter would. But Mirelle kept that thought to herself. Frankly, she still didn't understand David Morpurgo's kindness to her. She had brutally humiliated him when she'd broken their betrothal to wed another man. And yes, his anger and hurt would still flash out at times. But in many ways, he remained the caring uncle she'd once thought him, when she was growing up and she and Dolce had been best of friends. She was grateful to him even while wishing, more than anything, she no longer needed to be indebted to him.

"Besides, I have some interesting news I've just received," he continued, "an Italian letter and an article in the French press. Come down so I don't have to repeat myself. Yes?"

The question was phrased gently but was clearly a command. Unwillingly, Mirelle followed him into the garden where Dolce and her mother, along with David's brother Ezekiel and his wife Speranza were seated around a table, peeling peach slices and drinking white wine. They glanced up as David and Mirelle joined them. Ezekiel and Speranza both looked startled. Mama ducked her head and studied the tablecloth. Dolce's face hardened but then, glancing toward her father, her mouth curved upward in a smile that did not reach her eyes.

David motioned to a footman, who brought over two chairs. Mirelle slid into hers, knitting her hands in her lap and fixing her gaze on her white knuckles. Another footman brought two more crystal glasses. Mirelle shook her head when he began to pour wine into hers. The servant sniffed and moved on to fill up his master's glass.

After he took a sip of his drink, David pulled a pamphlet out of a stack of papers, ignoring the undercurrent of tension. "I was handed this a day ago," he said. "It purports to be a letter from a Jew to his brethren by someone called Mathéo." David smiled benignly at them all. "And I asked Mirelle to join us, since I think she'll be as fascinated as you will be, Dolce."

He paused, leaning back. "Let me start by saying that I suspect that this letter was, in fact, written by Bonaparte himself or by someone working closely with him."

Ezekiel shook his head. "That doesn't sound right, brother. Why would the general pretend to be a Jew?"

David inclined his head. "I agree that sounds odd. My sources made me consider it at first as just a piece of persiflage, a feint to cause trouble for the Ottomans, who have controlled our ancestral homeland for generations."

Mirelle couldn't quite grasp why David thought this pamphlet was so important, but she knew him well enough to wait patiently.

Then David added, "If my supposition is right, Napoleon is heading toward the East right now—to Syria or Egypt."

Mirelle sat up. The thought of Daniel sailing to either Egypt or Syria—to Israel—was breathtaking. No wonder she hadn't heard from him in so long! But then when would he be able to return to Europe? Possibly even return to her?

David continued: "Bonaparte has always supported emancipation for the Jews—with our seats on Ancona's municipal council, you and I are perfect examples of that, brother."

Ezekiel grunted.

"And we already know how skillful he is in using the press. He must have thought this appeal would be more effective if a Jew addressed his fellow Jews. If I've interpreted his intentions correctly, he's enlisting the help of Jews throughout the world to make our homeland a Jewish satellite of a greater French nation."

"To do what?" Dolce gasped. "Papa, you cannot be serious."

"Here, let me share the important part of this letter—then you can read the whole thing for yourselves."

David ran a finger down the sheet, then read: "'O my brothers! Let us reestablish the empire of Jerusalem. We are more than six million spread over the face of the earth; we have immense wealth; let us use all the means that are in our power to reunite in our homeland.'" He looked up. "Strong words, aren't they? Here, Zeke."

He handed the pamphlet to his brother, who read it, eyebrows raised in disbelief.

David turned his attention to two newspapers he'd placed on the table. "On its own, I might have dismissed the letter as nonsense. But the French press seems to be supporting it. Let me read you two installments of an essay from *Décade philosophique*, which I received yesterday."

He began to read a long essay, "Considerations on Egypt, Syria, and the English Power in India," which suggested that France use client states in the Middle East as a base to threaten England's hold on India. This piece, too, spoke of resettling Jews in the region.

"'We know how much they long for their ancient fatherland, the city of Jerusalem,'" David read out. He put the paper down, commenting in a voice of heightened excitement, "What an age this is for us Jews! First the French Revolution makes us citizens of France; then Napoleon frees us from the confines of the Italian ghettos. And now it is seriously being bruited abroad that we might regain our homeland in Israel! Something every Jew has longed for, for millennia. You and I included, brother."

"A pipe dream," Ezekiel scoffed. "When you consider how much the goyim still despise us, how can you give it credence, brother?"

"I would have thought so too, Zeke," David said, picking the paper back up. "But let me read from the second installment—this was published on April 19." He read out: "'Everywhere, they'—the author means Jews—'display sobriety, persistence, industry, activity. They have capital and commercial connections. These qualities and these means are not utilized as efficiently as they might be for their own benefit and for the broader society. It is therefore worthy of the attention of an enlightened government to consider whether it would be easy to do better in this regard, and thereby get for itself both advantage and glory.'"

Ezekiel just shook his head, clearly not convinced.

"Well, that's certainly a different attitude than how we're usually perceived, Papa—truly revolutionary. But what does it all mean?" Dolce asked.

Mirelle couldn't tell if she were truly interested or if she were just humoring her father.

"The author seems to think we Jews might be willing to underwrite the cost of restoring both Greater Syria—which includes our holy land—as well as Egypt," David explained. "Here, where is that paragraph? Oh, yes: 'Their fortunes are easy to transport; men and gold will flow; they will supply enough, not only to make industry flourish, but to meet the expenses of the revolution in Syria and Egypt.' What do you all think?" David looked around the table, clearly excited at the prospect. "If there is a movement to resettle us in our homeland, how can you and I, Zeke—or any Jew with means—ignore the call to help fund it?"

"Well," said Mama, "I'm not sure I understand all that. But it does sound grand. And you are always so generous, David."

"I'd need to be sure of what is truly taking place before I contribute, David," his brother argued. "It sounds dubious to me."

"But if Papa is right, Uncle Zeke?" Dolce asked. "Just think of what that might mean for us as a people!"

"Dolce is right," David said. "We would belong again among the nations, no longer despised as wanderers with no home. We could live as free men, creating a destiny that is wholly our own. No one telling us what we cannot do—able to farm, to own property, to observe our religion without fear of persecution."

Mirelle let the eager chatter wash over her. What *would* it be like to have the Jewish land of Eretz Israel restored? She pictured the desert sands, the palm trees, the stone buildings and striped nomadic tents she'd seen in etchings and books. A land, she had been taught, of milk and honey. She wasn't surprised at David's enthusiasm or willingness to finance the project. After all, hadn't he always put his hand in his pocket, extending it to help his fellow Jews? It was one of the things she'd always admired about him, one of the reasons she'd once tried to convince herself she'd be happy as his wife. But then, after Christophe . . .

She rose quietly, smiling in David's direction, and slipped away.

Nearly a week later, Mirelle was startled when Dolce finally acquiesced to a betrothal. Mirelle had watched her flirt outrageously for years, her swains beguiled by her blonde beauty, her poise, and, of course, her wealth. So she was startled when, one evening after a long day at the workshop, Mirelle retired to her lonely room to find Dolce sitting on a settee there, waiting for her.

"You do work exhausting hours," Dolce said. "Why this is what you've wanted all along truly escapes me."

"But it *is* what I wanted," Mirelle replied quietly. "And the workshop is doing well, which of course makes me happy."

Dolce laughed—that tinkling, insincere laugh that used to amuse Mirelle but now only raised her hackles. "That's marvelous," she said. "Strange and unseemly, but then, you've always had that unwomanly side to you. I remember when you begged your father to be allowed to work there, despite your mother and the rabbi's objections. What a different life you could be living, had you heeded them and married my father."

Mirelle sighed. That all felt so long ago. "Did you want something?"

"Just to tell you that I'm engaged to be married." She dangled a hand in Mirelle's face. A huge emerald and diamond sparkled on her ring finger.

For a moment, Mirelle recalled how exciting it had once been to be friends with Dolce. "That's wonderful!" she said, admiring the jeweled hand. "Who is the lucky man?"

Dolce smiled, seeming pleased by Mirelle's enthusiasm. "You wouldn't know him. He's from Florence, the son of one of Papa's business partners. Sansone di Lattes."

"Do you love him?"

Dolce's shoulders raised and her lovely mouth pouted. "Love? No. It's an arranged match. But a suitable one." She drew a small portrait out from her silken reticule and extended it to Mirelle. "Here, you can see what he looks like."

Mirelle studied the miniature. The man staring back had deep-set dark eyes and a brooding face. His curly hair waved back from a high, pale forehead. His lips were thick and he was dressed in the latest fashion. "He's handsome," she said.

"Would I marry anyone who wasn't?"

Mirelle handed the portrait back. "Congratulations. I wish you every happiness."

Dolce sat smiling for a moment at the miniature, then glanced up at Mirelle, eyes narrowed. "I've showed you his portrait so you'll be able to recognize him and stay away. He will be paying a visit soon. And when he does, I don't want him to meet you. Go to your *work-shop*"—she practically spit the word, making it sound like some kind of hovel—"or stay up here in your room. Is that clear?"

The nostalgic feeling of camaraderie fizzled. "It's clear."

Dolce rose, the portrait gripped in her hand. "Good. If he knew we were housing a strumpet, he might think twice. And besides," she looked Mirelle up and down, lips tight, "something about you attracts men, even if I don't understand what it is. I won't take that chance with Sansone. He's *mine*."

Mirelle was startled by the venom in her voice. "Honestly, Dolce, do you think any man you truly wanted would ever want someone else?"

One side of Dolce's mouth rode up and her eyes, already narrowed, nearly closed shut. "How soon you forget. Just stay away. Promise."

Daniel. Of course. Dolce had wanted Daniel.

"I promise," Mirelle said in a small voice.

"Good," Dolce said, her voice syrupy sweet. "That's settled, then." She turned and left the room, her silk skirts swishing along the tiled floor.

8

June
En route to Egypt

As the French fleet streamed out of Malta, the troops were finally told where they were headed—Egypt.

"Egypt?" Daniel asked Denon, confused. "Why Egypt, of all places?"

"It's a way of bedeviling the British," the artist explained as they stood on deck of *le Franklin*. "They think they control the entire Orient. We're going to show them otherwise." Denon swayed a little and caught hold of the railing as a swell pitched the frigate. "Certainly a better plan than attacking them head-on, which Bonaparte was ordered to do at first. I hear he spent some time in Calais and traveled up and down the coast. Upon returning from his reconnoiter, he told the Directory that they were crazed to think that the French could breach the island through Britain's naval defenses."

Daniel, like every other French boy, had grown up hearing stories of how British captains held sway over the seas, acting more like privateers than honest sailors. One of the sailors had told Pierre that the nefarious British Admiral Nelson was sure to be hot on their trail. Daniel could not think of the admiral—who'd lost both eye and arm under fire—without shuddering, especially now that they were all onboard a ship.

As the journey continued, stories circulated about Egypt's ancient riches. Denon confided to Daniel that Napoleon had asked the writers and artists among the savants to spread these tales to lessen the tedium of the passage. They spun elaborate stories and painted word pictures of the tombs of the mighty pharaohs, where abundant gold and silver lay buried, of the mighty pyramids and the mysterious Sphinx.

Daniel laughed when Denon waxed poetic. "You forget," he said. "My people built those pyramids when we were slaves in Egypt."

Denon's expressive eyebrows lifted. "It must feel strange, returning to a country where your ancestors were enslaved."

"It does," Daniel admitted.

"But of course," Denon added, "it wasn't you, personally."

Daniel didn't bother explaining how, every year at the Passover meal, his family would gather around the table and read the story of exile, enslavement, and escape from the Haggadah. "In every generation, we are obligated to see ourselves as though we personally came out of Egypt," his father would read out. What would his father and brother say, if they knew he was heading back to the land of the pharaohs? How would Mirelle respond when he wrote her about it?

He himself wasn't sure what to think about it. Certainly, there was a certain satisfaction in conquering a land that had enslaved his people. And the thought of actually seeing the antiquities Denon described couldn't help but excite him. But something about the whole expedition felt wrong, somehow. He just couldn't put a finger on what it was.

Denon, while quartered aboard *le Franklin*, often rowed over to visit those of his savant friends who were privileged to live on Napoleon's flagship, *L'Orient*. Upon his return, he would hold court on deck, regaling Daniel and the others with stories of how Napoleon was enduring the journey. The men were amused by his tales of Napoleon's custom-constructed bed. The general sought to evade sea sickness by sitting up most of the day in a bed fitted with casters, which swayed in rhythm with the ship. There he would read, write, and talk to his generals and favored savants. Every night he would gather the savants and his staff on deck, having previously decided on a topic that would comprise that evening's learned discussion.

Upon returning to *le Franklin* one night, Denon burbled over with laughter and couldn't wait to relate the story to the men. "Napoleon was leading a discussion about the possibility of life on other planets," he said, "and Junot was pulling faces and making silly quips. When the general chastised him, he pretended to fall asleep and snored so loudly he disrupted the conversation."

"Bonaparte couldn't have liked that," said Christophe.

"Like it? He kicked Junot, then ordered him off the deck."

Every evening the army band would strike up and the men would gather on deck to sing. It was a moment of rare amity among sailors and soldiers, who otherwise had little use for one another.

Because, for the most part, life onboard ship was a continual nightmare. If the trip to Malta had been hideous, cramped, and filled with queasy soldiers, it was nothing compared to the rough seas and the constant arguments that sprang up on this longer journey. The sailors openly sneered at the seasick soldiers, taunting them as they emptied their stomachs into the sea. Several of them, discovering that Daniel's company was largely made up of Jews, were even harsher, cursing them with foul names and antisemitic slurs.

"Christ-killers!" a midshipman muttered as he passed through the lower decks where Daniel's men were clustered. "You bring us nothing but *le malheur*."

"Yes, they do the devil's work for certain. We should throw them all into the sea," his fellow sailor agreed, face disfigured with a sneer. "*Tas de merde*, their stink makes my skin crawl."

Daniel was no stranger to such insults. Even after the Jews were given citizenship in France, there was no escaping the antisemitism that could make life hell on the streets of Paris. But during the last two years, he'd grown used to being accepted as just another soldier in Bonaparte's army. Being in such close quarters with the glares and muttered curses made his stomach roil. Despite his rank, nothing he would say—not his company's battle history nor the official French attitude toward them—would sway these men. He knew that. He thought of Odette, Christophe's devout mother, who still considered him devil spawn and openly mourned her son's lapsed Catholicism. Even Francesca Marotti, the Italian woman he'd grown to know and respect in Ancona, couldn't completely overcome her prejudice. This despite realizing that Daniel bore no relation to the hook-nosed, foul-smelling, untrustworthy picture of the Jew spread by her neighbors and the priesthood.

"Say nothing," Daniel told his men when they complained. "Keep your heads down. They can't do anything more than smear us with curses."

"We're as good as they are," Sebastian protested, enormous hands fisted by his side. "We should show them so."

Daniel grimaced. "A brawl onboard ship? They'll throw us into the brig. No fighting."

"And the brig would be worse than the way we're forced to live now?" Sebastian asked. But he was a good enough soldier to obey orders.

Of course, Sebastian was right. Conditions on board ship were atrocious. The air reeked of vomit, the food spoiled and the wine casks leaked. Rats boldly chased about below decks, the soldiers amusing themselves by catching them and throwing their wriggling bodies overboard. Within days, a swarm of fleas tormented the men, with no respite from their whizzing and biting. The men groaned at the incredibly tight quarters, shoehorned together with no escape from their fellows. Daniel spent as much of his day on deck as he could, but his duty required him to try and alleviate his company's discomfort. It proved impossible.

He had to admit that Christophe had an even more arduous task, for as a lieutenant of dragoons, he had horses to care for. Stabled in narrow stalls in the belly of the *le Franklin* with no way to exercise them, and with dwindling feed shot through with maggots, many of the steeds wizened and died. A dead horse had to be hacked up, bloody hunks of flesh hauled up and dumped overboard, lest the stench overwhelm the entire ship. Some of the men proposed eating the horseflesh, but after an abortive try with the first, its innards found to be crawling with maggots and its flanks worn so thin that bones protruded from its body, the idea was abandoned.

All this to reach Egypt? Daniel couldn't help but shake his head, still unclear exactly what the general's purpose was in setting out on this expedition. And he feared the worst was yet to come.

During the evening of June 22, fog rose in the early evening, making the French fleet look like ghosts haunting the waves. Daniel and Christophe, standing on deck, shivered at the damp air blowing all around them.

"They say it will take another week for us to reach Egypt," Christophe mused. "I'll be glad to be on dry land again."

"Dry land and something decent to eat," Daniel agreed.

"I don't even want to think about food," Christophe moaned.

Daniel sighed. "Remember those days in the Army of Italy before the general came? How we starved? Dug up dandelions to make a stew? I'd give anything for fresh dandelions."

Christophe's mouth twisted. "We complained then, too, didn't we? But then General Bonaparte arrived, and everything changed. Remember Italian cheese? Fresh vegetables? Meat?"

"Argh," Daniel exclaimed, clutching his empty stomach. "Talk about something else."

Christophe opened his mouth, but a distant booming made him snap it shut again. Both men looked around, startled.

"What was that?" Christophe asked.

Boom. Boom.

"Cannon," Daniel whispered. "Why cannon? Where's it coming from?"

Boom.

A clatter of footsteps as soldiers from both Daniel and Christophe's companies ran up to them. "What's going on?" Pierre cried. Through the mist of fog, Daniel could make out one of Pierre's fingers hooked into his wife's. She was trembling, hugging her too-big uniform jacket about her.

A sailor rushed over, treading on tip toe. "*Tais-toi!*" he hissed. "The British are about a mile distant from us. You must be absolutely silent!"

Louise moaned. Pierre put an arm around her shoulder. "Hush, little brother," he murmured.

"Go below decks," the sailor muttered. "Say nothing, do you hear? Not a word, not a sound!"

Daniel's men looked at him and he nodded. "Go on," he whispered. "As quiet as you can."

The men edged a step or two back, looking frightened. It was hard, Daniel realized, with a foe skulking in the darkness, an enemy who would rejoice if they were sunk to the bottom of the sea, perishing in the ocean's depths or disemboweled as shark food.

"Courage, men," Christophe told them in a soft murmur. "If we can remain undetected, we will prevail. It's completely in your hands."

That was smart, Daniel thought. Trust Christophe to know exactly what to say.

The night and the following day seemed interminable. The men huddled in their bunks, silent, barely daring to move. Fear that the British would realize how close they were to the French fleet exacerbated every noise. Every creak of the ship's floorboard, every cough was magnified tenfold, sounds echoing. It was ridiculous to think that the British could hear a shift of someone's cot, the hiss of someone's water in the piss pot, the soft sobbing coming from Louise's bunk. When a man fell asleep and began snoring, he was shaken awake, a hand clamped over the sleeper's mouth to keep him from crying out.

As Daniel lay silent in his hammock, his imagination took hold, seizing him in a cold sweat. He pictured the British discovering them. An outcry. Their guns would swivel around and pepper them with shot. The French would return fire, but to no avail. The British sailors, swords and daggers and muskets aloft, would board the ship to slaughter the French. Daniel forced his eyes open to stop the pictures forming in his brain, but they persisted in dancing before him. He felt, rather than imagined, being hauled up on deck, forced over the side. A gasp as cold water struck, battling the waves, tiring, finally sinking below. Air leaving his lungs.

Daniel knew from previous experience that such dire visions—anticipating disaster, the fear and dread he always felt before battle—were always far worse than the bout itself. Once engaged, he could starve his imagination, go from moment to moment, repositioning cannon, focusing only on what was directly before him. But this forced inactivity, this silent waiting, caused his heart to beat wildly and a pulse to throb in the hollow of his throat. He controlled his breathing with an effort, hoping his men wouldn't sense his fear.

And when he did manage to push his terror aside, thoughts of Mirelle plagued him. Would she hear of the disaster and mourn him? He regretted not ever telling her—at least not directly—of his love. Damn his diffident nature, his fear of losing her forever if he spoke out. She might never know, now, how he felt. Nor would he know if she returned his love.

He jerked with every sound of the guns, the constant *boom, boom,*

boom throughout the night. Daniel wasn't certain, but he thought the British must be using the cannon to keep abreast of the other ships in the fleet because of the fog. Why else waste ammunition?

Midday the next day, the sound grew softer, as if the ships were veering off. The men remained motionless, tensely waiting for the blasts to strengthen once more. But instead, they diminished, then faded to nothingness. And then, suddenly, just as the sun ducked down under the horizon line, cheering burst forth—loud, riotous shouts and applause. One of the ensigns clambered down to them, a grin plastered over his young face. "They've sailed in another direction," he said. "We're safe for now."

"Huzzah!" Sebastian cried, and the others echoed him, clapping one another on the back and tromping onto the deck where the sailors were lined up, lustily singing "La Marseillaise." The anthem was heard on the other ships in the fleet as well. Daniel joined in, belting out the chorus:

> *Aux armes, citoyens,*
> *Formez vos bataillons,*
> *Marchons, marchons!*
> *Qu'un sang impur*
> *Abreuve nos sillons!*

Onward, then, to Egypt and the glory that awaited them there.

9

June 28
Alexandria, Egypt

Esteemed katib,

May the peace, mercy and blessings of Allah be upon you and upon your master, the glorious Ahmad Pasha al-Jazzar.

I am honored that news of my writings on contemporary life has prompted you to request these accounts of Cairo—and yet, my first report will be, in fact, from Alexandria, whither my wife and I have traveled to visit my cousin, Baahir al-Sayed. As I believe you know, I am privileged to belong to a family that boasts several ulama, *well-known religious scholars.*

Alexandria, I am afraid to report, has fallen into disrepair . . . .

"Abd al-Rahman?" his wife interrupted him, coming onto the balcony where he had repaired to catch the cool sea breeze. "What are you doing?"

He looked up, annoyed. "I'm writing, Hasani. You can see that."

"Yes, but—to whom? You didn't agree, did you?"

He sat back, his fingers moving to his robe, pulling out his olive-wood worry beads and rubbing them between thumb and forefinger. He knew she was worried. He was, too, so his response sounded brusquer than he wished. "What choice had I?"

She sighed, shifting his ink pot out of reach. "Couldn't you have found an excuse?"

His heart warmed at her concern for him. "Do you think I didn't try?"

"But then?" She perched on the arm of his chair, her head nestling into the crook of his neck.

He wished they were home, where his cousin's family might not suddenly appear in the doorway. He kissed Hasani gently on the top of her head and pushed her from the chair. "I have no choice," he said. "One does not reject a request from al-Jazzar—not if one wishes to go on living."

"But to send him reports of what is happening here and in Cairo! You're a scholar, not a spy!"

He ducked his head. "Yet some would consider it an honor, wife. He's a man of considerable stature in the Ottoman Empire. And they say his *katib* is judicious in whom he asks to write such reports. And besides that"—he laughed, thrusting his worry beads back into his robe—"he pays well, much better than I could ever expect as a mere scholar."

While he knew he was wading in dangerous waters with these secret letters, he felt a frisson of excitement in this unaccustomed role. From the twist in his wife's lips, he could tell Hasani was not satisfied. A dutiful wife, she would acquiesce anyway.

Sighing, she reached down to caress his thick dark hair, stooping to kiss his cheek. "You know best, husband," she murmured. "I'll leave you to it."

He watched her fondly as she left the room, then reread the last sentence he'd written, "Alexandria, I am afraid to report, has fallen into disrepair . . ." And then he picked up his quill, pulling the ink pot closer, and continued his missive.

. . . *The signs of its deterioration sadden me. I write this in the hope that the Pasha might take a hand in restoring its past glory. For I am certain you know, Alexandria was once counted among the jewels of Egypt—a city crowned by its glorious lighthouse and famed library, both sadly no more.*

It was while Baahir and I were engaged on a debate of certain mystical practices and ancient mysteries that my cousin has studied extensively, feeling joyful as the sea breeze rose from the ocean, cooling this city which so many of my neighbors from Cairo visit during the hotter summer months, that a startling vision appeared.

Several European ships nosed into the harbor, all flying the insignia of the British. I counted twenty-five of them—a fearsome number, suggesting a possible attack. And I knew we could not defend ourselves, not with Alexandria's decaying walls and lack of fortifications caused by the neglect of our overlords, the Ottomans. We common Egyptians have hoped that the Mamelukes, who rule us with Ottoman acquiescence, would make amends for such negligence. But of course, it was too late for such measures, for the threat was now at our very doorstep.

I reached the dock just as a delegation of ten sailors rowed to shore. The ranking officer wore an eyepatch, with an empty sleeve tucked into his uniform coat. I realized that he must be the famed British Admiral Horatio Nelson, who had lost both arm and eye in battle, but who bravely continued to command despite his injuries. Would that such a man might serve in the army of Allah and become a defender of the faith!

The sailors disembarked into the crowd that had gathered, including several European tradesmen who reside in the port. These, however, had the wit to stand to one side, letting our leaders engage with the British.

One of the English sailors asked, in execrable Arabic, "Who is in charge here?"

The Turkish commander, Sayyid Muhammad Kurayyim, took charge and stepped forward to demand, "I govern this port. What do you want?"

The sailor translated, and the officer in charge bowed and spoke in a clipped language that caused several of the Europeans to murmur excitedly among themselves. "I am Admiral Nelson. We are on a mission to hunt down French marauders who may have landed here not long ago. A huge fleet. Have they passed by here? Have you seen them?"

As his words were translated, we Muslims looked at one another, not sure what to make of this news. The pause allowed me to make a study of the commander, who I am certain must interest you. His dark blue dress uniform bristled with medals and decorations, and his white powdered wig sat straight on his narrow head, topped by a high tri-cornered hat. He held himself erect, his remaining, hawk-like eye moving in all directions before coming to rest on Muhammad Kurayyim.

"A French fleet?" Muhammad Kurayyim finally responded. "We've seen nothing of them."

Nelson looked confused. "Is it possible we've overtaken them?" he asked one of his men, his gesture making his meaning clear even without the translation.

"There are no French here, except for those merchants that we allow to trade with us," one of the Mameluke officials replied. He flung an arm back to where the Europeans were gathered. "You see them here."

"Very well," Nelson said. He glanced over at the Europeans, bowing his head slightly.

Nelson motioned with his remaining hand, and one of his officers conferred with him. The admiral's lips twitched and *he turned back to Muhammad Kurayyim. "This French fleet are our enemies—and yours as well. If they arrive here, they will do so suddenly, and will attack and overtake you." He paused, sniffing as he surveyed the crumbling harbor fortifications. "You clearly don't have the defenses to withstand them. But we can remain on our ships and wait for them. When they arrive—and unfortunately, we are not sure in what direction they will sail from—we can defend you and repulse them."*

At that, I wondered how genuine the admiral was being. Was Alexandria truly in danger from the French? Or were the British the greater threat?

Now Muhammad Kurayyim whispered among his officials.

"I think we should let them stay," one of the Mameluke beys said. "Let them fight off this enemy. Save us the trouble."

"But what if this is a ruse?" another questioned, looking nervously toward the fleet of ships. "If we let them remain, they can attack us all too easily."

A ruse? I considered the possibility. The bey was not wrong: no good could come of allowing these Englishmen to loiter outside the city, their huge warships threatening the peace.

As Muhammad Kurayyim stood, undecided, Nelson spoke up again. "Sir. We need provisions—water and food. If we stay here to defend you and your harbor, we ask that you sell them to us. We will pay handsomely."

Several of the men nodded. I regret to inform you how I noticed some calculating what to charge on their fingers, hoping to cheat these gullible Englishmen. Surah 83 is clear on this sin: "Woe to those who deal in fraud."

Muhammad Kurayyim finally declared. "This is trickery on your part. There are no French ships—and we will not allow you or your ships to remain. Nor will we sell you any of our goods. You will leave and thus we hope to fulfill Allah's will."

The men who wished to profit off these Englishmen grumbled, and Nelson wasted much time arguing against Muhammad Kurayyim's decree. But in the end, the English force had no choice but to climb back into the rowboat. By Maghrib, as I knelt with my family for sunset prayers, the British ships had vanished past the horizon.

And thus I conclude this first—and eventful—report. The British have been dismissed, but it remains to be seen if the French, with greater ill intent, will follow.

Peace be upon you and upon our Pasha whom you serve so diligently, with the mercy and blessings of Allah.

Abd al-Rahman al-Jabartī

Adb al-Rahman reread the missive, nodding. He sprinkled sand upon it to dry the ink, then rolled it and placed it in a bronze tube beautifully etched with geometric patterns that he had purchased that morning in the market. One could not send al-Jazzar's *katib* anything less ornate.

10

June 30
Ancona

Not all days were difficult; in fact, some were intensely gratifying. Mirelle had so long wished to contribute to her family's legacy that she couldn't help but be happy when the ketubah workshop brought in new customers, when the documents they shipped out were minor masterpieces, when enough money piled up in the company's coffers to allow her to raise the men's pay or to purchase more extravagant supplies. Gold leaf, the darkest of black inks, parchment and vellum so soft that Mirelle sometimes ran her hand over the sheets in a kind of caress—all of these were her reward for her long days and careful management.

On good days she could forget her disgrace, ignore the whispers as she walked through the ghetto streets, pass by her mother and Dolce without flinching. Her workmen knew her worth and saluted her with warm smiles, heeding her instructions, trusting her judgment.

On good days, even the rabbi's visits couldn't touch her. And Rabbi Fano came frequently, at odd hours, early in the morning or late in the evening. He clearly wished to catch her in wrongdoing, to prove once and for all that he'd been right to prohibit her from managing the workmen. She wondered, sometimes, what might satisfy his prurient curiosity. An embrace with one of the men? A stolen kiss? The idea made her smile. The rabbi didn't know that her thoughts bent in an entirely different direction, toward Daniel, wherever he might be on this earth.

So she ignored the rabbi's peering into the workshop window and entering, unannounced, at all hours. She attended Shabbat services at the synagogue so no one could accuse her of ungodliness. Making her solitary way down the aisle and up to the women's section was hard, hard to seat herself on a bench, the women shifting their skirts aside as though she were contaminated. But she endured it, her mind busy with a list of next week's tasks to be accomplished in her true sanctuary, the workshop.

During one of these good days, when the quiet buzz of industry had settled upon the manufactory in the midafternoon, as she tallied up the week's earnings and thought contentedly of the fine shipment she'd send to the Netherlands that evening, a French officer entered hard upon his single loud knock on the door. He stood, uncertain, in the middle of the workroom. "Who is in charge here?" he demanded in rudimentary Italian.

Mirelle left her office. "I am," she replied in her fluent French. "What can I do for you, Citizen Captain?"

The officer reared back, startled. "You? A woman?"

Mirelle suppressed a grin. "Yes, sir. I am Mirelle d'Ancona and this is my workshop."

The captain, who had removed his tall shako cap when she approached, tucked it under his arm. "Is there a manager I can speak to?"

Mirelle sighed. Yet another man who didn't believe a woman could discuss business. She should expect it by now, but it still stung. She gestured toward Sabato, who had been standing to one side, watching them warily. "This is Sabato Narducci, my foreman," she introduced him to the officer. "You may speak with us both."

Of all the men in her workshop, she treasured Narducci the

most. He had been loyal to her father, had always supported her, was sincerely sorry during the last few years when Rabbi Fano and her mother had forbidden her to work there, and now, as her right-hand man, was completely reliable.

The officer looked relieved, handing Narducci a slip of paper. "We are levying increased taxes on all the businesses in Ancona, Signor Narducci," he said, keeping his eyes fixed on Sabato's face. "Rebels are plotting throughout Italy, some of whom threaten this city, and the French army needs additional funds to protect you."

Narducci handed the sheet to Mirelle, who looked at the figure and gasped. "You want—you realize that this is forty percent of our earnings, if not more?" she cried, incredulous. "How do you expect us to remain in business?"

Ignoring her, the captain's lips twisted as he spoke directly to Narducci. "You are Jews, aren't you? You always find a way."

"But forty percent!" Mirelle blurted. "You'll bankrupt us!"

Instantly, she realized she shouldn't have spoken out loud. The workers, hearing her, grew still, their faces swiveling toward them. One or two half-rose from their seats.

The captain eyed them cautiously, one hand on his sword hilt. "In a week's time, Signor Narducci," he said. "And make sure the accounts are in order. We know this is one of the most prosperous enterprises in the Jewish Quarter, so do not think to cheat us." He paused, the twist of his lips growing even more pronounced. "We know your Jew tricks."

Mirelle, heart thudding in her chest, barely heard the insult. Her brain was whirling, trying to calculate what this would mean to the business.

The captain replaced his hat and bowed to Narducci, turned briskly on his heel, and left. The foreman paid him no heed. Instead, he fixed his eyes on Mirelle's face, as if intuiting what was going through her mind. "What do you think?" he muttered as she led him into her tiny office.

"I'll do some calculations," she said. "If I'm right about the numbers—and if there are no more disasters—we may just be able to weather this. I must sit down with the books. Reassure the men, would you? Let them know it was just the shock that made me say—what I said about going bankrupt."

"Are you certain?" he asked slowly.

"Not certain, but fairly sure."

Narducci nodded, then returned to the workroom. He moved quietly from workbench to workbench. The men gasped out their questions, but his steady voice and a hand to the shoulder or arm calmed the most worried. Mirelle was already deep into the accounts, making notes. She let out a pent-up breath. The numbers, as always, fixed and definite, quieted her jangling nerves.

An hour later she picked up her head. The men were back at work, the peaceful buzz, the scratch of quills and the smell of paint drifting over to her. She thanked her lucky stars for Narducci. If they were careful—if she reneged on the men's raises—if they returned some of the more extravagant supplies and made do with what they had—if she herself took no income for the rest of the year—it was just possible that they might survive.

She shut her eyes at the long tally of numbers and repeated quietly to herself, "As long as there are no more disasters."

11

July 1
Marabout, Egypt

"Land ho!" came the cry from the sailor who perched high in the crow's nest of *le Franklin*, a looking glass held to his eye.

Daniel sighed with relief.

In an instant, the men crowded the railing, trying to catch a first glimpse of Egypt. It was still too distant, but excited chatter ran through the frigate. After weeks aboard this miserable vessel, every man was looking forward to standing on firm ground.

"Terra firma," Denon muttered, busily sketching the enthusiastic faces clustered about him, as well as the seagulls thronged about the ship, their shrill cries adding to the racket.

As they waited, Bonaparte's orders to the troops were read out. In them, he instructed the men to treat the indigenous Muslims with respect. "Act toward them as we have acted toward the Jews and the Italians; respect their muftis and their imams as you have the rabbis and the bishops. Have for the rites required by the Qur'an, for the mosques, the same tolerance that you have had for the convents, for the synagogues, for the religion of Moses and for that of Jesus Christ. The ancient Roman legions protected all the religions."

As he heard Napoleon's appeal for tolerance and respect, pride rose inside Daniel, just as it had so many times under the general's command. He had witnessed how General Bonaparte had freed the Jews in Italy, how he had made real the promises of the French Revolution, protecting them. Daniel understood—none better!—how important it was to treat the Egyptians with respect for their beliefs and their way of life.

They neared the fishing village of Marabout around midday. The small boats they'd spied that morning had scuttled back to shore, obviously panicked by the sight of the enormous fleet. In coordinated groups, the soldiers were loaded onto chaloupes and dropped with a splash into the churn of waves and spray. Loading the cannon in the longboat delayed Daniel's company, which finally set forth soon after the sun had sunk below the horizon, heavy artillery weighing down the narrow vessel. In haste to prevent some counterattack during the landing, the officers were ordered to cram as many men into the boats as possible. It meant arms, legs, torsos crowded against one another, jostling for space and overweighting the boats. Daniel's men clung to the edge of the craft as it tilted perilously in the water, waves whipping up and drenching them.

"*Nom de dieu de merde!*" Sebastian cried out as he pitched sideways. "What happens if the boat flips over, Lieutenant? I can't swim!"

Neither can I, Daniel thought. "*Tais-toi!*" he responded roughly, trying to exude calm and command when he felt neither.

In the stern, Louise sobbed loudly, her fright palpable. Pierre had an arm around her, whispering in her ear. Daniel wondered if the couple were sorry now that he hadn't stopped her from boarding back in Toulon.

A rough wave tipped the boat, almost capsizing them. A scream rose as the men reached for one another, gripping their seats and the edge of the boat.

"It's the cannon," another of Daniel's men cried. "It's too heavy! It's going to kill us all!"

"Toss it overboard," Sebastian growled.

A couple of men shifted as if to obey him.

"Don't you dare!" Daniel barked. "Leave it!"

"But, sir—"

"Leave it!" he repeated.

The men reluctantly slid back. The boat tilted again. One of the men, Marcus, fell into the water. He bobbed back up, gasping for air, and Daniel thrust a hand into the sea. "Grab hold!"

Two other men seized Marcus's jacket and pulled him up. He landed on the knees of several of the men, crushing them, dripping seawater.

Daniel wished it weren't so dark. *Were they close? How much longer—?*

Shouts cut through the blackness. Horrified, Daniel peered into the gloom as the chaloupe closest to them capsized, every man on board trapped under the waves.

"Save them!" Daniel jumped up, calling to the sailors who were propelling them forward. "We must—"

"Sit the fuck back down!" one sailor screeched. "Shithead landlubbers!"

The boat rolled beneath him, his balance perilous. Hands yanked him down.

"They'll drown!" he cried.

"We'll all drown if you don't stay in your seat!" The sailor let out a string of curses as he rowed against the powerful force of the waves.

Powerless, Daniel watched as some men surfaced from the water's depths, clinging desperately to the bottom of the overturned boat.

"*Au secours!* Help!" they screamed.

Pierre was counting aloud. "Eleven, twelve—" He paused, drawing in a jagged breath. "Sir, five or six men are still under the water! My friend Clément—I don't see him!"

I know, Daniel thought. *But what can I do about it?* "How much longer?" he asked the sailor.

"Hell if I know."

"Will they send someone to rescue those men?"

The sailor pointed at the water. "Too many of them."

Looking past his extended figure, Daniel saw even more bobbing figures struggling in the water, with others floating face down, limbs extended, bodies buffeted about by the choppy seas, already dead or dying. He closed his eyes, wishing he could as easily cover his ears. *How many lost?*

As the sailors' determined rowing brought them ever closer to shore, the shouts and calls for help grew fainter. Twenty minutes later, the boat scraped against the sand of the shore. The men, shaken but whole, clambered out, some falling to their knees and kissing the ground in relief. Daniel ordered them to pull the cannon out of the boat. That done, they collapsed on the beach.

What time is it? Daniel wondered. The darkness surrounding them felt palpable, the stars closer and sharper than he had ever seen before. It felt like an eternity had passed, but it couldn't have been more than a couple of hours since disembarking. He closed his eyes and muttered the Shehecheyanu prayer, "Blessed are You, oh Lord our God, King of the Universe, who has kept us alive, sustained us, and brought us to this season."

Daniel's company was settled near the general staff. The officers were grim-faced, arguing among themselves.

"Admiral Brueys told him the sea was too rough here, too far from shore, the coast lined with sharp rock reefs," one of them hissed. "But does he listen? Does he ever listen?"

"Would it have hurt for us to wait until morning?"

"How many men have we lost? Fifty? A hundred?"

"Bringing them all the way here just to plunge them into a watery grave. It's a scandal."

Daniel recognized the last voice as that of Junot, the newly made general of brigade whom he had gotten to know—by sight at least—during the Italian campaign. Curious why the staff was able to speak so freely, he craned past their small huddle, spying a bedroll and a snoring man lying on the sands of the beach.

So it was true. It was said the general could sleep anywhere, at any time, only waking when he decided to. There on the sand—mere feet from the still roiling waves that shrouded so many men lost—Napoleon was asleep.

Daniel was shaken by a heavy hand. "Get your men up! We're going to parade."

Groggily, Daniel sat up. "Parade? Now? What time is it?"

"It's just after three in the morning. Move it!"

Daniel rose, brushing sand off his legs and arms. Glancing over, he saw the general kneeling on the beach, talking with his staff, pointing to a map weighted down with rocks. "We need to take Alexandria immediately, before the British discover us here," he was saying.

"But sir—we don't have enough food—or water," protested one of his staff.

"Who's that?" Louise whispered to her husband. "Isn't he terribly old?"

Pierre leaned in to respond. "General Jean-Baptiste Kléber. We don't know him—he served near the Rhine, not with us in Italy. It's said he did well there. He's something like forty-four, maybe forty-five, and wanted to retire—but the general wanted him for this campaign."

Bonaparte whirled on the older general, knees digging into the sand, face red. "Do you think these men haven't marched on empty stomachs before? Learn to have the same faith in them that I have.

They won't fail me!" He stood, looking around. Suddenly, his eyes narrowed.

Daniel felt his stomach drop as he realized Napoleon was staring at the cannon the men had brought ashore. *What's wrong now?*

"Who's in charge of these men?" the general barked.

Daniel brought himself to attention. "I am, sir."

"What is this blasted cannon doing here? Didn't you get my orders to leave cannon and horses onboard? How the hell do you think you're going to transport that through the desert?"

Daniel recalled an order to leave the horses on the ship, but not the cannon. Had it been garbled in transit? He straightened his spine so he stood even taller. "Sorry, sir. The orders we received only spoke of the horses, sir."

"What?" Napoleon struck his forehead. "How the hell did you get across with that in the boat?"

Daniel wished now that he'd listened to Sebastian and thrown the cannon overboard. "With great difficulty, sir."

Napoleon snorted a harsh laugh, apparently tickled by his honest response. "I suppose I should commend you on your perseverance— but it's a hell of a quandary you've given us. You'll have to leave it here—along with any others." Napoleon turned again. "Lannes! Make sure the cannon gets back to—where? What ship?"

"*Le Franklin*. Sir." A bead of perspiration rolled down Daniel's back, despite the chill of the pre-dawn morning. With a supreme effort, he kept himself from flinching as Commander Jean Lannes glared at him. He stood frozen at attention until the general staff turned its back on him, as though he had ceased to exist.

12

JULY 2
ALEXANDRIA

Ethan stood at the entrance of the nearly deserted souk, watching the French soldiers march two abreast through the narrow streets. He was dressed as an Egyptian, in a long dun-colored robe that dragged through the dust, a keffiyeh wrapped around his light hair. His skin had darkened and his beard had grown during the overland journey from Constantinople. He'd driven his horses night and day, changing them only when they slowed and could no longer be encouraged to gallop, despite whip or spurs. He hated treating the beasts so harshly, but he wanted to reach Alexandria before Napoleon's fleet did. And he had—arriving in a mere two weeks, dizzy from exhaustion, just hours before Admiral Nelson landed and was turned away.

Ethan had watched from the shadows as pandemonium ruled the city streets, the people panicked upon hearing the French were en route. The souk thrummed with rumors as women emptied the market shelves and hefted buckets of water home from the city wells. The men congregated in the coffee shops, arguing over the foolishness of sending the British off, making wild plans to secure the citadel and tower. A group of teenage boys even went to the crumbling fortifications and desperately tried to shore them up, beating their chests and claiming they would hold off the French themselves if the cowardly Mamelukes could not—only to be chased off by irate city officials and sent home to their parents to be whipped.

It took only a matter of hours for the French to scale the walls and seize the city. Some attempt was made to defend it—shots rang out from the port—but to no avail. Alexandria's residents locked themselves behind the gates of their courtyards and the shuttered doors of their shops, praying for the safety of their children.

The squadron of soldiers marched off. Ethan surreptitiously followed them to the Citadel, where Napoleon had established his temporary quarters. The French flag hung over the entrance, drooping in the still air. A delegation of city notables were just leaving the building, their fingers curled around the Revolutionary cockades they must have been forced to wear, as if trying to hide the badges from public view.

A guard stood before the door. "Off with you," the soldier proclaimed in bad Arabic, brandishing his flintlock in an unmistakable gesture.

"I'm French," Ethan told him in their native tongue. "An agent of the Citizen General's. Let me pass."

The guard looked confused. "You're dressed like an Egyptian."

Ethan nodded. "Easier to pass through the streets this way. You've no idea what it's been like in this city the past few days."

The guard looked unconvinced. "I can't let you through looking like that. Someone will shoot you. Change your clothes and come back."

"Change my—? Look, there's no time," Ethan insisted. "I have important information for General Bonaparte."

The guard smirked. "Tell you what—you tell me, I'll tell him."

Ethan's lip curled. "He won't thank you. It's not good news."

The guard shouldered his weapon. "They'll kill you if this is a trick. Go on."

Ethan had to pass by three more guards, exchanging impatient words with each, before he was finally admitted into the general's antechamber. As he stood by the doorway, waiting to be recognized, he took a first curious glance at the general. Napoleon and some of his officers sat, shifting to find a comfortable position on piles of cushions surrounding a low table, drinking coffee and eating flat loaves of bread. While the others in their field uniforms towered over the shorter man, Bonaparte's presence dominated. His jacket was open in the heat, thin hair sticking to a damp forehead, a long nose and thin lips pulling down into a rounded chin. But it was his eyes, Ethan decided—dark, penetrating, potentially ruthless—that made him such a force in the room. Staring at him, Ethan was vividly reminded of the sparrowhawks that preyed on weaker birds in the forests and farms near his childhood home of Bischheim.

"I realize some of you still don't understand why we're here," Bonaparte was saying, his voice laced with impatience. "So let me explain. Again."

His officers groaned. Bonaparte pursed his lips in seeming frustration. But then he stood, and every man's eyes focused on him. Ethan found his own attention riveted. *What was it about the man?*

"Let's start with the obvious—the economic reasons." The general paced, hands clasped, sounding like a schoolmaster imparting a difficult lesson to ignorant students. "We could never hope to challenge the British navy. You know as well as I do that our naval fleet is nothing compared to theirs."

"Do we know this?" one of the generals asked. "Haven't we just escaped them?"

Napoleon glared at him. "Don't be a fool. We were lucky, no more."

"So what does this campaign have to do with economics?" someone else asked. "We're soldiers, not merchants."

The men laughed, a couple of them elbowing one another.

Bonaparte's eyes narrowed. "Do none of you see? Are you all that stupid?" He let out a long exhale before closing his eyes briefly, then started again. "Britain controls India and their valuable resources. Their exports from the East are the direct source of their wealth and strength as a nation—and are what allow them to invest in their military, especially the navy. They hold a monopoly over exports from India, shipping them through Egypt to England and other European countries. Through *Egypt*," he emphasized. "So what do you imagine would happen if we took this country? Blocked their trade? Weakened them in that way?"

The officers were suddenly paying close attention.

"And stopping the British won't only damage them but will strengthen the Republic."

"Yes, but why Egypt?" someone asked. "What about the Ottomans? Aren't they our ally? Can we really afford to challenge one of the few countries that support the Republic?"

"We've long considered conquering Egypt," Napoleon retorted. "Believe it or not, even Louis XIV proposed it. And the Ottomans aren't really in charge of Egypt, no matter what they claim. The Mamelukes have a stranglehold on the country, thumbing their noses at the Turks. The sultan will welcome our interference—Talleyrand will see to that."

Ethan's stomach knotted. What would Bonaparte say when he learned Ethan's news?

"Besides," Napoleon continued. He tilted his head toward the mosaic on the ceiling and his voice took on a different tone, no longer exasperated or teacherly. Instead, it grew richer, deeper, as if the general could see beyond to a future that stood just beyond his reach. "Besides, think of the great conquerors of history. Cyrus and Darius from Persia. Alexander the Great. Julius Caesar. Don't you want your names to figure alongside these men? Alexander brought savants with him as he conquered the world, so that his would be an intellectual as well as military victory. I have followed his example. Our savants will explore Egypt's ancient treasures, uncover the secrets buried in Egyptian tombs. Think of what they'll learn! Think of what distant, mysterious knowledge we'll bring back to the Republic." He paused, as if the vision was almost too much to contemplate. Then, with another deep breath, he continued, "And then, there's the freedom we'll bring to the Egyptians, now nothing more than slaves to these tyrants, these Mamelukes. Not just the Muslims, but the Coptic Christians, the Druze, even the Jews. Like the Italians, they'll be freed—and we will be the liberators who free them."

Ethan watched the officers' faces grow rapt, captivated by Napoleon's magnetic speech. He himself was impressed. No wonder Daniel and Christophe worshipped this man. How could they not?

Napoleon lowered his eyes from the ceiling, looking around the room, satisfied that his speech had won over his staff. He sank back down onto a cushion and took a long swig of coffee. "We should talk about the coming battle," he started, in a suddenly pragmatic voice, when the guard cut him off.

"Sir!" he said, snapping to attention. "An envoy from Agence d'Ancône requests entrance."

The general glared, clearly annoyed at the interruption. The guard sidled back into the corridor and Napoleon's gaze fixed on Ethan. "What information do you have for me?"

Ethan stared dumbly down at the general. Should he crouch to his level or remain upright? Napoleon relieved him of that decision by standing again, groaning softly as he stretched and cracked his back.

"Ridiculous that there's not a single chair in this entire building," he complained. "Come on, man, I haven't all day."

"Citizen General, I come to you direct from Constantinople, where I was charged with seeing Minister Talleyrand and learning how the Sublime Porte had received the information that you were en route to Egypt. And also to ascertain whether the viziers and other government officials accepted our assurances that you were doing so as an ally of the Ottoman Empire to rid the country of the tyrannical Mamelukes."

Napoleon nodded impatiently. "Yes. So?"

Ethan swallowed hard. "So, Citizen General, I learned that Minister Talleyrand had not arrived—and was not expected in Turkey at any time in the immediate future. No one there knows of your plans."

The general's face blackened and he twitched his hands behind his back. He paced the room, kicking at a cushion in his path. "That can't be right," he finally snapped.

"Citizen General—"

"That can't be right," he repeated, more emphatically this time. "This entire expedition was Talleyrand's notion. You were lied to. Deliberately misled. They didn't want it spread abroad that they accepted the idea of our invasion. That's all."

Ethan clamped his mouth shut. He'd been told that sometimes Napoleon didn't listen to reason. His handler at Agence d'Ancône— which, rather than the commercial concern it pretended to be, was quietly fomenting insurrection against the Ottoman Empire—had attributed the general's intransigence to his genius. "The man doesn't let mere facts stand in his way," he'd said. "He's a master at twisting them to suit his own conception of reality."

Napoleon continued to glare at him. After a moment of heavy silence, Ethan added, "I was here when Admiral Nelson arrived, sir, and overheard conversations explaining why the dock fortifications were crumbling and the city unprepared for assault. The Mamelukes . . . ."

Napoleon shook his head. "Why would you suppose I need that information now? We've conquered the city. Now, if you had some intelligence about what awaits us in Cairo, that might be valuable. But you don't, do you?"

Ethan stared at the floor for a moment, then raised his head to look directly at the general. Napoleon waved a hand as if to dismiss him. Ethan hurried to ask, "So what are your orders for me, General?"

"For you? You're clearly not competent enough to serve me. Go back to Ancona and let them decide what to do with you."

Ethan bottled up his rising indignation. He'd nearly killed himself to get the information about Talleyrand here, had endangered his life to listen to the chatter in the coffee shops, only to be so callously disregarded. "Sir," he growled, bowing low. And then, because he'd lived among the Egyptians for so many weeks, he couldn't help himself. "*Homaar*," he muttered.

Napoleon had turned away but whirled back at this. "What did you say?"

Ethan felt cold fingers climbing up his spine. "Nothing," he stammered.

"He called you a donkey," one of the other men said, looking amused. "It's a common Egyptian curse. Hello, Ethan."

Ethan hadn't noticed this narrow-faced man perched on his haunches behind the others. He was Jean-Paul Côté, one of Ethan's fellow students at *ecole Publique*. They had not been friends.

Before Napoleon could explode at the insult, Bourrienne intervened. "Sir, I hired this agent after reading his dossier at Sylvestre de Sacy's recommendation. He's an expert in Arabic along with an astonishing number of other languages. Let him help with the translation of your proclamation to the Egyptian people."

Ethan suppressed a grin at Côté's sudden intake of breath.

"I already have Arabic experts; why would I need another?" Bonaparte plopped himself back down on one of the cushions.

"He trained under de Sacy. Let him at least look at what they've produced."

Côté opened his mouth to protest, then thought better of it.

Napoleon brushed the air irritably in assent and Bourrienne led Ethan out of the room. As they left, Ethan heard the officers break out in fevered speech, trying to convince their commander to listen to reason, that it was dangerous to pursue this course if the sultan misinterpreted their actions. But Bonaparte retorted in a tone of sublime confidence: "If the truth does not bend in our direction, we must twist it so it does."

Bourrienne frowned, moving Ethan swiftly down the corridor. "We will most likely want you to head back to Ancona or to Paris— but not yet," he said. "Prove yourself more useful than you have up to now, yes? The general has no patience for incompetence."

Ethan's lips twisted. Despite his earlier spellbound reaction to Napoleon's eloquence, his fame as a writer meant that he wasn't accustomed to being so brusquely dismissed. "Are you so certain *I'm* the incompetent one?" he grumbled. But then, as Bourrienne shot him a startled stare, he added frostily, "Very well. I'll do my best."

13

July 10
En route to Cairo

Daniel shook his canteen again. The slightest trickle of water remained. He knew better than to drink it, as much as he longed to. Many of his men—the ones stalking in stolid silence before him—had guzzled theirs before the noonday sun reached its zenith. But being stuck in the middle of this snaking trail of soldiers meant that any well they found—which were few and far between—had already been drunk dry by the troops ahead of them. Others had been deliberately filled with rocks and sand by the fleeing villagers to torment them.

Daniel remembered the hardships of Italian marches when their commanders made them march thirty, forty miles in a single day. But in Italy there'd been shade and water from the streams, ripe fruit waiting to be plucked and eaten. Here, they broke camp in the hazy dawn with nothing in their stomachs, neither food nor water, company after company staggering forth in a long, disorderly line. Sweat dripped down Daniel's back, collecting under his armpits, his wool uniform sticking to arms, legs, torso. His flintlock and backpack were brutally hot, metal bits sizzling against his skin. Every step was an agony, heavy boots sinking into the desert sand, having to yank them free every time he forced himself forward. The Italian campaign was nothing compared to this hell on earth.

"What the hell is Bonaparte thinking?" gasped Maurice, his hand clasping his throat. "Sending us out like this."

Phillipe bent down and picked up a handful of sand, letting it run through his fingers. "Is this our *six arpets de terre*? Here, Sebastian, you take these six acres. See what crops you can grow."

"Save your breath and keep your mouth shut," Daniel retorted, feeling his mouth grow gritty the moment he opened it. He muttered the rest through clenched teeth. "Just keep marching."

Christophe's company rode past, horses kicking up dust. Daniel shut his eyes, jealousy nearly devouring him. His men should have been on horseback too. Or on those strange beasts called camels. But having talked to Christophe after parade, Daniel knew what had happened. The steeds onboard the ships—the ones that had survived the journey—had been brought ashore by boat. They were in bad shape. To supplement them, Bonaparte had negotiated with the nomadic Bedouin chieftains near Alexandria, buying three hundred horses and five hundred riding camels, as well as commissioning several experienced guides to lead the troops through the trackless desert. But then, the religious leaders in Cairo had declared an edict stating that every Egyptian was obligated to fight the invaders. So neither the promised transport nor guides ever materialized. Christophe said their own horses were skittish, nickering their displeasure at the burden of packs and riders, still malnourished and weak. But at least he was riding, not walking in this debilitating heat.

Daniel stumbled on. The wind picked up. A fierce surge of air battered his face, pushing his body back. The world was suffused with yellow grains of sand that prickled his bare skin, crept inside his sodden uniform. Over the howl of the wind, he heard horses neighing, rearing as they tried to turn away against the ferocious blast of air and dust. One of them bucked upward, toppling its rider, galloping off. The trooper lay covered in sand for a moment before dizzily rising to his feet, turning to look for the horse that had already disappeared beyond the cloud of sand. The soldier just stood there, a statue, as if undecided to chase after the steed or to join the men who were tromping forward. Daniel's company passed him by.

Daniel raised a hand to protect his eyes against the itching as sand crawled inside his eyelids and stuck there tenaciously. His men were coughing, bent over, some walking backward. Feeling tiny pellets slip down his throat, Daniel ached to cough but controlled the urge, somehow knowing once he started it would be impossible to stop. He forced himself to imagine biting into a lemon, so that saliva dripped onto his tongue. He swallowed compulsively. It didn't work after the first few times.

An hour passed, then two. The winds died down, but the sand clung to Daniel's eyes and clothing, penetrated inside his uniform, drying and itching against his clammy skin. His rucksack was heavy with it. Another hour, and then a shrill cry from the disorderly detachment before him made him rush forward.

Pierre was sprawled on his back on the desert sand, his face white. Louise crouched over him, imploring him to get up.

"What happened?" Daniel barked, barely able to croak the words from his arid throat.

His so-called orderly looked up, eyes wide with terror. "He just collapsed," she cried. "I can't . . ."

"Men are falling out up and down the line," Sebastian grunted, kneeling beside the prone soldier. "We can't keep going like this."

"We must," Daniel said. He didn't know what else to say.

"Then what do we do? Leave him?"

"*Six arpets de terre*," Phillipe muttered behind him, as if in a daze. "*Six arpets de terre.*"

Daniel knelt, taking out his canteen, raising the unconscious Pierre to a sitting position. He could see that his sand-crusted lips were blackened and peeling. "Who's got . . ." the words caught in his throat, and he cleared it and tried again. "Who's got water?"

The only response were head shakings. He uncapped his own canteen and tipped the tiny remnant of water down Pierre's throat. He was heartened as the man swallowed. "Water! Now!" he barked.

A couple of canteens were reluctantly handed up to him. Like his own, they held only drops. He poured them into Pierre's mouth, watched as his eyes flickered open.

"Can you stand?" he asked. "Walk?"

Louise hovered near as Daniel and Sebastian helped Pierre to his feet. The young sergeant was shaking all over.

"He'll never make it," Sebastian said.

The soldiers stood in a grim cluster around them. One look at their sullen faces made it clear: no one wanted to volunteer to help.

"Give me his gear," Daniel said, groaning silently at the thought of adding more weight to his own burden. "Take turns helping him."

"I've got him," Louise said, putting an arm under her husband's shoulders. She whispered something into his ear and he straightened slightly before slumping against her.

"She'll never manage," Sebastian scraped out in a rasp.

The confession hung in the hot, dry air, the men staring at Daniel, waiting to see how he'd react.

He cleared his scratchy throat. "At least she's got more *couilles* than the lot of you."

Sebastian's laugh was gritty and he cut it off, a hand at his throat. "You think she's got balls?" he gasped, somehow forcing the words out. "You're not wrong, young Daniel. We'll trade off. Here, Maurice, take the *orderly's* gear. And someone—Phillipe—you relieve the lieutenant in half an hour's time. Right?"

The men nodded. Daniel, despite realizing the men had hopped to Sebastian's command while ignoring his own, was too hot and exhausted to care. They lurched forward under the scorching sun. The winds had stilled and the company's mood seemed to have lifted, at least for now.

14

July 10
Ancona

Mirelle looked at the unappetizing contents of her luncheon basket and shook her head. Once again, the cook at the Morpurgo household had shown her disdain for the family's guest by packing food that would cause even the servants to turn up their noses.

Disgusted, her own nose wrinkled at the off smell, Mirelle covered the basket again. She couldn't eat this—*wouldn't give it to a dog*—and wondered if she could last out the day without food. But her stomach rumbled as if to tell her no, she needed to eat.

She slipped her hand into her reticule, finding only a few coins. Ever since the French had levied the inordinately excessive tax on the manufactory, she had stopped her own share of the weekly earnings. While that was a mere ten days ago, she was already finding it difficult not to have money to spend freely.

But a coin would buy her some bread—and bread would keep her full until she returned to the house for dinner. She sighed, realizing she might have to complain to David about the quality of the food his servants served her. Or else she might have to head back to the mansion for her luncheon every day. Both ideas tasted of defeat.

She'd think about it later, she decided, her stomach gurgling once more. Right now, she needed to buy something palatable.

She left the workshop and walked the few steps to the bakery that served the Jewish Quarter. Despite having been freed from living in the ghetto by Napoleon's heroic proclamation last year, the streets were still dark and narrow, overcrowded, bustling with mothers and children and tradesmen. The women pointedly ignored her, but that was nothing new. Raising her chin, she ignored them right back.

The bakery was unusually busy for a Tuesday even though there was only one other customer. Mirelle stood toward the back, watching and waiting. The baker bowed almost to the ground as he presented platter after platter to Signora Manelli. Aniseed biscotti and almond tortes, chocolate curls and *biscottini di roma*. Mirelle remembered the announcement at synagogue last week, proclaiming that the oldest Manelli boy would ascend to the Torah as a bar mitzvah that Shabbat. She wouldn't be invited to the celebration that followed.

Signora Manelli sampled the cookies and cakes, sniffing at each, poking and prodding. She chastised Antonio Baker that the tortes weren't sweet enough and the biscotti too small. Rearing back, Antonio Baker remonstrated with her, loudly arguing that his treats were worthy of nobles, princes, the Pope even. Mirelle was amused at the frenetic hand waving, the raised voices, the bantering and bartering back and forth.

But then Antonio Baker noticed her waiting in the back of the shop. "Jacopo!" he called toward the kitchen. "Come serve Signorina d'Ancona!"

The name startled Mirelle. Jacopo had been her brother's name. Her beloved brother, killed in the riots before the French troops came.

A tall young man ducked through the curtain that separated the front of the shop from the bakery in the back. He swept black curls off a sweat-drenched forehead, the cap that perched atop his head insufficient, his apron covered in flour. His sleeves were pushed up past his elbows and his forearms were thick with ropy muscles—probably earned from kneading loaf after loaf of bread.

Despite having lived in the ghetto all her life, Mirelle had never seen him before. Strangers were rare in the Jewish Quarter.

He moved to one side of the counter, and Mirelle stepped up.

"How may I serve you, signorina?" he asked, his voice melodic and deep. He fixed respectful eyes on her face and she flushed. Men didn't look at her like that, not anymore.

"Just a bread roll, please," she told him, extending her hand with the coin.

"Just a bread roll? Surely you want to sample my torta caprese? Or my cannoli? No one makes cannoli like I do."

The thought made Mirelle's mouth water. But she shook her head. "Another time, perhaps."

He studied her, his gaze traveling from head to toe. She knew her dress told him that she was, if not wealthy, at least well off. Perhaps he thought he could encourage her into spending more than her slender coin.

He winked at her. "Stay here," he said, and retreated into the kitchen.

Mirelle sighed. The bread rolls were just out of reach, behind the counter. She was tempted to lean over, take one, and leave the money behind. Before she could do so, he was back, carrying a platter filled with several different deserts. He held up a cannoli shell, stuffed with sweet mascarpone cheese.

"I am new here in Ancona, come from Capri to join my Uncle Antonio," he told her. "I'm afraid he is obstinate when it comes to my baking—says my deserts are too unusual for the Jews of Ancona. Will you help me prove him wrong by trying some?"

"Aren't cannoli originally from Sicily?" Mirelle asked, eyeing the one he held forth. She could just taste the crunchy shell, the creamy cheese filling.

"I refuse to limit myself to regional dishes," Jacopo said, standing tall and puffing out his chest. "I am a baker of all the world." He brandished the cannoli toward Mirelle. "Sample and see."

She stepped back. As amused as she was by his grandiosity, she wasn't sure he wouldn't present her with an accounting at the end of her "sampling" session. "Truly, I only have enough money with me for the roll," she admitted.

He waved an impatient hand at her. "You think I want you to pay for these tastes? Surely you don't mean to insult me." He leaned forward and lowered his voice, "You're far too pretty for that."

His flirting turned her ice cold. "Just the roll, please. And I must return to work, so if you wouldn't mind hurrying up."

The easy grin on Jacopo's face transformed instantly into a grimace. "I have upset you! You are offended! The last thing in the world I wished to do. *Mille scuse!*"

"I am just hungry, signore. And busy." She put the coin sharply down on the counter.

Abashed, the young baker put down the cannoli shell and reached for the roll, which he wrapped in brown paper, his strong fingers creating careful folds around it. And then, with a wink, he slipped the cannoli into the package as well. "*Mille scuse!*" he repeated, handing it to her.

She took it from him, nodded and left. The jingle of the shop bell echoed in her ears as she headed back to the workshop.

Returning to the Morpurgo mansion later that day, one of the footmen greeted Mirelle with a missive on a silver tray. "This came from the French barracks for you, signorina," he said.

A letter from Daniel! The difficulties of the day faded and she snatched at the folded pages, delighted to feel how thick they were. She had just mounted the stairs to the landing outside her room when Dolce emerged from her own, blocking her path.

"My, my," she tsked. "You're in a hurry."

Mirelle subdued an impulse to hide the letter behind her back or thrust it into her bodice. She was certain Dolce had already taken the opportunity to study the handwriting addressed to her. "It was a long day," she said. "And I want to change before the dinner bell."

"I see you received a letter this afternoon. How exciting!"

Mirelle let out her breath in a long exhale. "Just from my cousin."

"So you two are writing one another?"

The question was posed in sugary-sweet tones, but Mirelle saw Dolce's compressed lips, the slight flare of her nostrils. Mirelle recognized the look from their childhood days—back when they were the closest of friends. Dolce would wear it when she was angry at a servant, at another girl in the ghetto, or at one of the widows who tried so hard to capture her father's heart. Mirelle had always pitied the person on the receiving end—and now Dolce had turned the expression on her. Unsure how to respond, Mirelle simply said, "We are."

"Well, well, well. I didn't think you were on such terms."

"He's my cousin, Dolce."

"Yes, he's your cousin. But cousins marry all the time, don't they? And men don't usually write to single young women unless there is some understanding between them, do they?"

"It's not like that."

"Isn't it? Well, then, why not share the contents of this letter with us all? Surely we'd all like to hear what Daniel has to say. Why skulk away and read it in the privacy of your room?"

Mirelle itched to slap her. She'd waited too long for this letter to be wise. "You're just angry he's not writing you," she snapped.

Mirelle's mother came upstairs, frowning at their raised voices. "Girls. What's the trouble here?"

Dolce's smile reminded Mirelle of an illustration she had seen once in a book of exotic creatures, of an alligator, its half-eaten prey lodged in its maw. "Pinina, I'm glad you're here. Mirelle is engaging in a clandestine correspondence with her cousin Daniel. Surely an obedient daughter would show you the letter first. No?"

Mirelle controlled her impatience with an effort. "Mama, please let me go read my letter in peace. It's been so long since I've heard from him—"

But Mama put out a hand. Mirelle realized her mother couldn't back down—not in front of Dolce. Not with Mirelle's already tarnished reputation—a reputation that reflected so poorly on her mother as well as herself.

"I'll return it to you after I've made sure it's suitable for you, daughter. And you should not be receiving letters without my consent. Nor may you write to him without my reading what you write." She shook her head, eyes narrowed. "I cannot believe that after all the trouble I've taken to raise you properly, you've become such a hoyden."

Mirelle clutched her letter to her chest. "Mama, please!"

But her mother's hand remained extended. "Now, Mirelle."

Mirelle reluctantly surrendered it, fighting to keep the tears from overflowing.

Pinina tucked it into her apron. "I'll give it back after I've read it. *If* it's suitable." She turned and went back downstairs.

Dolce stood before her, beautiful features marred by more alligator-like gloating. Mirelle pushed past her, slamming the door, and standing in the middle of her room, her fingers curled painfully into the pads of her palms.

Two days later, Mirelle sat in the workshop in the dim early light of dawn, writing to Daniel.

Her mother had relented after seeing that the letter contained nothing more than an account of what had taken place in Malta. She handed the letter back at dinner and insisted Mirelle read it out loud—undoubtedly to show the Morpurgos that the correspondence was completely innocent.

David had been interested to hear how General Bonaparte had given the Jews of that island freedom of worship. "Of course," he had said, after a cringing Mirelle finished reading, "I had been informed by my business connections in Paris that Bonaparte's ultimate destination was most likely Egypt. Stopping at Malta only makes sense. One should consider the general's actions on that benighted island as another sign that the French Revolution means good things for the Jewish people. Perhaps we truly will see a Jewish homeland in our lifetime, Pinina."

"That would be a blessing indeed," her mother said, polite but indifferent. Her mother's interests—unlike David's or even her own—rarely extended beyond Ancona's Jewish Quarter.

Now, bent over the desk, Mirelle dipped her quill into the inkwell and wondered how much she should tell Daniel about her situation. Feeling she would burst if she didn't confide in someone, she began writing:

Daniel, I hope you are well. I was so pleased to read about Malta and the good work General Bonaparte did there to correct the errors of generations, especially for our people. I think of you often—more often, perhaps, than I should—and pray you remain safe.

I must admit I am struggling. Perhaps it was foolish of me to assume that once I took ownership of the workshop that my life would fall neatly into place. Remember how excited I was to finally be allowed to do the work? But I feel besieged from all sides—from the exorbitant taxes the French army is levying on the manufactory, from the whispers and sniggers I must endure due to my lost reputation, from the daily slights heaped upon me, particularly from Dolce.

Yes, from Dolce. For I have returned to live with the Morpurgo family. You can imagine how awkward. But after a particularly bad episode on the docks, when a man grabbed me—nothing came of it, so please do not concern yourself—I had no choice but to comply with Signore Morpurgo's dictate to live where he could protect me. And while I'm under that roof and cannot avoid her, Dolce is doing her best to spite me in any way she can. It's evident why. Despite her betrothal to a man from Florence, she's jealous, Daniel—angry that you did not return her regard and jealous of us. Does she have reason to be? That's the question that renders me sleepless at nights; the question I wish you would answer.

For, unbecoming and immodest as it is for me to commit my feelings to paper, to confess without waiting for your dec-laration—if in fact you intend to make one—I truly hope she does have reason for her jealousy.

Please direct your letters to the shop because the last one came to the mansion and Mama refused to let me have it until she had read it. It was innocuous enough, but I ardently hope the next one will not be.

Write soon, Daniel. And stay safe.

From your cousin who wishes you all good things, and more,

Mirelle

Mirelle blew on the wet ink, dusted the letter with sand, and sealed it. Looking up, she saw early morning light dappling the ghetto buildings. She put the missive in her reticule and left the shop before the men arrived for work, walking with determined steps toward the French barracks.

15

JULY 11
EN ROUTE TO CAIRO

Christophe impatiently held the leading rein for one of his troopers, who slumped in his horse's saddle, hanging onto the pommel to stay upright. Remy, upon waking that morning, discovered that his eyes were streaming pus.

"I can't see, Lieutenant," he'd cried out in sheer panic, rubbing his eyes with hands coated with tiny grains of sand. "I'm blind!"

Christophe had wiped the dust particles away, then moved his hand sideways across the man's face. Remy didn't even blink. "We'll get you to the medics in Cairo," Christophe had said, striving to sound comforting. It didn't come naturally. "You can hang on till then, right?"

"But how do I ride if I can't see? And what if one of those Bedouin tribes attack? I'd be a sitting duck!"

"And if we leave you here? Will you be any less of a sitting duck? You'd be dead in less than a day."

An aggravating amount of time passed before Christophe could convince the trooper that he had no choice: someone had to lead him. When he finally succeeded, the man asked, "Will you do it, sir? I trust you. The rest of them would lead me over a cliff just for a laugh."

So now Christophe was playing nursemaid. It meant he had to

slow down, ride behind his men. It was annoying. He preferred to lead, not follow, but it couldn't be long now. They had to reach Cairo sometime, right? And Cairo had to be better than that broken-down shell of a town, Alexandria, with its crumbling buildings and feral dogs snapping at your heels in the narrow alleyways. At least in Cairo they would find food. And water.

It had been days since he'd had a satisfying drink, something more than a few drops at a time. Even though the horses carried double the amount than those poor bastards on foot—Christophe grimaced, thinking of Daniel—he'd drunk all that days ago. The pace the commanders set was unrelenting, day after day of the sun beating down on them all, the poor, too thin horses stumbling and barely able to keep up.

And here he was now, stuck behind his men, eating the dust they raised, hot, thirsty, exhausted. He closed his eyes, swaying back and forth in the saddle, wishing he could drift off and escape this horrendous ride.

Just as he had nearly nodded off, someone cried: "Water!"

Christophe's eyes snapped open. He couldn't believe what he saw. A wavy line of blue rose out of the desert, looking like an enormous pool of luscious turquoise water. *Could it be?*

"Water?" croaked Remy. "Are they joking, sir?"

"They're not!" Christophe cried. "It's water. So much water, Remy. We'll be able to wash out your eyes. And drink! My god, drink! Can you believe it?"

The men, spurred on by the prospect of the cool, inviting lake, set off in a gallop. "Hang on, Remy," Christophe called as he urged his horse to catch up with them.

Remy sat upright, clutching the pommel. "Don't worry about me, sir," he called. "Just get me there!"

The pack of men rode as swiftly as they could, covering mile after mile, horses panting beneath them. Christophe threw Remy's leading rein to one of the other men so he could race ahead of them all, keeping an eye on that tantalizing strip of blue.

But then, suddenly bewildered, he pulled up on the reins. *Where did the water go?* He put up a hand to shield his eyes from the sun, thinking its rays were obscuring his sight.

His men halted their own horses, looking around, blinking. At the back of the pack, Christophe heard Remy asking, querulously, "What's happening? Why have we stopped? Are we at the water?"

"What the hell, Lieutenant?" Maurice said. "It—it disappeared!"

Christophe wheeled around, facing the troopers. "You all saw it, right? I didn't just imagine it, did I?"

The men murmured that they, too, had seen the water—which was no longer floating in front of them, teasing them. Just undulating dunes of sand scorching in the afternoon sun.

"Did we make a wrong turn, somehow?" someone asked.

Christophe turned his horse in a tight circle, scanning the horizon in all directions. All sign of the water had vanished. "I've no idea," he finally admitted. "It was there and then it wasn't."

All around him were moans and groans of complaint and disappointment. Christophe's throat tightened with a renewed sensation of dryness. *How was this possible?* He sat in the saddle for a silent moment, trying to figure it out. In the end, he had to give up.

"Onward," he commanded, spurring on his poor, wheezing horse. "Let's keep moving."

16

JULY 12
CAIRO

Esteemed katib,

May the peace, mercy and blessings of Allah be upon you and upon your master, the glorious Ahmad Pasha al-Jazzar.

This report will be lengthy, for there is much to impart—and you were kind enough to compliment my last missive, saying the picture I gave you of Alexandria was as important to your understanding as the events taking place there. So I will do my best to render a full description of what occurs here in Cairo as we prepare for the onslaught of the French marauders.

I traveled home from Alexandria the day after the French arrived, finding Cairo sunk in a similar state of panic. The souk closed at sunset, stalls shuttered. The men who generally sat outside the cafes with their hookahs and cup after tiny cup of rich coffee, huddled in their houses instead. The merchants doused the torches, plunging the streets and alleyways in shadow from the moment the sun went down. Despite the Aghā and Wālī publicly calling for the marketplace to remain open, sending boys out to rekindle the lamps so that the streets were no longer cloaked in trembling doom, no one heeded the call. The entire city is holding its breath, awaiting the invaders.

I myself was summoned to Ezbekyeh Square by a hand-delivered missive from Ali Pasha al-Tarābulsī. As I'm certain you are aware, the Pasha is a man of influence in the city. I had no idea what the wealthy man wanted from me, a mere humble scholar. But one does not ignore such a request.

The Square was crammed with people, and I soon realized that finding the Pasha in this crowd would be near impossible. I watched as the troops gathered under the banner of Murād Bey, whom the Amirs, the Qādī, and the sheikhs had declared as commander in chief, entrusting him to vanquish the invaders. My heart swelled with pride as I observed the enthusiasm of the soldiers willing to join the fray— nay, more than willing, eager. Such faith in Allah will surely vanquish the conquerors and leave Cairo to Muslim rule.

Cries of defiance rose from every corner. "Curse the French invaders!" was the most common. But I found most picturesque to be an officer, standing on a crate and waving his scimitar dramatically over his head, exhorting, "Slice off their heads and throw their bodies back into the sea from whence they came!"

Sword struck sword with a resounding clang as the troops practiced deadly feints, with much flourishing of weapons. The assembled crowd cheered, mothers and sisters ululating. Meanwhile, the armorers brought forth cannon and other lethal projectiles, rolling them into the courtyard, lining them up in deadly rows.

The Mameluke commander Murād Bey emerged to stand above the warriors on a balcony overlooking the square. "Brave men of Cairo!" he cried, raising a fisted hand for silence. "Heed me!"

The men moved to form straight lines, awaiting orders.

I offer you a brief description of our stalwart defender. Murād Bey is middle-aged, but his years seem only to have hardened him. Thick set, it is said that just one of his arms is strong enough to behead an ox with a single swing of his scimitar. A pair of ice-blue eyes blazed out of his pale face, which was crisscrossed with battle scars, his wiry, bushy beard a mix of dirty blonde and white.

As you must already know, esteemed katib, *Murād Bey rarely appears in Cairo, which he largely leaves to the governance of Ibrahim Bey. Murād Bey is in many ways the epitome of the Mamelukes who govern Egypt in the name of the Ottomans. Forgive me if you already know the man's history but seeing him standing before us in such a heroic stance made me think deeply about his background. Having been born in a poor village in the Caucasus, sold into slavery as a child, he trained in warfare and only earned his freedom and authority when his master died. I have heard stories of his cruelty and arrogance. And yet, I once visited Murād Bey's mansion in Jiza in the company of other Islamic scholars, and we ulema witnessed his gentler side: the chess-playing, musical man. Yet even as we left the palace, his impatient subordinates, brawny fighters cast in their master's mold, as harsh and brave as Murād Bey himself, elbowed and shoved us out of the way, showing us grave disrespect.*

But I digress and there remain important events to recount. As the hubbub in the square died down, Murād Bey's voice thundered out. "I praise each of you for your courage and your mettle! With Allah's blessing, we will meet these beardless degenerate cowards head on and make quick work of them, shall we not?"

A roar went up, echoing off the stone walls of the surrounding buildings. A forest of scimitars was thrust skyward. Soldiers pounded their swords and axes against their shields.

"They approach our city on foot, on camel and on horseback, as if no one has the power to stop them. I say, stop them we will!" Murād Bey continued. "Their blood will stain the desert sands."

The assembled crowd bellowed their approval, drowning out the bey's voice until he raised a hand to speak again.

"Yet another part of their force sails toward us in their ships. I have dispatched a fleet of splendid galleons and other battleships to confront them, manning these vessels with seaworthy sailors who have sworn to capture or capsize their armada! The bones of these degenerate infidels will be fed upon by tigerfish!"

You know, I am certain, that these ships are stationed in front of Murād Bey's palace at Jiza in dazzling array. But having personally seen the massiveness of the French fleet as they arrived to attack us, I was forced to wonder if they would be enough.

"Let there be no doubt," Murād Bey proclaimed to his forces, "that we will make an end of these French dogs. Those we do not slay by the sword will leave our lands whimpering, their tails between their legs. Allāhu ʿakbar!"

Another roar rose from the assembly, men and women alike, with cries of "Allāhu ʿakbar!" resounding from every corner. Weapons were raised on high. Drums and feet pounded, the women's shrill keening blasting eardrums. Murād Bey placed a hand over his heart in tribute to them all, then turned and reentered the house.

As I crept to the edges of the crowd, retreating from the noise and the tumult, I was approached by three men, all well-known in the city: Ali Pasha al-Tarābulsī, who oversees the military payroll for Murād Bey's troops, Nasū Pasha, a man of considerable wealth, and Sheikh Abd Allāh, who was arrayed in battle garb. With such stirring events taking place, I wondered at their desire to seek me out. Surely all three had more important tasks to attend to.

"As-salamu alaykum," I greeted them.

"Wa ʿalaykumu s-salam," they replied.

Ali Pasha al-Tarābulsī pointed to a rolled scroll in his hand. "This screed comes from the French bey. They tried to write in our tongue, but the language is convoluted. Can you help us make sense of it?"

Now I understood and was glad of their wish to see me, not merely for my own honor, but also because I would be able to relay the information contained within to you, katib.

They ushered me into a nearby cafe and lay the proclamation before me. I shall tell you of our conversation, as it may be useful to you to hear, but also have included the full text for your perusal.

"It says here that their purpose is to end Mameluke corruption and

free the Egyptian people from their rule," I explained after struggling with the poor Arabic for a time.

"Do we need an outsider to tell us how to govern our country?" sputtered al-Tarābulsī.

Nasū Pasha, patting a protruding stomach that spoke of a rich table, tilted his turbaned head to one side. "He's not wrong, though."

"Not so loud!" al-Tarābusī muttered. "You never know who's listening."

The Pasha's concern was well-founded, katib, and I hope you will not take offense if I tell you what we all think—for you instructed me to be candid, even if I relate opinions that you might not wish to hear. We know that the Mamelukes do not welcome criticism of their rule, no matter how much common Egyptians suffer under their tyranny. I trust in your promise of protection if I overstep.

But to continue with the French proclamation, I told them: "He assures us he is not here to abolish our religion." At that ridiculous statement, I pointed a finger skyward toward Allah. "As if he could."

Reading further, I could not believe that the words before me could possibly be correct. "Then he has the audacity to say that the French are faithful Muslims—because they destroyed the Pope's control of Italy, exiled the Maltese knights, and are allies of the Ottoman Porte."

Abd Allāh stuck his chin up. "They abandoned their own faith, didn't they? Silenced their church bells and threw out their priests. Does he think we're children, that we don't know that?"

"May Allah take their souls," Nasū Pasha murmured.

I bent my head to the page again. "It goes on to direct us how to act under their rule—to fly their flag and that of the Turks, continue to say our prayers, and to curse the Mamelukes." I hesitated, worried. "Do you think it's true he acts with the Sublime Porte's consent?"

Al-Tarābulsī flicked his hand outward to dismiss the thought. "Allah forbid."

I rolled up the proclamation, expressing my disgust at the hash of language, the redundancies and poor word choices. The scholar in me was offended at the ill-written wording. Arabic, after all, is an elegant language, with its rich vocabulary and poetic fluidity. No wonder the Qu'ran could only have been rendered in that exquisite tongue.

Then Nasū Pasha made an astonishing offer, saying, "We know you were at Alexandria when the Frenchman landed. We want you to chronicle their failed attempt to conquer us. As a scholar of some repute, the world will believe your account."

They offered a significant sum for this task, which I confess to you, wishing to be fully open and honest. After all, you pay me for these reports. I said I would happily write such a chronicle but turned down their offer of remuneration, telling them that my accepting money for the task could bring it under suspicion. It was tempting to take their money as well as your own, but frankly, doing so would compromise my integrity both as a scholar and as your agent. They pressed me but finally accepted my refusal.

Standing with the three men back out in the square, I nearly choked on the dust raised by the departing troops, clapping my hands over my ears at the din. Shouts of command filled the air, along with the clatter of hooves, drums setting up a pounding rhythm, and the rattle of cannon being pulled over the uneven cobbles. Swords glinted in the sun as they twirled in circles high above the warriors' heads, while occasional gunshots sent skyward were punctuated with cheers from the crowd.

But rumors were rife that others were sneaking out of the city—notables with their servants weighed down with bundles of riches on their backs, the merchants and poor scrabbling to leave unseen, knowing they would be cursed for their cowardice by those who remained to protect the city.

Al-Tarābulsī, pointing out a man and his manservant on horseback, taking the opposite roadway from the armed forces, asked, "What should we do about the cowards who are deserting us?"

"Fools," said Abd Allāh, watching them skulk away, "Don't they know they'll be attacked by bands of Bedouin the moment they leave the city?"

"We should consider an appropriate fine for those who betrayed our staunch defenders," Nasū Pasha replied, fingering his rich tunic, eyes glinting as if contemplating the new wealth the city might accumulate from these frightened families.

I was tempted to reprimand the man for his greed. A verse from the Qur'an occurred to me just then: "O you who have believed, do not consume one another's wealth unjustly but only in lawful business by mutual consent." But it was not my place, and Nasū Pasha would take offense. Besides, he was not altogether wrong. So instead, I said, "They are fools—and cowards too. For there can be no question but that the French threat will be eradicated in the face of our valiant fighters."

And to that, all three men chorused, "Mashallah."

This concludes my report to you, esteemed katib. I shall write more after we have vanquished the enemy and peace is restored to Cairo—for surely, the French cannot prevail over our loyal Muslim troops.

Peace be upon you and upon our Pasha whom you serve so diligently, with the mercy and blessings of Allah.

Abd al-Rahman al-Jabartī

17

July 21
Near the Pyramids

The Pyramids' pointed peaks towered over them. Positioned in battle formation, the troops were waiting for the warriors riding toward them. As the hours passed, Daniel had ample time for awe. The colossal structures rose out of the desert, monuments to dead pharaohs of antiquity. Daniel grew dizzy trying to count the rows of massive bricks that tilted up the sides of the Great Pyramid. Had his ancestors truly been forced to lug these blocks across arid sands, to build the enormous base and then climb ever higher into the sky? How many of them had perished, falling from unsteady scaffolds or whipped by cruel slave masters? Dying of starvation and thirst? The Passover story had never seemed so real to him.

But while he believed more firmly now in the story of his people's exile in Egypt, he refused to credit a fantastic story circulating around camp, namely, that some red apparition had invited Napoleon to descend into the largest tomb's depths, where he'd spent a long hour, emerging only after the general staff had grown increasingly anxious.

But having spotted his pale face as Bonaparte inspected the troops, Daniel wondered if something had in fact spooked the general in the interior of the Great Pyramid, something the great man refused to discuss. A year and a half ago, Daniel had seen how Napoleon reacted when he'd seen the miracle portrait of the Virgin Mary in Ancona, how he'd turned white in shock at her visage. The general might refuse to admit that he was superstitious, and Daniel had heard him chide his wife about her use of tarot cards and fortune tellers, but something about these otherworldly events clearly unsettled him.

Of course, this strange story might simply be due to other rumors floating about camp. General Junot had finally confronted the besotted commander, telling him that back in Paris, his beloved Josephine was cuckolding him with the retired soldier-turned-businessman, Hippolyte Charles, even showing Napoleon a letter filled with details of her adultery. Bonaparte, it was said, had cried out, "Josephine! And me six hundred leagues away!" He threw his hat on the desert sands and stomped off, muttering "Divorce—I must divorce her!" If he'd entered the Great Pyramid then, he'd likely stalked its depths in a white fury, emerging shaken at his disgrace. Others reported that he'd added, "I won't be the laughingstock of all those useless Parisians. I will divorce her. Publicly." He was not, Daniel suspected, a man who took betrayal lightly.

"Here they come!" Sebastian shouted, interrupting Daniel's reverie.

Daniel twisted about to see the long lines of Mameluke warriors riding toward them, their battle cries echoing over the dunes. The Muslim forces stretched across the desert sands, helmets glinting in the sun, cloaks waving in the breeze created by their brisk gallop, stallions harnessed with saddles decorated with sumptuous woven fabrics and chased with silver. Each one brandished a curved sword or saber, axe or spiked mace. Through his spy glass, Daniel noticed long-handled pistols tucked into sashes or hanging from their pommels.

"Such peacocks!" Pierre commented gleefully, a hand shielding his eyes as he squinted into the sun. "Look at all those colors—and that silver dangling around their necks. They'll be pillage aplenty when this is over, boys!"

Looking past the riders, Daniel swallowed hard, spying thousands of foot soldiers. To the west were the black kaftans of the nomads known as the Bedouin—the tented wanderers who had so brutally attacked the French soldiers during their hideous march through the desert. The French troops had only had mere hours to recover, but the promise of food and plentiful water awaiting them in Cairo had given them strength—and they were Napoleon's men, after all, eager for combat despite their enervated bodies.

The Egyptian defenders plunged toward them at a frighteningly rapid clip. Napoleon had ordered the soldiers into several tightly packed squares, each three rows deep. Daniel and his cannon stood at a corner of one. The unruly enemy seemed bewildered by this strategic formation, halting abruptly just outside cannon range. The two armies stood in uneasy silence, warily surveying one another.

Napoleon rode up, turning his back on the defenders. "Soldiers, forty centuries look down upon you!" he cried, one arm sweeping past the Pyramids. "I know you will prevail this day—standing firm in the face of the enemy in the tradition of Alexander's troops!"

A roar of affirmation rose from the French, buffeting outward on the wind.

As if to counter their enthusiasm, Mameluke horsemen rode up and down in front of the French forces, calling out, twirling their curved swords over their heads in skillful circles. One of them, with an impressive blonde beard and a turban like a mushroom top on his head, spoke at length, following his speech with the exhortation: "*Allāhu 'akbar!*"

"*Allāhu 'akbar!*" ran up and down the Egyptian line, as weapons were hoisted aloft and the men pounded their shields. "*Allāhu 'akbar!*"

While he knew no Arabic, Daniel recognized that they were saying, "God is Great." He had heard it called from the muezzin in Alexandria, and Cousin Ethan—who had sought Daniel out while they were docked, Ethan's appearance in that conquered city a shock—had translated it for him.

Daniel startled out of his contemplation as one of the mounted men rode too close. "Fire!" he called.

The enemy, struck by grapeshot, tumbled from his horse still holding the reins. The steed dashed dangerously close, the soldier dragged, face down, behind him. One of the French infantrymen slashed at the horse with his bayonet while another unloaded his musket into the man's back. The horse neighed, rearing precariously on its hind legs, then fell, blood gushing from its panting flanks. Another soldier thrust his sword into its head. The poor beast lifted its neck to let out one last, agonized whinny before collapsing in a sad heap.

The Mameluke soldiers galloped back to their ranks. More milling about, wild calls echoing in the still desert air.

Finally, the blonde, bushy bearded horseman, clearly the commander, rushed forward, his orders ripping out as a signal for the rest to follow.

Now that battle was finally upon them, Daniel couldn't help but be impressed by the charging calvary. As they approached, they wielded pistols, spears, and their curved swords, throwing emptied pistols behind them to be scooped up by attendants who reloaded them. But this show of bravado was no match for the French cannon, which took out many of the calvary and then the foot soldiers before they could even reach Bonaparte's squares.

Daniel's unit was particularly successful in striking down the men on horseback. Those who did make it through the barrage of grapeshot and cannon balls were met by sharpshooters kneeling in the formation's front line. Once these soldiers discharged their weapons, the infantry behind them fired over their heads, giving them valuable time to reload. The battle tipping in their favor, Daniel breathed more easily.

But was he judging the battle right? *"Allāhu 'akbar!"* came the frenzied cry of an Egyptian foot soldier who survived both cannon and artillery fire. A French soldier thrust his bayonet through the

Egyptian's chest. A second Egyptian, running next to him, sliced that Frenchman's neck through with his scimitar. The head, with its tall shako cap, rolled hideously in the dirt.

Daniel wiped smoke-filled eyes with the back of his hand, blinking away an unbidden childhood memory of the guillotine's merciless appetite. Shots rang out. With a wild shriek, the second Egyptian fell atop his enemy, clutching his chest.

The Mamelukes retreated from the onslaught, fleeing on horseback and on foot, sounding like squawking chickens in defeat. Daniel's heartbeat quickened. The day was theirs!

Napoleon ordered his calvary to follow close on their heels. Daniel watched as Christophe led his company, his sword slashing mercilessly through the ranks of running foot soldiers. The squares moved forward, their precise, choreographed movements a sharp contrast to the undisciplined Egyptian rout.

By battle's end, the desert was littered with dead soldiers, their blood running into the desert sand and staining the Nile River crimson. Daniel and his company were untouched—and triumphant. Knowing it was useless to try to stop his men, who considered it after all their reward for victory, he allowed them to move among the prone bodies. He couldn't help but flinch as the soldiers ignored any cries for mercy, finishing off those still alive with bayonet spears, reaching into their colorful garments for the silver they wore upon their chests, taking helmets and ostrich feathers from their turbans, curved swords and jeweled daggers, as battle souvenirs.

"We might have doubted Napoleon on the march, but there is no disputing he's a genius on the field of battle," Christophe said, riding up to his friend, his forehead seeping a thin trickle of blood from a scimitar thrust. "Such a glorious day!"

Daniel, distastefully watching his men rapaciously pillage the dead and the dying, wasn't completely sure he agreed.

18

AUGUST 1
ANCONA

"Good noontide, bella signorina!"

Seated in her office, Mirelle looked up from her accounts. Jacopo the baker's apprentice stood before her, a huge grin on his flour-dusted face, a basket of pastries wafting their tempting scent in her direction.

"I've brought you a treat today, Signorina d'Ancona. Do accept one of my Portuguese egg tarts. See how the custard is just baked—with a distinctive swirl of pastry on the bottom? I learned how to make these from a monk of the Jerónimos Monastery, in the beautiful city of Lisbon."

Mirelle's fingers itched to snatch the tart. "You are well-travelled for such a young man."

He waved it enticingly under her nose. "I considered it my duty to sample and learn to bake as many treats as I could. As I have told you, I am a baker of the world. Tragically, my travels were cut short for the same reason you buy only Antonio Baker's stale bread rolls." He leaned over. "No money," he whispered.

At that, Mirelle reared back in her seat. Had the entire ghetto realized the danger the manufactory was in? She had done her utmost to conceal their nearly empty coffers. But in addition to the avaricious taxes, orders had mysteriously slowed to a trickle. Some of the men were bound to the workshop until they paid back their years of training. She was actually considering releasing them from their articles, so they could seek employment elsewhere.

"I don't understand why you've chosen to visit me with your pastries," she said as sternly as she could. "Surely Antonio Baker doesn't want you gallivanting about the ghetto instead of baking."

"Antonio Baker is an old man, signorina. This is when he dozes off in the back of the shop—having risen at two bells to start the ovens and knead the bread."

"So there is no one there to serve your customers?" Now Mirelle's serious tone wasn't faked.

"Nonsense, of course there is. Don't you know that Antonio's granddaughter, Bluma, is behind the counter in the afternoons? He wants me to marry her, you know." Jacopo wrinkled his nose. "I'm sure other men might take her, but not me."

Mirelle studied his puckered face, shaking her head. "That's unkind."

"Unkind it might be, but do you really think I want to marry someone who can't imagine life beyond this ghetto—even if the gates are no longer there?" He shook the pastry, causing the slightest of ripples in the custard. "If I tell her about my home in Capri, she just stares at me. If I explain about the monk bakers in Portugal, she says it's a sin to learn from Catholics."

"Stop!" Mirelle put a hand up. "You mustn't blame her—she was raised to believe that. And besides, don't you wish to avoid the sin of *la'shon ha'ra*?"

"*La'shon ha'ra*?" Jacopo's bristly eyebrows raised. "Don't you know that gossip is the stuff of life for a baker? All those stories walking in and out of the shop?"

Mirelle flushed. So he did know. She had hoped the seeming respect he paid her whenever she visited the bakery meant that he, a newcomer to Ancona, had somehow escaped learning about her checkered past.

"Besides, sin?" he asked with a teasing tone to the question. "You sound just as devout as Bluma, rather than the enlightened young woman I thought you. All that piety twists your pretty mouth. It doesn't suit you."

She waved away the tart that he was still extending toward her. "Being kind is not necessarily pious. It's just . . . respecting someone, faults, mistakes, and all."

His smile faltered and she added, "I bid you good day, apprentice. I have work to do even if you do not." She took up her quill and lowered her eyes to her accounting book.

"Signorina." Sounding subdued, he placed the egg tart on her desk and took his leave.

She let the men depart early that afternoon since the few commissions they had were winding down. She entered the Morpurgo mansion, intending to head to her room and lie down. Her troubles made her head ache and she wanted to steal a nap before dinnertime.

But as she passed by the door of the yellow salon—always Dolce's favorite room in the house—she overheard someone say, "But my family has used the d'Ancona Ketubah workshop for three generations—ever since the shop was opened."

Mirelle recognized the voice: Giamila Renda, whose betrothal had been recently announced. Mirelle moved behind the salon door to listen.

"Well, so has my family," Dolce said smoothly. "Giamila, do take another biscuit while I freshen your cup."

"And isn't your father an investor in the shop?" Another bride-to-be, Ricca Mondella.

Peering through the doorframe into the room, Mirelle saw a sumptuous tea set out for the young women—all of them recently engaged. In addition to Giamila and Ricca, Mirelle saw Malca Garo and Benvenuta Margiotta.

Dolce laughed, her silvery tinkling floating out into the hallway. "He regrets it, believe me. When you consider her behavior . . ."

Heat flushed Mirelle's face. *Her.* No question who Dolce meant. Mirelle put a hand on the doorknob, fully prepared to burst in and confront them all. But before she could move, she remembered: she was a guest in the house. Common courtesy meant she had to pretend she'd never heard any of this. But while she shouldn't continue eavesdropping—which was not just impolite but nearly as devious as Dolce was being—she wasn't demure enough to creep away. She needed to know just how much harm her erstwhile best friend intended to inflict.

"After all," Dolce continued, "do you truly want your bridegrooms to consult her? I hear she meets with them in their homes—and who knows what happens there, behind closed doors?"

Giamila shook her head. "Not my Nathan. Dolce, I'm shocked you'd suggest . . ."

Dolce leaned over, placing long fingers on Giamila's knee. "I wouldn't have asked to speak with you all if I weren't certain that— that Lilith!—was seducing our young men. I can keep my own fiancé out of her clutches. But I can't sit by as it happens to anyone else, now, can I?"

"Why is she still living in your house?" Malca's head tilted to one side. "If you're so sure?"

Dolce sighed, taking a sip from her teacup. "Men are so weak. Even my father when it comes to Mirelle. After all she did to him— jilting him, making him a laughingstock in the community—he still brought her back home to live with us. After she'd consorted with a dock worker. Another Gentile—Italian this time. Shocking? Yes. Papa thinks he can save her from herself. But I know better."

"A dock worker?" Benvenuta asked, perching on the edge of her seat, a mixture of horror and prurient fascination lacing her tones.

"I'm ashamed to tell you so." Dolce leaned back, lacing her fingers together. "But it's true—and you need to know it. Your bridegrooms might well be tempted by her. I called her Lilith before—you all know the story, right?"

Mirelle watched as the four women shook their heads. She wasn't surprised—most maidens weren't told the story before their wedding and usually not even after that unless they showed some of Lilith's rebellious tendencies. Then the story of Adam's first wife would be related as a kind of cautionary tale. Dolce whispered the scandalous details—how Lilith had refused to lie under Adam. How, defying him, she'd uttered God's ineffable name, grown wings, and flown away. How she would suck the breath out of newborns. And—most importantly for Dolce's purpose—how she would visit men at night and tantalize them while they dreamt, causing them to spill their seed onto their bedsheets.

By the time she was done, three of the four girls were beet red: Giamila twisting her napkin, Ricca studying the floor and Malca the frieze on the ceiling. Benvenuta, however, fixed her eyes on Dolce's face, clearly relishing the details of the tawdry story.

Mirelle eased herself out from behind the door and quietly made her way up to her bedroom. Her head, which had ached before, was now pounding. *So this is why so many of our commissions are drying up.* Beautiful, wealthy, popular Dolce had great influence among the young men and women of the Jewish community. *This is nothing short of a calamity.*

19

August 5
Cairo

Ethan was bitterly disappointed in Cairo. Instead of the glorious ancient capital he'd dreamt of, filled with marble buildings and monuments to the pharaohs of old, the alleyways in the poorer sections where the soldiers were housed were narrow and choked with the smoke of a thousand cooking fires. Dust rose from sandals and bare feet. As in Alexandria, packs of dogs had free rein and snapped viciously at the soldiers' boots. The military doctor, Desgenettes, cautioned the troops and savants against the mutts' slavering mouths, warning that most were rabid and should be given a wide berth. The markets sold scant food fit for Western palates, and the houses of all but the wealthy were nothing more than narrow, dark dens. Children played in the alleyways, shouting out of mouths rife with blackened gums and missing teeth.

Ethan sometimes wondered why he didn't just set sail for France. A mere civilian, he was under no obligation to stay in this desolate place. But it irked him that his attempts to help the campaign had been so brutally disregarded. He told himself he would remain, even in the guise of a lowly translator, until he had a chance to redeem himself in Napoleon's eyes.

For he had an ulterior motive beyond simply wishing to completely change his life and get past his deep, unresolved mourning for the loss of his family. Writing about the Jews of France had played a role, however insignificant, to their gaining citizenship during the Revolution: citizenship for the first time in millennia in any European country, with all the rights and duties inherent in that privileged status. The part he had played a decade earlier had gratified him and he wished to take a similar role here in this foreign land.

He recalled his conversation with Sylvestre de Sacy when the man recruited him as one of Napoleon's Jewish agents. "There is a possibility that Bonaparte will wish to offer the Jews of Israel their own homeland in return for their support," the old scholar had said. "Such a thought is spoken of only in whispers and ultimately may not be true, Ethan. But considering your past achievements on behalf of your people . . ."

De Sacy had not needed to continue. Ethan wasn't certain such an event would ever happen. But if it did, he wanted to be there, to somehow influence the outcome. Even more than citizenship for the Jews of France, a Jewish homeland would change the destiny of thousands of Jews . . . .

A message from Paris had vindicated Ethan, informing General Bonaparte that Talleyrand had not departed for Constantinople and had no intention of doing so. Général de brigade Murat, who had witnessed Ethan's humiliation back in Alexandria, was kind enough to seek him out and tell him the news—adding, however, that Napoleon persisted in refuting the report. "He's blinded by his stubborn ambition," Murat groused. "The officers of the general staff are in near revolt over this filthy, pointless campaign, but he refuses to listen to anything we might tell him."

"Perhaps that is his strength," Ethan felt compelled to say, hoping Murat would report his disingenuous words to Napoleon, who'd then consider Ethan more favorably. "His tenacity and vision."

Murat shrugged at that. "He's tenacious, that's for certain."

"I wonder why Talleyrand didn't make the trip and ask for the audience with the sultan," Ethan mused. "Bourrienne told me that this entire expedition was the minister's idea to begin with."

Murat snorted. "Talleyrand? He wanted to stitch Napoleon up. After Italy, Bonaparte became the most popular man in France. The Directory fears him, is terrified he'll seize power. They want him out of the way. And you can't imagine any place on earth farther out of the way than Egypt."

"So Talleyrand convinced him?"

"Talleyrand played on his desire for glory, his sense of destiny. You've heard the general talk about why we're here. I remember you lurking in the hallway in Alexandria."

Ethan nodded.

"Where do you think all that eloquence came from? From books Talleyrand fed him and discussions the two of them had. So off Bonaparte went, panting to become the next Alexander the Great. With Talleyrand laughing up his lace sleeves the whole time." Murat shook his head. "That's not to be spread about camp, of course."

Ethan, promising to remain mute, wasn't sure what to think. Part of him felt sorry for the general. But there was still no mistaking how many men had suffered for his blind ambition. Or how many more would do so.

Murat invited Ethan to drink some thin wine he'd bought from one of the merchants who kept a bottle or two under the counter. "It's poor stuff, but better than nothing," Murat said. "Who knew that spirits were forbidden by these Muslim fools?"

Ethan had known that, and he also knew that Napoleon's bold publication that he and his men would convert to Islam to appease the local populace was stymied by that alcohol ban. The troops were also under the mistaken impression that Islamic doctrine required that converts be circumcised. As a Jew, Ethan thought wryly, had that last dictate actually been true, it would not have been a barrier for him. Accepting a glass from Murat, he entertained himself with the image of Napoleon's soldiers lined up, pants around their ankles, ordered to have their foreskins chopped. Smirking maliciously, he thought of the exquisite pain that the procedure would cause most of the men. Bonaparte's plan to convert the men was clearly nothing more than flimflam—a kind of toothless boast that the Muslims scorned and the French mocked. Was it possible the rumors of the Jewish homeland were just such rubbish? Was he wasting his time here?

Finishing the sour wine and bidding Murat farewell, Ethan passed by Daniel's quarters and stopped in. He found his cousin seated on his bedroll, eyes fixed on a letter in a kind of a daze.

"Daniel! Stand to your arms, man!" Ethan said, the laugh in his voice making it clear this was a joke rather than an actual command.

Daniel looked up, bemused. "Ethan. I didn't hear you."

"Clearly not. You wouldn't have heard me if I'd set off an explosive. What are you studying so closely? A letter? Is it—?"

"From Mirelle." Daniel's face lit up as though illuminated by a thousand candles.

"From Mirelle." Ethan perched on a campstool. "And what does our Italian cousin say?"

Daniel hesitated, then extended the letter to him. Ethan's eyebrows rose as he read it. "So. She cares for you," he finally said, handing the letter back.

Daniel nodded, lightly smoothing the page with the tips of his fingers, clearly ignoring the wealth of hesitation in Ethan's voice. "You agree that's what she's saying?" he asked eagerly. "I'm not just imagining it because I want it so much?"

"Could it be any clearer? She asks you to declare yourself." Ethan shifted slightly. "I do wonder, however, if she'd be so eager if she were not having such a difficult time back in Ancona. It was obvious to me even during the brief time I was there that the entire ghetto holds her in contempt. Perhaps she merely sees you as an escape from her tarnished reputation."

Daniel's forehead furrowed. "That's unworthy of you, Ethan! Having met her, how could you possibly suspect her of such duplicity?"

Ethan threw up a hand. "I admit, I don't like the thought. But you must agree, cousin, it's worth considering—before you commit yourself to someone who doesn't deserve it."

Daniel stared at him, nonplussed. "You've changed. You wouldn't have said something that harsh when I knew you back in Paris. I've noticed how hard you've become, how distrusting. Don't think I haven't."

Ethan shrugged.

"Did Adara's death hurt you that much?"

The question was a blow to the heart. Ethan set his jaw. "I don't talk about that."

"I don't mean to upset you."

Ethan softened his tone with an effort. "I know. But don't ever ask me about Adara again. Yes?"

"I was only . . ."

Ethan rose, hands fisted at his waist. "Ever, you hear me?" he bellowed.

"Fine!" Daniel stared, eyes wide in his shocked face, then looked down at his letter. "I'm sorry I mentioned her. It."

Ethan sat down, breathing hard. He gulped air, then added, "As for Mirelle, I would strongly advise you against giving your heart to her so unreservedly."

Daniel's eyes, shocked a moment before at Ethan's outburst, grew soft. "She has my heart already. She's had it since we met. And if she's in distress, all I want is to help her."

Ethan's mouth twisted to one side. But then he remembered how his own reason had fled when he'd fallen in love with Adara. Did he regret that sweet madness—considering how grueling the loss was now that she was gone? Would Daniel someday regret trusting Mirelle? But Ethan could tell: nothing he said now would make Daniel more cautious. "I should leave you to reply to her, then. Will you have her come join you?"

Daniel looked uncertain. "Here? To this barren wasteland?"

Maybe he didn't trust her love after all. "Didn't you tell me about the women who joined their men on this campaign? Would she not do as much for you?"

"She would, of course she would." Daniel smoothed out the letter. "You're right."

Ethan rose from the stool. "Well, then—"

But before he could finish his sentence, Vivant Denon burst into the tent. His face was filthy, coat and pantaloons rumpled, long lace sleeves fluttering about his wrists in tattered shreds. "Daniel! Did you hear?"

Daniel turned his head to stare at the artist. "Hear what?"

"Of the battle! Our sunken ships! How we're marooned!"

"What are you talking about?" Ethan demanded.

Denon dipped his head, clearly too distraught for the niceties of introduction. "You're Daniel's cousin, right?"

"Yes, but never mind that. What happened?" Ethan asked. Seeing that Denon was licking dry, chapped lips, he picked up the half-full canteen lying on the ground by Daniel's bedroll. "Here. Take a drink, first."

Denon tilted the canteen, gulping down the water. He returned it to Ethan, wiping his mouth on the back of his ragged lace sleeves. "Thank you." He collapsed onto the campstool that Ethan had just vacated.

Ethan sat on the edge of Daniel's bedroll. "Now. Tell us."

Denon exhaled, smoothing out his forehead. "Five days ago, I'd gone back to Napoleon's ship *L'Orient* at the request of some of my fellow savants. Monge and Berthollet wanted me to sketch some of the Maltese treasures we'd—er—liberated. To compile a record of them. Admiral Brueys had anchored the fleet in Aboukir Bay, apparently against Napoleon's wishes. The general told him to bring the ships closer to Alexandria—or even to depart for Corfu, for safety."

"Corfu?" Daniel asked.

"An island off Greece," Ethan replied.

"But the Admiral said that while Napoleon might be a brilliant tactician on land, he needed to trust a naval man to do what was right for the navy. I was serenely sketching below decks when I was sent reeling," Denon continued. "The flagship suddenly shook, the floorboards trembling, the sound of explosives deafening. Knocked onto my side, I lost hold of my pencil. The ship lurched again and it skittered across the tilted surface. The silver and gold chalices I had lined on the shelf rattled and I jumped up before they could fall on me. Tucking my drawing pad under an arm, I climbed to the poop deck and yelled, 'What's happening?'"

"What *was* happening?" Daniel interjected.

Denon ignored him. "Monge and Berthollet were standing at the railing. Seeing me, Monge pointed at the ships flying the Union Jack. Clearly, the enemy had moved so that they threatened both the port and stern side of the French fleet.

"'That fool Brueys!' Monge cried out. I could hear his voice trembling with fear. 'He's positioned us so poorly that the British managed to slip through the lines.'" Denon glanced at Daniel and Ethan. "Wait, I'll show you."

Denon grabbed some of the items laying on Daniel's bedroll—a brush and comb, a book, his spy glass, his hat and his revolutionary cockade—and arranged them as if they were the French fleet. He looked around, and Ethan gathered some of the men's objects to serve as the British ships, including a pipe and tobacco pouch. Humming the British national anthem, Denon pretended to sail them through, fore and aft.

"*L'Orient,* where we were, was anchored in the middle of the French fleet. We were assailed by cannon fire. Flying grapeshot and lead bullets whizzed past us. I seized Monge's arm, forcing him to crouch, then reached up to pull Berthollet down. Debris flew around us, pelting us with wood shards and shrapnel. Between blasts, I realized the upper sail had caught fire, then the mizzenmast. Parts of the burning sail fell to the deck just a few yards away." Denon reared back, as if the flaming sail had landed near him.

"Monge screamed, 'We have to get out of here!' and then I heard a cry on the upper deck and saw the Admiral collapsing in a heap, struck by a fatal wound.

"Berthollet was crying, 'What are we going to do? We're doomed!'

"I shook my head"—here Denon turned his head rapidly from side to side—"telling the frightened chemist to calm down.

"But then another cannon blast ripped through the air and blasted a hole through the rigging. It was then that I noticed paint cans left from when the poop deck had recently been painted. The flames were growing closer to them. I panicked. I knew that if the fire reached the paint, we were doomed.

"I pointed out the cans to Monge, and he started to gibber with terror. 'We must abandon ship!'

"I put a hand on his arm, hoping to soothe him. I knew we'd all be lost if both he and Berthollet remained this frantic. 'We must find a way off this deck, certainly,' I said, striving for calm."

Denon's lips twisted. "I would have thought two men of science and mathematics would be cooler under fire," he said, looking at Ethan and Daniel for their concurrence.

"All around us, sailors scrambled to extinguish the flames, but the fire pumps were flattened by an earlier cannon shot. The blaze was devouring the deck. One of the sailors grabbed my arm and cursed us all. 'Fucking civilians,' he cried. 'Get into the rowboat and save yourselves. The ship's going to blow any second!'

"We climbed over the side, down a rope ladder that was barely hanging by a thread. Every second I thought we'd be hurled into the sea, but we made it into a rowboat and were lowered into the choppy sea. The vessel was buffeted here and there, and I had to cling to my seat not to plunge into the rough waters. I grabbed hold of one oar, yelling at Monge or Berthollet to take the other."

Denon stopped to draw breath and swallowed some more water. "Don't you have something stronger than this?" he asked.

"Sorry," Daniel told him. "I don't allow spirits in the men's quarters."

"Continue, man. You were in the water," Ethan said, caught up in the savant's vivid retelling.

Denon sighed, tapping his head as though putting himself back in the rowboat. "The scene all around us was full of smoke—a constant barrage of bullet fire and cannon. Monge had gone pale and was next to useless rowing. Between us, Berthollet and I could hardly control the boat as we struggled to point it toward shore.

"And then," Denon said, rubbing his ears ruefully, "*L'Orient* exploded."

Ethan and Daniel both gasped.

"I swear, that blast must have been heard for fifty miles. Both navies halted in their tracks, shocked. For a full five minutes—maybe ten—absolutely no one moved. Not the French and not the British. I was paralyzed. My ears were ringing—they're still ringing. Then one ship after another went down."

"Went down?" Daniel exclaimed. "You mean, sank?"

"Sank, yes. The three of us barely made it to shore alive. I don't know what happened after that, but one thing's clear—we've no fleet left, none at all." He rose and paced the narrow barracks, visibly upset.

"No fleet left," Daniel said slowly, then repeated it, pronouncing every word. "No fleet left."

Ethan swallowed hard. How would this affect Bonaparte's mission?

"We're marooned here, aren't we?" Daniel asked, pale, his wide eyes fixed on Denon's face.

Denon hesitated, then nodded reluctantly. "I believe so, yes. It will be hard on us—no supplies from home, no communication with France."

"Dear God," Daniel moaned.

Ethan couldn't understand what had upset Daniel so much. After all, it wasn't the first time Bonaparte's forces had lived off the land. But then he saw Mirelle's letter clutched against his cousin's chest.

"I've no way to reach her," Daniel stammered. "She asks me to declare myself. Is waiting for my response. What will she think when my letter never arrives?"

Part Two

August 1798—December 1798

20

August 18
Cairo

Esteemed katib,

May the peace, mercy and blessings of Allah be upon you and upon the Pasha whom you serve so diligently.

You have asked me to send you my observations of the infidels currently occupying Cairo. It is a burden to relate how they, like fleas upon a mare, have embedded themselves in our very homes and dared to assume command of us. But because of their superior firepower, our Beys and Sheikhs have bowed to them in the most disgraceful manner.

What can I tell you of these foreigners, katib? Let me start with their disrespect for every civilized practice. Having beheaded their sultan and abolished religion in their own land, they have the audacity to claim themselves followers of the Prophet, may Allah's peace and blessings be upon him. Their commander, the Ṣāri 'Askar, does not even have a proper name. They call him Bonaparte, which means "pleasant gathering." We have not found gathering with him pleasant, for he struts about—having arrogantly housed himself in the home of Muhammad Bey al-alfi in the al-Sakit district—traipsing dirt from his muddy boots on the carpets. None of these nonbelievers have the sense or courtesy to remove their shoes or sandals when they enter a room. He barks orders and proclamations and expects us to kowtow to the French flag and the ridiculous ribbons they wear on their chests or in their hats.

These Frenchmen are filthy, there is no other word for it. They make their water and defecate in the streets and gardens, not even wiping themselves, or, worse still, using paper made sacred by writing. Several of the soldiers brought their women with them—women who show no modesty, who flaunt themselves, walking the streets gazing with lustful intent upon men, their thin dresses clinging shamelessly to their perfumed bodies. It is said that the Şāri 'Askar himself has insulted our women, calling them "Rubenesque"—a term that my new acquaintance, a Jew, says means unpleasantly fat. I for one would not trade the healthy curves of our faithful wives and sisters for a single one of the painted scarecrows the Frenchmen lust after.

Who is this Jew, you ask? I met him during the Breaking of the Dam, a day that these faithless ones made much of. He is one of the French translators who made such a jumble of the Şāri 'Askar's proclamation to us, but at least his spoken Arabic is tolerable. As I write a chronicle of these unfolding events, I realize it behooves me to make a friend of him, so that I can open a window into better understanding these Frenchmen. This new acquaintance should serve your purposes as well.

Abd al-Rahman stretched, then reread the last few lines. He had warmed unexpectedly to the French Jew, and was somewhat ashamed of any ulterior motives he might have in promoting their friendship. Yet, was it not part of his duty as a loyal Egyptian and Muslim, especially considering his task of documenting what the French did in their country, to discover what this interloper might tell him? Abd al-Rahman shook his discomfort aside and continued writing.

The Jew's history may interest you. As a writer during the French Revolution, he took up his people's cause and wrote essays supporting the idea of Jewish citizenship. Can you imagine, katib, *allowing the Jews such privilege? May it never happen here.*

I believe him to be more than a translator, with his own undisclosed motives. I saw him skulking among the merchants on the day that the British sailors came to Alexandria—woe upon us that we did not heed Nelson the Admiral's words and allow him to chase away these French dogs!

He recognized me as well and edged up to me, introducing himself and greeting me with more respect than I would have expected. He asked me to explain the significance of the Nilometer and I told him how fortunate we were this year that the Nile's waters rose to well above 16 cubits, as measured by the Nilometer. He said how grateful he was to be allowed to witness Wafa el-Nil, *even pronouncing the Abundance of the Nile holiday correctly!*

But I was less pleased with how the French elbowed their way into the festivities, making it more about them than about the yearly celebration of the Nile's rising. Their discordant army band insisted on drowning out our melodic wind instruments. Their soldiers stood in formation, arrayed in full military uniform, humiliating us by this reminder of their conquest of our poor country. The Ṣāri ʿAskar, standing with our dignitaries on a balcony overlooking the Nile, commanded his soldiers to take shovels and dig through the dyke into the Khalidj Canal rather than giving the task to honored Muslims. But we are our own worst enemies sometimes, katib, *for as the waters flowed forth, a cheer rose from all assembled. And then, to my eternal shame, came the pagan practice of casting an effigy of a virgin into the water as the Nile's bride. I hastily explained to my new friend Ethan that this was an ancient ritual that somehow had persisted through the centuries and had nothing whatsoever to do with the beliefs of true Muslims.*

The day ended with the Ṣāri ʿAskar casting gold coins into the canal and then a fireworks display. I am certain the French feel that, by forcing themselves into our festivities, they have shown us great regard, but I find their lack of understanding offensive. They have declared that they will also take part in the Birth of the Prophet celebrations. We shall see if they despoil that day as well.

And now I take my leave of you, having told you all I can.

Peace be upon you with the mercy and blessings of Allah.

Abd al-Rahman al-Jabartī

21

August 21

"Look at the dancing bear!" Christophe pointed at the animal that was being led through the marketplace, accompanied by two small boys, one tootling a flute, the other banging a drum. The bear, its neck encircled by a spiked leather collar, pranced about, showing its sharp yellowed teeth as it roared and groaned, to the delight of the people wandering the crowded souk.

The market-goers were in a holiday mood on this, the second day of the Birth of the Prophet celebrations, and Christophe was ready to enjoy himself.

Daniel shook his head disapprovingly. "Poor thing."

Christophe grinned, elbowing his friend playfully. "You're too soft, Daniel." Sometimes Christophe wondered how his friend survived the harsh realities of military life. He was certainly ill-equipped for it.

Daniel shrugged. Christophe had met up with Daniel just after breakfast, both having given their subordinates leave to enjoy the festive day. The markets were packed, French soldiers shoulder-to-shoulder with Egyptians and Mamelukes, gawping wide-mouthed at the various sideshows—trained monkeys, jugglers and magicians, even snake handlers and fire swallowers. At every corner, nearly naked fakirs—poor beggars who lived purely on alms—offered blessings to those who dropped a coin or two in their extended palms. Intoxicating scents of roasting lamb twirling on spits or sizzling on red-hot braziers, exotic spices piled high in canvas sacks, rich coffee and the cloying sugar syrup dripping on the thickly rolled pistachio and honey drenched pastries, all mixed with the pungent smell of perspiration and donkey dung. The clatter of heavy carts pushed through the rough-hewn cobbles and the hawkers' cries nearly drowned out high-pitched laughter and the atonal wailing of Arabic singers.

A cluster of men glared as Christophe and Daniel pushed through, navigating a curve in the souk. As they rounded it, Christophe spied a young woman trailing a gauzy pink dress over the uneven stone alleyway. His hand shot up. "Citizeness Fourès!" he called out. "Over here!"

The pretty Frenchwoman minced over, negotiating with a smile and a nod, a touch of an elbow here and the tap of a fan there, the crush of bodies that impeded her progress. Christophe noticed with amusement how the Muslims retreated at the sight of her, expressions sourly judgmental of her Western dress and the fact that she was unaccompanied.

When she reached them, Christophe picked up her gloved hand and kissed it gallantly. "My dear Citizeness, allow me to present my friend and fellow comrade, Lieutenant Daniel Isidore. Daniel, this is the lovely Pauline Fourès."

She dimpled and smirked at them both.

Daniel bowed. "Citizeness," he said. "I'm honored to make your acquaintance."

She giggled, covering her mouth. "Let me guess," she said, her eyes drifting over Daniel's uniform. "Infantry? No, that's wrong. I know—artillery!"

Daniel nodded and Christophe, grinning at his friend, said, "I'm sure the lieutenant could never guess what type of soldier you are. Go ahead, Daniel—guess!"

Daniel's brows rose and Christophe could sense his disapproval. It sharpened his teasing as he tilted a head toward the Frenchwoman. "Of course, it isn't fair of me to ask him, is it? He hasn't seen you in uniform."

Citizeness Fourès hid behind a quickly unfurled fan. "You are so naughty, Lieutenant Leferve!" she said, giggling again.

Christophe was reminded of the lightskirts he'd bedded throughout Italy and then on leave in Paris. Had Pauline not been married to one of his fellow officers . . .

"Am I to assume that the Citizeness came to Egypt with us?" Daniel asked. "That she boarded in disguise, as a soldier?"

Her dark eyes twinkled mischievously and, lowering the fan, she nodded. "Shocking, isn't it? But I am newly married, you see. How could I bear to be so soon parted from my husband?"

Daniel's expression relaxed as he admitted, "One of my men smuggled his wife aboard as well. They dressed her as my orderly. They too had recently married, and I admit, I looked the other way and let her slip onboard. It seems the two of you were not alone—I've heard nearly three hundred women were smuggled onto the fleet."

Christophe let out a low whistle. "That many? I had no idea."

Citizeness Fourès laid long fingers on Daniel's arm, confiding, "I wore a Chasseurs's uniform—my husband is a lieutenant in the 22nd Chasseurs—and sneaked onto the transport ship, *La Lucette*. You were much more astute, Lieutenant, than the officers there. I went undetected for the whole journey."

Christophe laughed. "It must have startled them after we reached Alexandria, suddenly discovering such a beauteous woman in their midst."

Christophe considered himself no mean judge of beautiful women and Pauline was exquisite. Soft blonde hair clustered around her forehead and fell in ringlets on her shoulders. Her wide mouth quirked up at either end, as if she had a delicious secret she might share. Her aquiline nose gave her dignity despite round, delicately tinted cheeks that made her seem barely out of her teens. Had she not been spoken for, Christophe thought again, he certainly would have tried his luck with her.

She turned to him, once more flipping open her fan and half hiding her face. "La, sir, you are too kind," she protested flirtatiously, casting him a coquettish look.

"Pauline!" came a roar from the end of the souk alleyway. "Where the devil have you gotten to now?"

Pauline skewed about, her seductive smile abruptly transformed into a look of annoyance. "I'm right here, Jean-Noël. Must you make the entire marketplace a present of my name?"

A fellow lieutenant in the calvary came striding up, roughly pushing a small boy out of his way. "You, Lefevre? What exactly are you doing with my wife?" He took her by the arm and pulled her abruptly against him, jamming her hip against his thigh.

"Hello, Fourès. A chance meeting, that's all," Christophe said, bowing. "I hope you're both enjoying the festival."

Fourès grunted, eyes narrowing as he studied Daniel. "And who's this?"

Pauline stepped sideways, threading her arm through the crook of her husband's elbow. "A new friend," she said, introducing them. "Lieutenant Daniel Isidore."

"*Another* new friend, Pauline? You've made quite a few since we arrived here," Fourès grumbled sourly.

"And why not?" Christophe asked gaily. "Who would not be honored to befriend such a perfect piece of nature? You should be proud of your wife, man. She's delightful."

Fourès glowered at him. "I've heard about you and women, Leferve. I warn you, my wife is no lightskirt. Understood?" He swiveled to face Daniel. "And you, Isidore. Am I clear?"

Christophe, tickled by the sudden flush that rose to Daniel's face, swiftly interjected. "My word of honor as a fellow officer. And you need have no fear of my friend here. He's not the reprobate I am—in fact, he's taken a vow of chastity until marriage. Haven't you, Daniel?"

Daniel's booted toe poked at a stone on the ground. "Leave off, Christophe."

Christophe laughed. "See? Pure as the driven snow."

A commotion at the other end of the alley distracted them and they craned their necks to see what was happening. Several Egyptians led General Bonaparte down the market street. The celebrating scrum of people almost magically cleared an aisle in the street for the delegation.

"That's Sheikh El-Bekri, the one in the ermine caftan," Fourès said, indicating with a tilt of his head. "They must be leaving the banquet he held at his home. I heard the poor general sat there mute for hours while the rag-heads first prayed to Allah and then made speech after speech."

"Are they ever not praying?" Pauline asked, laughing. "What is it—four times a day?"

"Five," Daniel corrected.

The three officers moved so their backs rested against a market stall, standing at attention as their commander passed by. Fourès grabbed his wife's elbow and pulled her beside him. Bonaparte ignored them, talking volubly through a translator to El-Bekri.

But suddenly, a few paces away, he turned, stopping short, and stared at Pauline. The men saluted. Pauline's demeanor was calm and unflustered as she dipped a low curtesy, lips twisting in a sweet smile. Napoleon stood still for a moment, contemplating her, then returned the men's salute and turned on his heel.

22

August 23

Ethan's head ached as he made his way to the palace of the Hasan-Kaschef Bey, one of the many Mamelukes who'd abandoned Cairo. He was glad it was early—just seven in the morning—because at least the heat was not nearly as oppressive as it would become later in the day.

The celebrations of the seventh New Year of the French Revolution had taken place the previous day, and Ethan had drunk too much and stayed out too long in the blinding sun. Bonaparte had seized the opportunity to show the Egyptians a glimpse of French culture, glad that the New Year followed the two previous Egyptian holidays so closely. The general arranged for the artist Jules Rigo to set up a wooden Arc de Triomphe in Ezbekiyah Square, painted with a mural of the Battle of the Pyramids. On the other end of the square a second arch was painted with the gold inscription in both French and Arabic, claiming, "There is no god but God, and Muhammad is his prophet." Ethan's new friend, Abd al-Rahman al-Jabartī, who had accompanied him, raised his eyebrows at that bold statement.

"He is merely pandering to us, no?" he'd asked, clearly meaning Bonaparte. "He doesn't truly believe in the Prophet, does he?"

Ethan shrugged. He had his own theories why Napoleon persisted in asserting his belief in Islam, but it would be a betrayal to share those traitorous thoughts with an Egyptian.

He'd been surprised, but pleased, that al-Jabartī had accepted his overtures of friendship. He suspected that, like him, the Egyptian had his own reasons for doing so. He knew al-Jabartī was writing an account of this episode in Egypt's history and Ethan's facility with Arabic would give him more insight into the French army's reasons for conquering the country. From what the Egyptian said, Ethan intuited that he and his countrymen were nothing less than incensed by their incursions, that as guardians of the land, they wanted to keep the country pure of foreign influence—and that they preferred Ottoman oversight to French, merely because the Turks and Mamelukes were fellow Muslims.

For himself, he had not given up on serving Bonaparte as more than just a translator. Perhaps this acquaintance would give him an entrée into Egyptian circles, allowing him to uncover information that would be useful to the general—and thereby winning his respect.

Ethan was amused by al-Jabartī's sour description of the festivities, his unhappiness at how long and how loudly the military band played, and his disdain at the portrait of Louis and Marie-Antoinette decorating the Square.

"Didn't you cut off their heads?" he asked. "So why are they part of your celebration?"

Ethan couldn't explain it, even to himself. Al-Jabartī was useful, however, in pointing out several dignitaries, including Jirjis al-Jawhari, the leader of the Greek Orthodox Christian Copts. Ethan could hardly believe the plump man's choice of garment, with its fur and filigree, and large, sun-ornamented buttons fastened from top to bottom of his robe. He wondered that the furred, tightly enrobed Coptic leader didn't melt in the heat.

"Look how happy these Copts are." Al-Jabartī sniffed. "They think you Frenchman have made them equal to the faithful. At least they've arrived on mules and not on horseback."

"They're not allowed to ride horses?" Ethan asked, struck by the odd social distinction.

"Of course not," al-Jabartī said derisively. "Neither the Copts nor the Jews. It is a privilege reserved for the believers of Muhammed."

Unless you're French and have conquered the country, Ethan thought, but didn't say aloud. Al-Jabartī's dig at the Jews made him remember what life was like before his people were awarded citizenship during the Revolution. Perhaps Napoleon would do the same for these disenfranchised people.

The morning's military exercises were followed by horse races, and then by a banquet Napoleon hosted for high-ranking officers and notables. Al-Jabartī left Ethan then, to return home. That night Ethan met up with Daniel and his artist friend, Denon, for the fireworks display. Just as Ethan lowered himself to sit on the ground next to them, Daniel said how sorry he was that the promised balloon accession hadn't taken place.

"Conté's balloon was sunk during the Battle of the Nile," Denon explained. "It's not easy to reconstruct with the feeble materials one finds here."

The three of them drank the contents of several bottles of wine that Denon had smuggled out of Napoleon's banquet. "It was interminable," he told them. "All those toasts!" He raised his glass in parody. "To the three hundredth anniversary of the Revolution," he cried, mimicking Napoleon's richly resonant tones. And then, in a nasal voice, "To the perfection of the human spirit and the progress of reason."

"Who said that?" Ethan asked.

"Monge, of course—delighted that tomorrow we'll be inaugurating the Institut d'Égypte. He's certain he'll be president, so of course he had to cheer on the progress of reason."

"Don't you admire reason?" Daniel asked. "Isn't that what the revolution was all about?"

"I did—until we were brought to this godforsaken country," Denon grumbled, swallowing more wine. "Where is the reason in our being here, exactly?"

Ethan grunted. He couldn't agree more. With Napoleon firmly ensconced in Cairo, he wouldn't need the support of the Jews in Israel, so his own reasons for staying were dwindling.

"Aren't you just jealous?" Daniel teased the artist. "Because Monge will be president of the Institute and not you?"

"Shouldn't it be me, after all?" Denon groused. "I am the oldest of the savants—and the most prolific. Look at all the drawings and paintings I've already created."

"But you're an artist, not a scientist," Ethan said. *And you're a friend of Bonaparte's wife, the wife who cuckolded him.*

"So?"

"So Napoleon fancies himself a mathematician," Ethan responded. "Of course he's going to appoint someone whose skills complement his."

"Besides, Monge was with him in Italy," Daniel chimed in.

Denon, craning his head to watch the first colorful explosion in the sky, just snorted.

The next morning, Ethan met al-Jabartī by the cluster of date palms in the courtyard of Hasan-Kaschef Bey's palace. The square was surrounded by balconies, some closed with ornate wooden fretwork, the others open to courtyard breezes. Curved steps led the two men up into a cool stone passageway. They explored the rooms, and al-Jabartī was intrigued by the laboratories.

"We should be seated on cushions on the ground like civilized men—and certainly not in here," al-Jabartī whispered when they entered, clearly upset by the space set aside for mathematics seminars, housed in the former harem. A flat platform had been erected to cover over the women's baths, and red cushioned chairs set around a table. "This room is sacred to the bey's concubines."

Ethan shrugged. He'd learned that the title of bey denoted leader or chieftain—but why every other Mameluke and Egyptian seemed to be honored with the appendage still mystified him.

The library in particular fascinated al-Jabartī and he lingered near the tidy shelves, running a finger along the books' spines. When the librarian invited him to take down a volume and sit to read, he burst out, "You mean anyone can read these books?"

"Of course," said the librarian. "They're for the edification and enjoyment of everyone."

"How did you possibly acquire so many in such a short time?" Ethan asked.

"Many are books that General Bonaparte brought to read during the journey," the librarian replied. "I'm told he brought hundreds of volumes with him. He's a voracious reader."

Al-Jabartī looked startled. "Of course, none are sacred books. No library is complete without the writings of the Prophet, without the Qu'ran."

Ethan had to stifle a smile as the Muslim tried to disparage the collection. He was reminded of the pious Jews he knew, who spent their lives reading and dissecting the Torah and Talmud. Devout Jews and Muslims might be more alike than they knew.

"We do have a few copies of the Qu'ran," the librarian said gently. "Including the one General Bonaparte brought with him—along with several copies of the Bible."

"I would not have suspected it," was al-Jabartī's only comment. But he looked nonplussed.

Leaving the library, they passed through a reception lobby into

the hall set up for the Institute's opening ceremonies. They sat in the
last row, so that Ethan could translate for his Egyptian companion
without disturbing anyone else. Milling about, the savants chattered
excitedly. Some had not seen one another since the French fleet had
delivered them to Egypt. Others, like Denon, Monge, and Berthollet,
had barely survived the disastrous Battle of the Nile. Ethan listened
as, reunited with their colleagues, the savants shared their discoveries, the measurements they'd taken, for instance, of the pyramids
and the Sphinx, or listed the varieties of flora and fauna indigenous
to Egypt.

Fifteen minutes passed, then twenty. The room turned restive.

Finally, Bonaparte walked in, his head ducked, hands clutched
behind his back, making his hurried way to the table covered with
an embroidered crimson tablecloth at the front of the room. He sat
in the middle, flanked by two savants. Monge sat on one side, and
Jean-Baptiste Joseph Fourier, another mathematician, on the other.

"They already voted on the officers earlier today," a voice murmured. Ethan looked up. Denon was sitting in the row before them,
perched sideways in his seat, his sketchbook at the ready.

"Did they?"

"Monge is president, Bonaparte vice president, and Fourier is secretary," Denon said. "You were right last night—Napoleon favored
the mathematicians."

Someone hushed him. Denon turned back around.

Monge called the first meeting of the Institut d'Égypte to order,
saying he was glad to see some Egyptians honoring them with their
presence, and that all were welcome. After some preliminaries, mem-
bers described their programs of study. Napoleon grew ever more
impatient. Finally, interrupting Dr. Desgenettes, he stood up, brandishing a piece of paper. "I have a list here of projects that I want
undertaken at once," he barked. "These are practical considerations
and necessary for the continued success of the military expedition."

Desgenettes's full round face flushed. "Citizen General, excuse me, but I'm not finished."

Napoleon waved an exasperated hand. "You can get back to whatever you were saying later. Unlike the rest of you, I have serious work to do, and this is dragging on too long."

Berthollet rose from his chair. "Point of order," he said. "General, the doctor had the floor. And frankly, I'm fascinated by his theories of how we can create new chemical formulations to combat plague in this primitive country."

Ethan, feeling al-Jabartī stiffen beside him after his translation, suppressed a grin. His new friend clearly didn't like the word primitive applied to his homeland.

"Plague? Chemistry?" Napoleon shook his head, annoyed. Then a thought stretched his lips into a grin as he proclaimed, "Chemistry is just cookery for physicians, and medicine the science of murderers."

The scholars gasped at the insult. Ethan translated and al-Jabartī murmured, "Such a lack of respect for your scholars."

Desgenettes slowly sank back to his chair, but Berthollet remained standing, his long, narrow forehead wrinkled and his fleshy nose flaring. "In which case," he spat out, "how would you define the science of generals?"

Al-Jabartī's eyes widened at the translation. "And now an egregious insult for your bey. Is this truly how you conduct yourselves?"

Ethan, who had witnessed contentious and even violent arguments break out at the French Assembly back in the early days of the Revolution, was unfazed by the dispute. He shrugged.

A flush raced across Napoleon's face and he glared at Berthollet like an asp ready to strike. "You presume too much upon our friendship," he began in hectoring tones.

Monge hastily rose, his chair clattering to the floor behind him. "Now, now," he said, running a hand through his always rumpled hair. "We will certainly continue with the good doctor's remarks later. But it is true that the general's time is not his own." He turned to Napoleon placatingly. "Please, Citizen General. Continue. We're all eager to hear your list."

As the general ran through it, Ethan marked Bonaparte's six points on the tablet he carried, rendering the list into Arabic for his new friend:

1. *Can the ovens the army uses to bake bread be improved?*
2. *What can we use to brew beer if hops are not available here in Egypt?*
3. *How can we make the water from the Nile potable?*
4. *What would be better here in Cairo—watermills or windmills?*
5. *What can we use to manufacture gunpowder in Egypt?*
6. *How can we improve Egypt's legal systems and education—especially considering the wishes of the general public?*

"Practical," al-Jabartī muttered.

After Napoleon finished reading off his list, Monge bowed toward him. "Wonderful suggestions, Citizen General. We will undertake them at once."

But Berthollet, clearly still smarting from his confrontation with the general, muttered, "Will we? Yet you were keen to investigate the optical illusion of seeing water in the desert where there is none. I didn't think anything could halt your progress."

Napoleon turned to the mathematician. "An admirable scientific investigation, Monge. Just put it on hold until my queries are satisfied." He thought for a moment. "The illusion needs a name, doesn't it? Do you have one?"

Monge nodded. "I'm calling it a *mirer*—mirage—from the Latin *mirari*, meaning to look at, to wonder at."

"Mirage," Napoleon mused. "A wonder—like so much of this country. I'll be fascinated to hear what you discover, my friend." Then, clapping Monge on the back, he added, "You'll all excuse me, I know. I have many tasks awaiting me today."

He made his way out of the room. As he reached the back where Ethan was seated on the aisle, he tapped him on the shoulder. "You. Come with me."

Bewildered and alarmed, Ethan stood and followed him out. He looked over his shoulder to discover that al-Jabartī was following too.

"What are you doing?" Ethan whispered, apprehensive what the general would make of his companion.

"What would be the point of my staying?" al-Jabartī responded calmly. "I can't understand what they're saying. Besides, I'd like to meet the Şārī 'Askar."

Ethan had to admire the man's audacity. "Come along then, but don't say anything to upset him."

Napoleon waited in the courtyard beside a central stone basin of water, green with algae and shimmering in the heat. He frowned when he saw the Egyptian. "Who's this?"

"General, may I present Abd al-Rahman al-Jabartī, a scholar and historian."

Al-Jabartī tipped his head, splaying one hand on his chest. "I'm honored to meet you, Şārī 'Askar," he said in Arabic.

Ethan translated.

"Not many of your compatriots joined you this morning, though all were welcome," Napoleon said. "Why did you?"

"I am writing a chronicle of the French occupation," al-Jabartī said. "And besides, it behooved me as a member of the faithful to learn more about advances in French science. For science and prayer are rivers that should join together as one."

Napoleon's eyebrows rose at Ethan's careful translation. "Occupation? We are here to liberate you from the Mamelukes. Make sure your chronicle reflects that fact." He paused. "But I like what you just said—about science and prayer as rivers. What was it, again?"

Ethan repeated it.

"Very wise. I may borrow the phrase sometime. Now," Bonaparte turned to Ethan, "I have an important task for you. I am dispatching Major Beauvoisin to Acre to meet with Ahmad Pasha al-Jazzar and deliver a letter I've written, asking for his support. You will accompany him as his translator."

Out of the corner of one eye, Ethan noticed al-Jabartī's face pale at the mention of the pasha's name. Ethan bowed. "Of course, sir. I'll let the major know I'm at his disposal."

"This is a critical mission, so do your utmost not to mess up this time, would you?" Napoleon strode briskly off.

"Well," Ethan said. "Finally, something to do. I'd best go find the major."

"Wait!" al-Jabartī grasped his sleeve. "Did the Şārī ʿAskar say Ahmad Pasha in Acre?"

Ethan nodded. "He did. I'm to travel with one of our officers to deliver a message from the general. Is there something I should know?"

Al-Jabartī's forehead creased. "Ahmad Pasha's nickname is Djezzar—the Butcher. Do you know why?"

"I don't know anything about him." Ethan said, frowning at the Egyptian's solemn face. "You say: the Butcher? That can't be good."

"It's not," al-Jabartī told him. "The man's a monster. He's vicious in war, but it's the duty of any good soldier to be ruthless in war. It's his private life that's horrifying."

"Is it so bad?" Ethan schooled his face to remain nonchalant. He wouldn't let this Egyptian see his sudden trepidation.

"It is. Hideous monstrosities. He bricks up enemies in the walls of Acre to die a slow, agonizing death. He has an advisor—Haim Farhi— whom he has maimed, carving off his nose and eye. He kills his wives when they anger him. And worst of all for you, he has a scimitar he keeps on hand, for messengers whose news displeases him."

Despite the tough exterior Ethan thought he'd perfected, he found himself swallowing hard. Was this just a ploy to frighten him? Or was al-Jabartī telling the truth?

Al-Jabartī eyed him regretfully. "I sincerely doubt he'll welcome the Ṣārī ʿAskar's message. Frankly, you'll be lucky to escape with your head."

23

September 2
Ancona

"It's too soon," Mirelle muttered as she walked back to the Morpurgo mansion. "It's just too soon, that's all."

She said it out loud to make herself believe it. For the past week, she'd swung by the French barracks every day to check for mail. She'd spoken with the young corporal who handled correspondence, but despite his assuring her that he would deliver any missive to the workshop personally—said earnestly and with a shy, admiring glance—she couldn't resist the daily walk.

Nor could she stop the thoughts that buzzed around her head like angry bees. What would Daniel write her? Had she been clear enough? Would he understand that she had, in effect, declared herself? Closing her eyes for a moment, she cursed the social conventions that wouldn't permit a more definite statement from her. Why couldn't she simply have written him and said *I love you and hope you love me. I don't know how we'll make it happen, but let's somehow wed.*

But a modest, unmarried woman couldn't be that blunt. And while Mirelle might not be perceived by her neighbors as deserving the term "modest" any longer, she didn't want Daniel to think of her as anything less.

Except—he might. He knew she had given herself—*only once!* she wanted to protest—to Christophe. Perhaps she'd misread Dolce's jealousy and her own hopes. Perhaps he wanted nothing to do with such a brazen woman. Perhaps he would write cousinly letters, to share his adventures—but would not dream of them standing together under a chuppah, exchanging vows.

And another thought tortured her. Perhaps he'd met someone else—someone sweet and lovely and untainted by another man's embrace. Someone he'd be proud to call his bride.

She mounted the steps to the Morpurgo home. "Too soon, that's all," she muttered again.

On her way through, she passed the library's open door, seeing David surrounded by newspapers. He looked up. "Mirelle!" he called out. "Come here, would you?"

She obeyed, trying to wipe away her troubled thoughts. David was discerning, especially where she was concerned—and she wanted to avoid his questions.

Just as Dolce's yellow salon was truly hers, the library was David's special province, a cozy room of deep red velvet chairs and a carved marble fireplace, shelves packed with books extending floor to ceiling on every wall. A ladder on wheels reached the highest shelves. When home but not in his office, David was most likely found here, perusing the stack of newspapers delivered to him daily, or reading one of the many volumes that arrived from booksellers in Holland, London, Rome, and Paris.

As she neared, she noticed an almost exalted look on his face. "Good evening," she greeted him, suddenly curious.

He flapped one of the newspapers in greeting. "Come in, come in. I want to show you something. I know none of you thought I was serious before, when I spoke about a Jewish homeland—but look at these papers, would you?"

She sat on a red velvet chair and took the sheet he brandished.

It was from the previous month, from the *Gazette Nationale ou Le Moniteur Universel*, known widely simply as *Le Moniteur*, the official newspaper of the French Directory. David had circled a passage:

> *The Jews see the French Republic as the veritable messiah that was promised to them. In this regard, they cite Isaiah who revealed that, upon appearance of such and such signs, there would be rebirth of the République judaïque and of the new architecture of the city of truth—Jerusalem—as the solemn meeting place of all the oppressed beings of the universe.*

"I'm not certain I understand," Mirelle said slowly.

"No? Remember I read out to all of you what the French press said back in June? About a Jewish homeland? And you were all skeptical. Certainly Zeke was. But these journalists take the idea seriously." He shuffled through the papers. "Starting with the German *Hamburgische Neue Zeitung*, which claims Jews are financing Bonaparte's foray into the Middle East. Then followed by these British papers—the *Evening Mail*, the *London Chronicle*, the *St. James Chronicle*." He laid each one on the low inlaid table between them as he named them. "If France's most fervent enemy is reporting on this, even if they're trying to discredit it, it must be true!"

Mirelle selected the paper on the top of the pile, scrutinized it, and replaced it. Her English was nowhere as good as her French. "And are they trying to discredit it?"

"Let me translate what they say in the *St. James Chronicle*: 'The wealth and numbers of the Jews in Germany, Portugal, Spain, Italy, and England, if moved politically, would be felt throughout Europe. It is lucky that the Jews are too shrewd a people to entrust their property to French protection.' Hah! As if the author knows what we will or won't do with our property!"

"So you'll support this Jewish Republic? You'll contribute?" Mirelle was struck by his vivid enthusiasm. While the Morpurgo family had always been a force in the local Jewish community, the scope of this endeavor seemed beyond even David's ken.

"I would like to," he told her, his tone shifting abruptly. "But of course, I've had some financial reverses lately. As have you."

A shiver climbed her spine. "The taxes," she stammered. "And fewer customers than we should have."

He eyed her, frowning, all his previous fervor dissipated. "I'm aware, *piccola*," he said dryly. "You know that I incurred debt to give you the workshop. As a wedding gift to my bride."

The chill extended down Mirelle's limbs as her cheeks grew hot. "Yes."

"And my own enterprises are being just as cruelly taxed as the manufactory. If this were a matter of pure business, I would ask you to repay me. But you cannot, can you?"

Mirelle shut her eyes. Was this his way of punishing her? And if it were, didn't she deserve it? Didn't she owe him repayment for the huge debt she owed him? She cleared her throat, opened her mouth, shut it again.

"No, I thought not," he said. "I acknowledge that this has nothing to do with your abilities, my girl. I know how skilled you are. But I'm a businessman. And as such, since I haven't gotten what I wanted from our bargain . . ."

"Can you give me more time?" she burst out, feeling cornered.

"And what do you think more time will do for you?" His voice had gentled, was almost kind. But his eyes remained as hard as flint.

She raised her chin, suddenly furious at being put on the spot. "You do realize a good deal of my problems stems from your daughter." She hadn't wanted to accuse Dolce, not while she was a guest under David's roof. But the threat to the workshop drove her to it.

"I do. Don't think I don't know what she's doing with those tea parties of hers."

"So can't you stop her? Talk to her?" Mirelle hated the begging tone escaping from her lips.

David leaned back, cheeks puffed out. "Dolce will be gone soon enough. Off to Florence, a happily married woman. With so little time left to me, I have no wish to force a confrontation. If she were your only problem, Mirelle, we could both wait her out. But she isn't."

"You mean, the taxes? I could afford them with enough customers. At least survive them."

"I don't mean just the taxes. I have heard rumors: our good friend Rabbi Fano is back at work undermining you."

Mirelle gasped. "But you said—you told him last year you wouldn't allow him to hurt the workshop! That you'd use your influence to stop him."

David's bark of a laugh struck Mirelle like a blow. "He's cleverer than I gave him credit for, *piccola*. He's been giving your workmen advice—and there's nothing I can do to stop that."

"Advice? What advice?"

"Advice on what to do if the d'Ancona Ketuba Workshop fails. They're not stupid, your artisans; they see that work has trickled off, that you're struggling. So they're looking for advice on how to apply for a different position. Whether to wait or to leave now."

Mirelle closed her eyes. It was all too much. And now she knew for certain that David would not save her if the worst happened. Why should he?

The next day she ventured into the bakery, driven by sheer hunger. She'd crept upstairs and into bed after leaving David's library, refusing dinner, pleading a headache. Her mother brought her some tea and bathed her temples with spirits of camphor. This unexpected tenderness nearly drove Mirelle to tears—reminding her how Mama had cared for her before Mirelle had shamed them both before the entire community. But when Mama asked why she was feeling so poorly, Mirelle couldn't answer. How could she tell her mother of her troubles in the workshop? She remembered how, when she'd prepared to run away with Christophe, she'd assigned ownership of the manufactory to Pinina. Her mother had torn the agreement in two. "Did you think to ask if I wanted it?" Mama had demanded. "Did you stop to consider that it would only bring me pain—make me miss your father even more? Or Jacopo? Or even you?"

So Mirelle just closed her eyes, pressing her mother's hand, insisting a good night's slumber would restore her spirits. And Mama, after moving a stray lock of hair off her forehead, rose and left without another word.

But sleep escaped Mirelle. She lay awake, eyes chasing the shadowy frieze of interlocked leaves on the ceiling, desperate to find an escape that eluded her.

She couldn't face David or Dolce at the breakfast table. So she'd crept from the house even earlier than usual, heading to the workshop, letting herself in and resting her head on her arms, feeling limp. While she jerked herself upright when the first workmen arrived, pretending to work all morning, by lunchtime her empty stomach forced her out.

The bakery bells at the door jangled, announcing her arrival. Jacopo, the baker's apprentice with her dead brother's name, stood behind the counter, his face lighting up as she approached. Mirelle reached into her reticule and put one of her last coins on the counter. "Do you have any day-old bread?" She hoped he'd sell her an entire loaf for the cost of a roll.

Jacopo let the coin rest in his palm. "Are things as bad as that?" he asked.

She stole a furtive look behind her. No one was in the store. Not that it mattered. The entire Jewish Quarter knew of her troubles.

"Worse," she replied. Tears welled up and fell, despite her trying to hold them back. Footsteps out on the street grew closer and Mirelle whisked her handkerchief from her reticule, hastily wiping her eyes. The string of bells clanged and a heavy tread entered the shop. Mirelle glanced over her shoulder and caught her breath. Rabbi Fano.

What is he doing here? He had a wife, two daughters. He had no business in a bakery in the middle of the day. *Is he here to gloat?* She raised her chin. "Good noontide, Rabbi," she said, forcing her voice to steady.

"Mirelle. It's good to see you, child," he proclaimed in his pulpit voice, then dropping to a throaty whisper. "I hope you are well? Prospering?"

He is here to gloat. She wouldn't let him see her crumble, despite her heart's rapid thudding. She backed away from the counter. "I'm well, Rabbi. Please do make your purchase."

He shook his head, limp gray hair brushing against narrow shoulders. "No, no, take your turn, child. You must return to the workshop. Far be it from me to interfere with *parnasa.*"

Parnasa. Business. That triumphant glint in his eyes. Her own narrowed and she drew in a deep breath. "Actually, Rabbi, speaking of *parnasa,* I have a bone to pick with you."

Now it was his turn to step back, a hand rising to clasp his chest as if in surprise. "A bone? I'm not sure I understand . . . ."

Anger rising, Mirelle reminded herself to sound calm. "I hear you've been discussing my business with my workmen. Surely it's not a rabbi's place to interfere with *parnasa.* To try and ruin a community business that has provided employment in Ancona for three generations."

His lips thinned in a sneer. "It is not me who is ruining the manufactory, Mirelle. We both know you are not fit to run it. You've never been fit."

Out of the corner of one eye, Mirelle noticed Jacopo walk out from behind the counter to lock the bakery door. A kindness that allowed her to be blunt. "Because I'm a woman?"

Rabbi Fano spread his hands out. "As I've said—repeatedly. But you refuse to listen."

Jacopo reached out as if to touch Mirelle's elbow in quiet support, but then, noticing the rabbi's baleful glare at his extended fingers, withdrew his hand. He disappeared behind the curtain into the kitchen.

"And more so," the rabbi said, a sordid relish lacing his tones, "because your reputation is soiled. You work with scribes who do holy work—*avodah kadisha*. How do you expect them to concentrate on their work when you are there to tempt them?"

Mirelle remembered how Narducci had countered that same accusation of the rabbi's. Was it already a year ago? "We do not hire men of loose character to work here," he'd said scornfully. "And any man who approaches Signorina d'Ancona with sinful intent will bear the brunt of our wrath and be turned off without a character. Trust me, she is safer here than anywhere else on earth." The memory of how the men had murmured agreement made her stiffen her backbone.

"If my reputation is soiled, Rabbi, you've certainly contributed your mite to the *lashon ha'ra* that won't let me repair it. Won't let me repent and move on."

"You accuse me of gossip?" His eyebrows raised as if in disbelief.

"I do. And of tempting my workmen to abandon me. You would be happy to see my business in the gutter. To see me forced to—" Mirelle paused. Did she dare? But one look at the rabbi's cold eyes and scornful lips gave her courage. "—to be the slut you think me."

He drew back, muttering *"B'li ayin hara"* under his breath, making a spitting sound three times to ward off the evil eye. After a moment he turned his back and went over to the door, fumbling at it and hissing as he found it locked.

Jacopo was there in an instant, turning the key and throwing the door open wide. Rabbi Fano stalked out and the baker's apprentice looked at Mirelle, whose white knuckles gripped the counter to keep herself from collapsing. Had she gone too far?

"Come." He took her arm and drew her behind the curtain. The back of the shop was empty, long worktables cleared and cleaned, all baking done for the day. Only a large bowl with a damp towel stood at one end, a yeasty smell rising from the bread starter to be used at sunrise. The hearth was swept of ash, the floors damp mopped. On the shelves were stacks of bread and cakes, boxes of cookies and biscuits. Eyeing them, Mirelle's stomach grumbled involuntarily.

Jacopo made her sit on a stool at the end of one of the tables, turning to the small fire still kindled in a corner of the fireplace and taking a kettle off the hob. Pulling down a container of tea, he poured the hot water over a strainer filled with the loose leaves, adding a heaping teaspoon of sugar and stirring it. Putting the cup in front of her, he pulled down a crusty loaf and cut a hearty slice, reaching for some soft white cheese, spreading it on the bread. "You've had a shock," he told her. "Don't say anything—just eat and drink."

"I can't pay," she said, casting a longing look at the simple fare. She didn't even feel embarrassed by what he'd probably overheard. Like the rest of the ghetto, he clearly knew how much trouble she was in.

"Have I asked? You're my guest. Eat, please."

Pride warred with hunger; hunger won. She bit the delicious bread and cheese. Nothing had ever tasted so good. She took a swig of the tea, followed by another mouthful of bread.

"Better?" he asked, sitting on a stool across the table from her.

"Mmmm." Her mouth was too full for words. She swallowed. "I can't thank you enough. For the tea and bread—and for being so kind despite what everyone says of me."

"Do you think I care about that? Yes, I know what's said of you—there's no way to avoid hearing it. But I think—no, I know—you don't deserve the scorn heaped upon you."

"But I did—I did—" She couldn't bring herself to say it.

"So what if you did? It's wrong to blame women for what men do."

Mirelle sipped her tea. So he thought Christophe had seduced her. She should tell him the truth—that she was as much to blame as Christophe. But it felt wonderful that at least one person in the community didn't cast her in the guise of a loose woman.

Jacopo sat silent, watching her. Then he said, "You're the strongest woman I know. I see how everyone in the city treats you. Yet you don't bow your head to them, don't accept their shame. Don't let them break you. If it helps, know that I believe in you. That I care."

The thought that someone—anyone!—cared was balm to her battered soul. She thought fleetingly of Daniel: how she wished he'd been the one to say words like these. Perhaps he would when his letter finally arrived. *If* it finally arrived.

She finished her bread and tea, soothed by both his words and her filling belly. "I can't thank you enough."

He put up a hand. "If you truly want to thank me, come back tomorrow at noon. I need someone to sample my new creations—after they've broken their fast. Yes?" He took some brown paper and wrapped the remainder of the bread and cheese. "And take this with you."

Mirelle knew she shouldn't, that at best it was charity, at worst it was—something else. But after all, she told herself, he had never asked for anything but her friendship. So she reached out a hand, laying it on his for a moment before taking the proffered package.

24

September 12
Acre

Ethan sat next to Major Beauvoisin in a coffee shop in Acre's bustling marketplace. The major moodily sipped the strong brew while trying to raise a breeze with a fan he'd fashioned out of a scrap of newsprint, listing once again his catalogue of complaints. "He still won't admit us. Still! After we came all this way—crossing the desert and then the sea on that wreck of a Turkish ship. And those shifty sailors. They would have killed us for the contents of our pockets if we'd let our guard down. Then making us stay in that flea-bitten inn instead of being hosted as befits a man of my rank in the Pasha's palace. And what does this petty tyrant do? Makes us kick our heels for days on end."

Ethan shut his eyes wearily. It had been more than a week since arriving in Acre, interminable days putting up with miserable quarters and waiting for Ahmad Pasha to respond to Bonaparte's message. And for Ethan to bear with the major's grievances, voiced almost hourly.

Beauvoisin was droning on. "Such a backward place. Filthy, like the people. And I've never met people who were so underhanded, so sly . . ."

Ethan felt rather than saw the person seated behind them lean forward. Opening his eyes, Ethan dropped his spoon and ducked to pick it up. He glanced over his shoulder at the small man who stared dreamily away, his own spoon clinking against the inside of his cup.

". . . and when I say sly, I mean they smile at your face and stick a dagger in your back."

"Major," Ethan hissed in a whisper, sitting back up, "someone's listening."

Beauvoisin slewed around in his chair, peering left and right. "Who?"

Ethan groaned inwardly. For someone with diplomatic pretensions, Beauvoisin had no subtlety. A true soldier—charge blindly, putting all his trust in his drawn sword.

"Who?" the major repeated impatiently.

"Behind me," Ethan muttered. "But maybe . . ."

The major half stood, peering over Ethan's shoulder. "Him?"

". . . don't look." Ethan sighed. "We probably should be more circumspect."

"That runt? You think he's a spy?"

"If he's not, someone else is bound to be. After all, you don't want your opinions to get back to the Pasha."

Beauvoisin slumped in his chair with a disgruntled groan. "Like I said—sly. Crafty bastards. What are we doing here? What's the point of this entire campaign anyway?"

That afternoon, Beauvoisin nodded off over a history of Greater Syria that he'd brought in his rucksack. He never managed to read past the first five pages. Ethan, robed in an ankle-length kaftan, a keffiyeh concealing his tawny hair, strolled through the market. Most of what he overheard was irrelevant—whether the rainy season would help the crops, why sesame prices had inexplicably risen—but as he leaned idly against a stall, one conversation startled him.

"Generous and devout, always giving to the beggars in the market," one man was telling another, shaking his head. "A true lady of faith."

"Hard to believe he dismembered her finger by finger before plunging his dagger in her throat. Before putting the poor woman out of her misery."

"Is it true it was simply because she wore a ring her uncle gave her as a present?"

"That's what I heard. A ruby."

"Djezzar's a maniac. You couldn't pay me to go near the governor's palace these days."

"My brother-in-law says . . ." The two men rounded a curve, disappearing from earshot.

Ethan sagged against the stall. He'd hoped that al-Jabartī's description of the governor's cruelty had been exaggerated; clearly it wasn't. Perhaps he and the major should be thankful they'd been denied entrance.

On his way back to the inn, he stopped for a cool drink of *sachleb*. Having first sampled the orchid root drink in Constantinople, he'd acquired a fondness for it. As he sipped, a man left an English newspaper on his seat. He picked it up. An inch-high headline jumped out at him.

TURKEY DECLARES WAR ON FRANCE

The sweet milky drink turned sour in his mouth. The English letters squiggled before his eyes and he slowed his breathing, forcing himself to focus. He read how Selim III, always before sympathetic to the French, was stunned to discover that his supposed ally had ventured into his territories in Egypt as a would-be conqueror. Therefore, the essay explained, the Sublime Porte now ranged himself with France's enemies, Britain and Russia. The end of the article announced that Ahmad Pasha al-Jazzar—Djezzar—had been appointed military governor of Greater Syria, with his capital in Acre.

No wonder he won't see us. Ethan tucked the newspaper into his robe and dropped some coins on the table. But before he could rise, someone tapped his shoulder.

"You are the French translator of Major Beauvoisin, are you not?" a hooded man asked him in fluent Hebrew. "Ethan ben Dovid?"

Ethan saw no reason to deny it. Trying to penetrate the thick cloak swathed about the man, he nodded, asking in the same language, "And you are?"

A twisted hook of a hand lowered the hood. Ethan gasped at the sight—the man's left eye was covered with an eyepatch, and instead of a nose, two holes gaped open in the middle of a deeply scarred face. "My name is Haim Farhi, and I am Pasha Ahmad's *katib*—his secretary, I believe you would call it."

Ethan rose and bowed. "I have heard of you. I did not know you were Jewish, however."

Farhi poked Ethan's arm with a gnarled finger. "I am, indeed, Jewish. And from the newspaper you just read, you know that we are now enemies. I am instructed to bring you to see the Pasha."

The room, which had been lively with chatter until now, seemed to go silent. "Right now? I will fetch the major."

Farhi shook his head. "Not the major. You." He looked over Ethan from head to toe. "But you had better change into European clothes first. The Pasha would not take kindly to your skulking around the city in Arabic dress."

"But the major is General Bonaparte's emissary, not me. I'm just his translator."

Farhi grimaced, his already grotesque face looking even more hideous. "I have my instructions, young man."

Ethan felt as if a freezing finger had been laid on his spine. Heart pounding, he asked, "Am I to be . . . ?" His head a muddle, he couldn't finish the question, couldn't even quite figure out what he wanted to ask.

"We're wasting time," Farhi said, not unkindly. "The Pasha will be angry if we don't hurry." A pause, then the *katib* added, "Well, even more angry."

Even more angry. Ethan wondered if this were his last day on earth. As they walked to the inn in somber silence, he found himself wishing he believed in an afterlife. The French Revolution had knocked all superstition out of him, or so he'd thought. Now he wondered if there were life after death, and if so, if he'd be reunited with his beloved Adara and their lost baby.

The major was not at the inn. Ethan scrawled out a note, changed his clothes, and, with dragging footsteps, followed Farhi to Djezaar's palatial home overlooking the harbor. Before they entered, however, he pulled on Farhi's arm. "How did you know where to find me?"

The *katib* laughed. "And you fancy yourself an agent of the French. We had you followed, of course. We've kept a careful eye on you since you visited the Grand Vizier in Constantinople. And I have my sources in Cairo, of course."

Ethan stifled a gasp. "You're joking."

Farhi shrugged. "If I can offer some advice, young man—you don't possess the shiftiness or guile required for espionage."

Ethan took hold of the door jamb, mortified. Had he been blind? Followed unawares ever since Turkey?

With a wry glance at Ethan's white-knuckled grasp on the doorframe, Farhi waved him inside. Ethan followed him down several snaking corridors into a green tiled antechamber, furnished with low divans and bustling with turbaned men, all obviously waiting to see the Pasha. From the expressions on their faces, not one of them relished the prospect.

And then he heard it—screaming from beyond the door. Like an animal in pain.

All chatter in the antechamber ceased instantly. Faces paled. Several inched toward the door. Two fled the room.

Ethan glanced toward Farhi, whose one eye was lowered to the floor. A man slid over to him. "Who's in there with him?" he muttered in Arabic.

Farhi responded in the same language. "God only knows."

"*Allah yuafiquna*," the man said, which Ethan silently translated as "God help us."

Another cupped his hands out before him and said, with a bowed head, "*Hasbunallah wa ni'mal-Wakil.*" Several men repeated the phrase with reverence.

Farhi said in Ethan's ear, "That means 'Sufficient for us is Allah, the best Disposer of affairs.' It comes from an Islamic *dua*, a supplication recalling when our forefather Abraham—whom the Muslims call the Prophet Ibrahim—was thrown into the fire by pagans. Abraham put his faith in God and was delivered from the flames."

Ethan wanted to ask the *katib* why he served such a brutal master, but before he could frame the question, a man was half-dragged, whimpering, from the room, blood streaming from both ears and from his mouth down his neck, his clothing sodden with it. A guard called, "Is the Frenchman here yet? The Pasha grows impatient."

"He is here," Farhi said.

Ethan felt as if both feet were welded to the ground. Somehow he found the strength to stumble forward. Farhi was two steps ahead. Ethan was startled at being led into a serene garden courtyard, a fountain trickling softly in one corner, greenery surrounding them. A servant was bent over a section of the courtyard stones, sopping up a pool of blood. A white bearded man wearing a rough grey robe and light brown turban murmured reassuringly to an unseen person through a grate of diamond-shaped plaster fretwork.

The bearded man turned as Ethan was pushed forward by the guard. "The translator?" he asked, his tone now harsh. He moved from the wall and sat under a date palm on a chair made from a simple plank of wood. This must be the butcher. Ethan breathed in deeply, trying to control his fear, to keep it from showing.

Farhi placed a hand on his breast and dipped his head in assent. "You have the letter?"

Farhi extracted it from his robe.

"You," said the Pasha, directing a baleful glare at Ethan, "read it to me. Slowly."

Farhi handed it to him. Ethan willed his hand not to shake. Knowing his duty, he would try once more to encourage the Pasha to admit the major. Clearing his throat once, twice, he bowed. "Great Pasha, a thousand greetings from General Bonaparte, who wishes you all health and prosperity. I am but a poor translator, Effendi. One whose presence cannot come close to praising you as you so richly deserve. Would you not prefer to see Major Beauvoisin, who has traveled all the way from Cairo to honor you in the general's name?"

Djezzar raised his eyebrows. "A silvered tongue, this one," he said to Farhi, who laughed. "Wings on his words like a bird in mid-air."

"A gifted writer as well, Pasha."

Ethan, startled, swiveled to stare at Farhi. How did he know?

Farhi smiled blandly at him, then turned back to his master. "After I learned of his skill, I read several of the essays he wrote during the French Terror. I was impressed by his flights of language."

Ethan's temples buzzed. How had his writing reached Farhi? Beauvoisin had labelled the people here crafty, but that description fell woefully short. For all his newfound friendship with al-Jabartī, Ethan had fallen into the trap of underestimating the people of this part of the world.

"So did he have a hand in writing that—that—?" The Pasha waved toward the letter still clutched in Ethan's hand. "Did you?"

Ethan was glad of the truth. "No, Effendi. In this case, I am merely the messenger." But then he recalled how al-Jarbarti had described Djezzar's beheading messengers with a special scimitar. He glanced at the curved sword hanging at the Pasha's waist and quailed inside.

"Well, then, read it." Djezzar picked up several sheets of paper from a stack next to him and began trimming them with a small knife, layering them together to form a rounded shape.

Ethan began to read, watching warily as the Pasha snipped through the paper, the knife slicing in rhythm with the words.

> We are no longer like the infidels of those barbarous times who were coming to fight your faith. We recognize it to be sublime, we adhere to it, and the moment has arrived when all regenerated Frenchmen will also become your believers.

Djezzar raised a hand. "Do you believe that, translator? You are a Jew, aren't you? Will you become a believer of Islam?"

Ethan felt his insides curl. He had no idea what to respond, his mouth opening and closing several times.

Djezzar laughed, but his eyes remained cold. "I thought not. Does your master think me a child? A fool?" His cuts grew less controlled, and when Ethan read out the next portion, the Pasha's anger made him rip instead of cut:

> Since my arrival in Egypt, I have reassured the people and protected the muftis, the imams, and the mosques. The Mecca pilgrims have never been welcomed with more care and friendship than I have shown for them, and the festival of the Prophet has just been celebrated with more splendor than before.

"How would he know?" Djezzar grunted, his eyes fixed on the page he was mutilating. "How dare he make light of our faith? Pretend to understand it?"

Ethan didn't answer. He continued reading:

> I send you this letter through an officer who will make known to you in his own words my intention to achieve a

good understanding between us, because the Muslims have
no greater friends than the French.

Ethan folded up the letter and bowed. "Effendi, Major Beauvoisin wishes nothing more than to follow his general's commands and speak with you on this matter."

The small knife clattered at Ethan's feet. "You dare presume to tell me what to do? You bring me this heathen tripe, these false claims about our sacred religion, and think I am fool enough to believe them?" The Pasha seethed. "Return to your Major and make him leave. If he continues to set foot in this country, I will throw him into a fire."

"But—" Ethan stammered.

"And make sure you depart with him."

Farhi put a hand on Ethan's shoulder. "Bow," he hissed, "and back out of the garden. Now."

Ethan, staring at the Pasha's flashing eyes and the thin line of his mouth, did as he was told.

"But what did he say?" Beauvoisin demanded, as Ethan threw clothes into a portmanteau. "Why won't he see me? Why do we have to leave in such a hurry?"

Ethan grabbed his Arab dress, stuffing it into the case. "Farhi said he would do as he threatened—burn us alive. Or throw us into a dungeon and forget all about us. Or post our heads on sticks on the seawall. We're lucky to still be breathing, Major. Believe me."

The major grumbled, "What will I tell Bonaparte? How can I tell him the Pasha refused to admit me—but saw you?"

Ethan shivered. "Be grateful. The man is terrifying. Come now—Farhi found us a ship that leaves in less than an hour."

As they made their way to the port, Ethan looked this way and that, trying to discern if they were being followed. He found himself jumping at shadows. Just as they were about to board the dingy that would transport them to Jaffa where they'd find a boat back to Damietta, a servant called for them to halt. Ethan's heart thumped.

"Which of you is Ethan the translator?" the servant asked.

"The one not in military dress, of course," Beauvoisin snapped.

The messenger turned to Ethan. "From the Pasha," he said, handing him a carved wooden box, then bowing himself away.

"A gift? From Djezzar?" Beauvoisin demanded, clearly affronted. "What really passed between you?"

Ethan fumbled opening the box. Inside, nestled in a nest of torn scraps, was a delicate bird shaped from layers of white paper, a bird with one torn wing hanging from its body, ripped instead of cut.

25

OCTOBER 20
CAIRO

Esteemed katib,

Before I begin my latest report, I must offer you a most sincere apology. When I last spoke with Ethan Dovid, I learned, to my chagrin, that you are of the Jewish faith. I had thought that you must be, like me and like the master you serve, a Muslim. I hope I have not offended you with my allusions to my own beliefs.

Abd al-Rachman rose from his low desk and walked over to the grated window, peering out on the busy Cairo street. Was his apology sufficient? He'd been startled when, peering through the few Arabic volumes in the library at the Institut d'Égypte, he'd found Ethan standing over his shoulder.

"I'm back—with my head still intact," the Jew had proclaimed, tapping his neck gaily.

"I'm glad to hear it," Abd al-Rachman replied. "I had my doubts."

They went to a coffee shop, where Ethan told him of his adventures in Acre. It was when he related how Haim Farhi had introduced himself that Abd al-Rachman had quailed.

"He's Jewish? The *katib* is Jewish?" he had burst out.

Ethan had stared at him, eyebrows raised. "Why does that matter?"

Abd al-Rachman thought back to the many times he had treated the *katib* as a Muslim in his missives. He gulped his coffee, burning his tongue. "I'm just surprised, that's all."

He hoped the *katib* had not taken offense—and yet, did it truly matter if he had? After all, Farhi was working for a Muslim, was living in a Muslim land. Abd al-Rachman returned to his desk, resolved not to mince his words just because the *katib* was a Jew. He picked up his quill again.

Yet, ironically, I must begin this report at the Mosque of al-Azhur in the medieval quarter of Cairo. For it was there, during early afternoon prayer—Dhuhr—that I first learned of the discontent burbling through the city. As I washed at one of the courtyard fountains, purifying myself by performing wudu, *I felt the peace of Allah descend upon me, something I fear you nonbelievers will never experience. I am too much in the company of the French, I told myself, as I set my intention for prayer: I must not allow myself to be contaminated by their godlessness.*

Finding a spot in the vast, columned sanctuary, standing on the lush red carpet stamped out in gold outlines to allow the faithful to stand and kneel unimpeded, I raised my hands to my ears. "Allāhu 'akbar," I heard intoned, together with hundreds of other believers. The transcendence of worship moved me, as it does every time I pray salah.

Katib, it is difficult for me to write without including such thoughts. If you are like the Jew I have befriended and whom you asked me to keep a watchful eye on, I believe you will forgive them. Indeed, as you serve our master the Pasha, you must be used to such references to our faith.

My meditative state was shattered, however, when, prayers completed, a lanky, sour-faced alim *stood to face the multitude, raising a fisted hand to demand attention. "Oh Muslims! Jihad is incumbent upon you. How can you free men agree to pay the* jizya *to the unbelievers? Have you no pride? Has not the call for revolt reached you?"*

Jihad! Holy war. I was stunned. I knew that the poll tax amounts for property and real estate—both private homes and public shops, bath houses, inns and more, had been announced the previous day, and grumbling had seized the city. But a call for war? It was fraught with danger—with a conclusion far from assured. Had my neighbors not seen the cannon, the rifles, the bombs of the French? How could they expect to win against such a fortified conqueror?

And yet, perhaps I should have predicted something like this. After all, no self-respecting Egyptian would wish to kowtow to a foreign power. At least the Ottomans and Mamelukes are Muslims. Not totally godless like these Frenchmen. The jizya *was merely a pretext. If not the poll tax, our discontented citizenry would have found another pretext.*

But I feared what rebellion would mean for me, for my wife, Hasani, and for our unborn child. The French have proven themselves vicious opponents, their well-trained troops backed by merciless commanders, at least on the battlefield. I am uncertain how they will react if the entire city rises against them— what retribution they will demand if they crush our revolt.

The worshippers in the mosque broke into frenzied groups, each louder than the next in their opinion. Their rancor rose, and in the tumult, harsh voices rang out. I moved from huddle to huddle, collecting their sentiments for this missive, as well as for the longer document I am writing about the French occupation.

"May Allah give victory to Islam!" cried one of the observant, followed by a fervent chorus of "Inshallah!"

"But the poll tax the French demand is actually lighter

than the one the Mamelukes imposed upon us," protested a merchant.

"The uluma *command us to kill the infidel! Shall we not obey?" countered another.*

A perfumer I know from the marketplace strode back and forth, his dagger half drawn from its sheath. "Make ready, oh stalwart warriors, and strike the godless everywhere!" he cried fervently. My nostrils were offended by the musky scent rising from his robe.

"We should not rest until French blood runs in the streets!" another merchant shouted, dancing from one bare foot to another.

"Nowhere Muslim swords have conquered can ever be governed by the faithless," a scholar I recognized added. "It is incumbent upon us to rid ourselves of the usurpers!"

White-robed imams passed through the crowds, reciting passages from the Qur'an in praise of martyrs—those who fell in battle and were promised paradise. "But do not think of those that have been slain in God's cause are dead. Nay, they are alive! With their Sustainer have they their sustenance," one proclaimed, then turned to glare at those who did not respond with the appropriate salute.

I swiftly clapped a hand over my heart in a show of devoutness. It was then I decided to leave the mosque and head home, treading warily as I noticed men forming clusters in the streets, echoing the shouts from the mosque and stirring the populace to prepare themselves for war. The cry of "Allāhu 'akbar" was repeated on every street corner. Women scurried through the marketplace, hastily piling food in their baskets as if preparing for a long siege, others standing, arms akimbo, shouting encouragement or ululating in heady enthusiasm.

You have told me that you appreciate not just my insights into the world outside my door, but also what I chose to tell you of my private life, so I will include what happened when I finally arrived home. My wife ran into my arms, fear contorting her usually placid face into a taut mask. I held her to me, hushing her gently, worried that her roiled emotions might somehow hurt the child inside her.

"They are saying in the souk that there will be war," she said. "You won't be pressed into fighting the French, will you? You'll remain safe at home with me?"

I loved her for her care of me and hastened to reassure her, despite not knowing where this would all end. "Let us hope we will come out of the next few days unscathed, dearest one."

"Yes," she whispered. "That is what we must hope."

She was holding back tears. I let her cling to me for a moment before stepping back and patting her on the shoulder. "I'm afraid we cannot predict what will come to pass, wife," I said, striving for calm. "How it will end, only Allah knows. Let us hope that wisdom and peace prevail."

"Inshallah," she whispered, then, straightening her shoulders bravely, repeated, "inshallah."

And now we wait, gentle katib, for who knows what morning will bring. Be certain I shall let you know whether our revolt against the French succeeds or—as I fear—if they will crush our attempts at revolt.

Ordinarily, I would close with a wish for peace, along with the mercy and blessing of Allah. But, not wishing to offend, I have asked my Jewish friend for advice—not, of course, telling him whom I'm writing. He tells me that the appropriate way to end my letters to a Jew is with that self-same desire for peace, along with a wish that the Lord blesses and keeps you. I must admit that the sentiment in your faith appears to be highly similar to that of my own.

Abd al-Rahman al-Jabartī

26

OCTOBER 21

At six in the morning, Christophe rode through the Cairo streets together with General Dupuy, the Governor of Cairo, and another five mounted cavalrymen. Reports had been circulating of an uproar in the city, and indeed, the sound of the muezzins from the minarets, unlike the now-familiar call to prayer, took on a frenzied air of exhortation. While Christophe certainly couldn't translate the words, he realized whatever was being broadcast sounded ominous.

As they rounded a corner, they were startled by the sight of dozens of Egyptians who were erecting a barricade, piling stones and timber and even tables and stools on top to block the passage while they cheered one another on. They had pulled their keffiyehs up to half-mask their faces, their stance fierce, determined. Shocked at the unexpected confrontation, Christophe saw they were brandishing swords and guns. Despite having faced the enemy countless times, he felt a twinge of fear that he immediately swatted away, like a pesky fly buzzing about his poor mount's twitching ears. What could these poor beggars and merchants do to them, after all? Untrained primitives who thought they could face down the glorious French army? They were in for a lesson.

Dupuy, riding in the front of the cavalcade, reared up and pulled on his mount's reins to stop short. "What is happening here?" he demanded. "Go back to your homes. What you are doing is unlawful."

The men behind the barricade let out a string of curses. One, in tortured French, told them to leave Egypt. "No infidels here!" he shouted, then translated his words back into Arabic to a roar of approval from the mob.

Dupuy coolly looked down his nose at them, clearly intending to intimidate them by his superior height in the saddle. "Go home and no harm will come to you," he commanded. "Stay and we will be forced—"

He never finished his sentence. A janissary—whom Christophe recognized by his tall white draped hat and red coat as one of the elite fighters of the Ottoman Empire—streaked from around a corner.

Thwack! He smashed General Dupuy in the nape of his neck with a club. The general toppled from his horse, sprawled in a heap onto the roadway below.

"*Allāhu 'akbar!*" The scream erupted from every throat.

Nerves on fire, Christophe backed his horse to protect the general's prone body. He reached for his sword. The men swarmed them, shouting and cursing. Christophe's sword sliced a cheek, an ear. Cries of pain rose, echoing in the narrow street. The Egyptians, heads moving rapidly side to side, sidled out of reach of his saber. Christophe sheathed his sword, reached for his pistol.

Pain. Sharp. Searing. A dagger suddenly bloomed in his shoulder. Christophe slumped forward in his saddle. Swift as the wind, the janissary slashed at Christophe's lifeless, dangling arm with his scimitar. Someone reached up, grabbed at Christophe's jacket. Pulled him off his horse. Another jolt of pain. The back of his head cracked against the street cobbles.

The cry of "No French here!" was the last thing Christophe heard.

When he regained consciousness, Christophe lay on a low bed in a dim room. He eased one eye open. The sun, barely discernible through a slit in closed curtains, was high in the sky. Noon or thereabouts. Someone with soft fingers was bathing his forehead and murmuring to him in an indistinct language. He lay for a moment, trying to remember what had happened.

As images of the clash came rushing back, both eyes flew open. Leaning over him was a young woman, maybe sixteen or seventeen. Large black eyes focused on his face as her soft hand applied a cool compress to his forehead. A gauzy scarf floated over dark curls that clustered around an oval face, her red lips puckered in concentration.

He moved slightly and groaned. His entire body ached. As he shifted on the pillow, pain radiated from the back of his head.

"You must lie still," the girl said in perfect French. "The doctor commands it."

"The hell with the doctor," Christophe snapped, struggling to sit up.

Her hand, still gentle, pushed him back. Why was he so damnably weak?

"You are wounded," she said. "Your arm. Your shoulder. Your head." As she spoke each word, her hand grazed those parts of his body, a butterfly's touch.

His arm was in a sling. It hurt like hell. He hadn't noticed it before she touched it. His head throbbed as he tried to turn it.

"Where am I?" he demanded.

"You are in the home of my uncle, Jirjis al-Jawhari. He is a leader of the Copts here in Egypt."

What the devil were the Copts? Looking around with bleary eyes, Christophe was startled to see a large icon of—was it Jesus?—hanging directly in front of him, along with symbols of the cross and a lion. "Are you Christians?"

The girl, seeing his eyes roam around the room, smiled. "Indeed.

That is our sacred Saint Mark, who brought the gospel to Egypt. You are in safe hands here. Sleep now. The doctor commands."

Damn the doctor, Christophe wanted to say, but the lure of sleep was too tempting. He shut his eyes and let darkness overwhelm him.

When he woke again, it was evening, the sun just peeking over the horizon. A stocky looking man was seated in the corner of the room, smoking a hookah. Christophe blinked a couple of times, taking him in. In the flicker of candlelight, the stranger was arrayed in vibrant orange, from his ornately swathed turban to his flowing robes. He had a neatly trimmed brown beard and moustache surrounding thick lips, dark eyes snapping with intelligence.

"So you're awake, young lieutenant," he said. His French was as flawless as that of the girl.

Christophe tried once again to sit up, but the girl moved quickly on stocking feet from behind a screen, pushing him down. "The doctor—" she started.

He took her hand and, with an effort, gallantly touched it with dry lips, startling her into silence. "—commands," he murmured. "So you've said."

"Ah," chortled the man in the corner. "You Frenchmen are always so gallant."

She reached over to a low table and poured some water into a cup. "Drink."

He was glad of the water, which had been freshened with slices of lemon. After swallowing, he handed it back to her and, regretting his prone position, greeted his host by tilting his head toward him, ignoring the pang of pain. "Sir. I am Christophe Leferve, a lieutenant in the French dragoons. May I know to whom I'm indebted?"

The man chuckled, his laugh jiggling his ample belly. "So formal!

I am Jiris al-Jawhari, who has been honored by your commander, the Şārī 'Askar, who permits my functionaries to continue to collect public revenue here in Cairo."

"You are Catholic?" Christophe's eyes again fixed on the icon of Saint Mark.

"Coptic—we were among the first believers of Christ, dating back to the days of the Roman Empire. We are not followers of your Pope—if indeed you follow the Pope, being as you are, a citizen of the French Republic which has, it is said, disavowed God." He smiled, as if amused at the thought.

The man's accented words were mellifluously soothing, and Christophe shook himself to stop from drifting back into slumber. "How did I get here?" he asked. "The last thing I remember was the attack in the street."

"Ah!" al-Jawhari put his hookah to one side. "You owe a life debt to my servant. He was fetching some material for Sappeira's latest dress and happened upon your body. Someone had dragged you into an alleyway and left you for dead. But my Mahmoud realized you were still breathing and had you conveyed to my house. A good boy, a devout Muslim, is Mahmoud."

"And then our doctor treated you," the girl said, a dimple flashing out as she smiled.

"Sappeira? Is that your name?" Christophe asked, bemused by the sweetness in her face.

She nodded, a second dimple appearing as her smile widened.

"Sappeira . . ." Christophe murmured. He was losing his battle with consciousness.

"Sleep again, then Sappeira will bring you some food," al-Jawhari told him.

"But what's happening? Do we have control of the city?" Christophe asked, his eyes shuttering closed.

Perhaps someone answered, but if they did, he didn't hear them.

27

OCTOBER 25

Daniel stared at a blank sheet of paper, ink drying on the quill he held. How could he possibly tell Alain that Christophe was missing and presumed dead? Would the letter even reach him? The British blockade, in effect since the Battle of the Nile, had halted almost all communication to France from Egypt. Sighing, he dipped his quill again in his portable inkwell when Ethan burst into his quarters.

"Daniel!" Ethan cried. "They found Christophe—he's wounded, but alive."

"How? When? But he was with General Dupuy, wasn't he? Didn't they kill the general and everyone who rode out with him?"

"I don't know the details, but somehow he escaped. A servant from al-Jawhari's household brought the news to Napoleon's headquarters," Ethan explained. "They didn't dare venture out beforehand, not with riots in all parts of the city."

"Al-Jawhari?"

"He's a wealthy Christian of some influence—Denon told me that it was his suggestion Bonaparte take over the palace of Muhammad Bey al-Alfi, right next door to one of his own residences."

Daniel, still soot-stained from dispatching round after round of cannon fire into the Al-Azhar Mosque to squelch the rebellion, his face lightly scarred from a French slug that had miraculously just skimmed his cheek, slumped heavily on his cot. "*Baruch HaShem*," he muttered. "I didn't know how I was going to tell his Uncle Alain that he'd been killed in battle. He's wounded, you say?"

"Wounded—and concussed. They're keeping him there for a few days more, so he can recover before reporting back to his company."

"I've leave for the rest of today. Let's go see him."

Ethan grimaced, shrugging. "I'll go with you if you like. But I've no great fondness for your friend, you know. Sometimes I wonder that you still do."

Daniel was startled. "What have you against him?"

"You forget, I knew him back when he was still bullying you at the printshop."

Daniel waved a dismissive hand. "That was so long ago! And he was misled by his mother. You can't still blame him for that."

Ethan's lips thinned. "And I saw your beloved Mirelle back in Ancona. He abandoned her to be castigated as a ruined woman, to suffer the slurs and insults of her community."

Daniel wilted a little under Ethan's harsh stare.

"It's hard for me to forgive that," his cousin continued. "Why have you?"

Daniel sighed at the still painful memories. But he had to be honest. "He was willing to marry her, Ethan. Willing to make amends. She was the one who didn't want that. And I can't help but be glad that she didn't. Don't you see?"

"Even so, he doesn't deserve your friendship."

"Don't you think I haven't told myself that? But despite everything, I forgave him. We grew up together, joined the army together. He was wrong, he hurt the woman I love. But despite everything, he's still my friend."

Ethan shook his head, lips compressed. "Like I said, I'll accompany you. But I'm not so forgiving."

Their walk through the shattered city took them to Ezbekyeh Square, where they hoped to hire a donkey cart. It was a long walk from Bulaq, where the soldiers were quartered, to Birkat al-Azbakiyyah. But when they arrived at the square, they found it deserted of trade, shops shuttered. A great wailing reverberated from the mourning men and women huddled together, surrounding mountains of severed heads piled high by the French as a warning against future rebellions. The smell of mutilated corpses decaying in the hot summer sun made Daniel gag. Flies swarmed the bloody heads, vultures and ravens picking at foreheads and cheeks. Small children and weeping mothers tried to shoo the predators away from the dead, but the vicious birds ignored them, feasting on the remains. The sight raised Daniel's gorge, and he had to swallow hard to keep down the contents of his stomach.

"They threw the bodies into the Nile," Ethan said through the handkerchief he'd raised over his mouth and nose. "Denon went to see the beheadings. He said the waters of the Nile ran red with their blood."

Daniel shuddered. "Our friend the artist has a morbid streak, doesn't he? This is barbaric."

Dark glares at Daniel's uniform made them hurry out of the square. Walking swiftly, they found a cart willing to convey them, though the driver spit at their feet and demanded triple the usual fee. The city was drenched in an ominous silence that raised the hair at the back of Daniel's neck. French troops marched stolidly through the streets, muskets cradled at the ready, booted footfalls echoing eerily.

It took nearly two hours before they reached Birkat al-Azbakiyyah, a neighborhood of palatial mansions, palm trees, and wide boulevards. It stood in great contrast to the poorer quarters of the city. Even the air felt different here, fresher. Daniel felt the tightening in his chest release. But his sense of relief fled when the driver spat again the moment he realized whose house they wanted.

"Coptics," he muttered. "Pigs and whoresons who steal our hard-earned wages. Degenerates."

Daniel blinked at the string of expletives as Ethan translated them. He was unused to hearing them applied to anyone but his fellow Jews.

Al-Jawarti's home was more palace than mansion, its white walls rising skyward from a thicket of palm trees and other greenery. A long flight of stone steps led to a wide porch, with arched doorways surrounding the front and sides of the building. Perched on top of the multistory building was a domed cupola.

Ethan pulled on the bell chord and a servant, in a blue robe and black tasseled fez, appeared almost instantly at the door. "*Nofri 'ehoou*," the servant said. Then, seeing their confused faces, added, "*Ahlan wa sahlan*."

"*Ahlan beek*," Ethan responded, explaining that they were there to see the wounded Frenchman.

"What did you say?" Daniel whispered as the servant brought them through the house and into a spacious inner reception room, disappearing to summon his master.

"Just greetings, although I have no idea what he said at first. I assume it was Coptic—a language I thought had died out. Like Latin."

"What in the world is—?"

Daniel's question was cut short as a young woman appeared, floating dreamily into the room. She wore an embroidered tunic over loose pants, long pointed sleeves draped over her hands, her dark hair only dimly visible through a gauzy veil. "You are friends of the French lieutenant?" she asked in melodious French.

Both men bowed. "He is, at least," Ethan said, nodding toward Daniel.

"Yes, good friends," Daniel said, relieved to be able to speak his native tongue. "May we see him?"

"I will show you the way." She led them down several cool corridors. She paused outside an ornate carved door. "You must keep your voices low and try not to excite him," she instructed them. "The room is being kept dim on purpose. He has a—what's the word?" She seemed to search for it, then smiled. "Ah, yes. *Commotion cérébrale.*"

"A concussion!" Daniel breathed. "Poor Christophe."

She opened the door and they walked in, stepping carefully to muffle the sound of their boots on the marble floor.

Christophe was propped up on a low bed, his head resting on a nest of pillows. His eyes were closed, but he opened them at the sound of their approach. "Daniel!" he cried, wincing at the volume of his own voice. Then, cooler, "Hello, Ethan."

Daniel sighed. He knew that neither his friend nor his cousin had any affection for one another; that Christophe was aware of Ethan's disapproval of him and consequently merely tolerated him for Daniel's sake.

"Hush!" the girl exclaimed.

"Welcome," Christophe said in a much softer voice.

Daniel crouched next to the divan. "My dear, dear friend, we thought you had died!"

"I'm not that easy to kill, it seems," Christophe murmured. "I'm delighted you're here. No one will tell me what's happening. All they say is not to worry, that the French have control of the city again. Is it true? I want to hear everything!"

"It is true," Daniel said. "But it was a rough few days."

"Please—do not disturb him," the girl pleaded once more. "He needs peace and quiet, not tales of rebellion and battles."

"Sappeira, I will become even more disturbed if I'm left in ignorance," Christophe declared, wincing again at his own strong tones. "Let them speak, would you?"

Sappeira. Something about the way Christophe's eyes lingered on her face reminded Daniel of Mirelle back in Italy—how Christophe had fallen in love with her modesty, so unlike the Italian lightskirts who had surrendered their virtue so readily to the dashing young

Frenchman. At least this maiden was Christian, not Muslim. If Christophe's mother, Odette, had been prejudiced against Jews, how much stronger would her hatred be for an Islamic bride?

Between the two of them, Ethan and Daniel told Christophe of the revolt. They described how rebels had ransacked Christian homes near Ezbekiyah Square, how they had made off with their meager belongings. How Napoleon had been out of the city when the revolt began, returning hastily when news of the uprising and General Dupuy's death reached him. How delicate scientific instruments from the Institute had been stolen or smashed, some of the savants killed. How Daniel's company had been dispatched to Ezbekiyah Square where a store of artillery pieces defended the city from the marauders, then at sunset sent off to heights overlooking Al-Azhar Mosque, where hundreds of rebels had set up camp.

"Napoleon's orders for the next morning were clear—we were to exterminate everyone in the mosque," Daniel said, keeping a careful eye on his friend's face, mindful of Sappeira's instructions not to upset him. But Christophe just demanded more details—wanting to know how the mosque and nearby houses were bombarded, how the French aimed fire at shops, houses, palaces and inns until nothing but rubble remained.

It had been sunset again when orders came to stop the attack. Ethan told how he was pressed into service as an interpreter when the community leaders presented themselves to Napoleon, pleading with him for clemency. "He told them," Ethan said, "that they had refused offers of mercy before, that they should have surrendered then—but now was time for vengeance." But then, he added, the general's orders for a cease fire contradicted his belligerence.

His men, however, Daniel continued, had revenge on their minds, and when they took the mosque, they trampled it with their horses, destroying everything they could find, tearing pages out of the Qu'ran and other holy books, even desecrating the building by drinking wine in it and defiling the holy building by breaking the bottles on its sacred floor.

As he related this part of the story, Daniel stole a glance at Sappeira and was astonished by her composure. She seemed as eager as Christophe for the bloody details. Her only concern was that the starkly dramatic story might upset her bedridden guest.

Ethan told them how it took until the next night before the final bands of rebels surrendered. Napoleon, who had promised to be merciful, was convinced by his staff that leniency would be interpreted as weakness—and so he dispatched his men to decapitate all the prisoners, resulting in the piles of bloodied heads now decorating the square and the floating headless corpses befouling the waters of the Nile.

When they finished their story, Christophe lay back on his pillows. Sappeira took up his hand, feeling for his pulse. "You must leave now." She shooed them out. "He needs to rest and regain his strength."

Christophe began to argue with her but subsided when she lay a long finger over his mouth. Daniel, bidding his friend a speedy recovery, was not surprised to find Christophe's eyes fixed hungrily on the girl's slender figure.

28

November 25

The days continued warm and pleasant, and, with the city swiftly brought back under French control, Ethan watched as the soldiers demanded more familiar forms of amusement. Tiring of the ubiquitous coffee shops and the dusty bazaar, they longed for the gaming rooms, the brothels, and wineshops of Paris. Most of all, they hungered for the comfort of women. The three hundred wives who had stowed away on the French vessels were, of course, largely spoken for, and, while happy to wile away a few frivolous hours flirting with their husbands' compatriots, a possessive arm at the end of the night would whisk them away to the spousal bed.

Napoleon must have sensed the men's discontent, Ethan mused, as he attended the opening of the Tivoli Gardens. The pleasure grounds were constructed in the spacious gardens of a former Mameluke palace once owned by Bey Ghayt al-Nubi. Ethan brought his Egyptian friend al-Jabartī to the opening, wondering how the devout Muslim would respond to Western amusements.

"This is nothing more than licentiousness," the Egyptian protested, after Ethan paid the entrance fee of ninety *nisf* for them both and they strolled about the illuminated gardens. Al-Jabartī averted his eyes from the European women promenading on the arms of their swains, but it was the Egyptian women parading themselves in Western dress that drew his ire. "Such immodesty," he raged. "You are contaminating our innocent women!"

The irresistible urge to tease his companion made Ethan repeat the rumor that Napoleon had been given the sixteen-year-old Zenah as a gift upon his arrival to Cairo by Sheikh El-Beikri, her father. "Surely the sheikh would not have made the offer if he thought Napoleon's attentions would despoil her, would he?" he asked, hiding his smile.

"Attentions? Depravity! One beheads such women and puts such panderers to the sword," al-Jabartī raged. "If this story is true, that is what will happen—mark my words."

Ethan shrugged. "I don't think she was to Napoleon's liking, anyway," he said. "Shall we have a drink?"

They were passing by a wineseller's booth. Al-Jabartī shuddered. "No," he said flatly.

"They sell coffee here, too," Ethan responded, to placate his friend.

Al-Jabartī 's shoulders released. "Perhaps a coffee."

The park was full of both innocent and illicit pleasures. Ethan was amused by witnessing it all through the Muslim eyes of his friend. As they passed the room dedicated to gambling, al-Jabartī murmured a verse from the Qu'ran: "'Satan's plan is to excite enmity and hatred between you, with intoxicants and gambling, and hinder you from the remembrance of Allah, and from prayer. Will you not then abstain?'"

"That seems overly harsh," Ethan commented. "Do Muslims abstain then from all pleasure?"

"Certainly not! We take great enjoyment in games and pastimes without the sin of exchanging money for them—surely you've seen the backgammon competitions and the chess matches in the coffee shops, the hard-fought wrestling matches. We glory in healthy competition. But money should be earned, not won."

Ethan mulled that over as he waved at Daniel and Christophe, who strolled down the pathway to join them, allowing himself a slight disapproving twitch of the lips at the dragoon's saunter. Christophe, whose right arm was still in a sling, had laid the fingers of his left hand delicately but protectively on Sappeira's elbow. Ethan blinked at her appearance. She was wearing a Western-style dress, but a more restrained version: high necked and long sleeved, draped by a figured shawl, an embroidered cap with a veil adorning her long black hair. Next to the flashy brilliance of the Grecian-styled high waists and flimsy materials worn by the French women and even some of the Egyptians, he couldn't help but applaud her modesty. A curious mixture of Western and Eastern clothing, Ethan thought, but it suited her.

Ethan introduced her to al-Jabartī, who nodded curtly and received an equally curt bob in response. The two then pointedly ignored one another as the small party walked the gravel paths, passing by a menagerie of exotic animals, including a growling spotted leopard and several hyenas, graceful gazelles and even a snapping alligator. A juggler made Sappeira clap her hands in childlike delight, while al-Jabartī seemed to almost approve of the skill shown by the fire breather.

They paused for some ices just outside the ballroom. Inside a waltz was being played and eager couples were sashaying up and down the dance floor.

"Will you dance with me?" Christophe asked Sappeira.

Al-Jabartī 's eyebrows drew together as Sappeira shook her head vehemently and flushed.

Ethan led al-Jabartī a few steps away. "Don't you believe in dancing, either?"

"Not this type of dancing," he said. "And not of Copts mixing freely with Muslims."

Ethan found his ire growing. Understanding the Muslim attitude toward life was all very well, but al-Jabartī was his guest, after all—and he was being rude. "One would think you'd disapprove of me, too—being Jewish. And French."

"You should know your place," al-Jabartī agreed. "This is a Muslim country, after all."

"Is it?" Ethan shot back. "The French conquered it, after all."

"To our eternal shame. But your commander claimed you would not interfere with our Muslim faith and traditions," al-Jabartī retorted. "Yet it seems like that is all you are doing." The Egyptian glared at him. "I am glad to have witnessed your debaucheries and corruptions, so I'll be able to write of them. But much more of this and my soul will be corrupted. So I'll bid you good night."

Ethan watched as the man stalked off. So much for his own diplomatic relations, he thought wryly. Would he ever understand these people? Turning back to Daniel and his friends, he heard Sappeira bashfully refusing Christophe's repeated requests to dance. But she seemed pleased at his persistence.

"Leferve!" a voice interrupted, and the small group swiveled to see a fellow calvary officer approach them, a beautiful woman on his arm.

Sappeira's eyes fixed on the woman, seemingly dazed. Ethan wondered how such a French beauty had suddenly materialized in the dusty reaches of Cairo. The impression she made was one of transcendent freshness. Her long blonde hair was caught up under a white lace cap, her thin white gown draped with a patriotic red and blue silk scarf. A red fan hung by a ribbon off her wrist. Her arms and chest were bare under a transparent gauzy collar and thin sleeves. Red drops dangled from her earlobes. Her lips were parted, showing perfectly white teeth—like pearls, Ethan thought. She exuded an almost unearthly quality in this musty, drab part of the world.

"Fourès!" Christophe greeted the chasseur, turning to bow. "Citeeness Fourès," he murmured, picking up her hand and saluting it formally.

Sappeira's eyes flashed at the gesture. The French woman quickly looked her over, head to toe, sneering a little. She seemed to consider the modest Egyptian as little to no competition for the men's attention.

Before Christophe could introduce Sappeira to the couple, General Junot suddenly appeared before them. Ethan thought he made a gallant figure in his full-dress uniform, his shoulder-length reddish hair and slim moustache giving him a devil-may-care look. Ignoring everyone else, he addressed himself to Fourès' wife. "Citizeness Pauline," he said, tones oozing familiarly as he threw out his chest, bedecked with medals, "you are invited to drink wine with General Bonaparte. I will escort you." He extended an elbow, clearly expecting her to take it.

Pauline Fourès drew back. "Please tell the general that while I am honored, I am otherwise occupied—with my husband and his friends." Her lips formed a tight line.

"You refuse?" Junot looked astonished. "Did you not hear me? General Bonaparte orders, er, wishes—"

Pauline turned to her husband. "Jean-Noël," she said. "I believe I have a headache. Can you please take me back to our quarters?"

Fourès, who had placed one dangerous hand on the hilt of his saber, nodded. "At once," he said, ignoring Junot's comically wide eyes and dropped mouth. He put an arm around her slender waist and drew her away.

Junot, beet red, muttered, "He has his heart set on her. She'll learn that all too soon."

"The general?" Christophe asked, sounding amused. "But aren't they both married?"

Junot grunted and turned on his heel. Ethan wasn't sure if the grunt was in answer to Christophe's question or simply one of frustration. But between al-Jabartī's disapproval and the sudden hint of lust emanating from their illustrious commander, the fairgrounds suddenly took on a distinctly sinister aspect, despite the firework illumination now brightening the night skies.

29

NOVEMBER 26
ANCONA

With the advent of cooler weather, Mirelle found herself forced to spend more of her time in the Morpurgo mansion whenever she left the workshop. And with a sharp reduction of revenue and the need to address the awful truth—that the manufactory couldn't continue this way—even the workshop stopped being a sanctuary.

The hoped-for letter from Daniel never arrived, and she despaired of it. Clearly, all her fears were realized—he didn't love her, he blamed her for her transgression with Christophe, he had never intended more than a cousinly correspondence. It was hard to face the artists and scribes in the workshop, whose accusing eyes haunted her waking and sleeping. She had failed them and they knew it. She hated every second she was forced to accept David Morpurgo's generosity, but she no longer had the money needed to rent even the smallest of rooms. And she had to watch as Dolce gloried publicly in her wedding preparations; buying expensive items for her trousseau, considering and reconsidering the ever-expanding guest list, selecting the musicians for the ball that was to follow, talking endlessly with Mirelle's mother about the food.

"Daughter," her father chided her once at dinner, as she relentlessly discussed which flowers she would carry, "we all take joy in your joy—but surely you might find a time other than our meals together to make these decisions."

"But Papa," Dolce protested, slanting her eyes toward Mirelle, whose gaze was fixed on her plate, "when else can I count on having you all gathered around the table? I want everyone to help me plan the perfect wedding."

"These are not matters for menfolk," her aunt told her. "Let be, child."

Dolce pouted prettily. Dolce's pouts were always pretty. "Oh! Well, I apologize to the menfolk, then," she said, squirming in her seat, drawing an appreciative chuckle from her fond papa. "I'm just so excited. To be standing in the heart of my beloved community, under the chuppah with the perfect man—I feel like my joy is bubbling over, that everyone"—and here she slid another glance through half-closed lids at Mirelle—"is as thrilled for me as I am."

David chuckled. "Of course we are, Dolce. But perhaps you should keep some of these arrangements secret, to delight your bridegroom—and your doting father?"

Dolce rose from her chair and ran to his, wrapping her arms around his neck. "You are right, Papa! I will." And a third glance, filled with gloating, was sent in Mirelle's direction.

Mirelle's sleep suffered. Her appetite suffered. She felt wan and unhealthy and unhappy. Her dresses hung on her, and she didn't have the funds to have them tailored to her almost too slender figure.

One afternoon Mirelle came back to her room to find her mother pinning the seams of one of her dresses, her sewing box by her side. "Put this on, daughter," she said around a mouthful of pins. "I can't bear watching you wander around the villa with your dresses practically falling off you."

Mirelle complied, standing stock still in the middle of the room, a tear dripping unbidden down her cheek. Her mother reached up and brushed it away. "Shush, child," she said in her gentlest voice. "It will be all right."

Mirelle drew in a deep breath. She wanted to protest, to weep, to cry out that nothing would ever be right again. But she straightened her back and stood silent, taking what comfort she could from the sensation of her mother's deft fingers pinning the dress around her.

It would be in one of these altered dresses that she finally met Dolce's intended. Sansone di Lattes strolled up to the mansion one evening, his arms full of red amaryllis, just as Mirelle was entering the house.

He was breathtakingly handsome, Mirelle thought, as she curtsied to his doffed hat and deep bow. His miniature was unlike portraits which often glossed over imperfections. In fact, it had barely done him justice. She recognized the dark curly hair, the high forehead, the slightly hooded, penetrating eyes. Standing as a foil to Dolce's blonde beauty, Mirelle realized, the two would make a striking couple.

"Good evening, Signorina d'Ancona!" di Lattes boomed, letting his eyes roam over her. "It is Signorina d'Ancona, is it not?"

"It is." Mirelle knew Dolce would be angry at this meeting, but how could she possibly help it? "And you are Signor di Lattes, I assume— the lucky man who will wed my"—here Mirelle paused, not sure how to title Dolce; *friend* felt wrong, *enemy* might be more accurate but couldn't be said aloud—"my kind hostess," she finally said.

"I am he! I've snuck away from my family business in Florence to spend some time with my beloved." He threw his arms wide, his bouquet shedding a few petals in his extravagant gesture.

Charming, Mirelle thought, *if a trifle flamboyant.* "I hope you have a wonderful visit," she said. "You will excuse me, I'm sure." She curtsied again and walked through the door, which was held wide by a stone-faced servant. Mirelle knew every word of their conversation would be reported to Dolce.

As she walked up the stairs to her room, she heard the hubbub of greeting below. She wished she could avoid dinner in his company and for a moment, contemplated asking for a tray to be sent to her room. But then, seated at her dressing table, she shook her head vehemently at her reflection.

Why should I hide? she wondered. *Haven't I repented sufficiently for my sin?* And setting her mouth in a firm line, she picked up a brush to tidy her tousled curls.

30

December 10
Cairo

Christophe was encouraged to visit al-Jawarti's mansion as often as he wished and to bring his friends along. It made a luxurious change from army barracks.

Sappeira made her home with her uncle, having lost both of her parents early in her life. She wouldn't explain the circumstance, no matter how hard Christophe pressed. He suspected it had something to do with her intense dislike of Muslims.

"She won't tell me," he said to Daniel one afternoon as they strolled the crowded bazaar alleyways together. He was searching for a trinket that she'd be willing to accept as a small token of his affection. Having memorized the list of things a devout Coptic maiden couldn't accept from a man—flowers, scarves, even sweetmeats—he hoped to stumble upon something small and innocuous. "It seems to pain her when I ask."

"So don't ask."

Christophe eyed Daniel's shrug with a frown. "But I want to know. I want to know everything about her."

"Ask her uncle, then."

His friend's curt answers bothered Christophe. Daniel had been this way ever since he'd met Sappeira. "You're angry with me. Why?"

Daniel shrugged again, his frown deepening. "What about that?" he asked, pointing at a display of ivory hairpins.

Christophe sidled over and looked at them. He picked them up, one at a time. Deciding on the most ornate pin, carved into curling leaves at one end, he shook a few coins from his pocket into his hand, raising them questioningly at the merchant.

The merchant shook his head.

"He wants more than this?" Christophe took another coin out and added it to the ones nestled in his palm.

The merchant shook his head again, then pointed at the button on Christophe's coat. "*Zurun*," he said.

Christophe, mystified, looked at his friend. Daniel laughed. "I've heard of this. They're afraid of our money. They think when the Mamelukes come back, they'll punish them for trading with us. But the buttons could have been taken in battle."

Christophe couldn't believe it. "He wants me to give him a worthless button?"

"*Zurun*," the man said again.

"Fine by me," Christophe said, plucking it from his uniform and extending it to the man.

The merchant handed him the ivory pin.

"*Shukran*," Daniel said, nodding. "That means 'thank you,'" he told his friend.

The merchant made a spitting noise through puckered lips and waved them away.

Christophe pocketed the pin. "Now. Why are you angry with me?"

"Who said I was?"

"Oh, leave off. How many years have we known one another? Something's bothering you."

Daniel shrugged. "I've seen this before. You're infatuated with that girl."

"And if I am? Is it a crime?"

"Only if you go too far. Again."

"You're thinking of Mirelle. Again. I've told you, that was a mistake." Christophe sighed. "Look, I promise. I won't do—*that*—again."

Daniel clapped him on the shoulder, his good humor seemingly restored. "Better not. Because I think al-Jawarti might chop off your balls if you do."

31

DECEMBER 11

Daniel, Ethan, and Christophe were lounging in the al-Jawarti center courtyard, sipping mint tea while Sappeira urged them to eat more sticky almond cookies, when al-Jawarti bustled in. The three guests rose and bowed.

"Ah!" al-Jawarti said, a grin lighting his round face. "So good of you all to grace my poor home with your august presence."

Daniel looked about him. In contrast to most Egyptians homes, this felt like the height of luxury. Was the Copt leader being modest merely to point out how splendid his home was? Something about al-Jawarti's effusiveness rubbed Daniel the wrong way.

"It is our honor and great pleasure to be here," Christophe responded, bowing again, while Ethan clasped a hand to his chest.

Daniel grinned. Smooth-tongued as ever, his friend. He was glad he had decided to keep an eye on him, to try and prevent Christophe from going too far, with this one at least. He wondered if Ethan were there for the same reason, considering his antipathy for Christophe.

Al-Jarwarti waved a piece of paper. "And I am honored to have you here at this instant, for your commander has sent a gracious letter to the Coptic community." He thrust the letter toward Ethan. "You know Arabic. Read and translate for your friends!" Seeing they were still standing, he lowered himself on a low divan piled high with pillows. "Sit, sit!" he urged.

Ethan unfurled the page, thick with seals and ribbons.

"'Citizen,'" Ethan began to read. Something in his expression and his almost instantaneous delivery made Daniel wonder if he'd helped render the missive into Arabic. "'I have received the letter from the Coptic People. It will always be a pleasure for me to protect them. Henceforth, it'—I assume he means the Coptic religion—'will no longer be degraded, and, when circumstances will permit, which I perceive to be not too far in the future, I will accord them the right to publicly exercise their religion; just as is the practice in Europe, where each person is entitled to follow his own belief.'"

Entitled to follow his own belief? Daniel thought of the silenced church bells back in France, of the ten-day week of the revolutionary calendar that erased all religious holidays, making it impossible for his family to attend synagogue on the Sabbath, of the fact that all clergy were forced to declare their loyalty to the French Republic first and foremost. Was that what Bonaparte meant?

"A sage decision by your so-wise commander," al-Jawarti interjected, rubbing his hands together. "A man of vision, of forbearance. May the day he promises come soon."

Daniel knew Bonaparte blossomed under such praise. Al-Jawarti had met with the general several times. Was this letter the result? But why was he being so suspicious? Word had arrived from Upper Egypt, where French troops were fighting to secure the land, that the Copts had been incredibly cooperative. Surely this was simply the general's way of rewarding the Copts for their support.

Ethan continued: "'I will severely punish those villages which killed Copts in the different rebellions.'"

Sappeira burst out, "Will he, indeed? Lieutenant Leferve, you serve a truly just and generous man! May he be blessed at the gates of heaven!"

Daniel wondered at the martial light glowing in her dark eyes. Was it a clue to what had happened to her parents?

"'As of today,'" Ethan concluded, "'you can announce to them that I permit them to bear arms; to ride on either donkeys or horses; and to wear turbans and clothing, as they themselves see fit.'"

Al-Jawarti reached up and adjusted his mushroom-like turban, which bloomed on his head in vivid cerulean. "Well, that's a relief," he chuckled. "Now I will not have to change my headgear when I leave the house."

Ethan handed back the missive, smiling. But then he sobered. "This is wonderful news for your community, Effendi," he said. "But I wonder how the Muslims will feel about it."

"They'll be angry," Daniel agreed, nodding. "Like the Catholics were in Italy, when General Bonaparte demolished the ghettos there."

"You witnessed that, didn't you? You were there?" Sappeira asked, hinging forward in her seat, then twisting toward Christophe. "And you, too?"

"We were both there," Christophe said. "It was a moving sight after so many centuries of incarceration behind the ghetto gates."

"We feel the same," al-Jawarti said, pressing a hand to his heart. "Centuries of repression end today. Surely your General Bonaparte is an angel sent from heaven to succor the oppressed. I will have special prayers said on his behalf this Sunday."

The pile of bodiless heads being pecked at by scavenger birds in Ezebekiah Square suddenly flashed in Daniel's mind. An *angel*? Once he had felt the same about the general—though perhaps not stated in such extravagant terms. But now?

32

DECEMBER 20

The days before Christmas were always strange ones in Revolutionary France, and those still secretly devout Catholic soldiers stationed in Egypt looked to the Coptic community to see how they celebrated. While Christophe had largely discarded his own faith—partially due to his Uncle Alain's feelings about the evils of all religion and mostly in rebellion against his overly pious mother—he was still curious. And aghast when he learned of their forty-three-day-long fast.

"We don't allow animal flesh to pass our lips during *Kiahk*," Sappeira explained as they strolled in a yet uncultivated part of the neighborhood, which al-Jawarti had presented to the Coptic Orthodox Church and on which construction of a cathedral had recently begun. "And we attend Midnight Praises, called *Tasbeha*, and the divine Liturgy. Would you like to come with us?"

"Perhaps some time," he told her, feeling diffident about any type of religious ceremony. "But seriously, no meat at all?"

She laughed, reaching up to gently touch the ivory hair pin that she had, finally, accepted after much pleading from him. "It is to show our devotion to our Lord," she told him. "Like our period of Lent, which Latins also celebrate, no?"

"Latins might. But I don't," he muttered.

She frowned. She had been glad to learn that he was raised Catholic, but sorry that he had discarded his faith so readily. If he weren't careful, it would cause an impassible breach between them. Just as Mirelle's Judaism had once done.

"But tell me about your Christmas," he said, returning to the subject. "It was one of my favorite memories as a child. We always went to midnight mass, of course—and Mama would bake *la bûche de Noël*."

"A tree trunk?"

He smiled at the little frown between her eyes that always formed when she was mystified. "A cake shaped like a yule log. Covered with chocolate and filled with cream."

"We have a *qurban*, a bread marked for the twelve apostles, which the priest uses for communion. And after the service, we distribute fried cakes, called *zalabya*, and go home to eat *fattah*, which is meat and rice served in a tomato sauce and flavored with lots of garlic."

"So that will be next week?"

"Next week?" Again that charming frown materialized between her liquid dark eyes. "No, no. It won't be for three weeks."

"Three . . . ?" Christophe thought she must be wrong, but he had always had trouble equating the Revolutionary calendar with the old one. Perhaps he had mistaken the date. Except he knew that Dog Day, the Revolutionary calendar title for December 25, was coming up next week.

But it wasn't important. Not when she was looking at him with those dimples flaring out of her sweet face.

33

DECEMBER 21

Now that the revolt had been put down and the army apparently settled into winter quarters, there wasn't much to do but sit around, drink, gamble, and gossip. And for Daniel, to fret.

He hadn't heard from Mirelle since he'd sent his last letter. He had been as crystal clear in his initial response as she could have desired:

My darling Mirelle,

As I read between the lines, your letter made my heart dance with joy. You are correct that Dolce understands my deep and abiding love for you. I am only sorry that her betrothal has not stopped her inexplicable jealousy. For I—a poor soldier—have nothing to offer her.

But I offer you all my nothing, my dear one. My heart, my very soul.

I enclose a letter for your mother, asking for your hand. I know not when we'll be able to wed, but I will come direct to Ancona as soon as I can. May the good Lord speed the day!

I will write again soon, but my head and heart are too full to pen more now.

Your devoted servant,
Daniel

Naturally he'd tried again, repeating his proposal of marriage in case she had not received the first letter—but was told that only official correspondence was permitted, due to the blockade. He'd asked Ethan to try and slip a missive into the diplomatic pouch, only to have Ethan laugh at him.

"I'm in disgrace, cousin—demoted to a translator, and a minor one at that. I haven't the influence needed."

He approached al-Jawarti, who seemed to be as successful a businessman as David Morpurgo was back in Ancona. Al-Jawarti listened to him sympathetically but shook his head when Daniel asked him to try and get the letter to Italy.

"I have no contacts in the Pope's country, my boy. We cut all connections with the Romans centuries ago."

He even tried al-Jabartī, Ethan's friend, dragging Ethan along to translate. But apparently the Egyptian had sworn off his non-Muslim acquaintances and Daniel received nothing but a quick shake of the head and al-Jabartī's retreating back.

So all he could do was wait, worry, and pray that she hadn't despaired of him.

He was kicking his heels in Christophe's quarters, waiting for his friend to return from a rendezvous with his newest infatuation. While Daniel still disapproved, he had to acknowledge that Christophe's obsession with the Coptic girl showed no sign of abating.

Of course, neither had Christophe's passion for Mirelle, not until the affair turned serious. While Daniel hadn't wanted Christophe to marry her, he had to agree with Ethan that Christophe's abandoning her to disgrace was appalling. Would he do the same to Sappeira?

The calvary quarters always smelled of horses—probably from the manure the soldiers tracked in on their boots. Unlike Daniel's soldiers, whose barracks were always kept immaculate due to his constant inspections, these men scattered clothes and hats about, littered boots, spurs, and whips on the floor, and hung furred capes untidily off the edge of camp stools. Daniel, feeling sick to his stomach at the unremitting odor of horseflesh and dirt, was about to leave when Christophe's fellow officer Fourès burst through the door and stalked over to his bunk. Growling under his breath, kicking a pair of boots out of his way, the man's face looked like a thundercloud.

He stopped short as he spied Daniel. "I know you," he muttered. "Don't I?"

Daniel rose. "I'm a friend of Christophe's. We met a couple of times."

Fourès seemed to have lost interest, turning away to pull a duffel bag out from under his cot. He tossed it with a grunt onto his rumpled bedroll.

"Is something amiss?" Daniel ventured, sitting back down.

Fourès turned to him. "What, don't you know? Doesn't the entire French army know of my disgrace?"

"Your—disgrace?"

"My wife. Napoleon. Don't you know?"

Daniel recalled how Pauline Fourès had walked away from the general's invitation at Tivoli Gardens. "But didn't she refuse him?"

"That's where I know you from! You were at Tivoli when that buffoon Junot first approached her. Yes, at first she refused him. But now . . ."

"Now?"

"He sent her flowers, cards declaring his eternal love. His aide-de-camp, Duroc, that smooth-talking bastard, brought her jewels and other expensive gifts, always bundled with some bit of poetry or praise for her beauty. And my wife has always loved being courted, loves flirting, loves being the center of attention." Fourès plumped himself down on the cot, placing his head in his hands, muttering through his fingers. "She can't help herself. He's turned her head, won her heart. I don't know what to do."

"But surely—" Daniel wasn't certain what to tell him. He looked at the man's bent-over figure with pity.

"And then—she betrayed me," he continued in a low voice rippling with agony. "Betrayed me."

Fourès told him how Pauline was invited, along with other French officers' wives, to a luncheon at Napoleon's headquarters. Champagne rescued from the general's depleted stores was passed freely. The meal was sumptuous, certainly when compared with the poor fare that was the only alternative in Egypt.

"The general sat next to my wife, whispered in her ear constantly," Fourès continued. "I was at the other end of the table, watching help-lessly as she flirted with him. Tapped him on the wrist with her fan. Constantly touched a new necklace—one I only learned later that he'd given her—of heavily worked gold filigree and diamond chips. I was surrounded by Junot and Duroc, who badgered me with talk of promotion 'if I were just sensible.'

"It was toward the end of the meal," Fourès continued, "that some-how, a jug of water was spilled on my wife's dress. On purpose, of course. She cried out. He jumped up, offered her his arm, told her he'd bring her to a room in the palace where she could repair the damage. Waved off anyone who rose to help."

"Didn't you go with them?" Daniel asked.

Fourès's face, already strained, scrunched as if in pain. "I started up, but Junot and Duroc each put a hand on my shoulder, forcing me to sit back down. Said I shouldn't make a scene. That the wise thing to do was to allow her—allow her—" At this, Fourès broke down, lowering his face back into his hands. While he didn't sob, his shoul-ders shook convulsively.

Daniel laid a sympathetic hand on his shoulder. Fourès shifted impatiently, dislodging the hand.

"The entire party watched as my wife and—that man!—compro-mised themselves. You should have heard the titters, the whispers, the hushed gossip that flew around the table. Minutes passed. It was nearly an hour before they returned. And such a return! Pauline's dress was replaced by another—a pink silk gown that I could never have afforded to buy her. Her hair was mussed, her color high. Napoleon preened as he seated her next to him again, pretending nothing had happened. But we all knew. *I* knew."

"Could you have been mistaken?" Daniel asked. "What did she tell you after you left?"

"She denied everything, of course—said he'd taken her out to the gardens because he was afraid that she was upset. Had to send out for the dress, so that delayed them further. Duroc had the audacity to say, in my presence, that appearances were more or less kept up. More or less. Hah! But I knew. And now . . . !"

"Now?"

"I'm being sent to Paris on a diplomatic mission. An important letter to the Directory, they say. An honor to be selected, they say. As if I don't know what they're doing. They want me out of the way so Bonaparte can have his affair with my wife without my interference. I'm to report to the *Chasseur* and depart on the twenty-eighth. Even if I go and return immediately, Napoleon will still have three full months to despoil my wife—ruin her reputation, make a cuckold out of me!"

The Biblical tale of how King David lusted after Batsheba and sent her husband off to war to be killed flashed into Daniel's mind. Would Fourès's story turn out to be just such a tragedy?

Fourès jumped up, knuckling his eyes furiously. "And I've no choice. It's an order and I'm a soldier. So I've got to pack."

"But . . ." Suddenly, Daniel was confused. "Surely you don't live here in officers' quarters, do you? Don't you have a place of your own with your wife?"

Fourès's face darkened further. "We fought and she kicked me out. Told me to get my temper under control and until I did, to sleep elsewhere. So I moved in here."

"I see." Daniel sighed. "I'm sorry for your troubles."

Fourès, busy piling clothing into his duffel bag, looked up. "Thank you. It's a relief to tell someone. Everyone else is laughing at me." He shrugged. "Even your friend, Christophe. Everyone thinks it's a joke."

Daniel's straightlaced upbringing made him recoil at the thought of two married people carrying on in this unseemly way. Christophe and the other soldiers might consider any woman as fair game, as a diversion from the battlefield, but surely that couldn't apply to married men? Yet, Daniel thought, at least Bonaparte had some excuse. Josephine, it was said, had betrayed him first, treating his devoted love for her as a mere bauble to be thrown away. Daniel knew he was heartbroken at her perfidy. That he intended to divorce her the moment he returned to France. So he, at least, might consider himself a free man. But then again, to poach another man's wife? Surely that was inexcusable.

Rousing himself from his reverie, Daniel shook his head, standing up again. "I wish you well," he said, starting for the door.

"If I can ever do something for you, let me know," Fourès said.

Daniel froze, then turned back. "There is something . . . ."

PART THREE

JANUARY—MARCH 1799

34

January 11, 1799
Ancona

Despite saying almost daily that he needed to return to Florence, Dolce's fiancé lingered in Ancona. It would be the last visit he said he could make before their May wedding, and he seemed in no hurry to leave his beloved.

Or to leave Mirelle.

Her initial spark of defiance, sitting down to dinner with him back in November, burned ever more fiercely. Mirelle smiled grimly at Dolce's displeasure every time Sansone di Lattes enjoyed her company. He insisted that the three of them walk together—"for surely," he told Dolce, "we need a chaperone, and who could be better than your little houseguest?"

Whenever he presented Dolce with a gift—a bowl of exotic fruit, a pearl necklace, a bouquet of flowers—he would give Mirelle a token: a single piece of fruit that he'd pluck out of the bowl, a pearl bead pin, or a solitary flower he'd deliberately select from Dolce's garland. He would present the gift to Mirelle with a deep bow and a sly smile, as if he realized how much it irked his betrothed.

She shouldn't have allowed herself to be a pawn in his game, but her anger at Dolce still smoldered. But what was di Lattes's objective? Perhaps he was training his fiancée to recognize him as her master, though Mirelle knew full well that it was a fruitless quest. Dolce would never succumb to anyone's command.

Dolce kept her displeasure under tight control, sweetly admiring his attentions toward "her poor, poor friend," and seconding his requests to have Mirelle join them with insincere smiles plastered on her face. Mirelle, hearing the poisonous undertones, turned the invitations into a game of her own; she accepted some and refused others—but never let Dolce predict which answer she'd give. And there was satisfaction in watching Dolce's long fingers curling into fists, fingernails cutting into her palms, both when Mirelle agreed and especially when she demurred—for then Sansone di Lattes would sweetly plead that she change her mind and encourage Dolce to join her entreaties to his. At least Mirelle was exacting some punishment for all the harm Dolce had done—and was continuing to do—to the workshop. Mirelle couldn't help but be amused at Dolce's frustration, an amusement she had to work hard to hide.

Only Mama discerned her little game, but she didn't interfere. Mama, Mirelle knew, had her own opinions about Dolce, few of them complimentary. David Morpurgo, so astute when it came to business matters, merely thought the rupture between his daughter and his once-beloved Mirelle was finally being repaired.

"I knew it would only take time for the two of you to become friends again," he said one day as the girls put on their hats and prepared to walk to the dockyards with di Lattes. "It was a good idea of mine, having you return to stay with us, Mirelle, wasn't it?"

Mirelle dipped her head, tightening her lips to close them on words that couldn't be voiced to her kind host.

Dolce raged at Mirelle when she was certain no one else would hear her. "I told you to stay away from him, didn't I?" she hissed one evening, when Mama was downstairs discussing the coming week's menus with the cook and her father was out making late business calls.

"Are you so unsure of him?" Mirelle countered. She was seated on a chair near the fireplace, reading a book by the light of the flames.

"Unsure? Of course not!" Dolce tossed her blonde curls. "But every man is susceptible to the temptation of a loose woman. To a Lilith."

Mirelle's eyes narrowed. "You've called me that before. Don't think I don't know what you've been doing, trying to dissuade my customers from buying from the workshop."

Dolce's eyebrows rose. "Trying? Surely I'm succeeding."

The problem was that she *was* succeeding. Commissions had dwindled to almost nothing. And the next quarter's taxes were due at the end of the month—which would force Mirelle to close the workshop. She and Sabato met about it almost daily, staying late in the evenings after the rest of the men left for the day. They reviewed every step they could take to delay having to shutter the shop—cutting back on supplies, reducing the men's hours. They considered wild schemes, such as moving the entire enterprise to another city. But again and again, Mirelle's honesty about the numbers forced them to acknowledge that they were nearly bankrupt.

"I remember you telling me how my grandfather nearly ruined the manufactory because of his lack of business ability," Mirelle said sourly, rubbing the back of her neck one evening as she considered the useless plans they'd scrawled on scraps of paper littering her desk. "And you praised me for my gift with numbers. Is it not ironic that I'm the one who has failed?"

"It's not your fault," Sabato told her. It was a sentence he often repeated, especially at the end of these sessions.

But she knew better. If it weren't for Dolce and her poisonous tongue, for the rabbi and his wheedling advice to the men—both directly due to their hostility toward her—they could have survived the French taxes. During her grandfather's time, it had been Morpurgo family assistance that had saved them. But now David Morpurgo hadn't the slightest interest in lifting a finger, never mind helping financially. In fact, Mirelle often wondered during her sleepless nights, if he didn't take a secret joy in watching her flounder. Watching her fail.

So she took satisfaction where she could, playing di Lattes's game and frustrating Dolce. It was the bitterest of pleasures. Her conscience pricked her, but she quieted it. She needed *something*, she told herself.

Despite his several attentions to her, it was a shock to find di Lattes seated in the manufactory one morning, waiting for her.

"I've come to discuss a ketubah with you," he said. "The richest, most ornate ketubah you can possibly create." He leaned forward in his seat in her small office, whispering. "It's to be a surprise for my bride."

A surprise for Dolce? Considering how many brides she'd discouraged from using the services of the d'Ancona Ketubah Workshop, Mirelle knew Dolce would despise the gift. Was it possible di Lattes was ignorant of that fact? For half a minute, Mirelle considered turning away the commission. But this is *parnesa*, she told herself, quieting that persistent inner voice that told her this could not end well. As a businesswoman, she had no choice but to accept.

Di Lattes spent a considerable amount of time with her that morning as they discussed the gold overlay and deliberated on the extravagant ornamentation derived from both the Biblical illustrations and from nature. He spoke softly, almost whispering, so that she was forced to lean in to hear him. He insisted on visiting the stock room with her, fingering the pages, choosing the heaviest vellum, approving the brilliant colors. He toured the desks to see the men at work, to select the best scribe and most artistic of craftsmen.

Di Lattes insisted on paying in full, in advance. "For I must return to Florence tomorrow. I've stayed here, enjoying your company too long. I will only return for the wedding." He paused, his eyes on her face. "I am loathe to leave. You've made this a lovely interlude."

"You mean, Dolce has," Mirelle stammered.

"My exquisite bride! She'll adorn my home beautifully, will she not? A wife almost worthy of the place in society I will give her." His eyes didn't move and Mirelle suddenly felt a shiver run up her spine. Was that Dolce's future? To be an adornment?

"But you, my dear," di Lattes leaned closer. "You must come and visit—soon. And stay."

Mirelle swallowed hard before responding. "I'm not sure Dolce . . ."

He laughed, touching her elbow. "And if she doesn't know?"

He couldn't mean what she thought he meant—could he?

"I'll write you," he said, upsetting her further.

Standing, he extended a hand across the desk, taking hers and kissing it, then turning it and letting his lips linger on the palm.

After a moment's shock, she snatched it away, taking refuge in a conventional farewell. "I wish you good fortune." She signaled over his bent body for Sabato to come into the office. "And here is Signor Narducci, who will see you out."

After di Lattes had left, Mirelle sat at her desk for a while, her hands folded on her account book. Eventually she flipped open the book, recording the sale. Because di Lattes had been so generous—not to say extravagant—his payment would nearly allow them to meet the demand for taxes. How to make up the shortfall? Where before it had seemed impossible, now just one or two commissions would save them.

And then she had an idea. She picked up the order form once more, thinking how to make it work.

35

JANUARY 13
CAIRO

Denon, back from one of his many trips to Egypt's upper reaches, dropped into the barracks late one afternoon. "I've been invited to Napoleon's table this evening," he told Daniel. "He wants to hear a first-hand account of how our forces are doing. I'm bringing several of my sketches of Upper Egypt with me to amuse his guests. Why don't you come and help me carry them?"

Daniel shook his head. "Come with you? Without an invitation? I couldn't."

Denon shrugged. "He won't care. It's not like he doesn't invite half a dozen savants and officers every night—to say nothing of the ladies. If he asks, which he probably won't, I'll tell him I had invited you to spend the evening with me and didn't want to disappoint you." He glanced around the barracks, shaking his head. "After all, what possible attraction is there moldering in this flea pit?"

Truth be told, Daniel thought, Denon's invitation would rescue him from yet another evening of deadly boredom, kicking his heels in the dusty, flea-invested room. Was that worth the risk of offending his commander? Looking about him at the spartan quarters, the men dicing irritably in the corner, he sighed. "If I get into trouble . . ."

"I'll take the blame. Come on, young Daniel! It will be a lark."

So Daniel attired himself in his dress uniform—scruffy and worn as it was—and the two set off to Napoleon's mansion headquarters.

Entering the palace deserted by the Mameluke Muhammad Bey al-Alfi, Daniel expected to see Oriental furnishings similar to those in al-Jawarti's home—low divans, piled cushions, mosaics on the floors and walls. Instead, he was stunned to see a scene that—except for the tiled floors and walls—might well have been at home in a Parisian salon. Velvet furnishings and inlaid tables were scattered about. Wax candles burned in sconces, in clusters on side tables, and in crystal candelabras. Officers in dress uniform, civilians in pantaloons and short jackets, ladies in diaphanous gowns that clung to them, all bustled around. The only indication that they were not in Paris was that some of the male guests were attired in long robes and turbans. Daniel bowed toward al-Jawarti, who smiled benignly at him without interrupting his discussion with a French major. A buzz of conversation permeated every corner of the room. Denon brought Daniel over to the tight circle of savants, who were trading discoveries and theories. It didn't take long for Denon to monopolize the conversation, recounting his exploits with the French troops in Upper Egypt. Daniel, who had heard as much of this as he cared to on the trip over, headed toward an Egyptian servant dressed in Western livery and powdered white wig, circulating with a tray of wine glasses.

As Daniel stood to one side, sipping the full-bodied vintage and watching the crowd, an exquisitely well-appointed Frenchwoman sidled over to him. "Lieutenant, you look terribly out of place. Are you here alone?"

In any other circumstance, Daniel would have avoided such a forward woman. But recognizing her as the wife of General Desaix, he smiled instead. "I was brought here by the artist Denon, Citizeness Desaix, but yes, I'll admit that I'm not entirely comfortable in such grand surroundings."

She looked around her, sniffing. "You call this grand? It's a far cry from how I grew up. This entire country is filthy and run-down, don't you agree?"

Daniel, not sure how to respond, simply nodded, noting the thin ribbon of scarlet she wore around her neck—a symbol that, despite her noble birth, she had barely escaped the guillotine. He'd seen a similar ribbon around Josephine's neck back in Italy.

"Amable!" someone called out, waving an enthusiastic fan in her direction. "My dear!"

Citizeness Desaix sighed. "That's Marie Garnier. Such a prattler . . . Marie, my darling!"

Citizeness Garnier waddled up. Unlike her slender counterpart, she was wider than she was tall. Nonetheless, she wore the thin column dress that was now in vogue, a wide sash crushed under an ample chest, making the gown look more like an overstuffed potato sack than fashionable garb. Ostrich feathers waved in her frizzled curls and rogue bloomed in circles on her powdered cheeks.

The two women pretended to kiss, lips hovering over sallow skin. "How are you, darling?" Marie Garnier cooed, then, taking a greedy glance at Daniel, added, "And who is this delightful young man?"

"I was just asking him to introduce himself," Citizeness Desaix replied. "Lieutenant?"

Daniel bowed, wishing he were anywhere else. He forced the polite blather to his lips. "Charmed, ladies. I am Daniel Isidore. Citizeness Desaix, I was honored to serve at the Battle of the Pyramids alongside your husband."

"Ah, yes." Amable Desaix stifled a yawn. "And now he's chasing that dreadful Murad Bey all over Upper Egypt. I should have a word with your friend, Citizen Denon, whom I believe went with him."

"In fact," Daniel said, "after dinner Citizen Denon will display several of the sketches he's made of ancient monuments while accompanying the general."

Another stifled yawn. "Oh? Ancient monuments? What a dreadful country this is."

Citizeness Garnier must have decided that Daniel was not worth her attention, for she pulled Amable aside. "Have you seen her yet today? Wait until you see the pearls he's given her."

"Oh, I saw them yesterday. Is she wearing them again today? How gauche."

Daniel started to edge away from the women, but Citizeness Desaix hooked his arm. "They'll be announcing dinner soon. Will you take me in?"

Trapped, Daniel bowed. He stood listening to their gossip, which centered on the scandal rocking French Cairo. After Jean-Noël Fourès had left for Paris a few weeks ago, bearing Daniel's letter to Mirelle with him, Napoleon had moved Pauline into an apartment next to his own. He was said to visit together with one of his officers for dinner on most nights, abandoning the officer to brandy and a cigar while he and Pauline retired to the lavish bedroom he'd furnished for her.

"Did you see her outfit when she rode out with him two days ago? Dressed up in a general's uniform and wearing a tricolor sash as a bonnet?" Citizeness Garnier breathed.

Another woman overheard and broke away from her circle to join them. "And the troops cheer her on. Calling her La Generale."

"Or Clioupatre," said another, as the two groups merged. "With those blonde curls!"

"I don't know who she thinks she is," Citizeness Desaix added, fingering the thin red ribbon. "Daughter of a clockmaker and his peasant wife. Did you know she worked as a milliner before Fourès married her?"

Daniel grew increasingly uncomfortable at the gossip. He'd heard much of it before—in much more vulgar terms as the soldiers bandied Pauline's name about, listing her myriad attractions. But she did seem to revel in the attention, just as her husband had said.

Pauline would organize picnics in the desert, suppers with Napoleon's staff officers, expeditions to the Pyramids. She was ostensibly the hostess of this dinner party, with its display of Denon's sketches. Napoleon's guests might take it all in stride, Daniel reflected, listening uneasily, but his upbringing made him uncomfortable with the lax manners of fashionable Paris. The same thoughts that he'd had while watching Fourès pack his bags chased once again through his mind. Both Napoleon and Pauline were married, pledged to another. Even if the general had sworn to divorce his wife, even if he was suffering at Josephine's cuckolding of him, did that give him the right to make love to another man's wife? Daniel pitied Fourès, sent away with dispatches, with nothing to do during the long sea voyage except contemplate his disgrace. And it made him wonder: this general whom he had once admired so fiercely—was this how he acted in private life? Once again he thought of the Biblical story of King David, who also misused his authority to dispatch Bathsheba's husband when he wanted to bed his wife. David was punished by God, who refused to allow him to build the Temple as a result of his sin. But the French Revolution had done away with religion—so who now would hold Bonaparte to account?

Finally, as the chatter ran in circles around the tasty morsels of innuendo, Napoleon appeared, a resplendent Pauline on his arm. She was wearing a seafoam green gown, and was sprinkled with emeralds, sparkling in her hair, dangling from her ears, and twisted with seed pearls in a tight choker around her slender neck. She clung to him—or him to her—as they conversed with the company. They paid special attention to Denon, applauding him for his coolness under fire.

"It's merely that I'm absorbed in my drawing, General, Citizeness," Denon replied with a dramatic wave of his hand toward the sketches set up in a corner of the room. "Bullets and flashing scimitars and even rockets can do little to disturb me when the muse demands my attention."

Bonaparte clapped him on the back. "I had my doubts about bringing you on this expedition, Denon. I'm glad my"—he stopped himself, then recovered, "—my people convinced me that you would be an asset."

Daniel recalled hearing that Josephine had been the one to put Denon's name forward. Seeing the flush rise to Pauline's face, it was obvious she knew it too.

"But before art—meat!" Napoleon said. "Pauline, my dear, are we ready to sit down?"

"We are, Citizen General," she said, then jumped a little as Napoleon's hand flickered over her derriere. She tittered at his touch, then said, in her grandest manner—her voice climbing like a little girl pretending to be a lady—"Ladies, gentlemen, officers—dear guests. Please do follow me."

Napoleon blatantly encircled her waist and ushered her out of the salon and into the dining room. Citizeness Desaix smiled at Daniel, who offered her his arm. Before the Revolution, Daniel recalled, there would have been precedent as to the order in which they sat at the table. Here, while the staff officers did go first, there was some confusion as to who should precede whom. With Citizeness Desaix on his arm, Daniel was among the first to be seated, not far from the general who eyed him for an uneasy moment. Daniel willed himself not to flush under the eagle stare.

But luckily, Napoleon must have decided the young officer was not worth his attention and turned away, toward the plate of barley soup being served. Did the general think he was the Citizeness's latest flirt? The notion made him shift uncomfortably in his chair.

The long table covered in snowy white linen filled the narrow room. Chairs—not all matching—were tightly packed from side to side. The plates were of the finest china and the wine goblets of thin crystal. How in the world had Napoleon gathered such riches here? Silver candlesticks set at every other place illuminated the room and there were even hothouse roses set in shallow silver bowls. Daniel wondered once more if he had somehow been transported back to Paris.

The conversation emanating from the top of the table was a mix of Napoleon's pronouncements and brusquely barked questions. Pauline, as hostess, was seated at the other end of the long table, chattering away, showing off her new jewels, and making promises of ever more extravagant entertainments to the young officers who sat on either side of her.

"What do you think of a barge ride down the Nile?" she asked, her lips quirking up at the corners of her mouth, turning her head from side to side to include them both.

"Like Cleopatra?" one of them said. "How wonderfully apt."

Her tinkling laughter carried up the table, and Napoleon interrupted one of his officers to call out, "What's so amusing down there?"

"Oh, this dear boy says my idea of a barge ride down the Nile makes him think of Cleopatra, Napoleon. It's funny, don't you think?"

Napoleon's eyes narrowed as he scrutinized the officer, who squirmed. But the general's face softened seeing Pauline's obvious enthusiasm at the compliment. "I'm afraid, my dear, that such an expedition is out of the question until we get better control over the fellaheen and the Bedouin tribes. I've reports that they are still attacking our troops."

"Oh, that's too bad." Pauline pouted. "But you know best, Citizen General."

After the soup course, plates of chicken and beans were served. Daniel was surprised by this rustic meal, but then remembered seeing Napoleon eating the exact same dinner back in Italy. The general was certainly enjoying the food, rapidly dismembering his chicken and stuffing it into his mouth, sometimes even mid-comment or question. The staff officers sitting near him—for there weren't enough women to disperse them equally between the men—seemed resigned to the peasant fare.

Unexpected shouts sounded from just outside the dining room. The room hushed as everyone looked toward the door. It burst open and Jean-Noël Fourès rushed inside, closely followed by Napoleon's guards. Fourès, face and uniform smudged with dirt, stood panting.

Pauline gasped.

"What is the meaning of this?" Napoleon roared.

"We couldn't . . ." one of the guards stammered.

"Lieutenant Fourès! Why are you not en route to Paris with your dispatches? How dare you barge in here, interrupting me and my guests? Explain yourself, man!"

Fourès, a hand at his side, bowed ironically. He did not salute.

Napoleon stood, his chair scraping the tile floor. "Is this how you present yourself to your commander in chief? Have you no respect for command?"

"No sir," Fourès said in ice-cold tones. "I do not." He strode over to where his wife was sitting, huddled fearfully against the back of her chair. He slapped her face, the ringing sound of the blow echoing through the narrow room. "Nor have I any respect for whores. Which, I regret to say"—he slapped her other cheek, and she collapsed in her chair, shrieking and sobbing—"my wife is."

"Guards! Escort this man to the stockade!"

Fourès pulled his saber from its sheath. "Not until I've had my say, General!"

"How dare you! Guards!"

Fourès brandished the sword and the men stepped back warily, their heads craned toward their commander.

"Shall I tell you how I come to be here, General?" Fourès hissed "Don't you want to know?"

Napoleon took a step toward the still weeping Pauline, but thinking better of it, stopped and placed his hands behind his back. "You have three minutes," he said coldly.

"That will suffice. I was on board the *Chasseur*, per your orders, *sir*.

We were intercepted by the British ship, the *Lion*. The sailors were all too happy to tell me how you were housing and bedding my wife. *My wife!*" Fourès spit onto the floor, with a baleful glance at Pauline, who held her reddened face in her hands, sobbing. "Not that they told me anything I didn't already know. They gleefully said they would send me back to Egypt so I could reclaim her." His voice dripped with scorn. "As if I'd want the slut back."

"She'll divorce you," Napoleon said. "You've struck her before witnesses. She'll have no difficulty obtaining a divorce."

And then what? Daniel wondered, sitting stock still along with the rest of the guests, paralyzed by the scandalous scene. Would the general divorce Josephine, with all her political connections in Paris, and marry this unsophisticated child, with her soiled reputation?

But perhaps Bonaparte truly loved her, the way Daniel loved Mirelle, whom he would marry no matter what anyone else thought of her. No matter what she'd done in the past.

"Let her!" Fourès shouted, sheathing his saber. "I want none of her!"

"And your dispatches? Did the British take them from you?"

Fourès reached inside his jacket and let a sheaf of papers fall to the tiled floor. Mixed among them, Daniel realized with a wrench to his heart, was his letter to Mirelle.

"Guards!"

This time, Fourès put up no resistance as the guards led him away. Napoleon stomped out of the room. One of the staff officers scooped up the dispatches. Daniel watched, wondering if someone would read his heartfelt letter, and if they'd have the decency to return it to him.

Pauline, her sobs echoing around the room, hurried after the general.

"What? No sketches of ancient monuments?" Citizeness Desaix murmured. "I'm desolate."

36

JANUARY 14

Christophe was in love.

He was no newcomer to love, having felt its pang and pull before, especially back in Ancona, with Mirelle. Yet that emotion, or rather, infatuation, had not lasted. Religion had been against them, of course, but it was more than that. Having won the prize, it had somehow lost its luster.

Daniel had more than once accused him of this, saying of Mirelle: "She's something you'll never have. You like the challenge more than the girl." But when Christophe had, against all odds, made her his own, when Mirelle, frightened she was pregnant, agreed to marry him, she then discovered it was only a scare and released him from his promise. And he'd felt nothing but relief. He recalled asking her why their love had faded. "Because we're from two different worlds, I suppose," she'd told him. "If we'd truly loved one another, we might have bridged the gap. But what we had—it only tricked us into thinking it was love. It wasn't real."

Christophe would swear on a stack of Bibles that what he felt now for Sappeira was real. And yet—were the obstacles between them no less great than what he'd experienced with Mirelle? Sappeira's religion was important to her and both she and her uncle insisted that it bore little relation to the Roman Catholicism that Christophe's mother still obsessively observed. He had flinched at the idea of bringing Mirelle home to his mother. Would the fact that Egyptian-born Sappeira worshipped Christ be enough?

And what did it matter if his mother accepted Sappeira or not? Would Sappeira even be willing to go to Paris with him? To live where everything was different, strange?

But he could not see himself remaining in Cairo once his tour of duty was over. And surely, if she loved him as much as he loved her, he assured himself, Sappeira would be thrilled to come with him. They would make their own home together. Love, this time around, would be enough.

Thoughts like these propelled him to Sappeira's uncle's home as often as duty allowed. He felt fortunate to be stationed in Cairo rather than chasing about the country as so many of his compatriots were doing. While there was no glory to be had in kicking his heels in this squalid capitol, he had ample opportunity to visit his new love.

One morning, when one of the interminable parades of the Hussar regiment was cancelled because Murat apparently was feeling ill, he rode to al-Jawarti's mansion. His spurs rattled as he strode down the long corridor to Sappeira's favorite drawing room. His heart pounded at the thought of seeing her once more. But then, on the room's threshold, he was brought up short.

Ethan was seated with her side by side, looking cozy on a couch, the two of them huddled over a massive book. Both were shoeless and Sappeira had covered her long hair with a scarf.

"What the devil?" Christophe blurted before he could stop himself.

They looked up, startled. Ethan's face hardened at the sight of him. While he and Ethan rubbed along for Daniel's sake, Christophe had long intuited that Ethan disapproved of him for some reason—so naturally Christophe didn't like him either. But for Daniel's sake, Christophe let the older man's sidelong glares and slights slide off his back unchallenged. Until now.

Sappeira, on the other hand, smiled from ear to ear, every one of her adorable dimples deepening. "Welcome, Lieutenant!" she cried, shifting the book to Ethan's lap and rising. "I didn't think you would visit today. Didn't you tell me the regiment was on parade this morning?"

Christophe bowed. "I didn't realize you were entertaining other company," he said, with a suspicious glance toward Ethan.

Ethan cast his eyes up over the book, looking faintly amused. "Sappeira has been kind enough to teach me some of the Coptic language," he said. "We both thought you were otherwise occupied."

"Parade was cancelled," Christophe said shortly. Then, the full implication of Ethan's words striking him, he added, "Sorry to dis appoint you both."

"Disappoint us? What can you mean?" Sappeira asked, looking bewildered, sitting back down.

"You clearly weren't expecting me to interrupt your tête-à-tête," Christophe replied, sprawling on a low divan across from them. "Don't let me disturb you."

Ethan's lip curled. "Well, if you're sure. Sappeira was just explaining how the language—somewhat like ancient Latin or Hebrew—is primarily used for prayer. But like them both, people once spoke it in everyday conversation."

"How fascinating," Christophe drawled.

Sappeira stared at him uncertainly. "We don't want to bore you. We can do this another time."

"Not at all." Christophe straightened up, wanting her to understand that his rudeness was directed at Ethan, not her. "Please, do continue."

Sappeira shifted the book back to rest on both their knees. "This is the Agpeya, or our Book of Hours," she explained to Christophe. "We pray from it seven times a day."

"Like the rag heads?" Christophe asked.

He couldn't tell whether she frowned at the insulting name or the comparison. "Not like the Muslims," she said. "More like you Latins."

"I'm not . . ." Christophe started, but then Ethan interrupted him.

"Many religions have set times to pray. Observant Jews pray three times a day."

Was it Christophe's imagination, or did Sappeira shift away from Ethan slightly at that remark?

"We're reading one of the Old Testament psalms, which Ethan is already familiar with in the original Hebrew. This particular copy of the Agpeya contains the various readings in both Arabic and Coptic, which makes it easy for Ethan, since he is already fluent in Arabic," Sappeira continued explaining.

"How fortunate for him." Christophe threw a baleful glance toward his rival for Sappeira's attention.

Ethan smirked, seeming to recognize how annoyed Christophe was—and clearly amused by it. Christophe clenched his fists, hiding them under his thighs.

"Since the lieutenant doesn't seem to mind, shall we continue?" Ethan asked.

Christophe was determined to wait the lesson out, sitting stolidly as they read out the Coptic psalm, comparing it with the Arabic, while Ethan recited the Hebrew, which he clearly knew by heart. Damned show-off! Not able to follow a single word, Christophe grew increasingly frustrated. They were shoulder to shoulder over the volume, with Sappeira pointing out the words. At one moment, Ethan lay his hand over hers, speaking softly in some foreign tongue or other, and Christophe growled deep in his throat.

"Is something wrong?" Sappeira asked, raising her head.

Ethan's hand did not move.

Did she not realize what was happening? But her dark eyes reflected only dismay at the harsh sound he'd made—and her innocence.

"Not at all," Christophe said, inwardly cursing Ethan, whose hand was still on top of hers.

Nearly an hour elapsed before they were finished—one of the slowest hours of Christophe's memory. But Sappeira finally closed the book and slid her scarf off her head, feeling for her slippers under the couch. Ethan slipped on his boots, which he had lined up near the door.

"Thank you, dear lady," he said, bending over her hand, throwing an audacious grin toward Christophe. "I hope we can continue my lessons soon."

"I'd be delighted," Sappeira told him, a smile lighting up her happy face. "You really have a remarkable talent for languages."

Christophe, who had risen with Ethan, stood awkwardly waiting for him to leave. Sappeira smiled at him. "I'm afraid I have some chores to attend to," she said, dismissing them both. "Please do come again soon, Lieutenant Leferve."

He could barely contain his frustration. "I had hoped you might spare a few minutes for me."

"Not today," she said firmly, escorting them both to the door. "Another time."

As soon as they left the mansion, Christophe grabbed Ethan's arm. "What the devil was that?"

Ethan shook his arm free. "What was what? You were there. It was a lesson in the Coptic language. What exactly do you suspect me of?"

Christophe wanted to punch his smug face. "Are you trying to pay court to my girl?"

Ethan slewed around, lips compressed. "*Your* girl? Do you have a claim on her? Are you betrothed? Or—do you intend to despoil this one, too? The way you did my cousin?"

How many cursed cousins did Mirelle have, anyway? "I don't need to defend my actions to you," Christophe blustered. "Just stay away from Sappeira."

"Do you have any idea the predicament you left Mirelle in? How she's shunned as a loose woman because of your *actions*?" Ethan glared at him. "I've never understood how Daniel could bear to remain friends with you after what you did. I've put up with you because of him. But I'll tell you this—if you think to do the same thing to that innocent child—"

"How dare you?" Christophe raged. "You don't have to tell me that she's innocent!"

"—I'll go to her uncle. I'll tell him what you are. What you've done."

"You won't!"

Ethan thrust his chin up defiantly. "Won't I?"

His soldier's code made it imperative to answer the insult and demand satisfaction. Christophe jerked one of the white riding gloves out of his belt. He stepped forward and raised the glove.

Ethan moved out of reach, eyebrows arching upward. "Are you challenging me to a duel?" he asked, his tones overlain with sarcasm. "Don't you know Bonaparte has forbidden them? What will your commander say when he finds out?"

Christophe smacked the glove against his own palm, nostrils flaring. It was true. He'd be put in the stockade if word of a duel leaked out. He shouldn't risk it. But he was too furious to think logically.

"Are you planning on killing me?" Ethan asked acidly. "I've no experience with swords or firearms, you realize. You might as well just stab me and have done with it."

"If you were a man instead of a coward—"

"And who should I ask as a second?" Ethan interrupted, continuing to mock him. "Daniel? How do you think your childhood friend would feel about that?"

Christophe clenched the glove, creasing it in a tight fist. He knew Daniel would disapprove, might even refuse to act. "Goddamn you to hell, Ethan Dovid," he muttered, turning on his heel and stalking off.

37

JANUARY 15
ANCONA

For Mirelle's plan to work, she needed a chaperone.

At first she thought perhaps she could simply hand the task over to Sabato Narducci. But, as wonderful a foreman as he was, he didn't have the persuasive power needed. They'd never had to play the role of merchant before, Mirelle thought bitterly. If you were marrying in Ancona, it was always understood that the d'Ancona Ketubah Workshop would fashion your ketubah.

No, she would have to do it herself. But with her reputation, she couldn't visit any of the betrothed men alone, not at their businesses, not at their homes. If she were seen entering their door, her already soiled status in the community would be confirmed. She'd be that Lilith Dolce loved labeling her.

But who would be willing to accompany her? Their old servant, Anna, had left Ancona once Pinina could no longer afford her. None of the Morpurgo servants had any sympathy for her. For a couple of minutes, Mirelle considered asking her mother, or Arianna Narducci, Sabato's wife. But both would disapprove of putting herself forward in such an unwomanly way.

Mirelle was walking in the market near the docks, contemplating her problem, when she saw Francesca Moratti selling eggs at her usual stall. The Catholic woman looked troubled. Mirelle approached her.

"Good morning, Signora Moratti," she said. "Is all well?"

Francesca's hand went up to the wooden cross she wore around her neck. "Signorina d'Ancona. Do you want some eggs?"

"No eggs for me this morning. Where are your children?"

At that, Francesca released the crucifix and wiped her eyes on her apron. "At home. Both have the fever."

That winter, influenza had swept through the city. It wasn't the deadly illness that often visited—and it wasn't the plague that periodically decimated the town. Mirelle couldn't understand why Francesca seemed so upset.

"They're young. Surely they will recover," Mirelle said.

Francesca let her apron drop back to her waist. "The babe can't breathe. He burns with fever, refuses to drink or eat. I want to buy a tonic for him but it's too expensive." Her shoulders sagged. "They're all I have, Signorina."

Mirelle thought for a moment. Two of the Morpurgo servants had been stricken with the illness, and they'd been prescribed a tonic. Remnants of the medicine might well be stored in the house.

But she didn't want to raise Francesca's hopes if she couldn't find it. "I see. I wish them a full healing, Francesca. I'll pray for them."

Francesca rolled her eyes. "Don't you think I'm praying for my children day and night? Prayers don't seem to make any difference, this time. I don't know where to turn."

Mirelle couldn't believe what she was hearing. The pious Francesca shedding her belief in prayer? She placed a comforting hand on the woman's arm, then walked swiftly away.

The bottle of tonic was right where she thought it would be, in the kitchen storeroom. It was half full. Certainly enough for a toddler. Mirelle felt guilty taking it, but surely it was tzedakah—charity.

She told herself she would not ask for anything in exchange, but if Francesca offered . . .

She hurried back to the market. The sun was setting. A year ago, that would have meant she would have been forbidden to walk the streets of Gentile Ancona, but the ghetto gates had been torn down and the Jewish community given the freedom of the city, day and night. Mirelle blessed General Bonaparte and his forces—including Daniel—for demolishing them.

At the quay, Francesca was packing up. It didn't look like she'd had much luck selling her eggs that day. Mirelle thrust the bottle of tonic at her. "Here. For your babe."

Francesca looked at her, suspicious. "What is this? Some kind of Jewish witchcraft?"

Mirelle sighed. Francesca's prejudice against Jews still surfaced at inopportune times despite having gotten to know both Daniel and Mirelle. Perhaps her childhood upbringing would always be too strong to entirely overcome the tendency to believe they were the devils the priests and townsfolk thought them.

"It's the tonic to help your child breathe. The servants in the Morpurgo household had the same fever, and Signore Morpurgo brought the doctor to see them. They recovered quickly after taking it."

Francesca took the bottle. "Why are you giving me this? I can't pay you for it."

Mirelle sighed again. "I'm not asking for payment. You helped me when I needed it, out on the docks. Besides, I don't like to think of your little one suffering. Be careful with the dose—this was made up for adults. Don't give him too much."

Francesca eyed it, still suspicious. The liquid in the mottled glass bottle was dark and viscous. "What's in it?"

Glad she had overheard the doctor when he'd handed it to her mother to give to the servants, Mirelle ticked off the ingredients on

her fingers. "It's a mixture of licorice, vinegar, oil, treacle, and a tinc-
ture of opium. It should clear his phlegm and allow him to breathe—
and help him sleep." She mentally reviewed the doctor's instructions.
"You should also boil water and hold his head over it—not too close.
Let him breathe in the steam."

Francesca held the bottle up to the dying sunlight, turning it to all
sides. "If it hurts him—"

Mirelle shook her head. "It shouldn't. Just don't give him too
much."

Three days later, Francesca came to the workshop, keeping her head
ducked low to avoid the surprised stares of the workmen. Mirelle
brought her into her small office.

"It worked!" Francesca said. "I've come to thank you."

"The babe is better? I'm glad." Mirelle smiled. Part of her longed to
ask for her favor, but that wasn't how charity was supposed to work.
True charity was offered anonymously—something Mirelle couldn't
have done. At least she had volunteered the tonic without being asked
for it.

Francesca glanced out the office door. The workroom was half
empty, the hours of work for all the men having been severely reduced,
along with their wages. "It's so quiet in here," she observed.

Mirelle stiffened. She hated that her misfortune was so obvious.

"I wish I could help you in some way," Francesca said, looking left
and right at all the vacant seats. "Return the favor."

Mirelle closed her eyes. Surely it wasn't wrong to ask when the
offer was given freely. "You can."

They left the workshop and headed to Nissim Badalassi's silversmith manufactory. The charcoal ablaze in the smithy overheated the room, even in the middle of January. Along the manufactory's sides were shelves of the cups, plates, receptacles, and vases that Nissim so lovingly crafted, gleaming in the firelight.

Nissim was alone, the very state Mirelle had both hoped for and dreaded. He was sawing a shape from a large piece of sterling silver but put it aside when he saw the two women come through his back door.

"Ladies?" he asked, sounding uncertain, glancing at the cross around Francesca's neck.

Mirelle gathered her courage and smiled. "Signore Badalassi, I've come to see you because there has been a misunderstanding. I believe Dolce Morpurgo has told your betrothed, Malca Garo, that Dolce won't have her ketubah made at my workshop. But here"—she reached into her reticule and unfolded di Lattes's order form—"you can see that's not true."

Badalassi studied the page and his eyebrows rose. "Congratulations, Signorina. That's a very elaborate ketubah. But Malca wants me to have our ketubah made in Rome."

Mirelle nodded. "I'm aware. But is that what you want? After all, your father and grandfather ordered their ketubot from my father and grandfather. I'd hate to see you break that tradition, just because of a mistake. And you know the ketubot we create are the most splendid in the world. Why go elsewhere when we're right here?"

Francesca, who had been silent throughout, chimed in. "Isn't it the man's job to make these arrangements? In my religion it would be."

Mirelle wanted to kiss her.

Badalassi stared at Francesca, his forehead puckered. "Signorina, why did you bring this Catholic woman with you?"

Mirelle forced a smile. "Salacious rumors persist in circulating about me. I assure you, they are both unkind and untrue. Signora

Moratti kindly agreed to accompany me to make sure there wouldn't be more of them."

Badalassi nodded. "I see. Well, if I were to order my ketubah from you, it couldn't possibly be as richly festooned as di Lattes's."

"Of course not." Mirelle nodded, feeling hope rise like a bird fluttering in her chest. She was careful to keep her voice measured. "We get an order like this one perhaps once every couple of years. But I wanted you to see that Dolce Morpurgo's ketubah will definitely be created in my workshop. So why shouldn't yours and Malca's?"

"I'll have to think about it." Badalassi said. "Talk it over with Malca."

Francesca sniffed, looked as if she were about to say something, then folded her lips together. Badalassi glanced at her, withering a little under her obvious scorn.

Mirelle rushed in before Francesca's derision could stiffen his back and turn him stubborn. "Please don't delay. Your wedding is soon, isn't it? I want to make sure your ketubah is as beautiful as any of your exquisite silver items." She nodded toward the shelves of glinting objects. "As a fellow craftsman, you know that takes time."

Badalassi looked gratified. "I'll decide today and come to the workshop tomorrow." He glanced again at Francesca, eyes narrowing as if disregarding her contempt. "After I talk to Malca about it."

Mirelle smiled, bowing her head. "I'll hope to see you tomorrow, then."

Heading out of the smithy, Mirelle and Francesca repeated the visit to all the prospective grooms. A few had already commissioned their ketubah from another shop, but the others promised to think it over, particularly after perusing di Lattes's generous order. By late afternoon, when Mirelle bid goodbye to her chaperone, she felt certain that she had saved the workshop.

A week later, Mirelle was startled to be summoned downstairs just as she was about to prepare for bed. She quickly replaced the pins in her hair and followed the servant to the drawing room.

Her heart froze. Seated there was Rabbi Fano, partaking of a cup of wine and aniseed biscuits together with David Morpurgo and Dolce. Her mother hovered in the background.

"Ah, Mirelle!" the rabbi greeted her.

She disliked the expression on his face—smug, with an edge of gloating. Looking around, she noticed Dolce's white face, her quivering lips. What could have so perturbed Dolce, who was always in control, no matter what? David's face was like stone, his jaw clenched, his eyes snapping with anger. Mirelle glanced at her mother, whose hands were fluttering and eyes downcast.

"I asked Rabbi Fano to come here because we have a matter of grave concern to discuss with you," David said slowly, grinding out his words as though they were wheat in a mill.

Mirelle couldn't imagine what he was talking about. Was it the tonic she'd taken? Or the fact that she'd been soliciting business all about the Jewish Quarter?

David took a paper out of his vest pocket and extended it to Mirelle. "This came for you."

She stepped forward, her heart lifting unexpectedly. "From Daniel?" she breathed.

Dolce glared at her. "Are you expecting a letter from Daniel?" she asked, her voice like a knife.

Mirelle wished she hadn't said it. How many months had it been, after all?

"Read it," David commanded.

With shaking hands, she unfolded the piece of paper. It contained an invitation from di Lattes to come to Florence for a visit in the months before the wedding. No, not for a visit. To stay, to become the man's paramour. Shocked, she felt the heat rise to her cheeks as she read his brazen words.

> *I know you are having difficulties living with my bride-to-be. It hurts me to think you must suffer so. I will provide you with apartments that match your beauty, clothe you in the richest garments, surround you with luxury. You would be my dearest secret, my loving, lovely lover. Use the money I gave you for that foolish ketubah to travel to me. Do it soon, as I long for you. I will transport you from the consequences of your sullied reputation and give you everything you deserve—and more.*

"How dare he!" Mirelle burst out, crushing the paper between her hands. "I assure you, I did nothing to encourage such—such—I don't have the words to describe how disgusted I am at this—this indecency!"

"You are quite the actress, Mirelle." Every sharp word Dolce spoke was coated with scorn. "Don't think I didn't see you using your wiles to tempt him from me. Yet another man you've managed to seduce. To take from me." She broke down, pulling out a handkerchief, covering her face. "Do you hate me so very much?"

David moved over to the sofa where she was sitting, putting an arm around her shoulders. "Hush, child. Hush."

Dolce buried her face in her father's shoulder. "What did I ever do to her, Papa?" she sobbed.

David kept his daughter in a close embrace as he looked up at Mirelle. "You deny it?"

"Deny what?" she demanded, feeling as though she were sinking into a nightmare.

"Deny enticing him. Deny tempting him to spite my Dolce."

"Of course I deny it! What do you take me for?"

At that, the rabbi, with a sly smile, rose slowly from his chair. "We know what you are," he hissed. "We've always known it."

"Known what? Say what you mean, Rabbi." Mirelle thrust her chin in the air, words stumbling out of her mouth unchecked. "You have wanted to hurt me ever since I thwarted your attempts to keep me out of the workshop. You spread rumors about me—*lashon ha'ra!*—that have ended with this—this insult! This insult I did nothing—nothing!—to merit." She drew a deep breath. "I sinned—once! Once! I have repented for that sin a thousand times. And despite that, despite my wish to redeem myself, you take pleasure in my pain. You are glad this man insults me! Despite your holy office, Rabbi, you want me nothing but harm!"

The rabbi shook his head, her attack wiping the remnant of a smile from his face. He spoke slowly, enunciating every word. "You grievously wrong me, child. And, as usual, you are forward. Unable to see that it is your unwomanly nature that brought you to be so soiled."

Mirelle felt faint. Even her own mother had inched away, standing with her back to the wall, mopping her eyes with her apron. She had no one. For a fleeting moment, she thought of Daniel. Wished for him. But even he had abandoned her.

Putting out a hand, she blindly groped her way to an empty chair and stood, swaying, holding onto its back. "I did not tempt him," she said through clenched teeth.

Dolce's throbbing protests cut through the room. "I won't marry him," she cried out. "Not after this! I won't!"

David held her close. "Not if you don't want to, my poor child. We'll talk about it later. But men do"—he cast a scornful glance in Mirelle's direction—"need to sow their wild oats. It's natural. Especially when they find a woman who is not careful of her virtue."

Dolce picked her head up off his shoulder. A harsh glow had entered her sapphire blue eyes, and a feverish tinge outlined her high cheekbones. "She leaves this house. Today."

"We'll talk about it later," David said, soothing Dolce by rubbing her arm.

"I may have a solution for Mirelle," the rabbi unexpectedly said. "A path for this wayward child to redeem herself in the eyes of our community."

Utter silence. Then Pinina said her first words since the entire debacle began. "Truly, Rabbi? But how?"

38

JANUARY 15
CAIRO

"But why won't you allow me to at least kiss you?" Christophe demanded. "Don't you love me?"

"Love you?" the girl repeated, her eyes resting on the hand that gripped her elbow.

He let it go. "Yes, love me. I adore you, beautiful one. But you will not allow me to show you how much. No gifts, no speeches—not even a chaste kiss on the cheek."

"That's not how a man acts, not among my people." Sappeira rubbed her elbow.

Christophe groaned. "Then tell me how. Teach me. I'm willing to learn."

"If my father were alive, you would address him. Since he is not, you must speak with my uncle. But I doubt you'll have any luck with him."

Perhaps now was the time to ask. "What happened to your parents, Sappeira? Won't you at least tell me that?"

She walked away, looking sideways out of one of the arched windows into the courtyard. A bitter tone entered her voice. "They were slaughtered, together with many more of my village. The Muslims wished to cleanse—that was the word they used—to cleanse. I cannot . . ."

She broke down, her voice trailing off, a single tear trickling down her cheek.

Christophe felt his heart break for her. Striding over, he reached up and touched her cheek, whisking the tear away. At just that moment, al-Jawarti entered the room.

"What's going on here? What are you doing?" he demanded, his face purpling.

Sappeira struck Christophe's hand from her face, then ran from the room.

Christophe turned to the irate Coptic. "She was telling me about her parents. I meant no dishonor. I was merely consoling her."

"By touching her? How dare you! I've been too lenient, allowing you Frenchmen the freedom of my home." Al-Jawarti pointed at the door. "You will leave at once and never return."

"No!" The word was forced from Christophe's mouth. "You cannot part us. I love your niece, Effendi."

"Love?" The scorn in al-Jawarti's voice was palpable. "I've seen what you Frenchmen call love. Dallying with Egyptian women, decking them out in Western clothing, making them false promises to entice them to your beds. Your own commander seducing a married woman. At least she is a Frenchwoman. Your compatriots sully the honor of these foolish women, women lost to all sense of what's proper. Trust me, they will be cast aside, ruined, once your forces leave. But you will not so compromise my niece!"

Christophe drew himself up. If the man knew his history, especially what he had done to Mirelle, he would never be able to convince him of his true feelings for Sappeira. He had regretted his seduction of Mirelle before, but now Christophe could only be grateful al-Jawarti was unaware of his reputation. And since there didn't seem any other way to win Sappeira, he squared his shoulders and asked, "What if I offered my hand and my heart in marriage? What say you to that?"

"You think I hold my niece so cheap? What are you but a godless soldier—a man who disavowed even your own Latin faith? Were you still a Latin, that would be at least something. But you are nothing—a man without belief!"

"I believe in your niece. I believe in our love. You cannot tell me that she doesn't love me."

Al-Jawarti, who had been nearly nose to nose with Christophe as they argued, stepped back, his face suddenly ashen. "You cannot pretend that she told you she loves you. She is a good girl and would never admit to such a thing without the sanctity of betrothal."

Christophe nodded. He regretted the fact that Sappeira's uncle was correct. He had never managed to get her to admit her feelings. But he would stake his life that she loved him. She must!

Desperate, he said, "And if I convert to your faith? Would you allow me to address her then?"

Al-Jawarti stared at him. "You do this only to win the girl. You are not sincere."

It was true, he was not. But he would do anything for Sappeira.

"Let me talk with your priests. Let Sappeira be my religious guide. I promise you, my intentions in adhering to your faith are honest and forthright."

"All because you love her?"

"All because I love her."

Two days later, Christophe waited, impatient, as Daniel finished his noontime parade of his men on the barren stretch of land outside of the barracks and dismissed them for lunch. They trooped off, and Christophe rushed up and grabbed his friend's arm.

"Congratulate me, *mon ami*—I'm a married man!"

"You're a what?" Daniel pulled back.

Christophe grinned at the flabbergasted expression on his

childhood friend's face. He waved a hand before his eyes, showing off the thick gold ring adorning it.

Daniel clutched his hand, turning it this way and that. "Married? To whom?"

"To Sappeira, of course. Who else?"

"But . . . have you thought about this?"

"Of course I have, you fool! I've thought of nothing else since looking up into her sweet face after I was wounded." Christophe snatched his hand back, annoyed. "I'm surprised you ask."

Daniel shrugged. "I've seen you in love before, you remember."

"God, will you never let that go? Is Mirelle all you ever think about?"

Daniel stared at the rocky path for a long moment, then picked his head up. "Are you actually married?"

Christophe grinned again. "In a church, no less—this morning. Can you believe it?"

"What church? Where?"

"Saints Sergius and Bacchus Church—and look, I'm sorry I couldn't have you there as a witness. I just didn't know—I mean—" Christophe grimaced.

"What church is that—Coptic? Did you think having a Jew there would upset the priests?" Daniel grinned. "You could be right." He thought for a moment. "I can't picture you getting married in a church. What was it like?"

Christophe grinned. "Well, first of all, this church—it was ancient. Built supposedly on the spot where the Holy Family rested when they fled into Egypt. Icons of Jesus and the saints all over the place. The ceremony itself was impossibly long." Christophe groaned as he recalled what felt like hours of standing and kneeling. "I won't bore you with the details."

"No, I'm fascinated. Tell me."

"Oh, lord, there was incense and interminable prayers and readings, and then they anointed us with oil . . ."

"What? Like King David?"

"Al-Jawarti said something about us being treated like royalty, because we were now the king and queen of our new household. Believe me, I was as surprised as you are. But the"—here Christophe laughed—"crowning glory were the two crowns. They were these heavy, elaborate gold crowns—one for each of us. I must say, Sappeira looked like a princess in hers. We didn't get to keep them, more's the pity. They draped me in a white cape—a chasuble, it was called—because I'm also the family priest of love, or some such." Christophe shook his head. "Honestly, I could hardly stop myself from laughing at some moments. It was all so ludicrous. But I'd have stood a lot more of it to be able to call Sappeira my wife."

Daniel smiled at that. "And you say all this happened this morning?"

Christophe nodded.

Daniel shot him a strange look. "So why are you here, then? I mean—congratulations, Christophe, and I'm thrilled for you, but shouldn't you be with your bride?"

Christophe groaned. "That's the absolute worst of it—and I didn't know it until al-Jawarti told me a couple of days ago, when I begged for her hand. We're not supposed to touch one another for the next three days. Something to do with deepening our spiritual bonds and uniting our union with God. I mean—I've waited this long and now I have to wait another three days?" He clutched at his hair in mock desperation.

Daniel laughed. "Poor fellow! Now I know you truly love her if you're willing to put up with that. Let's go toast your marriage, then!"

"Let's! We're both supposed to fast for three days too—but if you think I'm going along with that rubbish, you're crazy!"

As they strolled toward the mess tent, Christophe humming the wedding march, Daniel grew pensive. "I'm surprised there isn't a big wedding celebration. Did al-Jawarti balk at throwing you one?"

"Oh, it's going on right now. Women making these odd wailing noises, men jabbering away in Arabic, everyone stuffing their faces while I'm supposed to look on, starving. I got bored, so I told al-Jawarati I needed to report to my commander and tell him about my marriage."

Daniel's jaw dropped. "What? You didn't get permission from your colonel first? He's going to court martial you."

Christophe laughed. "I decided I couldn't risk him saying no. I may just go straight to Murat. He's more liberal about these things than straight-laced Garnier. Here, come with me for moral support, would you? Word in the barracks is that Murat is visiting his tailor today—that always puts him in a good mood."

Daniel grinned. "I wouldn't do it for anyone but you, Christophe. I'll let Sappeira know if they toss you into the stockade. It'll be my wedding present to you both."

Laughing, they changed direction, heading toward the center of town where Murat's French tailor had his store.

39

Esteemed katib,

I realize I have been delinquent in writing these reports, but since deciding that I was in danger of being corrupted by these revolutionary French attitudes, I have held myself aloof. So after writing you about the failed revolt, I have had little to say.

I can tell you that I've been to their so-called Egyptian Institute several times to peruse their bookshelves. They've books about the Prophet, upon whom be mercy and peace, and about his Companions, and even a translation of our Qu'ran into French, although what use that is to them when they profess to be godless—and proud of it—I don't know. Their scientific efforts have been admirable, of course, and I hope we Muslims can profit from their discoveries.

They do, however, continue to do us considerable harm, particularly when it comes to our women. It is bad enough for the foreign women to stroll about like whores, but worse still when Egyptian women don Western dress and run after officers. Surely such loose women will reap the consequences of their illicit behavior.

It is hard to blame the soldiers and officers, however, when their own Ṣāri ʿAskar takes a married woman from her husband and places her in his bed. And this the man who claimed to be Muslim! It is inconceivable!

Yet one must wonder about General Jacques-François de Menou, who commands one of Napoleon's five divisions in Egypt. Having married the daughter of the wealthy Egyptian, Zubaidah bint Muhammad El Bawwab, he converted to Islam, accepting the new name of Abdallah de Menou. His behavior is such that one feels his conversion to Islam may in fact be genuine. The French soldiers and officers, however, mock the man on nearly every occasion. So much for the Ṣāri 'Askar's protestations that the French forces respect Islam!

And just today, having a cup of sachleb with Nasū Pasha, I heard that another officer, a dragoon, was accepted into the Coptic faith, chiefly doing so to marry the niece of al-Jawarti. I know you will forgive my observation, having been so forbearing up to now, that these Frenchmen seem incapable of distinguishing between the faithful and the Copts, the Bedouin, or the Jews. Their philosophy is to treat everyone, despite their religion, all the same. I feel certain such bizarre tolerance will lead to their ultimate downfall.

My main reason for writing you, however, is to report that we here in Cairo are hearing rumors that the Sublime Porte has appointed your master, Ahmad Pasha al-Jazzar, to take on the French. Inshallah, may the Pasha make short work of them and deliver us from the infidels.

You may not be aware that, according to Nasū Pasha, who is in a position to know, the Ṣāri 'Askar is about to head into the desert again, to head the Ottoman forces off. Perhaps this information will help al-Jazzar prepare for an attack. Not a military man myself, I can only hope this tidbit of news will be of use—and of course will continue to send more information as I learn it.

Wishing you peace, along with your Lord's blessings,
Abd al-Rahman al-Jabartī

40

Daniel realized that Christophe was right. Murat was delighted by the marriage. Draped by his new uniform jacket, with its higher-than-regulation red collar, gold florets and trim dripping everywhere, he clapped Christophe on the back and demanded wine of the tailor for a toast right then and there.

"To the bride!" he boomed. "What's her name again?"

"Sappeira," Christophe said, raising his own glass. "To my angel, my love!"

All three quaffed the sour wine. Murat then volunteered a two-day leave for the groom. "For the honeymoon!" he chortled. "May it be sweet!"

When Christophe told him of the Coptic tradition of abstaining for three days, Murat burst out laughing. "Let your leave start on—what?" He counted on his fingers. "This Monday, then!" And he scrawled out the pass on the back of one of the tailor's order forms. Handing it over, he added, "You'll want to be back with your company by Wednesday. Not sure when we're heading out."

"Heading out, sir?" Christophe asked.

But Murat just waved him off. "Go back to celebrating, man!"

As they left the tailor's, Daniel caught Christophe's arm. "How are you going to break the news back home? And what happens when your tour of duty is over? Have you thought about any of that?"

Christophe just shoved the pass into his jacket and shrugged. "I'll write to Mama, of course. She'll be delighted with my darling, don't you think?"

Christophe had said almost the same thing about Mirelle, claiming that his mother would love her. "Who wouldn't love Mirelle?" he'd asked and Daniel now choked back the comment that a Coptic Egyptian bride might displease Odette nearly as much as a Jewish Italian one.

"And when we march? Will she come with us?" Daniel persisted.

"Nonsense! She'll stay here with her uncle. Do you think that's what Murat meant? That we'll be getting new orders soon?"

From the gleeful lilt of his friend's voice, Daniel realized once again how different the two of them were. He would have been worried about leaving a bride behind, not knowing if he'd ever return to her. But for Christophe, the idea of being on the march again was exhilarating.

"And when we return to France?"

Christophe punched him on the shoulder. "What a worrywart you are, Daniel. There's plenty of time to think about all that."

Daniel let it go. Perhaps Christophe was right—and besides, it wasn't his problem. Wishing his friend well once again, he clapped him on the back and sent him back to his wedding celebration.

41

FEBRUARY 8

Ethan had no idea what to expect when he was summoned to present himself to General Bonaparte.

The news from Greater Syria—especially the land that he thought of as Eretz Israel—was not good. Even in his lowly translator's station, reports trickled back of Pasha Ahmed—Djezzar the Butcher—being given command of the Mameluke forces. It was said the pasha boasted of how he would liberate Egypt from the French, chucking their infidel bodies into the sea or slashing them to bits for the vultures to feast upon. Ethan could almost hear him saying it.

But that had happened a month or so ago. So why did Napoleon want to see him now?

As he kicked his heels in the antechamber, Ethan thought about his distraught cousin. He'd found Daniel drinking arak all alone in a dimly lit Egyptian café the previous evening. Spirits were prohibited to the Muslim faithful, but that didn't prevent cagey Egyptian café-keepers from keeping a bottle or two for their French patrons.

"I love her and she'll never know it," Daniel had muttered, pouring himself another glass. "This damned British blockade . . ."

Ethan grasped Daniel's wrist just as he was about to throw back the drink. "We'll find a way," he said. He snapped his fingers for the café owner. "Strong coffee. Now," he barked. "And take this glass and bottle away."

Daniel was so dispirited that he didn't even resist. He drank the dark brew and sipped from the carafe of water the proprietor deferentially placed by the tiny coffee cups. Sobering, he agreed to head back to his barracks. "You know what it's like," he said as they walked the narrow Cairo streets. "You lost the woman you loved."

Ethan glared and Daniel flinched. Realizing it, Ethan patted his cousin's shoulder.

Adara's memory wasn't fading, but her loss and that of their still-born child were no longer as acute. Ethan wouldn't have given up their handful of years together despite the depths of his mourning. Sympathetic to the pain heard ringing in his cousin's voice, Ethan occupied himself now in thinking of ways to dispatch Daniel's letter to Mirelle as he awaited his audience with the general.

When he entered the office, Napoleon was sitting behind a huge desk, his head cradled in his hands, his shoulders sagging. Ethan thought briefly of the scores of duties and decisions that rested solely on those shoulders. No wonder Bonaparte looked weary.

His secretary, Bourrienne, asked, "Ethan Dovid? You accompanied Major Beauvoisin to see Ahmad Pasha al-Jazzar?"

"I did, sir," Ethan said, standing awkwardly before the desk.

Bourrienne waved him to a chair, but before he could sit, Napoleon shot up. Ethan hesitated, then straightened.

"Al-Jazzar saw you and not the major, right?" Napoleon barked.

Ethan nodded.

"Speak up, man!" The general moved out from behind his desk and approached Ethan, standing mere inches from his nose.

Ethan willed himself not to step away. "He did, sir."

Napoleon placed his hands behind his back and began pacing the room. Ethan kept still. The room was cold—the iron stove in the middle of the room was unlit—but beads of sweat popped on his forehead.

"Why was that?" Napoleon's tone changed, turning curious rather than commanding.

Should he tell the general the truth? But what choice had he, really? "I believe it was to insult you, sir."

"I think so too." Bonaparte nodded briskly, then turned again to pace the room.

Ethan waited.

"Tell me everything," Napoleon said, snapping a finger at Bourrienne. "Lucien, take notes. Leave nothing out, no matter how insignificant you think it."

Ethan related how they had arrived, how days had passed with them being unable to gain an audience with the pasha. He spoke of how Haim Farhi had found him at the café and brought him to Djezzar's palace.

Napoleon interrupted. "Tell me more about this—what did you call him? *Katib*? He's a Jew, you say?"

"Yes, sir. He serves the pasha, despite having been mutilated by him."

"Mutilated?" Napoleon stopped short, his head jerking back. "Mutilated how?"

"His eye was gouged out and he lost his nose entirely to the pasha's cruel whims. He may have had other wounds inflicted as well. The Muslims give Djezzar the nickname of the Butcher. As I waited for my audience in his courtyard, the pasha maimed another man—I don't know why. He was dragged out past me with his face streaming with blood from knife wounds." Ethan shuddered. "I still have nightmares about those screams."

"I see." Napoleon sounded thoughtful. "Continue."

Ethan told him the rest—how angry Djezzar had been when

Ethan read Napoleon's letter and how he had banished both him and the major from his city.

Napoleon's forehead wrinkled slightly. "But I don't understand," he pondered, as Ethan completed his tale. "He should have been pleased by my affirmations of his faith."

Ethan shook his head. "He was not. Decidedly not."

Napoleon took another turn around the room. Bourrienne put his quill down beside the page, blowing softly on it to dry the ink.

"Lucien, read him Reynier's report," the general said, settling himself back behind the desk.

Ethan, not invited to take a seat, remained standing.

Bourrienne nodded, putting his account of Ethan's encounter with Djezzar to one side and picking up another piece of paper. He read how General Reynier's troops had captured a Mameluke runner, who told them that El Arish was under Ottoman control.

"El Arish is a mere twenty-two miles from the Egyptian fort we occupy at Katieh on the edge of the Sinai desert," Bonaparte interjected.

"The messenger also told Reynier that the pasha has occupied the Ottoman provinces of Ramleh and Jaffa," Bourrienne concluded.

Ethan wondered why he was being given this information. Usually civilians weren't privy to military intelligence. The fact he was being trusted with it made him brave enough to ask, "It's true, then? The Porte has made Djezzar the commander of Greater Syria?"

Bonaparte gritted his teeth. "This is all Talleyrand's fault. If he had only seen the Sultan when I needed him to."

Ethan had to choke back the urge to remind the general how he'd reported this back in July.

A clock on a side table chimed the hour. It was four o'clock.

Bonaparte smacked the desk with both hands and leaned forward. "Never mind all that. I have another mission for you."

42

Opening the door to his home, Abd al-Rahman was shocked to see Ethan standing there, holding out a wrapped package. They hadn't met since Ethan had brought his cousin along, to ask for his help in dispatching a love letter.

"*Ahlan wa sahlan*," Abd al-Rahman said uncertainly. It was incumbent upon him to welcome his guest, even while he wondered what his purpose was in coming.

"*Marhaba*," Ethan responded, peering past him. "I'm sorry if I'm intruding. But I wanted to say farewell before I left the city. The general is sending me on an important mission. I'm not sure if I'll return."

"But how did you find me?"

Ethan smiled. "You once told me that you lived near the souk on the Street of the Tentmakers, south of the Bab Zuweila gate. I went to the souk and inquired of you among the merchants. The stall keeper who sold me this candy knew how to direct me." He thrust the wrapped package toward Abd al-Rahman.

"I will give this to my wife," he said. "Please, enter." He gestured, escorting Ethan down a dim hallway into a sparsely furnished inner chamber, with a single divan, a rag rug running the length of the room, and tufted cushions scattered about. The walls were studded

with overflowing bookcases, while books littered the floor next to a
low desk covered with paper.

"Your study?" Ethan asked.

"Yes. Do sit down. I'll ask Hasani to bring refreshment." He left the
room and sought out his wife, handing her the package and telling
her about their unexpected guest.

She unwrapped it. "Nougat!" she exclaimed, happily.

"Bring some coffee if you would, wife. Do you mind meeting him?"

She smiled. "Not at all. Exciting, isn't it? Meeting a foreigner?
You've mentioned him so often, I already feel I know him."

He returned to the study to find Ethan kneeling on the floor,
examining his books. Hurriedly, Abd al-Rahman gathered them in
his arms. "I apologize for the room's untidiness. Please know it's not
Hasani's fault. I ask her not to clean in here when I'm in the middle
of working on something."

"Those books are about the French. About Europe." Ethan sounded
bewildered as he rose from the floor and sat on the divan. "What
exactly are you trying to learn? Can I help?"

"I want to understand the culture better. So I am accurate in my
chronicle of your occupation of my country."

Ethan's face hardened. "Is that the real reason you befriended me?"
he asked brusquely. "And after you learned what you wanted to know,
you dropped me, didn't you?"

Abd al-Rahman was taken aback. Of course, there was some truth
in Ethan's accusation. He could not, of course, tell him about his
reports to Farhi. "Certainly it is one reason," he said slowly.

Ethan rose. "Then I will trouble you no longer."

"You are too abrupt, my friend."

"Friend? I thought we were friends. But you're saying not."

"I'm saying—"

His response was interrupted by Hasani, properly concealed by
the drape of her veil and long dark robe, carrying a tray with coffee,

nuts, and the nougat. She moved awkwardly and Abd al-Rahman rushed to relieve her of her heavy load.

Ethan stared at the heavily pregnant woman, then quickly lowered his eyes. His frown deepened, startling Abd al-Rahman. "Will you introduce me to your wife?" he asked correctly, his voice polite despite his glum face.

Abd al-Rahman was impressed, as always, with Ethan's knowledge of Islamic manners. "Yes, of course. Ethan, I am delighted to introduce you to my wife, Hasani. Hasani, this is Ethan Dovid, a French Jew, fluent in our tongue."

"*Salam Alaikum*," Ethan murmured, his eyes fixed on the tiled floor.

"*Wa Alaykum as-salam*," Hasani said cheerfully, her own eyes averted. "Please, have some coffee. May I pour it for you?"

"I would prefer you didn't bother." Ethan's voice seemed oddly full of grit, as though it were hard for him to clear his throat and speak naturally.

Both Abd al-Rahman and Hasani froze at the man's rudeness. "But surely," Abd al-Rahman said, trying to keep his tones polite, "you'll honor my house by partaking of some refreshment?"

Ethan turned toward him. "I don't want her to stoop, not in her condition," he muttered.

Hasani flushed red and fled the room.

"There was no need to be so indelicate," Abd al-Rahman reproved him.

"I apologize to you both," Ethan said, sounding abashed. "But it is a dangerous time for her."

"Dangerous?" Abd al-Rahman studied Ethan's face, noticing his clenched jaw and the wrinkle of concern between his eyebrows. What ailed the man? "Why do you say that? Her condition is natural, surely."

Ethan shrugged. "I should go."

But now Abd al-Rahman was intrigued. "No, no. Please. I'll pour the coffee. Sit."

Ethan sat on one of the cushions, staring at hands knit together in his lap, knuckles white. Abd al-Rahman poured him out a cup and placed it gently before him. Ethan nodded thanks and blew on it.

"Something troubles you, my friend—and yes, I consider you a friend despite our differences of religion and nationality. What is it?" Abd al-Rahman leaned forward.

Ethan said nothing.

"I realize now I know nothing about your home life," Abd al-Rahman persisted, probing to find the reason behind Ethan's odd reserve. "Are you married?"

Ethan flinched, sipped the coffee, and put it down abruptly. "Hot," he said. Then, after a long moment that Abd al-Rahman refused to fill, he added, "I was married. She died in childbirth."

"I am sorry. When was this?"

Ethan shut his eyes. "Two and a half years ago."

"And you mourn her still?"

"Every day. Every hour." The words sounded as if torn from him in a torture chamber.

Suddenly, the hard shell Abd al-Rahman had sometimes seen wrapped around Ethan snapped into place. The man had never recovered from the loss of his wife. "You must have loved her very much."

Eyes still shut, Ethan nodded. "Very much. She was everything to me." He paused, drew a harsh breath, then resumed. "I was poor and she the daughter of a wealthy, prominent man in the Jewish community of Alsace. It was nothing short of a miracle that I won her hand. We were so happy every day, especially during the months that she was pregnant with our child. Both perished." He looked away, his face pale.

"And you are wretched still. Yet does not your tradition prohibit such a long mourning?"

Ethan's eyes opened. "It does, but the heart does what the heart does. I assume Islam does not favor such self-indulgence?"

"It does not." Abd al-Rahman headed for his bookshelves and pulled out a volume. Quickly riffling through it, he found the passage he was looking for. "Here, I think this might be helpful," he said, pointing. "You are discontented because you have been alone with your grief, which means you have invited Shaytan—the devil— to become misery's company. You've grown hard and mistrustful, thinking that if your beloved can be taken from you, other friends and even lovers can be as well. Isn't that right?"

Ethan shrugged. "Perhaps, but why should I burden anyone with my grief? You never knew Adara. Why would you care about my loss?"

"You cared enough about me and my countrymen to learn our language, our customs. You extended a hand of friendship. I may not have known your wife, but I know you. My wish for you is that Allah might offer you comfort—if not by that name, then by the one you call him."

"That is kind of you," Ethan murmured.

Abd al-Rahman was glad to note that the Frenchman's face looked less haunted. "Perhaps we might try a small experiment," he said. "You are a scientific people, one that treasures reason above religion. So tell me about her—how you met, how you won her hand. We will see if your recounting lightens your heart's burden."

Ethan hesitated. "I'm not sure . . ."

"Just try," Abd al-Rahman insisted.

Ethan sighed deeply, a breath that seemed to rise from the very core of his being. "Very well. But please, let me first apologize to your wife. I would ask her to join us if you have no objection."

Abd al-Rahman nodded and left the room to fetch Hasani. As he reentered the room a few minutes later with his wife in tow, he noticed that Ethan had closed his eyes and locked his fingers together, as if summoning up visions from his past.

Ethan apologized to Hasani, careful to avert his eyes as he did so. She waved his apology away, looking compassionately at him out of the corner of her eyes, for Abd al-Rahman had explained the reason for Ethan's rudeness. Abd al-Rahman tenderly helped her sit down, banking pillows behind her.

"I was an ambitious young clerk who loved to write more than anything, working for Cerf Berr, Adara's grandfather, when I first realized I was in love . . . ," Ethan began his tale. Over the next half hour, he related the difficulties of the match—the disparity of wealth and social position, his being sent to Paris to chronicle the Revolution and how it affected the Jewish people. "Not unsimilar to how you are writing about the French in Egypt and the effect it is having on your society," he added, nodding at Abd al-Rahman.

"I loved her but nearly lost her," Ethan continued. "Her grandfather—who supported my writing—was opposed to our match. We were unequal in social standing, in wealth. And she herself wavered. But then . . ." Ethan trickled off, looking into the distance.

"Then?" Hasani prompted. Abd al-Rahman smiled at his wife's eager face. He knew how much she loved a romance.

"My writing was controversial. Often criticized in my community. I was summoned to a Jewish court, on the charge of heresy, facing excommunication."

Abd al-Rahman was horrified. Excommunication! He knew his friend's ideas were radical, in keeping with this Enlightenment of the French, but this seemed a step too far, even for a nonbeliever. Holding his breath, he waited for Ethan to continue.

"Adara supported me through my trial, came to Paris especially to be with me. And when it was over and I was vindicated—she could refuse our love no longer."

"So then she agreed to marry you?" Hasani asked, breathless.

Ethan cracked a bitter smile. "Indeed. Her grandfather saw that she loved me as much as I loved her and sanctioned the match."

Abd al-Rahman ached to ask what Ethan could possibly have written about that so threatened his community but realized this was not the time. The Jew's face had lightened as he told the story of his beloved. He wanted him to find comfort, not confrontation.

"But then . . ." Ethan continued more somberly. "She lost our first child. A miscarriage. And the doctors said we should not try again, that it would be too dangerous, for her and the child both. But I wanted a son."

Hasani glanced down at her protruding belly, her face now troubled. "Inshallah," she murmured.

"And I was punished for my selfishness." Ethan ducked his head. "I lost them both."

Abd al-Rahman understood now that guilt colored Ethan's grief, not just grief alone. "If you were my brother in Islam, I'd know what to say to you." He rested a hand on Ethan's shoulder.

Ethan raised his head, brushing away the hand. "And what exactly would you say?" he asked, reverting to the hard, ironic tone that Abd al-Rahman now recognized as his protective shell.

"My wife has invoked the will of Allah—inshallah. Surely everything that happens is Allah's will and decree. That article of faith is what makes us accept whatever fate comes our way—good, bad, even tragic."

"That might work—if I believed in Allah—or even in God." Ethan's shoulders hunched.

Not believe in God! Abd al-Rahman was horrified. He knew Ethan had been affected—one might say contaminated—by the free-thinking ideals of the French, but surely he still had some core beliefs remaining. He half-stood, anxious to escort him from his home and away from his wife.

But Hasani put a hand on his arm and forced him back to his seat. "I feel for you, then," she told Ethan softly. "What a sad world you inhabit. Have you no hope of being reunited with your wife after death? Surely that thought must be a comfort to you."

Ethan, in blatant disregard of Muslim customs, stared straight at her. "You are kind," he stuttered. "And it would be a comfort—and yet . . ."

"Why not think on it? And realize that your beloved wife's death has some purpose in Allah's will," Abd al-Rahman said. "Or God's will, if you prefer to call him by that name."

"I will consider it," Ethan said, his voice gentle again, rising. "And even if I cannot bring myself to fully believe it, you have both tried to help me and I appreciate it. It has helped. I hope to see you again— that is, if I ever return to Egypt."

"Ah, yes—your important mission for the Ṣārĭ 'Askar."

Abd al-Rahman was astonished at the sudden exultant look on Ethan's face.

"Yes. I should not tell you, but you'll learn about it all too soon. Bonaparte is offering the Jews of Israel his protection—even giving them a homeland of their own if they support him. You Muslims have never been without your own countries. You don't know what exile is like."

Abd al-Rahman was horrified but strove not to show it. "But Palestine—your Israel—is a Muslim country now." For all Ethan's knowledge about Islam, did he not understand this basic principle—that once taken by the Muslims, land should remain Islamic in perpetuity?

Ethan didn't seem to realize the import of the statement. "Like Egypt?" he asked gaily.

Abd al-Rahman's face froze. But Ethan, looking at his pocket watch, may not have noticed.

"I must go," he said. "If I do not see you again, know that I wish you both well."

"Inshallah," Hasani said as they ushered him to the door.

43

February 8
Ancona

Mirelle sat in the Morpurgo drawing room, fiddling with the laces of her new dress. Mama had made it for her as a surprise. Mama's renewed affection was one of the slight consolations Mirelle felt during these odd, troubling days. The fact that David had allowed her to remain under his roof was another. His conditions were harsh, however: she was to avoid Dolce, be served all her meals in her room, and had to allow him to close the d'Ancona Ketubah Manufactory in a manner befitting its long legacy.

A week ago, she forced herself to walk past the workshop. She would carry the devastating image of the shuttered windows and doors, the empty rooms, the sign on the door announcing that the business had been wound up and was for sale, as a bruise on her heart for the rest of her life.

As she waited for Jacopo, she recalled the sensation Rabbi Fano's words had created the night her world had shattered to pieces.

"I may have a solution to that," he had said, electrifying the room. "A path for this wayward child to redeem herself in the eyes of our community."

It seemed that, despite his altercation with her in the bakery, the rabbi had paid close attention to the baker's apprentice and how he had silently supported Mirelle. After a few days passed, Rabbi Fano had repaired to the bakery at closing time and questioned Jacopo closely. He repeated what had transpired to a rapt audience. Even Dolce settled down and listened, though her mouth remained screwed tight, her eyes shooting daggers.

"I asked him," Rabbi Fano said, "what made him have such a care for you, Mirelle. After all, he was a stranger to Ancona. He told me that he liked your independent spirit." At this, the rabbi laughed ruefully. "Not a quality I admire in a woman, as you know. But when I—forgive me, child, I had to be certain he knew—mentioned your reputation, he shrugged and said there was an imbalance in society—that a man who is intimate with a woman is merely considered to be sowing his wild oats. So why shouldn't it be the same for a woman?"

Mirelle's mouth dropped, staring at the rabbi's smiling face. Was this the same man who, just moments before, had labeled her a loose woman?

But then the rabbi shook his head. "Naturally I didn't agree and we argued about it for a while. In the end, we agreed to disagree. I must admit, he's a charming fellow, even if he's been indoctrinated by the new thinking that's tainting so many of you young people." The rabbi took a sip of his wine. "He is fond of you, apparently, Mirelle. And would be willing to wed you."

"To—wed me?" A cold hand took hold of Mirelle's heart.

"And best of all—he will be leaving Ancona in a few months' time. Heading back to Capri to start his own bakery. He says he and Antonio Baker have never agreed on his more radical notions, so it's better that they part."

"Why is that best of all?" Mirelle asked stiffly.

"Because you'll never recover your reputation while you're here, Mirelle. Isn't that obvious? But in a new city—where no one knows you—where you'll be a new bride—you can start afresh." The rabbi sounded almost kind, nodding his head rapidly, his thin gray hair brushing his narrow shoulders.

"In a bakery." She had to force the words out of her mouth. "But what of the workshop? My workshop?"

The rabbi reared back. "Your workshop? I can't believe you still . . ."

"Mirelle." David slid away from Dolce and swiveled to stare at her. "The workshop will need to close."

"No, it won't! Not with the new commissions I managed to secure, using . . ." The sudden realization hit her like a blow. If Dolce refused to marry Sansone di Lattes, Mirelle would have to return his extravagant fee. And the taxes were due on the last day in January. There was no possibility of paying them and keeping the workshop open. "But—my workers. I can't desert them."

David's lips thinned. "I'll find them occupation, make sure none of them are harmed by this. After all"—he glanced at Dolce, who sat, her eyes still shooting sparks—"this is partly my fault for not stepping in. Not stopping my daughter's mischief."

Dolce's nostrils flared. "You blame me?"

David sighed. "Only because you're to blame, daughter."

At that, Dolce rose, hands fisted at her sides. "*I'm* to blame? *I'm* to blame? With everything she's done to me, you blame me?"

Mirelle closed her eyes. What was the point of saying anything?

Dolce knocked hard against Mirelle's shoulder as she fled the room. Footsteps sounded on the staircase. The slam of the door echoed through the house.

Mama turned to Mirelle, eyes full of unshed tears. "You see, daughter? You could have wed the wealthiest man in Ancona. Now you'll settle for a baker. I'm sure he's a nice boy, but it wasn't what Papa and I wanted for you."

It wasn't what Mirelle wanted, either. The workshop once had been all her ambition but that was gone. She wanted Daniel—but he didn't want her. He would have written to her by now if he did. Her chest aching, she said, "Yes, Mama. I'll settle for a baker. Jacopo has been very kind to me."

Jacopo came in now, beaming, bearing gifts of tortes and cannelloni that Mama took, laughing, off to the kitchen. Mirelle never had to fear going hungry ever again.

"I've been writing to my brother in Capri," he said even before he sat down. "He says he'll find us premises with rooms above. They won't be anything like this"—he looked around, seating himself too close to Mirelle on the sofa—"but we'll be cozy, *mia sposa*, at least until the little ones come along. Perhaps by then we'll be able to afford a house."

Mirelle shifted away slightly. The thought of children raised a lump in her throat. *He's been so kind to me*, she reminded herself. *It's not his fault I don't love him.*

He reached over and took her hand. "You seem sad again. I know losing the workshop has been a blow, but soon a whole new life will begin for us both. Can't you smile for me?"

She forced a smile, painfully stretching the edges of her lips upward. At least he seemed satisfied by the attempt.

Mama bustled back into the room, seating herself in a corner, taking out her darning.

"We'll travel through Italy on our way to Capri. A bridal tour. Here"—he pulled a paper out of a pocket—"I've made a list of the cities I'd like to visit. As a baker of the world, remember?"

She recalled his grandiose ambition and her smile softened, growing more sincere. She took his list.

"We'll make a roundabout journey, starting in Venice. You'll love Venice."

She swallowed, remembering the ball where she had first met Christophe. And Daniel. "I've been to Venice."

"Have you?" He reared back, staring at her. "Did you eat *fritole* there?"

The memory of her and Dolce in Caffè Florian, being plied with the fried, sweet dough by all of Dolce's admirers, laughing, listening to the musicians in St. Mark's Square, almost undid her. She nodded, blinking hard.

"Delicious, no?"

She nodded again, clearing her throat. "They were. And then? Where will we go after that?"

He outlined an ambitious tour—through Verona and Milan, down through Florence and Rome, each time mentioning a distinctive pastry he wanted to sample—*sbrisolone, pantone, schiacciata Fiorentina, tartufo.*

"Then we'll head to Sicily, where the *sfogliatelle* are"—Jacopo kissed his fingers and let them fly, dramatically, into the air—"and from there, it's a short boat trip to my island of Capri. You'll love Capri, Mirelle!"

"A baker's dream of a honeymoon," Mirelle said, his enthusiasm breaking through her lingering sorrow. "I'll have to be careful, Jacopo, or I'll grow fat."

He took hold of her wrist, feeling the bones protruding through the skin. Despite her future having been settled, she still wasn't eating well.

"You are too skinny, *cara mia*. Certainly too skinny for a baker's wife. One look at you behind the counter and they'll wonder if my pastries and breads are any good."

Behind the counter. Her future. She pictured a plump version of herself, handing out cakes to the housewives of Capri, whining children clinging to her skirts. The image was so strong that she flinched.

"Mirelle?" He looked concerned. He was a dear man. Kind, caring. Surely it wouldn't be as terrible as she feared.

"Tell me more about our tour. How long will it take?" she asked. "Where will we stay?"

He described his plans to her, his hands dancing, his words washing over her. Mama, busying herself in the corner, nodded happily. Her daughter's future at last assured, her relief was palpable. As for Mirelle, she played with the laces of her new dress, a frozen smile plastered on her lips.

44

FEBRUARY 21
ACRE

Daniel was thrilled to find himself in Eretz Israel. The entire trip had happened so quickly, with Ethan presenting himself at his barracks and telling him to pack, and then they had to travel by camel hired to take them to Alexandria, to a Turkish boat that would transport them to Jaffe, and from there, to move up the coast to Acre. Daniel, Ethan said, was coming along to protect him.

"I can't just leave my men," Daniel had protested.

"Isn't that sergeant of yours—Sebastian, right?—able to take your place for a few weeks?"

Daniel knew that was undoubtedly true. But what would it say about his command if he just deserted the men? Then he had an idea. He found Sebastian outside their barracks, dicing with the men, and pulled him aside.

"You've long deserved a field promotion," Daniel told him. "If you do this, I'll make the recommendation."

The corners of Sebastian's lips compressed. "Do you think you're the first to offer me this? I'm happy where I am, sir. But I'm happy to babysit the men so you can have this little adventure."

Daniel, while still uncomfortable, decided it was too good an opportunity to pass up. "It won't be for long," he said, looking away.

"Take as long as you want." Sebastian clapped him on the back. "We won't miss you—much."

Daniel and Ethan left Cairo, both garbed in Arabic robes. Daniel spent much of the journey in silence, afraid to open his mouth and reveal that he spoke only a few words of Arabic.

Having arrived at last, Ethan and Daniel were led into a courtyard to await their audience with Haim Farhi. The cobbled pink stones underfoot were shaded by palm trees, and in the center, a fountain surrounded by a low, blue mosaic wall burbled invitingly. A young servant moved soundlessly on slippered feet, setting down a shallow bowl of dates and figs, along with a flagon of wine and another of cool water on a low marble table. With a fluid gesture of his hand, he invited them silently to partake.

"*Shukran*," Ethan said, thanking him with his hand on his heart, bowing slightly.

"You are welcome," the servant said in fluent French. He smiled at their startled expressions and slipped away.

"Wine or water?" Daniel asked his cousin, moving forward, his boots clattering loudly on the cobbles.

"Water. I want to keep a clear head when we speak with Farhi. From everything I've observed, he's the brains behind Djezzar's brute strength."

Daniel poured water for them both, then picked up a date. "What will you say to him?" he asked.

Ethan patted his breast pocket. "I have General Bonaparte's letter here, promising the Jews in Israel his protection—even hinting at a possible homeland. I suspect that Farhi's reason for staying with the Pasha despite his cruelty is to protect the Jews of Acre—and of all of Syria. This despite Djezzar's vicious caprice, including Farhi's own scars."

At just that moment, a broad shouldered, slender man came out to greet them. His turban dipped strangely over the left side of his face and Daniel realized it did so to conceal Farhi's missing eye. Daniel's gaze moved lower, settling on the blank space in the middle of Farhi's face. Two dark holes were all that were left of his nose. Daniel couldn't help but shudder.

The man, seeing his aghast expression, laughed, then spoke in French. "Your companion didn't warn you that I am disfigured?" he asked, turning to face Ethan's carefully composed expression. "He, at least, has no reason to be surprised by my poor face."

"I did tell him, and apologize if his discomfort offended you," Ethan said. "My young cousin was certainly aware of what you have suffered at the hands of the Pasha."

"My master has a hasty temper and a jealous disposition, that is true," Farhi said calmly, then added in icy tones, "but that does not mean that I should betray him."

Daniel and Ethan looked at one another. Ethan hastened to say, "We do not wish you to betray the Pasha for that reason, esteemed *katib*. Rest assured, we have more persuasive arguments to make."

"And I am ready to hear them." Farhi sat himself down on a low cushion, folding his legs comfortably, signaling to Daniel and Ethan to do the same. Daniel wished the man had brought them inside. Despite the shade of the palms, the day was sweltering hot, and his clothing stuck uncomfortably to the back of his neck and his moist arms. He lowered himself on a blue cushion, resting his knees against his chest.

Before Ethan did the same, he pulled the general's letter out of his chest pocket and extended it to the *katib*, bowing. "Perhaps it is best for you to read my general's proposal in his own words," Daniel said, moving back and sitting down.

Farhi took a moment to read the letter silently, then shook his head, looking at the two Frenchmen. "Is your general insane?" he asked.

"Effendi?" Ethan's eyebrows rose.

Farhi returned his gaze to the letter for another beat of silence. "I am impressed by his Biblical knowledge," he said finally. "I thought the French were a godless nation now. Yet Bonaparte spouts Isaiah and Joel as though he were well versed in the prophets."

"We are not all godless," Ethan said smoothly. "My cousin here and I are Jews, emancipated during the French Revolution. My cousin is a soldier who was present when Bonaparte broke open the ghetto gates of Italy. We are certain that Napoleon is sincere in all he says."

Daniel kept his face under tight control. His doubts about Bonaparte formed no part of his duty, he told himself. And yet, he couldn't help wondering if Ethan's assurances were anything more than another of Napoleon's tricks. With a sudden pang, he longed for the simpler days when he believed in the general—when he took part in tearing down those ghetto gates and marched from victory to victory with the intrepid French Army of Italy. The days when the worst of his doubts centered around Bonaparte's pillaging of the grand palazzos and churches, loading the carts with treasure that were intended to rescue the bankrupt Directory—but which enriched the general's own coffers, too.

But now? Witness to the senseless campaign that had squandered the lives of his compatriots on the desert sands, dying of thirst and heat prostration, having seen the mountain of headless corpses in the great square in Cairo, having watched him dallying with a married woman—Daniel could no longer fully trust the general's word.

"I must have time to consider this," Farhi finally said. He rose, folding the letter and tucking it into the broad sash that bisected his long gown. "I will arrange for quarters for you so we can talk after dinner tonight. You will be my guests, of course."

"We are honored," Ethan said. "And hope to convince you to support the general, for we know your words have weight with the Jewish community. But before we retire, my cousin has a request."

Daniel pulled his letter to Mirelle out. "I need to find a way to have this letter delivered to Ancona in Italy," he said. "Is it possible to find a messenger who will give it safe passage? It's—it's important."

Farhi took the letter, his disfigured face lightened by his smile. "A matter of the heart, I portend?"

Daniel ducked his head. Ethan laughed. "You've guessed it, Effendi."

Farhi gestured to the servant who had been standing in attendance in the doorway. He handed him the letter and spoke a few words in Arabic. "Love must find a way," he said. "We will do our utmost for you. But now you should rest."

"Come with me," the servant murmured.

Daniel and Ethan followed him into Farhi's residence.

Three hours later, Daniel awoke to the sound of pouring water. Raising himself up to his elbows, he smiled to see a young servant boy bustling about his room, filling a large copper basin.

"Will you wash to refresh yourself, Lieutenant?" he asked.

"How do you know my rank?" Daniel asked, surprised.

The servant laughed. "My master does not entertain guests without full knowledge of who they are."

"Your master might well know," Daniel said slowly, "but I remain surprised that you do. Are you not a servant?"

"I am a member of the *katib*'s household. He has raised me and educated me, and I am honored to serve him."

Daniel realized he had no idea what that actually meant but decided to let it go. But he was still curious. "How old are you?"

"I am fifteen, Lieutenant. And you?"

Taken aback by the direct question, Daniel's eyebrows rose. "Nearly twenty."

"Not that much older, then. Especially as we grow to manhood here much more rapidly than you do in the West."

"Do you?" Daniel was amused by the young man's brashness. "I wonder why."

The boy shrugged. "We live our lives on a scimitar's edge. No one knows from day to day what tomorrow brings."

"We soldiers might say the same," Daniel said, looking around the chamber. "I certainly would not have suspected yesterday that I would be so well housed and cared for."

The room was large and airy, opening to three quarter windows barred with exquisite ironwork grills. The walls were unadorned except for thick white plaster, the floor tiled in beige and white, cool underfoot. Several cushioned divans were scattered about the room, piled with pillows exquisitely embroidered in colorful needlework, punctuated by shiny small beads and tiny mirrors.

"Come, take your ease in the bath," the boy said, "for my master prefers his guests not to stink."

Daniel laughed and willingly removed his heavy robe. The boy gathered it up in his arms. "We will do our best to launder your garments, Lieutenant," he said. "In the meantime, I will bring you something cooler to wear." Arms full of Daniel's dusty and sweat-stained clothing, he slipped from the room.

Daniel lowered himself into the basin, grimacing a little at the heat of the water. But after a moment's discomfort, he let his muscles relax and leaned against the rolled towel placed at the bath's edge. Despite his lengthy nap, he felt his eyes closing and let his head fall back, groaning softly at the pleasure of the steamy bath. His thoughts flew to Mirelle and he had to chide himself to stop wishing she was there with him, sharing the sensual delight of the hot water.

The boy returned several minutes later with a pair of thin white pantaloons, a blousy white shirt, and an open gown of some buff-colored fabric. He helped Daniel out of the bath and dried him with a large, fluffy towel, then directed him to cover his nakedness in the light garments.

They were incredibly comfortable—more like night clothes than proper dress. Daniel blushed as the boy brought out a bright red sash, tying it around him, completing the ensemble by draping the open gown over his shoulders.

"I don't feel decent," Daniel muttered.

"Nonsense," the boy replied, his fingers straightening the gown. "You are very well dressed now."

Dinner was served at eight o'clock, long after the sun had dipped beneath the horizon. Ravenous, Daniel sat down at the long board. His host placed him next to a modest young woman wearing Arabic garb. "My daughter Miriam," Farhi said in terse introduction. Ethan, as the primary emissary, was seated next to a plump woman of older years, whom Daniel realized was Farhi's wife. She, too, was swathed in a modest veil and long gown.

There was an empty seat next to Miriam and another next to another girl, who sat a few places removed from Ethan. Daniel could not tell whether everyone at the table were family. He assumed not; there were too many of them.

He was startled when two young servants entered and approached the table. One was the boy who had helped him bathe and dress. He sat in the seat next to Miriam. Ethan threw a similarly curious glance down the table at the second boy.

"My youngest sons," Farhi said, looking amused at the Frenchmen's bewildered expressions. "Benyamin and Nathanel."

"But they . . ." Ethan started, then closed his lips tight.

"I sent them to wait on you, yes," Farhi said. "One learns a great deal about someone when they think you are a servant."

Dinner was a leisurely meal, with Farhi asking probing questions about Bonaparte. Toward the end of the repast, as strong coffee was served with fresh figs, their host related how Napoleon had left Cairo on February 10 to head off Djezzar and his troops, telling them what he knew about the French forces' recent victory in El Arish.

"Mustafa Pasha was in command—perhaps not the best choice. Your forces sieged the fort for more than a week. The walls were just breached yesterday, I'm told. I admire your General Bonaparte—he lost a mere two-hundred men to our nine-hundred."

"You're very well informed," Ethan commented, splitting a fig open.

Farhi shrugged. "I had better be," he said, touching a damaged cheek. "My master does not tolerate mistakes." He was quiet for a moment. "I admit, I was surprised by the mercy Napoleon showed these men."

"Mercy?" Daniel couldn't help his surprise. Mercy was not a quality he attributed to Bonaparte.

"My agent told me that he allowed hundreds of soldiers—somewhere around eight hundred, he estimated—to swear on the Qur'an that they would not serve in Djezzar's army and not return to Syria for a year. And then he freed them."

Daniel thought for a moment before commenting, "A wise strategy, for after all, what would he do with them all? He's on the march—how could he possibly keep so many captive or feed them? He'll have trouble enough feeding the troops."

Farhi helped himself to more coffee. "Wise or foolish? I wonder. These men fear my master far more than the French, and they have reason to do so. Does Bonaparte think they will not rejoin Pasha Ahmed's forces when the Butcher calls for them?"

Daniel had no answer for this. Farhi rose.

"Let's go into the courtyard and discuss your general's so-called proclamation to the Jews, shall we?"

They trooped after him. The chill night air made Daniel shiver as they seated themselves under the stars. Seeing it, one of Farhi's sons brought him a blanket and arranged it over his knees.

"So." Farhi lay the document in his lap, smoothing it out. "Let me read from the last part of this document if you'll indulge me:

> *Rightful heirs of Palestine!*
>
> *The great nation which does not trade in men and countries as did those which sold your ancestors unto all people (Joel, 4:6) herewith calls on you not indeed to conquer your patrimony; nay, only to take over that which has been conquered and, with that nation's warranty and support, to remain master of it to maintain it against all comers.*
>
> *Arise! Show that the former overwhelming might of your oppressors has but repressed the courage of the descendants of those heroes whose alliance of brothers would have done honor even to Sparta and Rome (Maccabees 12, 15) but that the two thousand years of treatment as slaves have not succeeded in stifling it.*
>
> *Hasten! Now is the moment, which may not return for thousands of years, to claim the restoration of civic rights among the population of the universe which had been shamefully withheld from you for thousands of years, your political existence as a nation among the nations, and the unlimited natural right to worship Jehovah in accordance with your faith, publicly and most probably forever (Joel 4:20).*

Farhi put the document in his lap. "And I repeat what I said earlier, young sirs—is your master insane? And does he think we're fools?"

"Do you think he's not sincere?" Ethan asked. "After all, in Italy . . ."

"He freed the Jews of Italy, yes—I grant you that. But he also came to Egypt proclaiming himself a Muslim. Does he not realize that one of the chief tenants of Islam is that once they have conquered a territory by the sword, it can never be returned to the infidels? And we Jews, young men, are infidels in Muslim eyes."

Farhi sat back for a moment. The moonlight fell on his maimed face, the shadows playing on his wounds making Daniel shake at the hideous sight. He hid his revulsion by shifting the blanket higher.

"Besides, who is he going to rouse?" Farhi continued. "Wait until you see the old holy men in Jerusalem, begging for alms in the streets, spending their days solely absorbed in study of our ancient texts. Does he truly think these weak and wizened men will take arms against the Turks?" Farhi shook his head. "In fact, I've been told that the Jews of Gaza fled at Napoleon's approach—that in Jerusalem, Rabbi Moses Mordecai Joseph Meyu is encouraging the Jews to do the deputy governor's bidding, to throw up ramparts against the approach of the French troops."

"We're heading to Jerusalem from here," Ethan persisted. "Don't you think this proclamation will stir them? Haven't we waited for more than a thousand years to recover our homeland?"

"Is Bonaparte the Messiah? For these men are spending their whole lives waiting for a Messiah—the only being, they believe, who can restore us to our homeland. But Bonaparte? A man who discarded his Catholic faith, embraced the godless precepts of reason, pretended to be a follower of Islam? Who would credit that Bonaparte believes in any religion at all? Any religion but war, perhaps?" Farhi grew heated. "He hasn't even the Christian excuse of the Rapture to justify his claims—having the Jewish people return to their homeland to presage the Second Coming of Christ. I'm sorry, ben Dovid, but this is nothing but foolish and misguided ranting. I expected better from him, frankly." Farhi extended the proclamation to Ethan.

"That's yours to keep," Ethan said. "For you to consider. You are an intelligent man, a man dedicated to the support of our people. How can you side with the Muslims against such a promise?"

"I'm a realist, not a dreamer," Farhi said now. "I know that such promises can vanish—will vanish, the moment your general leaves these shores. Take your document away. If I were found to have it in my home or on my person, my pasha would inflict further wounds on me—perhaps even behead me."

"Then I'll certainly take it back," Ethan said, rising from his seat and tucking the document into his tunic. "I'm sorry if we've wasted your time."

Farhi's lips curled. "You haven't. You've given me some insight into my enemy. Not what you wanted to do, I grant you."

Daniel stood as well. He knew Ethan was bitterly disappointed at the *katib*'s reaction. As much as Daniel, too, wished for a Jewish homeland, he frankly couldn't see Napoleon delivering on such a grandiose promise. Then again, he mused, he would never have thought the general would have demolished the gates and emancipated his people in Italy. And Ethan had been at the French Assembly on that miraculous day when the Jews of France were granted citizenship. Perhaps his cousin was right. Perhaps there might yet be another miracle—the most wonderous one of all.

"You can sleep here tonight," Farhi said. "Tomorrow you can head to Jerusalem, though that will be as fruitless as this. But I know you have your orders."

"I'll accompany Ethan to Jerusalem," Daniel said. "And then I'm to rejoin my regiment."

"If I'm correct, you'll be heading to Jaffa, then," their host said. "Be very careful. There is plague right now in Jaffa."

45

MARCH 4
JAFFA

As Daniel rode up to Jaffa to rejoin his regiment, he was startled to see two heads displayed on pikes, their revolutionary tricolor ribbons still pinned to their hats. Blood stained their faces. The enemy hadn't even the decency to close the bulging eyes of one or shut the gaping jaw of the other, his circled lips probably at the shock of being slaughtered.

"Who the hell are they?" he asked Sebastian, dismounting and throwing the reins to one of his soldiers. He noticed the men of his company, along with every Frenchman around them, were seething with anger.

"They," Sebastian said between clenched teeth, "are the emissaries we sent with our offering of peace and conditions of surrender. And that's what they did to them!"

Daniel sighed. "Nothing surprises me any more in this benighted country."

Jerusalem had been as much of a disappointment as Alexandria or Cairo—its walls crumbling, beggars on every street corner, tattered residents impoverished. The rabbis they had visited were, just as Farhi had described, poor shriveled skeletons of men, annoyed at having their hours of study of the Talmud disturbed. Those who granted them an audience rebuffed their call to support the French. They flat out refused the suggested reward of a Jewish homeland.

"What?" quavered Rabbi Moses Mordecai Joseph Meyuchas, who had been instrumental in telling his followers to throw up ramparts to keep the French at bay. He sat in the private study of his yeshiva with a dozen favored scholars, all bending and swaying over their books, mouthing lines of the Mishnah and Gemara. Ethan and Daniel had passed through a room crammed with earnestly studying school-boys, earlocks bouncing, small mimics of their elders. "You want us to proclaim a Jewish state before the coming of the Moshiach? God will one day, in his own time, return the Jews to their land and give us control of it, but this will only happen when Moshiach arrives."

"But who's to say that time is not upon us?" Ethan argued.

"You clearly have not read the Song of Songs, clearly do not heed the three oaths the people of the world took when we were exiled from this land."

"Three oaths?" Daniel, who had only nodded politely when intro-duced, couldn't resist the question.

The rabbi's voice took on the sing-song quality of the surrounding Talmud scholars. "When we were sent from our land, the peoples of the Earth made three sacred oaths to God, two by us Jews and one by the Gentiles. We Jews promised not to 'storm the wall'—in other words, not lay claim to the Land of Israel—and not to 'rebel against the nations,' which is clearly what you are asking us to do. The third oath was made by the *goyische* nations, who promised God they would not oppress Israel too much."

"Not oppress Israel?" Ethan broke out. "What do you call the Inquisition? The blood libels? Burning our books? Locking us inside our synagogues and torching them? The humiliation of our people having to wear Jewish insignia or live behind closed gates?"

"I've heard of you, ben Dovid," the rabbi countered, pointing a wrinkled finger at him. "You achieved worldly fame as an essayist during the French Revolution. A *shonda* to use your God-given abilities to promote such evil. You are among the *apikoyris*—the heretics—who want us to abandon our faith and assimilate among the goyim."

"I simply . . ."

Suddenly, the rabbi seemed to unbend his ancient bones, straightening, his gaunt face catching the firelight, looking almost prophetic. "I will not have it!" he thundered. "And you will leave my yeshiva at once before your pollution can spread further!"

A second, younger rabbi, Rabbi Abraham Pardo, was more practical in his denials. "Do you know what the Turks will do to us if we do this? What Ahmad Pasha would do? What a massacre he would order?" He sliced a finger across his throat.

A third, Rabbi Nathan Soloman, invoked the false messiah, Shabbetai Tzvi, who had caused such an uproar in the Jewish world back in the 1600s. "We don't need such a disruption to what is truly important, young men," he'd said. "Only through *tikkun olam*, repairing the world through study and charity, can we bring about the Messianic age. Then, and only then, can the Kingdom of Jerusalem be restored. We must focus on these and leave the great political movements of the world to the goyim."

Somehow, word that Haim Farhi had refused to keep a copy of Napoleon's proclamation had made its way to Jerusalem. His influence was as potent as Ethan had feared it would be. Not a single Jewish leader would accept the proffered document, a couple even throwing it into the fire. Only one Jewish merchant, headed for Germany, tucked it away, saying he'd have it translated and dispatched in the diaspora.

Daniel, recalled to his duty, left Ethan on the road to Safed, where his cousin confessed to scant hopes for a better reception among the mystics of that mountain-bound retreat. The bitterness that seemed to have lifted from Ethan when they'd started out on their mission had now returned full force with its seeming failure. Daniel was frankly glad to part from him.

And now, standing outside of the city of Jaffa, Daniel felt the suppressed fury emanating from his fellow soldiers.

"It's not just that they beheaded our messengers," Sebastian explained while they set up the cannon on the south side of the city's fortifications. "I don't know if you heard of how Bonaparte freed hundreds of Mameluke soldiers in El Arish after making them swear on their holy book that they wouldn't fight us."

"In fact, I did hear something about it," Daniel replied, remembering Haim Farhi's surprise at Napoleon's mercy.

"Well, we were in Ramleh on the way here when these Capuchin monks approached the general, letting him know that those same bastards were headed straight here to Jaffa, to bolster the troops here. Breaking their vow. I mean, what soldier of honor does that? Bonaparte's spitting mad and who can blame him?"

It wasn't just the general who was spitting mad. The siege lasted two days before the walls were broken down and the fight moved to the streets. Jaffa, full of stony stairways and tight corners, had ample places for the polyglot collection of enemy soldiers to hide— Turks, Syrians, Mamelukes, even hired mercenaries—firing upon the Frenchmen or lunging out with daggers and swords.

"These barbarians don't understand the rules of warfare," Christophe panted, happening upon Daniel in the melee. "Once your walls are breached, you surrender. Why the hell are they still fighting?"

So the French made them pay dearly for their stubbornness. Once a truce was called, they let loose with a vengeance. The narrow walls of the city rang with screams for help; French soldiers slaughtered soldier and resident alike, raping and pillaging.

Appalled at the violence, Daniel tried to control his men. "Stop!" he called as they abandoned their cannon and began to clamber over the broken walls. "That's an order!"

"No sir," Pierre retorted, as the rest of the men ignored Daniel's command and, arming themselves, moved forward into the city. "You can court martial us if you'd like, but we're heading in."

What would Christophe have done? But Daniel knew his friend didn't share his squeamish nature and would never have tried to stop his own men from the pillage. The fortunes of war, Christophe would have said callously. Helpless to halt the men, Daniel followed them into the city, hoping at least to contain them. But even that was beyond his powers.

"*Koon raheem!*" he heard, called by a child whom Sebastian skewered with his sword before stepping over his corpse.

"*Ya Allah!*" A woman, possibly the child's mother, bent over him, wailing and sobbing. "*Hafizani Allah min almawt!*"

"I'll show you what Allah will do to you," another of Daniel's soldiers said between clenched teeth. And he threw the sobbing woman down, yanking up her skirt and unbuttoning his trousers.

"Jean! Stop!" Daniel screamed, yanking at his arm.

But Jean merely shrugged himself free and climbed atop her, pushing the boy's sprawled body out of the way. Daniel, aghast, couldn't stand there and watch. *What would Mirelle think of me if I did?* He fled, the woman's cries of pain and Jean's animal grunts echoing in his ears, chasing him from the house.

The streets were no better. Blood pooled in the alleyways, heads and bodies shattered by gunshot or by being shoved against the stone walls of the city. Men, children, women, lay on the cobbles after being stabbed or shot, gasping in agony. Shrieks for help, for mercy, were ignored by the rabid Frenchmen, whose bloodlust and desire for revenge drove them to ever more hideous atrocities. Daniel staggered from street to street in a daze, witnessing the cruelty, helpless despite his repeated attempts at stopping it. With every step, he confronted a new horror—throats slashed, girls violated on top of the bodies of their mothers, smoke rising from the houses the avenging troops lit

on fire, the metallic smell of blood and the smoldering fog so perva-
sive that Daniel felt them choking him. Soldiers fought over the loot
they'd collected from the bodies of the dead and dying, from the
houses they'd sacked.

The French terror lasted for hours, an entire day in the blazing
sun, then lit by torches, lanterns, or simply conducted in the dark
shadows of a moonless night.

Rounding a corner toward daybreak, Daniel entered the courtyard of a mosque, where he released the contents of his stomach in
a torrent of vomit. Wiping his mouth, he looked up to see the army
surgeon, Dr. Larrey, staring at him, a scalpel in his hand, blood staining his apron-covered front.

"You! Don't just stand there being sick. If you have any bowels of
compassion, help me!" the doctor snapped.

Larrey, disgusted by the actions of the French troops, had turned
the mosque into an aid station, where he had herded some of the
wounded and was treating their injuries. Daniel, grateful for anything he could do, went out into the streets to bring others to the
comparative safety of the mosque.

"Leave your sword and musket here, man!" Larrey called as he
headed out. "They won't trust you if you're armed!"

Daniel wished with all his heart he spoke Arabic, for at first
the residents refused to come with him, fearing for their lives.
Casting back to the few words he knew—the ones that were closest to Hebrew—he repeated "peace" and "mercy" over and over,
"Salam, rahma," spreading his hands wide to show that he meant
no harm.

He managed to persuade a few—a pitiful few—that he wanted to
help. He dragged them into the courtyard, leaving them there for
Larrey, heading out again. He was starting to feel the heaviness in
his gut lift when suddenly a youth, perhaps thirteen or fourteen,
brandishing a scimitar that was too heavy for him, faced him down.

Caught on the curve of a narrow stairway, littered with the bodies of young girls, Daniel couldn't escape the vengeful boy.

"*Salam!*" he shouted.

But the boy, his teeth bared, a gash over one eye, moved steadily forward, growling curses under his breath.

Why had he left his weapons behind? Daniel looked about for something to defend himself with, stooping to pick up a large rock.

The boy, with a primal cry, leaped forward. But before he could slash at Daniel, he seemed to fold in on himself, slumping onto the stairs with a cry of pain. Blood oozed out of him and, moaning, his eyes flickered, then shut. His head fell forward. Dead.

Standing behind him, his flintlock smoking, was Christophe.

"What in the world are you doing out here unarmed?" his friend demanded, his filthy face drawn into a grimace, eyes flashing.

"I'm trying to help them!" Daniel cried. "What did you kill him for? He was only a boy!"

"Jesus! A boy with a sword, you idiot! What's wrong with you? Help them? Daniel, you're a soldier!"

"Yes, a soldier, not a murderer, not a rapist, and not a looter!" Daniel flung back. He could see the gold glinting, peeking out of a sack his friend had thrown over his shoulder.

"They don't deserve any better, any of them!" Christophe said. "If you knew what they'd done to Sappeira's parents . . ."

Daniel was silent, thinking back to the rabbi of Jerusalem who had argued for *tikkun olam*. How was this repairing the world? And why was he here, now? What did Egypt or Eretz Israel have to do with the principles of the French Revolution?

And what would Mirelle think? He had thought of her constantly through the wretched day and night, knowing that she would have condemned the soldiers. Would the small help he had managed to offer the poor citizens of Jaffa have redeemed himself in her eyes?

"It's almost sunup," Christophe said, callously kicking the boy's fallen body off the stairs, swatting at the fleas that swarmed around the corpses' heads. "I've orders to round up my men and get them back to camp—you do, too. Let's go."

46

March 8
Ancona

Mirelle thought seeing the manufactory empty would be among her worst memories, but then she learned that David had arranged for it to be sold to another owner—who immediately hired back nearly all of her workers—and she thought her heart would break.

"It's the best possible outcome for everyone," David told her, as he sat her down in his library to sign the papers transferring the shop to a scribe from Milan. "He's not even changing the name, since, being in Ancona, the d'Ancona title is still accurate. So in a way, your grandfather's legacy will live on."

But without me, Mirelle thought. The rabbi, Dolce, her mother—they had all won.

She pushed the pages across the table to David. "If that's all?"

"No, wait," he said. "You should understand that the sale of the premises has brought you a small sum—a dowry. Even after you pay back the debt you owe me, enough is left over for you and your fiancé to put toward your new bakery when you get to Capri. Or save it, invest it for your children. You'll know best how to use the money, *piccola*."

Once upon a time, Mirelle would have pored over the numbers, made sure they were tallied accurately, understood how much of a dowry she would have. Now she just felt numb, aching as if there were ground glass in her stomach. She pushed her chair back and in doing so, let a newspaper article David had clipped fall to the floor.

She stooped and picked it up, then found herself arrested by the report. She read:

Buonaparte, it is said, has issued a Proclamation to the Jews dispersed in Africa and Asia, inviting them to restore the Kingdom of Jerusalem. He has armed a great number of Jews and formed them in Battalions; and now threatens Aleppo.

"So your dreams of a Jewish homeland seem to be coming true," she told David, handing him back the paper. "If I've understood the English, that is."

David looked perturbed. "One thinks it might be, but it's hard to know, what with the British blockade stopping any genuine flow of information from the region. I wish I could put someone reliable there, to discover what is really happening."

Mirelle nodded, rising from her seat. But before she could leave the library, she suddenly stopped cold and turned. "British blockade?"

David was staring at the article. "Yes, of course, child. Didn't you know? The British have blocked the Egyptian ports pretty much since the French landed—and now the ones off Eretz Israel. Even the French Directory has been stymied, I hear. Why do you think you haven't heard from your cousin? I know you were writing him." He glanced up, eyes arrested by the look on her face. "Mirelle? You've gone pale."

"British blockade," she repeated.

"Yes. I thought you knew," he said.

She felt dizzy. Turning, she collapsed into one of David's velvet chairs.

"Mirelle?" He rose from his seat. Reaching across his desk, he pulled the bell to summon a servant. "Fetch some water," he instructed the man.

A pitcher and a glass materialized in an instant. David himself poured it out and handed it to her. "Drink," he told her.

She sipped. The fuzzy feeling dissipated, replaced by her heart pounding so loudly that she could almost hear it. She clasped a hand to her chest. "He might have written, then," she said.

"Who? Daniel?"

She nodded, carefully putting the glass down on the side table next to the chair. "All this time, I thought . . ." She knit her hands in her lap.

Comprehension lit David's face. "You were waiting to hear from him."

She closed her eyes.

"And you thought, because he didn't write . . ."

Silence.

"Mirelle. You were mistaken about love before," David reminded her. "I grant you, this time it's a man worthy of you. But you haven't seen him in more than a year."

"I know."

David knelt beside her. "And you've agreed to marry another man." He laughed deep in his throat, the sound bitter. "It seems we're repeating history here, *piccola*."

She nodded again, wretched. She had been betrothed to David, despite their age difference, despite thinking herself in love with Christophe. Because her mother had so fervently wished it so, because it would save the workshop after her father's death. But her feeling for Christophe—that quick-burning infatuation—was nothing like the deep, clean, abiding ache in her heart for Daniel. Nothing like the certainty that she would love Daniel until the day she died. "It's different," she said.

He rocked back on his heels, his face impassive. "That may be. But even so . . ." He rose, walking back to his desk and seating himself behind it, looking as if he were cleaning his hands of the entire morass.

She excused herself from seeing Jacopo that evening, pleading a headache. She'd used the excuse often enough that everyone believed her. Instead, she sat in her room, trying to consider what she should do.

It wasn't a matter of thinking about what she wanted. She knew that was Daniel, without a shadow of doubt. It was a matter of how to extricate herself from this betrothal, hopefully without hurting the kind man who had been willing to take her, flaws and all. Was that even possible?

And if she could, what next? She wished for some form of magic, to transport herself to the same land, the same city, where Daniel was fighting against the Sultan's forces. Was he commanding one of those Jewish battalions the British newspaper spoke of?

But what if he were dead? What if he'd been shot, or stabbed, mortally wounded, his lifeless body left to molder on a foreign battlefield?

Or—possibly worse still—what if he'd found a bride worthy of him among the Jews of Egypt or Eretz Israel? What if he were happily married?

No, she scolded herself, that wasn't worse. If he had, she wished him well.

She did.

The headache she had lied about showed every sign of becoming real. She moved from her chair to her bed, lying down and closing her eyes, trying to catch hold of her revolving thoughts, to conceive of a plan that would deliver her from her current nightmare.

47

March 10
Jaffa

Daniel woke to the sound of the muezzin calling the faithful to prayer. He rolled over on his bedroll on the beach, trying to dismiss the terrors of the French rampage which had haunted his wakeful hours during the long night and plagued his dreams when he finally drifted off.

We'll be on the march soon, he told himself, looking forward to shaking off the dust of this accursed city. *This will all be just a terrible memory.*

The chanting meant it was dawn. Daniel, sitting up, looked out on the calm turquoise sea. The sun was peeking over the water beyond the rocky point of the harbor, staining the clouds pink and yellow. Small craft bobbed in the waves and, after so many days of bloodshed and agony, peace had descended once more over the city. Daniel took a deep breath of sea air, the salt tickling his nose.

He rose, leaving his suspenders to dangle over his trousers. Bare chested and bootless, he took a towel and shirt from his rucksack, making his way down to the seashore for a quick dip. He rolled up his trouser legs and stepped in, waves lapping his ankles. The salt water was fresh and cold and he splashed his chest and arms, rubbing briskly with a bit of soap.

He woke his men and walked them to the area where the mess tents had been set up. Food was plentiful in this part of Eretz Israel, and they feasted on flat bread, a pungent bowl of yogurt, olives, and the oranges picked from groves just beyond the city.

As they headed back to camp, they spied a long line of enemy soldiers being marched down to the south side of the city at bayonet point.

"Infantry. Bon's men," Sebastian said, pointing at the soldiers herding the prisoners.

"Are they letting them go?" Jean asked. "Are we making the same mistake we made at El Arish?"

"Bloody *bougnoule*," Pierre muttered. "We should kill them all."

The sense of well-being that had settled upon Daniel at dawn faded slightly as he listened to his men grumble. "They asked for mercy," he told them. "And the general promised they wouldn't be harmed if they surrendered."

Pierre's face hardened. "They have no honor and don't deserve mercy." He spit on the sand.

Daniel didn't respond. He'd heard all the complaints that keeping so many prisoner—there were thousands penned up in temporary cells—would deplete the army's rations and force troops who would be better used in fighting to guard them. *But Bonaparte gave his word*, he reassured himself silently.

Just past noon, as Daniel and his men prepared for an inspection, they heard the first gun shots.

"Target practice?" Sebastian asked, peering toward the harbor.

"Now? When our ammunition is so low?" Daniel shook his head. "Pierre, go see what's going on."

Pierre loped off and the rest of the men turned back to polishing their boots and belt buckles. He returned, breathless, in a few minutes. "They're executing the turban heads!" he gasped out.

"They're what?" Daniel stared at him. "You must be mistaken."

"I'm not! They're going to kill all the prisoners!"

An excited clamor broke out, several of the soldiers surrounding Sebastian. The sergeant pushed through the group and turned to Daniel. "The men want to go see, sir. May we?"

Daniel didn't want to let them gawk at the slaughter. But remembering how they'd shrugged off his orders during the sack of Jaffa, not wanting a repeat of his command being so blatantly disregarded, Daniel gritted his teeth and nodded. They ran off, like schoolboys let out for some treat. Feeling sick in the pit of his stomach, Daniel thought back to the gleeful crowds that had gathered in Paris to watch the guillotine take aristocratic heads, how they would cheer as the blade severed noble necks. *Is something twisted in their souls—in the hearts of most men?* he wondered. *Or is it me who is lacking?*

He realized that if his men were all there, he had no choice; he had to witness the carnage along with them. With dragging steps, he followed the ricochet of gunfire to a bluff where his men had gathered, together with an excited crowd of other soldiers.

Daniel walked up to a fellow officer. "Who ordered this?"

"Who do you think?" the man said, sounding gleeful. "Who else but our commanding officer? Who else would dare?"

Daniel still couldn't believe it. "Despite promising them mercy?"

The officer shrugged and moved off.

Daniel watched, heartsick, as group after group of prisoners were led to a slight rise overlooking the seafront. The French infantry soldiers shouldered their rifles and fired. Bodies dropped into the waves, turning the sea crimson. Then another group was moved into position and the macabre spectacle repeated. As the afternoon waned, the order came down to bayonet the prisoners instead, to save on bullets. The executions slowed, Bon's men having to move closer to the condemned to dispatch them.

Around him, Daniel heard bets being taken. "That one's going to fall first. No, that one." Money exchanged hands and the men cheered for their choices, like at a horse race.

He tried hard not to think of Mirelle.

Pleas for mercy and compassion echoed off the beachfront buildings. A crowd of Jaffa's residents gathered. They collapsed onto their knees on the sand, watching, wailing, beating their chests. They were surrounded by the French, threatened by drawn guns, shouted at to return to their homes. Despite the danger, most stayed, hugging their children to them, throwing curses at the soldiers, their cries for mercy unheeded.

Daniel lost count how many thousands of men were slaughtered in this way. Mid-afternoon, a group of Mamelukes broke free. They scrambled down the rise, dashed into the water, diving desperately under a breaking wave, floundering with quick strokes away from the shore.

"Catch them!" General Bon boomed. "Into the boats, men!"

Soldiers from the infantry unit clambered aboard the small craft, rowing hard. Coming close to the frantic swimmers, they slashed at their churning backs repeatedly with bayonets. The men in the water gasped, struggling to keep afloat, finally succumbing to the water's depths. Circling around the harbor in their boats like sharks drawn by the smell of flesh and blood, the Frenchmen butchered the Muslims without mercy, not allowing even one to evade death.

Toward day's end, Daniel noticed several of the groups remained composed as they awaited slaughter. Watching their brethren die, they lay their hands over their hearts and spoke quietly. Curious, Daniel sought out one of the translators. "What are they saying?" he asked, pointing to a nearby group.

"They are asking one another for their blessing and saying the Shahada, the affirmation: 'There is no god but Allah, and Muhammad is his messenger.' They're also reassuring one another that as *shahid*, martyrs, they're guaranteed a place in Jannah, paradise."

Daniel flinched as one of these groups were led forward. Bayonets pierced one chest after another. With a push, the wounded Muslims were shoved into the sea, water spraying upward as their bodies disappeared beneath the waves. Those still alive were left to bleed to death or drown.

Afternoon shadows lengthened as the sun scudded behind thickening clouds. Bon had to keep yelling encouragement at his men, who wearied of the repeated killings, of the toll it took on their sword arms. It seemed as if there was no end to the slaughter.

The sun was setting when Daniel turned away, sickened by the sight of the sea, stained with blood, lifeless bodies washing up on the shore. He walked back to camp, his ears filled with the groans of the dying. He noticed the sunset. Where the dawn had been bright with yellow and pink promise, the sky now was ominously purple, the red globe of the sun almost obscured by the thick, low-lying clouds.

48

March 11

After Christophe's wedding announcement, the flamboyant, romantic Murat made a kind of pet out of him—looking for him on the parade ground, including him on missions that no lowly lieutenant had any business being invited to. At first, Christophe was uneasy at the attention, but soon enough he realized it might well be a way to advance through the ranks. He decided to make the most of it.

So it didn't surprise him to be told to report to General Bonaparte's party that afternoon. But this mission, he realized with discomfort, was more dangerous than most and held none of the glory of the battlefield.

The group headed to the Armenian Saint Nicholas Monastery to visit their sick troops. Several French soldiers had been infected with bubonic plague since their assault on Jaffa—suffering hideously from fever and chills, growths in their groin and armpits. The doctors had counseled Napoleon to stay away.

"Nonsense," he had growled. "These are my men. They've given their all to me. Can I do any less?"

Christophe, having heard Daniel rant about yesterday's massacre of the prisoners, wondered idly if this gesture was meant to repair the general's reputation with the men. Not that most of them cared if the

ragtops lived or died. But those burdened with a troublesome conscience, like Daniel, had sent up a murmur around the camp, queasy
over exterminating these men.

"They deserved it," Christophe countered when Daniel had pointed
out that they'd been promised mercy. "They broke their vow not to
fight us."

"Not all of them," Daniel argued. "Not most of them. Most weren't
at El Arish."

In the end, they'd reached an impasse and Daniel had skulked
away, his anger at the general's broken promise and frustration with
Christophe's callous attitude still simmering.

The monastery was just off the waterfront, its heavy wooden doors
set in a stone archway, topped by a cross. Many of the sick soldiers
lay on cots in the open courtyard, exposed to the brutal sunshine.
Christophe, entering at the rear of Bonaparte's train, clapped his
hand over his mouth and nose, the putrid smell of infection turning
his stomach.

"We're happy to do what we can for your men," said the abbot,
leading the general from bed to bed, his sandaled feet shuffling on
the uneven stones.

Napoleon nodded briskly. "We appreciate it. And thank you for
allowing our doctors to tend to them."

Christophe saw Dr. Desgenettes lancing a boil in a man's armpit.
The pus spurting out of it ran down the soldier's body, turning rancid
in the air. Christophe gagged.

"Desgenettes!" Bonaparte called to him. "How are my men doing?"

Desgenettes put the lancet down on a blood-stained tray the
monk held. He walked over. "I'd be doing better if I could shift some
of these men upstairs and out of the sun and wind," he growled.

"Why can't you?" Murat asked.

"The beds are all occupied," the Abbot said patiently. "I've told the
doctor this."

Napoleon shifted his gaze from one side to the other, surveying the open courtyard. "What if we put a covering on top? A tent, for instance?"

"It would need to be a large tent, but it would help." The second military doctor, Larrey, came up to the small group.

"Mine is the largest tent in the army, isn't it?" Napoleon asked. "Murat, send one of your men to fetch it."

"But, General? What will you do?" Murat asked.

"I'm sure I can manage," Bonaparte said testily. "I've made St. Peter's Church my headquarters while we're in Jaffa anyway. Hurry up, man!"

Christophe hoped that he'd be the one sent, to escape the foul air of the makeshift hospital. But Murat pointed to another of his men. "You heard the general!"

The man scampered off, looking relieved. Christophe couldn't blame him.

They continued their tour of the sick men. Some of them, devastated by high fever and chills, didn't respond to Napoleon's greetings. Others forced themselves out of their stupor to sit up and salute. One, draped only in a sheet at his waist, pushed himself out of his cot, standing on unsteady feet.

"Good man!" Napoleon exclaimed.

"Sir, it's an honor," the soldier gasped. "I was with you in Italy."

"You see, Murat? Give me more soldiers with the heart and courage of this man and together we'll conquer the world." Napoleon moved forward, as if to clap the man on his back.

Murat grasped his shoulder. "Sir, please don't take the risk."

"The risk? When these men have given me their all? What's your name, soldier? Where are you from?" But despite his bravado, Napoleon kept his hand at his side.

Christophe noticed the man was staying upright only with difficulty, his legs trembling.

"Florent Berger, sir, from Vienne."

"Vienne, eh? Good farmland there. Sheep farming mostly. And now you've got this pestilence. Desgenettes!"

The doctor, who had hovered at the edge of the small contingent, stepped forward.

"Desgenettes, when will this man be able to return to his company?"

The doctor pushed damp curls off his red, sweaty face. "General, he's quite ill."

"Ill? Nonsense! Look at him!"

"I have," came the doctor's dry rejoinder. "He's afflicted with the buboes that are common in this disease. Here, look." And he reached over and extended the man's arm upward.

Napoleon stepped forward. Murat again grabbed his shoulder. "General!"

But the general shrugged him off, and with his right hand, traced the swelling under the armpit. His entourage gasped. Christophe wasn't sure what to think—was this gesture raw courage or simply the act of a fool? Would the general take sick? What if he died?

Christophe flicked a hand again at the fleas that seemed to be everywhere in this unfortunate country, and which were swarming over the pools of pus and blood left in open bowls throughout the courtyard.

Berger's legs buckled beneath him, and Desgenettes helped him lie back down on his cot. "Rest, man." Then he turned to the general. "Sir, may I urge you to wash that hand?"

"Certainly," Napoleon said coolly.

An orderly ran up with a basin and the general dunked his hand inside, swishing it around for a moment before reaching for a soiled rag to dry it.

"I'd advise all of you to bathe when you return to your quarters. Sea water is a wise precaution," the doctor told them.

Christophe couldn't wait to dunk himself in the sea. Hadn't they spent enough time here?

"I wish you all a speedy recovery," Bonaparte called out, as he turned to leave. "We need you all restored to your companies, fit and ready for battle!"

The abbot accompanied him to the door, murmuring a blessing. Bonaparte bowed his head. Then, just as they were about to leave, he unbuckled his sword and handed it to the surprised abbot.

"For your courage and kindness in tending to my men," Napoleon told him.

The abbot stared at the sword for a long moment, shifting it in his hands. Christophe wondered what he might be thinking. After all, this was a man of peace.

But then the abbot spoke. "You honor us, General. We will do our best to care for your brave soldiers."

Feeling relief as they left, Christophe realized his neck was itching. He reached inside his collar and scratched the raised bumps. Damn fleas.

49

MARCH 13
ANCONA

Nearly a week had elapsed since Mirelle had realized the British blockade might have prevented Daniel's response to her declaration. Despite any lingering doubts, she wanted to believe he must care for her. Certainly she cared for him. And knowing that, she couldn't marry another man.

So the first thing she had to do was to break off her engagement.

She walked to the bakery at closing time. Jacopo's face lit up as she entered, the bells at the door jingling merrily. "*Cara mia*," he greeted her. "I'm just about done here."

"Good," she replied, trying to stop the guilt she felt from showing on her face. "Do you want to take a walk with me on the beach?"

He smiled widely, flashing white teeth. "Wait, wait, wait!" he sang as he rushed around, cleaning flour and dough from the counters and the floor.

Bluma, the owner's plump granddaughter, glared at Mirelle while stowing unsold bread and cakes in baskets to take to the poor.

Perhaps he'll wed her after all, Mirelle thought.

Jacopo went into the back of the shop, then took Mirelle's elbow and led her out of the bakery to the tinkling of bells. Under his arm he balanced an unwieldy wrapped package. "Today's experiment," he said, shifting it to a more comfortable position. *"Pane di Altamura.* Did you know that the poet Horace once mentioned it?"

He really is a dear man, Mirelle thought with a pang. She hated the idea of hurting him.

"You know who Horace is, don't you?" He squeezed her elbow with his free hand.

"I do." In an effort to distract him, she asked, "Tell me more about your experiment."

He launched into an explanation of how the centuries-old bread was shaped like a "priest's hat," how the mixture of semolina and flour gave it a unique, coffee-like smell, how it would remain fresh for nearly two weeks. She nodded, pretending to listen.

They reached the shore, deserted aside from a few seagulls. Breathing deeply for courage, she interrupted his explanation of how he'd mixed sea salt into the ingredients. "Jacopo. I have to tell you something."

Good-naturedly, he grinned at her. "Of course, *cara mia.* Should we walk or sit? Shall we sample my bread?"

Knowing it would taste like dust and ashes, she shook her head. "Let's walk," she said. "We can eat the bread later—if you still want to."

"If I . . . ?" A line puckered his forehead. "What would stop us?"

"I can't marry you," she blurted. "I'm in love with someone else."

He stopped short, removing his hand from her arm. "What do you mean?"

The consternation and confusion on his face tore at Mirelle's heart. "I'm so sorry."

"Sorry? I don't understand." He shook his head rapidly from side to side as if to clear it, then repeated, "What do you mean?"

She launched into her explanation, words tumbling out of her mouth, knowing she wasn't making much sense to the poor man who stood there, mouth open, wide eyes staring at her uncomprehendingly. She didn't think she'd ever mentioned Daniel to him—why should she? So every part of her story was new to him. And painful.

"Was he the man who . . . ?" he finally asked.

She shook her head. "No. Daniel would never. That was his friend—a Christian. And a terrible mistake."

"But the rabbi told me you loved me." Jacopo's foot dug in the sand.

"He said that I—" Mirelle swallowed back her annoyance at Rabbi Fano. "He had no right to say that," she stammered.

"You don't love me?" He couldn't seem to look at her.

She shook her head again. "I'm sorry. I don't. I liked you, I still like you, but it was never love. I thought I had no choice but to marry you, to leave Ancona." She bit her lip. "I never wanted to hurt you."

He raised his gaze then, eyes raking her face. She stood still, keeping her head upright despite the urge to hide her face in shame. Whatever he saw there must have convinced him. He turned and walked away, swiftly heading back to town.

She lingered on the shore, heart sore. After a half hour of wishing she could do something for him, she retraced her steps. Just as she was about to reach the quay, she noticed a noisy flock of seagulls picking at something on the beach. Drawing closer, she saw it was the *pane di Altamura*, its wrapping ripped open, the birds fighting one another to snatch at pieces and fly off with them.

After a solitary dinner in her room which she couldn't swallow, she sought out David in his library. He was seated with his brother, who glowered at her. Ezekiel had never understood David's affection for her and felt, along with Dolce, that she should have been forced to leave after di Lattes's letter had been discovered.

"David?" she ventured. "May I speak with you?"

He was seated comfortably in his favorite reading chair, flanked by several wax candles. In his lap was a much-loved book of poetry. He lay it aside reluctantly. "Go ahead."

She glanced at Ezekiel.

"Does this need to be private?" David asked, and at her nod, said, "Zeke, do you mind?"

His brother rose, muttering under his breath, and stalked out of the room.

"There goes my peace for the night." David sighed, looking after his brother's retreating back. "What can I do for you, Mirelle?"

His impatience was evident from his tightened lips and the index finger tapping the arm of his chair. She rushed to answer, remaining upright despite his waving her toward a seat. "You said you wished you had someone reliable in Israel to let you know what was really going on," she said.

"So?"

She stretched out her arms. "While I may not always have been reliable in your eyes, except perhaps in the workshop, I'd be willing to go and report back to you."

He leaned back, eyebrows rising. "You?"

She ducked her head. "Me."

He considered her for a long moment. "Sit down, would you? I don't like craning my neck."

She sat, knotting her hands tightly in her lap.

"You want to go to Israel. To go to where a vicious war is being waged. Just to report back to me if anyone is taking General Bonaparte's offer to the Jews seriously?"

She flushed. "No, not just to do that."

"To find Daniel." He said the words matter-of-factly, but his eyes narrowed and lips thinned.

She nodded. Warmth crept up her neck and into her cheeks.

"In the middle of a war. By yourself?"

"I suppose so. If I must."

"And how exactly do you propose doing that? How would you get there? How would you find him? And what if—forgive me, Mirelle— what if he's been killed in battle?"

Mirelle shifted uneasily. "I've asked myself the same questions. I don't have answers to any of them. I was hoping—as your agent—that you could help me figure out at least the first few."

"And finance the trip? You must be joking."

She glanced at him, uneasy. Now, in addition to the narrowed eyes, a vein throbbed in his forehead. "No. I would use the money from the sale of the workshop. It wouldn't cost you anything. I looked at the numbers; there should be enough. I just need help finding my way there."

"You would spend your dowry on this journey. What does your betrothed think of all this?"

The edge of anger in his voice reminded her of when he'd first learned she planned to run away with Christophe. Trembling, she hastened to say, "He's no longer my fiancé. How could I marry him when—when I have hopes of another?"

"I see." A world of pain lingered in those two words. "You've told him?"

She nodded. "It upsets you. Why?"

He spoke slowly, picking his words with care. "Mirelle, everything you've done has hurt people. Me. My daughter. Your own mother. And now this poor boy." He sighed. "If you leave and find that Daniel doesn't care for you—or worse, is dead—I don't want you to return. I'll help you, but only on the condition that you never come back to Ancona."

Tears streamed down Mirelle's cheeks. She couldn't believe what she was hearing. Never return to Ancona?

He stared out the window that let into Via Astangna with unfocused eyes. "Let me think about how to get you safely to Eretz Israel. I don't know—a woman, traveling alone—it won't be easy." He thought for a moment. "If there is a chance that the French forces will establish a Jewish homeland in Jerusalem, perhaps you can find a haven there. But I'm afraid it's just a chimera, a dream we will never realize."

Mirelle wiped her wet cheeks with her handkerchief, clearing her throat. "I will let you know, either way."

David nodded, picking up his book. "Fine. Go now. We'll talk more in a day or so."

50

MARCH 19
MOUNT CARMEL

Church bells were ringing incessantly. In his stupor, Christophe felt their vibration throbbing in his aching head, his aching limbs. Struggling to open his eyes, all he saw around him was a haze of white—white cots, whitewashed walls, men lying, moaning, draped in white sheets. Picking up a hand, he saw he, too, was encased in white; a sheet covering him, a gown of white swathed around his body. Moving hurt. His throat was parched, as if he'd swallowed the desert. Through the slit of his eyelids, which was all he could force open, he saw brown-robed men and women moving softly through the crowded room.

Why wouldn't the bells stop? He tried to sit up. Every bone in his body hurt, a deep-rooted pain that seemed to beat in time with the bells. Someone came over to him, supported his back, murmured softly. He couldn't distinguish the words. A wooden cup was held to his lips and he drank, grateful to feel the liquid slip down his throat. He tried to mutter his thanks but was hushed and helped to lie back down.

But he couldn't lie still. Despite the pain that ripped through him with every small movement, he tossed and turned. The pillow he lay on was burning hot; the sheet covering the cot was rumpled beneath him, damp and clammy, sticking to him. He couldn't find a comfortable place to rest. A gentle hand touched his forehead, followed by a wet cloth bathing his face, his neck, his wrists.

Where was he? How had he gotten here? Closing his eyes against the relentless glare of white, he felt relief when the bells' tolling finally ceased. The dampness applied to his body started to irritate him and, with a motion weaker than he could fathom, he pushed it away.

"Rest now," came a woman's voice. Whoever it was had been kneeling beside him, and she rose, moving away. He slit his eyes back open, focusing on the worn stone floor and her bare feet padding off to the next bed.

When he woke, it was the middle of the night, and the bells were tolling again. He called out for water and another brown-robed figure—a man this time—came over to him, holding a candle aloft in one hand. The flickering flame hurt Christophe's eyes. Again water was tipped down his throat, but the cup was removed before his thirst was quenched. He tried to pick up his hand, to grasp the man's wrist, but his hand, dangling out of his cover, wouldn't obey in time. The man, shielding the candle, moved away.

"Water!" Christophe croaked again. "And make the damn bells stop."

But no one returned. In desperation, he closed his eyes and let sleep overtake him once more.

Morning. Someone tried to spoon some gruel into his throat, but he couldn't swallow. Giving up, the brown-robed woman gave him more water. He gulped and gulped, letting the excess run down his throat.

"Where am I?" he rasped.

"In the Stella Maris Monastery on Mount Carmel," she said in a soothing voice.

"I'm sick?"

She nodded. "I'm afraid so. It's the plague."

Shutting his eyes, he damned Murat and Bonaparte to hell and back for exposing him in Jaffa. That must have been where he caught it. He felt the lump in his armpit. Reaching under the sheet, he felt another in his groin. "Buboes," he said.

She sighed, sympathy clear on her round face under the wimple.

"Am I going to die?" he asked.

She straightened the sheet, tucking him in. "Some survive," she said calmly. "It's in the hands of God and the Holy Mother. I'll send one of the Brothers over to pray with you."

He lay back, feeling heat radiate from his body, his head aching. He thought back to the climb up Mount Carmel when he first began to feel ill.

The steep climb up the mountainside was grueling. The day was overcast, but still the French forces gasped, the foot soldiers panting. The long trail of soldiers snaked their way up through the scrub, through the trees that clung to the sides of the cliff. At least there was ample shade.

Even on horseback, Christophe felt dizzy. He'd ridden up more challenging mountain ranges in Italy, but something about this ascent settled in the pit of his stomach, nauseating him. He wondered idly if his horse would put a foot wrong, if they'd both topple off and fall into the foggy valley far below—or in the sea just beyond. Somehow, the thought stuck and wouldn't leave, no matter how absurd he told himself it was. Would he survive such a fall? Repeatedly he shook his head, trying to chase away the odd fancy. His body felt woozy, detached. His back began to ache, then his arms.

Finally at the top, he dismounted and stood for a moment, holding onto the reins and leaning against his horse's flank, trying to catch his breath. His body hurt, and, leaning over, he retched into the path.

"Christophe?" he heard, as if from a distance.

But before he could answer, a terrible yell echoed through the mountainside. Keeping the reins clasped in his hands in case he fell, certain he might tumble off the mountain if he did, he looked up at the peak. General Bonaparte stood there, a spyglass clasped to his eyes, and was cursing and shouting. "Send a messenger!" Christophe heard him call, and a courier clambered onto his horse and recklessly dashed down the mountain.

Christophe skewed around and saw, as if in a dream, two warships barely visible through the fog, flying British flags in the harbor.

"Our ships will never make it, General," one of the staff officers said. "Our messenger will never warn them in time."

"They will," Napoleon insisted through clenched teeth. "And he must."

But neither messenger nor ships were in time, and, clinging onto his horse, still feeling strangely distant from the scene, Christophe watched the nightmarish spectacle of eleven French ships—which he knew were heavily loaded with siege weapons, cannon, armament, and other vital supplies—sailing serenely around the curve of the mountain to fall into the trap the British warships hadn't even needed to set.

"Why don't they see them?" someone cried.

"It's the fog, you dolt. Jesus, get out of there! Go back!" Junot yelled.

Bonaparte just stood, his spyglass clutched in his hand, paralyzed, as his staff officers screamed and cursed. The British warships moved to confront the French ships, guns blazing.

A sudden chill struck Christophe as he watched one, two, six of the French ships captured. He could barely stay on his feet, was shaking from head to foot. "Leferve?" someone said.

And then, nothing, until he was awakened by the church bells.

One of the monks came over, clasping a book in his hand. "Sister Mary Concessa said you wanted someone to pray for you."

Christophe shook under the covers, his teeth chattering. Part of him wanted to shout at the monk to leave him be, but then he thought of his mother, who used to sit by his side when he was ill as a child, the beads of her rosary slipping smoothly through her fingers as she prayed for him. She would have wanted him to let the man pray. So he inched his head downward, feeling the tremors grip his chest.

The brother fetched a blanket and lay it atop him. "O Merciful Lord," he intoned, "visit and heal Thy sick servant, this poor man, now lying on the bed of sickness and sorely afflicted, as Thou, O Savior, didst once raise Peter's wife's mother and the man sick of the palsy who was carried on his bed: for Thou alone hast borne the sickness and afflictions of our race, and with Thee nothing is impossible, for Thou art all-merciful." He paused, but perhaps intuiting that Christophe didn't have the strength to acknowledge the prayer, said amen himself, rose and left.

Christophe tried to lie still, despite the icy cold. All around him other men groaned and cried out, for their mothers, their sweethearts. Christophe thought of his new wife far away in Cairo, of her smile, her laughter. He realized, as if a dagger had pierced his chest, breaking through skin and bones to puncture his heart, that he might never see her again.

Part Four

March—June 1799

51

MARCH 22
ACRE

E than stood at the dock, watching the frantic residents of Acre trying to board the ship to Istanbul. A notice by Djezzar had been proclaimed throughout the city, telling anyone who was not a combatant to leave the city or face being slaughtered. The pasha, clearly thinking a long siege might be imminent, wanted as few bellies left to feed within the walls as possible. The gates were already barred and the only exit was seaward—and the only ships manned by Muslims. Ethan, on his own recognizance, had found a different way out, a gap in the walls narrow enough to go overlooked, but he was staying for as long as he could, hoping to find information to help the French forces.

He draped a keffiyeh over his head, low on his forehead and obscuring his mouth. He kept to the shadows, noting when British Commodore Sir Sidney Smith disembarked from the *Tigre*. Both that ship and the *Theseus* had been anchored in Acre for several days, positioned so the guns on their broadsides would repel any French attempt to take the port. Ethan's eyes widened when he heard Sir Sidney speaking to someone with a French accent. This short, stocky man stood proudly, even though his head barely came to the chest of the much taller commodore. He lapsed occasionally into French phrases, excitedly pointing at certain points along the walls. Ethan, moving as close as he could without calling attention to himself, realized they were talking about artillery positions.

Who could he be? The mystery was compounded when one of Haim Farhi's sons joined the two men, telling them that his father was eager to speak with them both. A janissary came up to greet them as well, sent by Djezzar, and Ethan strained to hear the introductions. The Frenchman bowed, grandly, and told the Turk that his name was Louis Edmund de Phelipeaux.

"Is it true," Farhi's son asked, as he ushered them out of the quay, "that you were in the Ecole Militaire together with Bonaparte?"

Phelipeaux nodded. "Indeed. We vied for top honors in the class. I was awarded them, while Buonaparte—which was his name back then, a filthy little commoner from Corsica—only attained a third. I'll best him here, too."

"Phelipeaux!" Bonaparte shouted when Ethan told him what he'd seen and overheard. "That runty little bastard! He said he'd best me, did he? We'll just see about that."

"But who is he?" Duroc, the general's aide-de-camp, asked.

Ethan suppressed a grin, realizing that Duroc had avoided responding to the general's "runty little bastard" line. Of course, Napoleon was nowhere as short as the enemy press liked to pretend. But he wasn't tall, either.

"He's a cursed aristo who was in my class at the Ecole Militaire. I think he must have bribed the officers to get first in class—I was certainly better than him in just about everything. And those aristocrats hated me, anyway." Napoleon waved an irritable hand. "But I'm not surprised he's with Sir Sidney. You don't know the story of how Phelipeaux helped that damn Brit escape, when we imprisoned him in Temple Prison?"

Duroc shook his head.

"It's too long a story to go into right now, but we captured Sidney and his ship after he'd burned our fleet in Toulon. Phelipeaux, along with other Royalists, disguised themselves as guards and absconded with him, pretending to take him to another prison. Traitors, all of them!"

"Could he actually be a threat, General? If you studied together . . . ?" Duroc asked hesitantly.

Napoleon threw out his chest. "A threat? Nonsense! We'll take Acre in a few days, just like Jaffa. How could it be otherwise? And if I manage to capture the bastard, all the better. He'll hang for his crimes against the Republic." He turned to Ethan. "Can you get back into the city?" At Ethan's nod, he said, "Good. Bring me any information you can on their fortifications, their supplies. They took our cannon at Haifa—where are they employing them? Where are they most vulnerable? Yes?"

"General, I'm not trained in military matters. Perhaps I should show someone else . . . ?" Ethan started, only to have his words freeze on his lips as the general glared at him.

"You're not refusing to go, are you? I need someone with your knowledge of languages. Take someone if you must—but you go, too!"

Daniel was busily placing cannon at the farthest point where they would still strike the walls. Both he and his men thought they wouldn't be effective enough here, but the command had come down from Napoleon himself.

"He's in a stupid hurry to break through and take the city," Sebastian said. "Not even digging trenches deep enough. You should hear what the engineers think. And why the hell aren't we waiting for the siege guns to be brought up from Egypt? Those damn Brits took ours, didn't they? Does the general think they won't use them?"

Daniel sighed. His sergeant was only repeating what the rest of the army was saying. Why was Napoleon being this impatient? He remembered the lightning attacks in Italy, the way the general had moved swiftly from victory to victory. But somehow Daniel knew the same tactics wouldn't work here. Not against an enemy like Djezzar.

As they shifted the cannon, a horseman rode up. Thinking it might be new orders, Daniel looked up, then gaped in shock.

"Christophe! You're alive!" he cried.

"Barely," his friend said, dismounting with a groan. He kept hold of the reins as if he needed a tether to stand upright.

Daniel reached out and hugged him, clapping him on the back. He could feel how gaunt his body had become, how shaky his limbs. "What are you doing here? Shouldn't you have stayed to recover for a few more days?"

"God, no," Christophe said, disengaging from Daniel's embrace. "It was hell there. I got away as soon as I could stand on my feet."

"But you're still not well!"

"I wasn't going to get well there, not watching soldier after soldier die, thrashing in pain, crying out." Christophe shuddered.

"But you'll live?"

"I'm one of the lucky ones. It's a hideous death." Christophe shut his eyes for a moment, then opened them. "But Murat is well? Bonaparte? That's hard to believe. It's all their fault I caught this damn pestilence back in Jaffa."

Daniel didn't know what to say.

"How did you know I was sick?" Christophe asked after a moment of silence.

"Remy from your company told me. I still can't believe you're alive, Christophe."

Christophe grunted. "I can't, either. Listen, I've got to report in. And then dash a letter off to my wife." He hesitated. "I'm glad I didn't write her when I thought I was going to die. One of the nuns said she'd send a letter for me—but I thought, as long as I didn't write, there was still a chance. Looks like I was right."

Ethan sought Daniel out at dusk. He found him sitting over a dinner of mutton and wild greens, hunkered next to a small fire. Seated next to him was someone who looked familiar and yet not. It was a shock when he realized he was looking at Christophe—but a Christophe with sallow, hollowed cheeks and dark shadows under his eyes.

"What the hell happened to you, man?" he exclaimed before he could stop himself.

Christophe, who was breaking off a piece of the local flat bread, grinned. "Plague," he said, stuffing the bread in his mouth.

"And you survived?"

Christophe, his mouth full, just nodded. Ethan looked over at Daniel, eyebrows raised.

"It's a miracle." Daniel moved over, gesturing to Ethan to sit.

He squatted next to the fire, waving away Christophe's offer of bread. "I ate earlier," he said. "Listen, Daniel, I need you to come with me into Acre."

Daniel's eyes widened. "Are you crazy?"

"I'm supposed to report back to Bonaparte on the disposition of cannon there. I know how to get into the city. I may be able to understand what they're saying, but I don't know enough to make sense of artillery placement. But you do."

Daniel shook his head. "And if we get caught? Didn't you see the head hoisted over the wall, of the messenger the general sent into Djezzar? Don't you remember what you told me about how brutal he is?"

"Is it any worse than facing him on the field?"

Daniel pursed his lips. "Maybe not. But this is a siege, which means cannon is critical. I can't leave my position. Certainly not leave my men."

Ethan sat back. But Christophe, his suddenly blazing eyes looking too large in his overly thin face, burst out, "I'll come with you!"

"You?" Ethan scrutinized him in the light of the flames. Despite his sudden eagerness, Christophe looked exhausted, weak, spindly. And besides, they had never fully repaired the rift that had opened between them the day Ethan sat with Sappeira to learn Coptic.

But Christophe seemed to have forgotten all that. Perhaps because he had won the fair lady. "Look, Daniel's right. He's got to stay with his men. But until the walls are breached, my men and I are merely standing by." Christophe shrugged. "And to be honest, I'm not sure I'm going to be much use on horseback for a bit. But I can help you. I'm not the expert Daniel is in artillery placements, but I've been with the army long enough to know what Bonaparte needs. Let me come!" He seemed to radiate excitement. "It will be a lark!"

Ethan turned to look at Daniel. "What do you think?"

"First of all, I'm no more an expert than he is. Second, he's always been crazy—no, not crazy, intrepid. As long as you can rein him in, you couldn't ask for anyone better."

Christophe stuffed another piece of bread in his mouth, gulped down the mutton on his plate, and stood up, swallowing. "When do we go?"

52

April 2
Kythira, Ionian Islands

Mirelle stood in the port of Diakoftis, on the southern-most Ionian island, Kythira, looking out on the crystal clear sea. She wore a light traveling dress and carried a small portmanteau, which was all David suggested she take with her. "You'll be able to buy what you need once you arrive in Jaffa," he said.

The choice of traveling from Ancona to Kythira was the result of much deliberation. David had enlisted the help of his reluctant brother, who thought the whole plan ludicrous. Mirelle suspected that Ezekiel only gave in when David explained that she wouldn't be returning to Ancona, no matter what. They'd discussed the options of Portugal, which was struggling to remain a neutral port, or sailing into Constantinople, which would take her through Muslim territory, or heading to Athens, where ships came in and out nearly daily. But Athens, too, was owned by the Ottoman Empire, while the Ionian Islands had previously been the property of the Venetians. So once France conquered Venice, they owned the islands as well.

But perhaps that, too, was being contested. The Turks, having declared war on the French and allied with the Russians, might easily eye the southern-most tip of Greece as easy pickings. That was David's major hesitation. But, as he told Mirelle, "The best thing is that they speak Italian there. Because they were owned by the Venetians for so long."

Mirelle hadn't thought about the difficulties of language. Nor had she considered the ramifications of a woman traveling alone until David handed her a band of gold to place on her left ring finger. "Tell anyone who approaches you that you're making the journey to join your husband," he told her. "That should stop most fops from bothering you."

Most but not all. She perfected an indignant glare when she was accosted by men who obviously considered any lone woman to be fair game. And the one time that didn't work—when she was backed into a corner of the ship's deck by an overly amorous sailor—she let out a piercing scream. He fled from her, muttering curses over his shoulder.

The tedious ocean trip had given Mirelle time to dwell on painful memories. Mama clung to her and wept when she learned that Mirelle would not marry Jacopo—and cried even harder when Mirelle told her that she'd been effectively banished from her home.

"At least in Capri I could have come to you when you had babies," Mama had sobbed the first night they revealed the plan, everyone sitting in Dolce's favorite yellow salon. "Now where will you live? What will you do? What happens if Daniel doesn't want you?"

"Oh, Daniel will want her," Dolce put in, not realizing that her spite calmed the worst of Mirelle's fears. But then she maliciously added, "Unless he's dead."

Mirelle set her lips together. Despite trying to hide her pang of apprehension, she winced at Dolce's ice-cold glare. Her childhood friend, who always made life bend to her whims, was now much to be pitied. For Dolce, sophisticated enough to recognize that men do need to sow their wild oats, had reconciled with her fiancé. As long as he wasn't sowing them with Mirelle, Dolce had decided the benefits of the match outweighed any future mortification.

Di Lattes's wealth and his position in Florentine Jewish society made him equal in status to her father—perhaps more than equal, since Florence was a superior city. Dolce would be the reigning queen of Jewish Florence, her father had insisted repeatedly. She'd decided to agree with him.

Clearly David didn't want his beloved daughter to break the engagement. And perhaps he didn't fully understand how di Lattes would treat Dolce—as a mere ornament adorning his home. Having watched his warped style of wooing, Mirelle wondered if he would try and break her spirit, might indeed trot out some of his paramours before her to demonstrate his mastery. Mirelle still had enough feeling toward her friend to feel sorry for her. But there was no point in trying to dissuade her.

David was right, she'd thought morosely as she leaned out over the railing on the quay, gazing listlessly at the blue waves. All she'd ever done was hurt the people she loved.

The day of her departure nearly broke Mirelle's heart. Even the constrained nights when the Jews of Ancona had been locked behind the ghetto gates seemed dear to her now. She had never traveled anywhere before but Venice. She'd never had another home but Ancona. And now she was leaving it—leaving willingly, perhaps, but barred from ever returning.

David had booked her on the boat that ferried her to the distant Greek island. Now it was up to her to find one that would head her in the direction of Jerusalem. Scouring the various newspaper accounts of the French battles, she and David had decided that Jerusalem was the most logical place to start her search for Daniel. After all, if there were Jewish battalions and if the French had already seized control of Aleppo, they would be in full control of the ancient city. And there Mirelle would best be able to assess whether the reports of a Jewish homeland were more than just words on newsprint.

But sending her to this tiny outpost might have been a mistake after all. For all the ships in the harbor were Turkish and Russian. And none of them looked friendly or willing to take passengers.

Not sure what to do, she approached a cragged-faced fisherman who was mending nets on the side of the quay. "Good morning," she greeted him tentatively in Italian.

He looked up, touching his cap as he noticed her traveling dress. "Signora?"

She was about to correct him when she remembered the gold band on her finger. "I'm looking for passage to a port in Syria"—she knew better than to call it Eretz Israel, which would identify her as a Jew—"and I don't see any vessels that might take me."

"Most of the ships were chased off," the man said laconically, spitting a plug of tobacco on the wooden planks of the quay. "The Turks now claim they own the islands."

"There are no ships taking passengers?" she asked.

He thought for a moment. "Chased off, like I said. But my brother-in-law is due in a couple of days from now—he sails on a Portuguese schooner. He goes back and forth from Lisbon to Beirut, stopping here on the way. You can buy a passage with him."

Mirelle had pored over maps with David and knew Beirut would serve her purpose, even if it meant entering Ottoman territory. That was almost inevitable anyway. She could head directly from there to Jerusalem—and, hopefully, somehow discover where Daniel was fighting. "Is there an inn where I can stay until he arrives?" she asked.

He directed her to a small hostelry that housed travelers. The innkeeper eyed her small bag with some disdain but was happy enough to take her Italian money. Dinner would be served, he said, at seven o'clock. When Mirelle asked about the other meals, he shrugged and said, "There are plenty of tavernas on the island."

Having long finished the contents of the basket of victuals packed for her back in Ancona and as the local church bell had just chimed one o'clock, Mirelle decided to walk about and find one. Seated on the quay, she sampled a tangy fish soup that the taverna owner called *kakavia*. Just as she finished it, she was startled to hear someone speaking in Yiddish behind her. She swiveled in her seat to see a bearded man in a dark coat and flowing white collar, a wide black hat on his head, together with a plump woman in a modest gray gown, buttoned up to her chin, with a white fichu and cap.

Mirelle's parents rarely if ever spoke Yiddish at home, preferring Italian. But clearly this couple must be Jewish. She stood and greeted them. "*A gutn mitag,*" she said, following it, in French, with "good afternoon."

The couple looked her over cautiously, the woman paying particular attention to her hand with the ring. "Good day to you," the wife said in strangely accented French, volunteering nothing else.

How could she let them know she, too, was Jewish? She didn't want to blurt it out. But then she remembered the necklace that she had tucked under her dress. She fished it out and let it dangle close to her throat. Their eyes widened as they saw the Jewish star and they began to babble in Yiddish to her.

She raised a hand, looking around. "Please. French, please."

They must have realized the need for caution and switched to heavily accented French. "Where are you from?" the woman asked.

When she told them she was from Ancona, they both grew excited. Indicating that she should sit at their table, pushing aside their empty dishes, they told her that they treasured the ketubah that they'd had made there for their wedding nearly thirty years ago. They grew even more excited when they learned that Mirelle's grandfather had probably created it. "We are from Amsterdam," the husband said. "I teach in a yeshiva there."

The wife introduced them—Rav Wim Kluytmans and Mevrouw Hedy Kluytmans. "Why are you here all alone?" she asked in a motherly fashion, with another glance at the ringed finger. "Where are your companions? Your husband?"

"I am traveling to rejoin my husband—he is in the French army," Mirelle said.

"Shh!" Rav Kluytmans hissed. "Not so loud! You never know who might be listening."

"And you?" Mirelle asked more quietly. "Where are you going?"

Almost as one, the couple looked over their shoulders before shifting their chairs closer. "To Eretz Israel," Rav Kluytmans murmured. "We are going to Jerusalem."

Mirelle scraped her chair in. "I'm headed there as well. I have promised to find out if . . ."

". . . if this crazy French general really means to establish a Jewish homeland?" Mevrouw Kluytmans whispered. "That is our purpose too."

"You must travel with us," the Rav said. "It's not safe to be a woman alone these days."

"Really, child, we insist," his wife said with a determined jerk of her rounded chin.

53

April 20
Jerusalem

The siege of Acre was taking longer than the general had hoped, and despite other French victories—in Nazareth, in Cana, and at Mount Tabor—the Ottoman, Arab, and British resistance (directed by Sir Sidney by sea and Haim Farhi by land) meant that the troops were mired on the outskirts of the fortified city.

This despite all the good intelligence Ethan and Christophe had brought the general. They reported on how Phelipeaux had concentrated his guns exactly where Napoleon tried to breach the walls, how the outside walls of the moat were reinforced with stones, rising almost thirty feet high. When Napoleon's first feint was defeated, they witnessed Djezzar's execution of a hundred Christian residents of the city, the bodies tossed into the sea. The general heard the reports, his face stony, refusing to credit most of it.

"It's as if he won't believe anything can stand in his way," Ethan said to Daniel. "As if the only truth is the truth he creates in his own mind."

But Napoleon was at least casting about for allies. He wrote to Bashir Shihab II, the Emir of the Druze, who refused to commit to either side until a clear victor emerged. And he reissued his Proclamation to the Jews, which is why Ethan had traveled to

Jerusalem on the eve of Passover, hope once more kindling in his heart. This time, Bonaparte was actually in Eretz Israel. Perhaps that would help tip the scale.

While the holiday might be perceived as a bad time to disturb the rabbis of Jerusalem, Ethan recognized why, strategically, the general had chosen it. After all, did not the Passover Haggadah say: "This is the bread of destitution that our ancestors ate in the land of Egypt. Anyone who is famished should come and eat, anyone who is in need should come and partake of the Passover sacrifice. Now we are here, next year we will be in the land of Israel; this year we are slaves, next year we will be free people"? The text spoke directly to welcoming him as a stranger—and how persuasive was the passage of becoming a free people after more than a thousand years of wandering?

The evening he arrived, he approached the yeshiva of Rabbi Meyuchas, where the rabbi was hosting a seder. After identifying himself as a visitor to the city, he was brought into the yeshiva's crowded dining hall. The seder had yet to begin, though most of the students and their families were already seated. The rabbi himself sat at a long table in the front, surrounded by many of the city's Jewish notables. The women were seated behind a partition—a *mechitza*—a kind of trellis that allowed them to see into the room and partake of the ceremony but not distract the men.

As Ethan was led up to a spare seat, a woman's shocked voice called out, "Ethan? Ethan ben Dovid?"

He recognized that voice! He moved quickly to his side of the *mechitza*. "Mirelle d'Ancona? Is that possibly you?"

A gasp and a sob. "Yes, I'm here. Oh, dear cousin, are you well? And can you tell me if . . ."

The rabbi's student escorting him interrupted. "The rabbi wants to begin. Please come."

"We'll talk after the seder, Mirelle," Ethan managed to say before being ushered away.

It was nearing midnight before the service was finally over and the last piece of matza eaten. Fueled by the four cups of wine everyone drank, the students were encouraged to argue, just like the scholars of antiquity, and their debates were long-winded and fiercely fought. The entire hall rocked back and forth in sheer joy, singing many, many stanzas of their favorite Passover songs. While Ethan couldn't help but be infected by their delight, he was impatient to learn why Mirelle was in Jerusalem.

When the last of the singing petered out, the men headed into the clear, cool night, the women started stacking the Passover dishes and clearing the remains of the meal, brushing matza crumbs off the tables, prodding cranky, half-asleep children awake. Ethan first arranged to visit the rabbi in the morning and then sought out Mirelle. She was arguing with a large woman who stared suspiciously at Ethan as he approached.

"But he's my cousin, Mevrouw Kluytmans," Mirelle was saying. "I *must* speak with him!"

The woman crossed her arms over an ample chest. "It's late and the Rav is exhausted. And you are in my care—I will not just leave you here with a man!"

Mirelle looked like she was about to weep. "Let me just arrange a time to meet him. Please?"

Mevrouw Kluytmans scrunched up her double chins. "I'll do that." She turned to Ethan. "We must go. We're staying with Rabbi Meyuchas. You can visit us tomorrow afternoon."

She grabbed Mirelle's forearm and pulled her away before she could say anything more.

The next morning, Ethan made his rounds of the rabbis. This time, despite his trotting out the verse from the Haggadah, they were even less willing to listen to him.

"We've been warned that there will be reprisals if we even think of supporting the French troops," Rabbi Pardo told him. "Take your proclamation away. Even just speaking with you puts me and my community in danger. Don't you know what Djezzar is capable of?"

Ethan did know and he shuddered, remembering. After his passionate arguments failed, he rolled the documents and tucked them away, his heart sinking. He'd have to return to Napoleon and let him know that he'd failed to convince them. That there would be no Jewish homeland.

Or was he required to return? Not for the first time, Ethan toyed with the idea of abandoning his obligations as one of Bonaparte's agents. He could head home to Paris or even Bischheim and find employment there. He wasn't a soldier. Now that this last hope had faded, nothing but his own sense of duty was keeping him in this backwater of a country.

But first, he had to find out why Mirelle was in Jerusalem. It was the last place he expected to see her. Sitting in Rebbetzin Meyuchas's parlor, he waited for her. Half a dozen small children—curly-haired toddlers who grasped his knees and made faces, little girls who tittered at him—wandered in and out. Before his conversation with al-Jabartī and his wife, he would have flinched at this assault of little ones. Now, somehow, the constriction that had squeezed his heart for so long had loosened, and he was able to grin at their antics.

Finally, Mevrouw Kluytmans sailed into the room, her protruding blue eyes full of doubt. He rose, bowed, and introduced himself.

She sat on a rickety wooden seat across from him. "So, young man. Mirelle tells me you are her cousin. You know her husband, yes?"

"Her . . . husband?" Ethan was shocked. Was Mirelle married? His thoughts flew to poor Daniel, wishing he could spare him this discovery.

An older girl bustled in, carrying a decanter of wine, a plate of Passover almond cookies, and small wine glasses on a tray. She set it down and pushed the children out of the room. "With Mama's compliments and she'll be in soon," she said in rapid Yiddish.

Merouw Kluytmans waved away the wine Ethan offered to pour. "Of course her husband," she persisted. "Is it possible you don't know of him?"

Before Ethan could reply, Mirelle burst into the room, her skirts clutched in her hands, showing her stockinged ankles. Merouw Kluytmans tsked, scolding her as if she had a right. "Mirelle! Such an undignified manner! So immodest! What will our guest think of you?"

As Ethan noticed the gold band glinting on Mirelle's finger, a heavy weight pressed on his chest. He thought of all the times Daniel had tried to write to her and proclaim his love. Had his last letter, the one Farhi had promised to dispatch, ever reached her? Mirelle must have given up on hearing from him and married someone else. Is that why she was here in Jerusalem? Had her husband brought her? Was she married to this woman's son?

He rose again to bow, but Mirelle, ignoring the older woman, ran full tilt into him, hugging him fiercely. He heard Merouw Kluytmans' shocked "*oh meyn Got*" and, giving Mirelle a slight squeeze, slipped from her embrace. "I hear congratulations are in order," he said.

"Congratulations?"

"On your marriage."

"Oh, that!" Her face lit up.

She must really love her husband, he thought. Poor Daniel.

But instead of explaining, she did something unexpected. "Merouw Kluytmans, I'm going to take a walk with my cousin. I'll bring Tzitta along to chaperone."

Merouw Kluytmans's brow puckered, but she said nothing. In a few minutes they were walking swiftly down the stony street, the girl who had brought the wine trailing behind discreetly.

"Mirelle, what are you . . . ?" Ethan began, but she cut him off mid-sentence.

"Daniel. How is Daniel? Have you seen him recently? Where is he? Is he—Ethan, is he alive?"

She sounded breathless, half-ecstatic, half-terrified. He stared at her flushed face. Then he answered calmly, "He was fine when I saw him in Acre a couple of weeks ago."

"Oh, thank God!" she exclaimed, swaying as if weak at the knees.

"Mirelle, are you all right? Should we find a place to sit?"

Tzitta rushed up. "There's a stone wall in the next street. You can sit there."

Ethan took Mirelle's arm and supported her as they turned the corner. He helped her up on the stone wall. Tzitta walked off, giving them as much privacy as a chaperone could while still keeping them in sight. Mirelle threw her a kiss.

"Mirelle?"

The words came tumbling out. "I'm not married, Ethan—the ring was for my protection while I traveled. It was David Morpurgo's idea. The trouble is that Merouw Kluytmans and her husband, the Rav, think I'm Daniel's wife."

"Daniel's wife." Ethan was beginning to understand.

"He's not married, is he? I was so afraid—when he didn't write . . ."

Ethan laughed, joy for his young relatives flooding his heart. "Oh, my dear, dear cousin. If you only knew the agonies he went through because of the British blockade. He was devastated because he couldn't respond to your letter. Married? Daniel? No, no. A thousand times no."

Her face looked like it was lit by a candles, her eyes glowing by their light. She clasped her chest with both hands. She tried to speak, but clearly words wouldn't come.

He let the glory of the moment sink in, then grinned at her. "But do you know who is married, cousin? Christophe!"

54

MAY 4
ACRE

The troops were told midday to prepare for an immediate attack. Daniel hustled his men into position, employing the new cannon and ammunition that had arrived just days ago from Egypt.

"What's Bonaparte doing?" muttered Sebastian, who was in a foul temper, his arm infected from the slash of an enemy's scimitar earlier in the month, when Daniel led a group of men to collect round shot the British fleet had fired at them. Napoleon promised the men ten to twenty sous for every bit of ammunition they could reuse; the price based on the heaviness of the ball. Neither Daniel nor Sebastian had seen the Turks before they burst out upon them. The French soldiers were lucky when Daniel immediately ordered them in a strategic retreat, so they didn't lose a single man. But many, like his sergeant, were wounded.

"What's he doing?" Sebastian repeated, his brows compressed in pain and annoyance. "We're in the exact same spot we've been for the last few attacks. Does he think Phelipeaux isn't wise to him?"

Daniel frankly agreed, but he had his orders. Morale, which had lifted considerably when news of the victories in the Galilee reached the men, had plummeted again. Too many had been killed or wounded, too much disease was decimating the troops, and this siege was taking weeks and months, not the days the soldiers had been promised. For some reason, Bonaparte simply refused to change his strategy. Daniel, whose admiration of the general had long since dwindled, now wondered if his triumphs in Italy had been due to luck rather than skill.

Looking up, he saw Napoleon now standing on the crest of the hill that he often used as an outpost, the spy glass at his eye winking in the early sunlight. *Doesn't he know the enemy can see him as well?* Daniel wondered, just as a flash of fire and the whizzing of cannon balls split the air.

As Daniel's men watched helplessly, hearts in their throats, a ball struck a group of soldiers huddled together near the general, while another barely missed Napoleon. Two of his aides-de-camp threw themselves upon him, forcing him to the ground. Cries of pain rose from their location. *How many did we just lose?* Not Bonaparte, for he stood after a moment, brushing the dirt off his uniform.

"He lost his horse one day standing there," Pierre muttered to no one in particular, rubbing his shoulder where he'd been wounded in Italy. "And earlier this week, they fired a musket ball at him and sent his hat flying."

The chorus of discontent that rose as the men complained about their commander had to be stopped. "Shut up and let's get this lot shifted," Daniel barked. "We don't want to be caught flatfooted when they give the command to fire."

55

Late in the afternoon a huge explosion was followed by a raucous shout. After weeks of trying, the French finally breeched the walls near the tower, which had been Bonaparte's target all along.

Christophe, who had been riding his restive steed up and down just behind the engineers and the artillery, cheered along with the rest. Finally, some real action! He'd been too long idle. At first, he'd enjoyed his forays into Acre with Ethan, but his enthusiasm waned as the intelligence they brought back didn't seem to make a difference to the general, who doggedly kept trying to break down the tower walls. He and his men had been deployed in setting out scarecrows and puppets to draw British fire and reveal their gun positions. While it was dangerous work—a few were shot when positioning the decoys, and Christophe had lost his favorite battle-hardened horse—there was no glory in it. But Christophe mentioned to Murat that he knew the alleyways and twisting marketplace of Acre intimately because of his sorties in the city. So Murat put him at the forefront of the first line of attack, promising him a promotion after a successful battle.

"Follow me, men!" he shouted now, urging his horse recklessly through the flurry of French fire and into the moat that the defenders had dug. The thunder of hooves, the shouts of the infantry behind him made him grin, heart pounding.

He was just about at the breach in the walls when he spied the mass of Turks running swiftly to confront them. Djezzar stood on the walls above, bellowing, exhorting his men forward. In a moment, they'd be overrun.

"God damn it! Fall back!" came the call from his colonel. Gritting his teeth, Christophe wheeled his steed around. Trapped, momentarily, by the thick mass of the infantry, he twisted and turned to reach the far side of the moat, his men galloping close behind. They scrambled out and back outside the walls to safety.

Boom. The British gunships opened fire. Christophe actually saw the round shot headed in his direction. He tried to pull up, but his new horse, frightened by the tumult, refused to heed. Pain struck him as shot pelted his shoulder. A musket ball lodged in his chest, another in his horse's flank. Screaming as the world seemed to vibrate and pulse around him, the reins slipped out of suddenly useless hands. He toppled, falling headlong to the ground. The horse fell atop him, trapping his legs underneath the flailing, screaming beast.

56

MAY 5

Daniel headed over to see Sebastian, struck with a musket ball in the fleshy part of his forearm. Once at the infirmary, he found Christophe lying unconscious, the doctors deciding whether they needed to amputate both his shattered limbs.

"Can't you save at least one leg?" a horrified Daniel asked Dr. Larrey.

"Look around you," Larrey growled impatiently. "We've no time to waste. If we ship him off to the monastery the way he is now, the legs will fester. He'd just die of gangrene on the way. This at least gives him a fighting chance to survive."

Larrey motioned to the surgeon, who callously whistled under his breath as he brought out his saw and placed it halfway up Christophe's right thigh. The flesh streamed with blood as he sliced into it. At the sound of tines grinding on bone, Daniel clenched his jaw, his gorge rising. He fled the tent, resolving to return that evening to make sure his friend had survived. If he survived.

He walked slowly back to his quarters, his heart heavy, thinking of Sappeira in Cairo, of Alain and Odette in Paris. He rubbed at the battle grime on his face and hands. He needed to grab a towel and find a safe spot to wash. His stomach grumbled, reminding him he'd spent more than a day on the battlefield without stopping to eat. But the gore he'd just witnessed meant he would probably just vomit it all up again. Maybe later.

Walking into his tent, he saw a woman dressed in Arabic robes sitting on his bedroll, her eyes downcast. His cousin Ethan, similarly attired, stood beside her. She lifted her head at his approach. He blinked, once, twice. Was he dreaming? "Mirelle?" he croaked.

She jumped up, seized him. "Oh, thank God, thank God, you're alive," she cried, clutching him tight.

His arms slid around her waist. He couldn't breathe, couldn't think. She couldn't be here. She was here. No, it was impossible. How in the world had she arrived? Here, of all places?

It had to be a dream. Or perhaps he had died on the battlefield and gone to heaven. No, there was no heaven. But feeling her cling to him, her cheek tucked against his own—in a way, it was a kind of heaven. He closed his eyes, held still, relishing whatever illusion this must be.

But Ethan, chuckling, woke him out of his trance. "Yes, she's really here," he said. "Let go of one another and I'll explain."

Daniel took his arms from Mirelle's waist but grasped her elbows, refusing to release her. At arm's length, he could see her more clearly. Her clothing made her look like a stranger: a long mud-colored robe, a green scarf covering her hair and draped around her neck. But her dear face hadn't changed, despite looking thinner, exhausted. And when she spoke, her sweet voice brought him right back to Ancona.

"Ethan thought this dress was the safest way for us to travel from Jerusalem," she told him shyly, stepping back to smooth the rough garment with her palms.

"You're lovely," Daniel breathed. "Lovely."

The corners of her beautiful mouth turned up as she surveyed him from head to toe. "And you're filthy. My poor Daniel, was the battle terrible? I was so frightened, hearing the guns firing, the ground pounding beneath my feet, knowing you were in the middle of it all."

She reached up, lightly touching the faint scar on his cheek, a remnant of the Cairo revolt. "You weren't hurt, were you?"

"An old wound—and a minor one. But you shouldn't be here. It's not safe," Daniel said. He looked at Ethan, who was watching them both, a huge grin on his face. Daniel suddenly recognized the cousin he'd grown up with in that smile. "Why did you bring her here?"

"Aren't you glad to see me?" Mirelle asked in a small, troubled voice.

"Glad?" Daniel took hold of her elbows again. "Glad doesn't even . . . I don't have the words. I don't believe . . . how in the world . . . ?"

Ethan laughed. "I'd better explain. I'm not sure either of you can make sense right now."

And he did explain—and then Daniel washed and changed and brought them both to the mess to eat. They ignored the curious glances the other soldiers sent their way. From there, they went to the hospital tent to see Christophe. He was awake, sodden from the opium the doctors kept pouring down his throat to soothe his pain. He didn't understand why Mirelle was there, but he was happy to see her—clasped her hand and spoke muzzily about his wife and how glad she'd be he wasn't dead.

Daniel approached Dr. Larrey. "Does he understand he's lost both legs?"

Larrey shook his head. "It often happens that way. It will be a shock when he does realize it. But for right now, it's a mercy he's still oblivious."

"What happens to him now?"

"We'll send him to the monastery on Mount Carmel. The monks will take good care of him. When he's healed, we'll ship him back to France."

"His wife is in Egypt, you know."

Someone screamed for the doctor, shrieks of pain rising from one of the cots. "Not my problem," he said over his shoulder, moving off.

Mirelle, who had schooled her face in gentle lines during the visit, burst into tears the moment they left. Pulling her to one side, Daniel put an arm around her shoulder. "It's all right, sweetheart. Christophe's strong. He'll recover. Lots of soldiers lose limbs."

"It's just so awful!" she wept, resting her head on his chest. "Christophe, of all people!"

He nodded, keeping her close.

As soon as Ethan left them to report to the general, Daniel walked with Mirelle through one of the nearby orange groves. The grove's citrusy scent perfumed the air as he took both of her hands. The sun was long gone, but a full moon and the twinkling stars lit their path.

"You'll marry me, won't you?" he asked. He should be more eloquent, but he was too weary to do more than speak from the heart. "You know how much I love you, don't you?"

Her smile flashed out, but then wavered. "Even though I'm a fallen woman?"

"Do you think I care?" He saw the pain and bitterness etched on her face. "I don't."

"I didn't think I did, either," she said slowly. "But then I had to live with the consequences." She slowly pulled her hands from his. "I want to marry you, of course I do. Why else would I have chased you over two continents? But I don't want you to be stained with my sin."

"With your sin?" He was indignant. "That's ridiculous."

She stared down at a half-rotten orange that had fallen from one of the trees. "I've hurt people. People I love. People who cared about me. I couldn't bear it if I hurt you too."

"The only way you could hurt me is by not marrying me." He led her over to a fallen log and helped her sit, then perched beside her. "I've done nothing but dream of you—of marrying you. Of making you my wife." He put a finger under her chin and raised her face, her cheeks damp with tears. "Say you will."

She nodded, once, twice. It was answer enough. He put his arms around her, gathered her against him, kissed her.

Ethan reported to Bonaparte, told Daniel and Mirelle that he'd received a tongue lashing for his failure, and said he wasn't sure what he'd do next. "I'm useless here. Maybe I'll head back to Cairo. Maybe I'll figure out how to go back to Paris. I need to think about it."

"Should you take Mirelle with you? It's not safe for her here," Daniel asked.

But Mirelle clung to him, fingers digging into his arm. "I'm not leaving you. And it's not safe for you either. I mean, look what happened to poor Christophe." She shuddered.

"Mirelle, you can't stay here," Daniel retorted, suddenly feeling the weight of responsibility settle on him. He still couldn't believe she would be his wife. "We're in the middle of a siege."

Should he tell her how disenchanted he was, how the sack and slaughter of Jaffa had sickened him, never mind the nightmarish desert crossing, the piles of heads after the Cairo revolt? Would she think him a coward if he confessed how much he hated it all? He couldn't do it, couldn't risk diminishing himself in her eyes.

57

MAY 8

Mirelle married Daniel three days later, a drumhead wedding attended by Daniel's men, conducted by General Dommartin, who commanded Daniel's artillery company. Mirelle told Daniel that it was the most romantic ceremony she could have imagined. Neither of them wanted to wait for a religious ceremony, though Daniel did promise her they'd be wed again by a rabbi under a chuppah the first chance they got. But Mirelle was perfectly happy with the civil ceremony, which was necessary anyway if they ever planned to live in revolutionary Paris.

Mirelle dressed in a cream-colored gown with an overlay of gauze and blue embroidery on the sleeves and at the bottom of the skirt. It was wrinkled from the weeks it had spent at the bottom of her portmanteau, but even so, Daniel caught his breath upon sighting her, making her smile mistily. A lace veil was cast over her dark hair, caught up with clusters of iris and narcissi. She blushed, noticing that Daniel couldn't keep his eyes off her. He, of course, was attired in his dress uniform, boots, buckles, sword and scabbard polished to a shining gloss by his men.

The night before, Mirelle had burrowed in her portmanteau, find-ing a small wooden box and taking something from it. Smiling, she stood before Daniel and opened her palm. In it nestled a gold band. "From David Morpurgo," she told him. "To keep me safe and unmolested during my journey to you."

Daniel took it, still warm from her grasp. "I will keep you safe, now," he murmured, and she knew it was a sacred vow.

Standing on the seashore, buffeted by the sound of the waves and the gulls, they clasped hands as General Dommartin read out the contract of marriage, which they both signed. Mirelle felt almost giddy with joy as she inscribed her name, her dress and veil fluttering in the breeze. Daniel placed the ring on her finger and kissed his bride. The men cheered, then formed an arch with their sabers for the newly married couple to walk through.

Dommartin pulled the new couple aside. "Listen, Isidore. I can't free you from duty—we need every man we've got—but I can give you a temporary reassignment. Consider it a wedding gift. We can't have this lovely lady worried about you on the battlefield, at least not during your honeymoon."

Mirelle wanted to kiss him. Later, Daniel explained that rumors had long circulated around camp that Dommartin disapproved of Bonaparte's expedition to Egypt and wouldn't be averse to his failing.

"What about heading back to Cairo?" Dommartin asked. "Working with the savants there? They're a pesky bunch. Or," he said before Daniel could answer, "a better idea. The garrison in Jaffa needs support. Building up the fortifications there, keeping an eye on the supplies from Cairo, sending us what we need. It's mainly desk work and certainly more tedious than being in the field . . ."

"That would be perfect," Mirelle said. And she did kiss him, twice, on either cheek.

The general squeezed her before turning her loose. "Consider it done. And I can see," he said with a laugh, "who is going to wear the pants in *this* family."

He then toasted them with a glass of wine before heading back to duty. Ethan took Daniel's emptied glass and lay it on the sand for the bridegroom to smash—the one concession they would make to Jewish ritual, Daniel said.

But Mirelle knew of one other concession, a surprise she had for him. After feasting with his men, they returned to the tent that had been moved to the farthest reaches of the camp, giving the newly married couple as much privacy as possible. Daniel reached out his arms to embrace his bride, but Mirelle forestalled him, hunting around in her portmanteau once again, carefully bringing out a roll of parchment.

"It's one of the ketubot the workers made when they thought I was marrying David," she told him, kneeling and spreading it out carefully on his bedroll. "They never added the bridegroom's name— and trust me, I would never hold you to the excessive amount David promised me, were we ever to divorce."

It was an exquisite document, a cream-colored parchment deco- rated with intertwined flowers, two lovebirds sitting atop marble col- umns, drawn in gold, silver and jewel tones. The amount—a hundred thousand scudi—made Daniel's eyes widen.

"You want me to sign this? But will it be valid, without a rabbi witnessing it?"

"I wanted to show it to you. We can wait—of course we can—until we're married by a rabbi."

Daniel fingered the document. "It's perfect," he whispered. "And so are you."

Somehow, the ketubah floated from the bedroll to the sandy ground and lay there. It would be a while before either one of them thought to rescue it.

58

MAY 21
JAFFA

Daniel had barely established himself at the French headquarters in Jaffa before news arrived that Bonaparte was retreating from Acre and heading back to Egypt. Messengers sent in advance of the army told a sad tale of how the wounded and sick with plague were often abandoned.

"What will happen to them?" Mirelle asked that evening in the small stone house Daniel had commandeered. The home was located on the outskirts of the city, which was still floundering under bubonic plague. He forbade her to venture into the city, bathing himself nightly in the sea before entering their quarters, bringing home whatever they needed and could not buy from the outlying fruit groves or from local shepherds.

"It's obvious," he replied. "If the Turks take the city back, they'll be slaughtered."

Ahmad Pasha Djezzar was taking swift and brutal revenge on the Christians and Jews who had supported Bonaparte or were reported to have done so. The reports that trickled in of massacres on the people of Tiberias and Safed were heartbreaking.

"Will we return with the troops to Cairo?" Mirelle asked.

Daniel didn't have an answer for her and couldn't conceive of what would be safest. The idea of taking his new wife on a march across the Sinai and Nitrian deserts knotted his stomach. But would she be safe here if Djezzar attacked? During restless nights, watching her slumbering face lit by the moonlight filtering through the stone-lined window of the little house, he almost wished she were safely back in Ancona, despite how she'd suffered there.

Two evenings later, Daniel stood high on the walls of the city where the garrison had new orders to demolish the city's fortifications they'd been restoring for weeks. He spied the huge mass of troops pitching tents on the shore. They were clearly keeping their distance from the plague-ridden city. Daniel climbed down and walked to the camp, looking for his old company. He found Pierre and Sebastian, among others, and asked about the retreat.

"You're lucky to have been spared it," Pierre told him almost glee-fully. "We put whole villages to the torch as we marched through. And looted them, of course. You wouldn't have had the stomach for it."

Daniel flushed. He knew his men had thought him weak when he'd tried to stop the plunder of Jaffa. He was relieved not to be in command of them any longer.

"Which means the enemy won't pursue us at our most vulnerable, during the march back," Sebastian added.

Daniel's felt the sergeant's eyes resting on his hot face.

Pierre's voice grew more somber. "To say nothing of leaving our sick and wounded on the roadways."

"I'm lucky I could walk," Sebastian said, putting a hand to the arm in a sling. "I can still hear the poor wounded bastards pleading with us to take them along. 'I don't have plague.' And: 'If you have an ounce of compassion, don't abandon me to the mercies of the Turks.'"

"I'm still horrified that we lost to a barbarian like Djezzar!" Pierre moaned. "Can you believe Bonaparte just gave up?"

"Why the hell he kept insisting on attacking the same place is beyond me!" Sebastian grumbled.

"Morale is low, I take it?" Daniel asked.

"Low! Couldn't be any lower." Sebastian fiddled with his sword hilt. "And if you think anyone's looking forward to a desert crossing in late May . . ."

The thought made Daniel wince. "I'd better get home to my wife," he said. "She won't know why I'm so late."

"Henpecked already!" Sebastian crowed. "Didn't I tell you, Pierre—his wife's got him all tied up in her apron strings."

"At least," Daniel retorted, "I didn't sneak her on board *le Franklin* in an orderly's uniform." He grinned at Pierre. "You'll be glad to get back to Louise in Cairo, won't you?"

Pierre nodded. "Will you bring Mirelle with you?" he asked. "On the retreat?"

Daniel kicked at the sand. "Not sure what my orders will be."

Pierre walked off, but Sebastian took Daniel by the arm. "We miss you, lieutenant. We may tease you sometimes about your disapproval when we take our reward for victory—"

"Plunder and pillage, you mean," Daniel shot back.

Sebastian half-shrugged, "Call it what you will. It's what soldiers do. But it's not as if we don't respect you for wanting us to do better."

Daniel stared at him. "I thought you all thought me a weakling. When I think of Christophe . . ."

Sebastian shook his head, lips pursed. "You'd do better not comparing yourself to him all the time, you know. He's daring and dashing, sure, but dangerous on the battlefield. He forgets that his first responsibility is the safety of his men. You never forget that."

Daniel's face warmed, and he dug a foot back into the sand.

"You're shaping up to be a competent officer. Maybe quieter than some, but always reliable. That counts a great deal with the men. Sir." Sebastian clapped him on the back and walked off.

As Daniel started toward home, gratified by Sebastian's words, he passed a knot of officers, their voices loud and angry. Slowing down to listen, he identified the head military doctor, Desgenettes, arguing with Napoleon.

"If I were in your place," Napoleon was saying, "I would put an end to the suffering of our plague patients."

"How, exactly?" Desgenettes demanded, crossing his arms over his chest.

Napoleon shrugged. "You realize what danger they represent to the rest of us, don't you? If I were in their place, I would think it a favor to be mercifully dispatched. Don't you have enough opium to do the job?"

The doctor looked horrified. "I do not. And, as far as I'm concerned, my duty is to preserve life. Not take it." He turned on his heel and stalked down the beach.

Napoleon glared after the doctor, his face black, his chin jutting out.

"I may have enough opium, sir," said the French pharmacist, Royer.

"Yes, but who will administer it? You?"

"I know someone who might—the Turk, Hadj Mustafa. He's enough of a physician to do it."

Daniel moved swiftly on, not wanting to hear Napoleon's response.

A day later, Daniel stood outside the Armenian monastery, watching as the plague cases that had survived the march from Acre were moved inside. He, like the men who were carrying them in on litters, wrapped a kerchief over his mouth and nose. Unlike Christophe, whom he hoped was recovering in the Mount Carmel monastery, Daniel had never seen bubonic plague up close, and he was sickened by the look of these poor souls with their black pustules, the sickly odor wafting on the air, many of the men moaning in pain or delirious with fever.

"How many patients are there, now?" he asked one of the orderlies who had carried them in.

The man pulled down his mask and Daniel stepped back, wary of possible contagion. "I didn't count them, but it looked like about forty," he said. "Believe me, I just wanted to get out of there as quick as I could."

Daniel couldn't argue with that.

A day later, as the troops began to move out, Daniel received his orders. "I want you to stay with the calvary who will remain behind to guard the wounded and ill, the ones we can't yet move," Dommartin told him, leading the artillery troops on horseback. "You'll leave by boat when that's all done, along with Murat's men."

But the very next day, at dusk, Daniel was told to prepare to leave by morning. "We're done here," Colonel Garnier told him.

"Done? But the men in the monastery?" Daniel said, startled.

Garnier laughed. "Poor devils. They're all gone now—or will be by morning." He strode off.

Daniel, remembering the conversation he'd overheard between Dr. Desgenettes and the general, rushed to the Armenian monastery. But before he could steel himself to step inside the infected space, the Turkish physician, Hadj Mustafa, came out of the building with the French pharmacist, Royer, beside him.

"We have enough left over for the men at Stella Maris?" Mustafa was asking.

"Plenty," Royer said. "Desgenettes lied to Bonaparte, saying we didn't have nearly enough. But this is a better death than being tortured or beheaded by your countrymen."

The Turkish doctor shrugged. "The fortunes of war, my friend. But my faith counsels me to have compassion even for you infidels."

Royer grimaced at the assertion. "Of course, you've been paid well for your services here."

Mustafa laughed deep in his throat, spreading both hands wide, palms upward, in a gesture of compliance.

The two men moved on, and Daniel rushed inside. The monks were walking up and down the aisles of the hospital cots, administering last rites to any of the men still able to receive them. Others lay in a stupor, arms dangling listlessly out of the beds, while the corpses which had succumbed to the heavy dose of opium were covered head to toe with thin sheets.

Daniel stumbled back out. He brought up the contents of his stomach into the sea. *This is the last straw,* he thought bitterly. *How can I continue to serve a man who so callously disposes of men loyal to him?*

He remained, kneeling on the sand, recovering from his bout of nausea. The ocean breeze cooled his sweating brow. Wiping his mouth with his handkerchief dipped in sea water, he rose and brushed the sand off his legs, then started back to the little house, to prepare Mirelle for the journey. But then, something that Mustafa had asked struck him like a blow to his stomach: *"We have enough left over for the men at Stella Maris"*?

Stella Maris was where Christophe lay, recovering from his wounds.

That night, Daniel sat Mirelle down on the stone step leading to their little house and told her that he planned to make the trip up to Mount Carmel, to find Christophe and deliver him back to Paris. Somehow.

"Those are your orders?" she asked, looking at him wide-eyed, clearly unsure.

He wondered for a moment if he should lie to her. But he couldn't do it. "They are not," he said. "My orders are to return to Cairo with the calvary."

Her eyes grew even wider. "But won't you be considered a deserter?"

He stared out at the orange grove. In many ways, this was a beautiful country. But it had broken his heart. "Mirelle—I just can't serve Bonaparte any longer."

Her forehead scrunched up. "But . . . but why not? Surely after what Sebastian said . . . ?"

He swallowed, once, twice. "That just makes this harder. There's so much I haven't told you." He stared at the ground, afraid to meet her searching eyes. "In Italy, the general was amazing, invincible. One felt honored following him. But here—here it's been as if he's wearing blinders, ignoring all the pain and suffering he's caused." In a rush of words, he described the desert crossing, the thirst and heat, the men who fell out during the march, the ones who committed suicide rather than go on. He told her about Jaffa, about the rape and pillage and wholesale slaughter of the people there, the execution of the soldiers who had been promised mercy. By the time he finished, tears were streaming down her cheeks.

"But the worst thing," he continued, his voice breaking, "the worst thing . . ."

"The worst thing?" she prompted him, taking his hand.

He described the scene in the Armenian Monastery, how Napoleon had urged Desgenettes to use opium to murder his own plague-ridden soldiers, how the doctor had refused. "As Sebastian said, an officer's first duty is to the safety of his men. How could Bonaparte have betrayed them all like this, after they risked life and limb for him? It's monstrous." Daniel paused, thinking. "He must have gone to the Turkish doctor instead. He administered the killing draught. And now—the Turk's headed to Stella Maris. Where Christophe is."

She'd turned pale. "But Daniel, if you desert, won't they shoot you?"

"They'll have to catch me, first," he said. "I'll make sure they don't. But I want you to go with Ethan to Paris. He'll take you to my parents."

She wiped her face and sat up straight. "Absolutely not. I'm not leaving you."

"Mirelle, be sensible. How can I do this if I take you with me?"

She stood up. "How can you do this alone? You don't speak Arabic."

He'd already considered this. "I'll avoid people. Stay off the main roadways. With luck, I won't need to speak at all."

"And you actually think that will work?" She shook her head, her lips tightening. "I'm heartsick at the thought of Christophe's death, but I can't lose you, not now!"

"So you want me to simply give up on him? I wouldn't have thought that of you!" He rose, striding into the grove to contain his sudden spurt of anger.

But she followed him, reaching for his arm, pulling him to her. "You're right," she said slowly. "I know you can't give up on him. I don't want you to. But if you're asking me to be sensible, you need to be too. I've made a dangerous trip already—with Ethan. What if he comes with us?"

Ethan. It was a brilliant stroke. After the failure of the Proclamation to the Jews, his cousin planned on finding his way back to Paris. Finding a ship that would take him was proving impossible, so he decided to travel overland to Beirut. He hadn't left yet but if they were to convince him to go with them, they needed to find him. Now.

They located Ethan packing his belongings at the nearly deserted army camp.

"Yes, I'll take you," he said. "But you shouldn't just desert, Daniel. They'll shoot you if they catch you. Isn't there another way?"

"I don't plan to return to the army," Daniel said stubbornly. "I never should have joined."

Ethan shrugged. "They would have just conscripted you in a year or two." He turned to Mirelle, who was neatening his small store of shirts. "What do you think?"

She looked up from the pile of clothing. "Even if he's eventually going to desert, we should delay the army knowing as long as possible. Long enough for us to leave the country, to find somewhere they can't track him down. Can't we think of a reason for us to go north?"

Ethan nodded. "I was planning on traveling through Acre, to see Haim Farhi once more. He sent me a message, asking me to come to see him. I'm not sure why, but the general has agreed that I should. He doesn't know that I don't plan to return, of course. But it's a good excuse. I'll tell your commander I need you to come with me. And we'll go to Stella Maris on the way."

59

MAY 30
MOUNT CARMEL

Gasping, they reached the summit, Mirelle almost doubled over from the stitch in her side. Daniel put an arm around her waist and she melted to see the concern in his eyes.

As they climbed, she had been silently pondering the words David Morpurgo had chastised her with—how she had hurt people. She knew he was right. Somehow, she needed to make amends. But even with the guilt she carried, despite the trouble and danger surrounding them, she couldn't help the bubble of happiness inside her, being there with her husband, knowing he loved her as much as she loved him.

His confession about Napoleon, his decision to desert the French army, had shocked her at first. General Bonaparte was revered by the Jews of Italy, having freed them from the restrictions of the ghetto. And they had both been brought up to do their duty. It was one of the things she loved about Daniel. Yet, the more she thought about it, the better she felt about his choice to desert. Naturally the man she loved wanted nothing to do with the violence and destruction the army—any army—brought in its wake. He told her about the rabbi who'd preached *tikkun olam*—repairing the world. How could that be done in an army uniform, at the point of a musket, or through the collision of a cannon ball?

What would their future hold? She had no idea. But they would face it—together.

"Water?" Daniel asked, handing her his canteen.

Gratefully, she drank. "Do we know how far away we are now?"

Ethan laughed. "Look over there." He pointed.

She followed the direction of his finger. The square pink stone building glowed in the sunlight, surrounded by cypress and palm trees. Serene and quiet, it was smaller than Mirelle had expected—certainly less grand than the cathedral she'd grown up with but never entered back in Ancona. A cobbled walkway led them up to the narrow entrance. The stone tiles under their feet echoed strangely. The foyer and sanctuary were deserted.

"Hello?" Ethan called. "Is anyone here?"

No response. The three exchanged glances.

"I don't know much about Catholics, but wouldn't someone be on hand to greet pilgrims?" Mirelle asked, her voice wobbling.

"Perhaps they're supposed to observe silence," Ethan ventured. "But something doesn't feel right about this."

Heading upstairs and rounding a corner to the sick ward, Mirelle suddenly gasped. As they reached the doorway, they stood face-to-face with Christophe. Propped up in a chair, he cradled a musket on his legless lap, the stumps wrapped tightly in bandages, his uniform jacket draped over his hospital gown.

His eyes widened at the sight of them. "What the hell are you doing here?" he snapped.

"What in the world?" Ethan asked, his mouth dropping open. "Why aren't you in bed?"

Daniel reached for Mirelle's hand. "And what's with the rifle?"

Mirelle glanced past Christophe, toward the cots of groaning men.

"Where are the monks, Christophe?" She looked at Daniel, worried. "Are we too late? Have they been poisoned?"

"Poisoned?" Christophe stared at her. "Poisoned how?"

Daniel explained about the Turkish doctor who'd administered opium in Jaffa and who was supposedly on his way to do the same here.

"Hasn't come," Christophe said, shifting uncomfortably, his face contorted. "Would have been a mercy if he had."

Mirelle, seeing the pain on his face, picked up a pillow from an empty cot and placed it under his stumps. The touch of the rough bandages unnerved her, and she struggled not to let it show on her face.

He sunk down a little, shoulders relaxing as the pillow took some of the strain. But his voice was no less harsh as he said, "You must leave. Now."

"What? Why?" Daniel demanded, putting out a hand toward the musket. "And where are the monks?"

Christophe pulled the musket back to his chest. "Gone. Bloody cowards. Not that I blame them, not really. They couldn't have prevented the Turks from slaughtering us—and most of these men are dying, anyway."

"The Turks?" Ethan exclaimed. "The Turks are on their way?"

Christophe nodded. "That's what the monks were told by some of the villagers. Djezzar wants revenge on every Frenchman he can get his hands on—and we're easy pickings."

Ethan shut his eyes. "Then you're doomed. Djezzar is merciless."

"So you need to get out—and I mean now!"

"Not without you," Mirelle cried. "We came here for you."

Christophe reached out a hand and touched her arm. His smile was bitter. "I won't leave these men. Death doesn't scare me, not anymore." His eyes flickered down to rest on his stumps. "But you and Daniel—you have so much to live for. And I need you to write

Sappeira, tell her how I loved her. Tell her not to mourn. After all, what kind of husband would I have been to her, in this shape?" He swept his free arm over his legless lap. "She's better off without me."

Daniel set his jaw, moving his own rifle from his shoulder into his hands. "Ethan, take Mirelle. I'll stay."

The cry was forced from the very depths of her being. "You can't!"

But as they stood there, frozen in indecision, the room started to shake, as if from the rumble of a hundred feet. Wild cries reached them through the open windows.

"Daniel, go," Christophe said, through whitened lips. "Tell my mother and Uncle Alain what happened to me. Tell my wife that I love her. That I want her to love again, to have a happy life. That I will look down and bless her from the heaven she believes in."

Daniel put up a hand as if to stop his words, but Christophe shook his head and continued: "You love Mirelle, and she loves you. How can you abandon her? Staying here means certain death."

"But how can I . . . ?" Daniel looked haunted. "Christophe, let us carry you out."

The entrance door below was wrenched open. *"Allāhu 'akbar!"* The cry of fervent voices reverberated around the hall.

"Too late!" Christophe cried. "There's a back stair—there!" He gestured toward it. "It will bring you to the sanctuary. The stairs lead down to the grotto. Hide there!"

"We'll be trapped!" Daniel hoisted his musket up and pointed toward the door.

Mirelle blanched. Christophe, who had shifted his gaze toward the commotion downstairs, now glanced at her, a wry, brave smile crossing his face, breaking her heart. "I do this for love of you, sweet Mirelle," he told her softly. He turned his musket on his friend. "She needs you, and you know you can't save us. We're doomed. Go or I'll shoot you. Move—now!"

Ethan grabbed Daniel's arm. "It's our only chance. Come on!"

Daniel seized Mirelle's hand and the three of them dashed past the cots of the sick and wounded. Mirelle felt ill, thinking of the cruel death that awaited the soldiers, horrified especially for Christophe, her first love. Finding it hard to draw breath, she wondered if she'd made this harsh journey only to die in the arms of her husband. *If so,* she told herself, *it was worth it.*

The grotto—a bare cave where the prophet Elijah had supposedly lived—was tucked underneath the altar in the sanctuary. A marble monument stood in the middle, and the three of them huddled behind it. Daniel pulled Mirelle into his arms, whispering into her ear, "I love you."

She nestled against him, his heart beating rapidly against her chest. "If we don't survive," she murmured, "know that I'm not sorry."

He clasped her closer, one hand clutching his musket.

From far above, shots rang out, screams and cries of triumph mixing together. "They're killing them," Ethan muttered, flinching. "Christophe must be dead already."

A tear trickled down Mirelle's cheek. Daniel flicked it away with a finger, his jaw set.

Mirelle wondered how long the slaughter would last, wondered if the Turks would search the rest of the church. It seemed like hours that the three of them crouched there. The thud of boots descending made her cling even closer to her husband.

"I love . . ." she started to say, but he hushed her.

The Turks were in the sanctuary now, arguing, shouting. Ethan listened closely. Then—as if by miracle—the soldiers tromped out of the church, their victory yells ringing in Mirelle's ears.

"Wait!" Daniel hissed as she started to rise. He pulled her back.

Minutes ticked away. Finally, Daniel stood up. "I think it's safe now."

"We were saved by their faith," Ethan said solemnly. "They wanted to come down and search, but someone said they shouldn't go into the holy site of Ilyas—that's what they call Elijah—as warriors. It would be a desecration."

Mirelle felt as if her legs couldn't hold her. Daniel supported her as they crept out into the sunlight. The monastery, which had been wrapped in unnatural stillness earlier, now seemed haunted by the silence of the dead.

"Shouldn't we give Christophe a proper burial?" Mirelle asked.

Daniel and Ethan exchanged glances. "I'll go up," Daniel said. "Stay here."

He left and Mirelle heard him climbing the stairs. He moved slowly, with long pauses between halting steps.

"Won't he need our help?" she asked Ethan.

He shook his head. "He wants to spare you. The Turks aren't—gentle."

Daniel returned a few minutes later, his face green. "They took their heads, chopped their bodies into bits. Flayed them into pieces," he said. "It would be almost impossible to identify Christophe among the mess of . . ." He didn't finish.

Mirelle felt dizzy. She shut her eyes, putting a hand to her throat, another to her roiling stomach. Opening them, she saw Daniel staring at her, concern written on his face.

"Let's get out of here," he said quietly.

She stumbled out into the quiet courtyard, gagging at the trail of bloody boot prints the Turks had left in their wake.

60

June 6
Acre

A week later, they were at Haim Farhi's home in Acre. Daniel had hushed Mirelle when she'd protested coming.

"Surely he's an enemy," she'd said. "What if he delivers us to Djezzar? Why do we have to go there?"

But Ethan had reassured her. "He's a fellow Jew. He asked me to come and I have to admit, I'm curious why. You and Daniel don't need to accompany me, you know."

"If you're going, we are as well," Daniel insisted. "We won't abandon you to Djezzar. But I think you're right—Farhi isn't the type to betray us."

Daniel had been morose ever since they descended from Mount Carmel and made their way up the coast, keeping out of sight of the Turkish forces and the British ships. He mourned his friend, wishing he could have delivered him from such a gruesome end. He wasn't the only one. Mirelle wept for Christophe, trying to hide her tears from him. Before leaving the region, they would need to write to Sappeira. At least, Daniel consoled himself, Christophe had had the joy of his marriage to her, even for such a short time.

Daniel grieved even as he wondered what was next for them. Their future was still hazy. They needed some time to be still and consider. Perhaps they could find some peace at Farhi's home.

And indeed, they were welcomed as friends, not enemies. Mirelle, forewarned about the *katib*'s mutilated appearance, was able to look him right in his one eye as he bowed over her hand. Farhi congratulated Daniel on his beautiful bride, celebrating the new couple with a glass of wine in the inner courtyard before sending them off to rest. After dinner that night, they returned to the courtyard to discover why Farhi had made his unusual request.

"I've heard from most of the rabbis in Eretz Israel," he said. "They have decided it will be safest for them to pretend there never was a Proclamation to the Jews from General Bonaparte. Djezzar has already ruthlessly sanctioned riots in the Jewish Quarters of Tiberias and Safed. They want the violence to stop—and if he discovers they even spoke to you about this . . ."

"So that is the end of the dream," Ethan said sadly. "I knew it could not come to pass, of course, when I was in Jerusalem, but this makes it final."

"I must write to David Morpurgo and let him know," Mirelle said.

"I can find a way to get that letter to him," Farhi said. "You must be discreet in how you tell him, however. Can you do that?"

Mirelle nodded.

"We certainly won't tell anyone," Ethan agreed. "And I don't think General Bonaparte will say anything about it, either."

"He doesn't look back," Daniel added. "Not him."

"My sources tell me he's halfway to Cairo right now," Farhi told them. "Pretending that he was victorious here. I've had to convince Djezzar that the newspaper accounts and the general's declarations of triumph are simply so many lies. Otherwise, he would chase after the French troops to disprove their claims."

Daniel shifted in his seat, staring at the stones underfoot.

"What is it?" Mirelle asked, softly.

"I just wonder—Bonaparte never needed to lie before. Not in Italy. But here—this entire expedition has been a disaster. A mistake."

"One also wonders what he'll do next," Farhi nodded. "From my reading of him, he won't let this mistake stop his ambitions. Whatever they may be."

Daniel waved an impatient hand. "He's welcome to them. I want no part of them, however."

"No." Farhi looked at Daniel out of his one eye. "What will you do now? All of you?"

"I'm going to return to Paris as soon as I can find a way back. Probably go to Beirut and find passage there," Ethan said. "I am certain there are interesting days ahead for the French Republic—and much to write about."

"So you are going to write again?" Mirelle asked. "My papa would be so pleased to hear it." She hesitated for a moment, then added, "And so would Adara."

The darkness that Daniel had noticed at any mention of Ethan's wife flickered swiftly over his cousin's face, but then he nodded, half smiling. "I believe she would be," he said softly.

"And you?" Farhi asked, his one eye fixed on Daniel's downturned face.

Daniel hesitated, but then decided to gamble that Farhi would not betray him to the French. "I can't return to France—I'd be shot as a deserter. Mirelle can't go home to Ancona. And we don't want to stay here."

"You do realize," Farhi said slowly, "that I can find a way to let your commander know you were at the monastery during the attack. Which means they'll assume you're dead. So you're free to go and do whatever you want."

Daniel nodded. He had wondered the same, but it seemed callous to use the massacre in that way. Yet what would Christophe have wanted him to do? Christophe's last act of friendship had been to save them—for Mirelle's sake, whom he had once loved. For Daniel's sake, for all the years they had shared. Daniel would honor his friend's sacrifice.

Mirelle met his gaze, her face alight. "So we only need to decide where to go," she whispered.

"If I were in your shoes," the *katib* said, "I'd consider the new world. I've heard Jews are not persecuted there. That freedom of religion is guaranteed by the new American republic."

"America?" Flabbergasted, Daniel considered the possibility. "But what would I do there?"

"Daniel." Ethan laughed. "You're a printer. You'll find work as a printer, of course. Eventually own your own shop. Which Mirelle can manage."

Mirelle drew in a deep breath, looking excited.

"I can arrange for a passage for you both," Farhi said. "The sooner you leave the country, the less chance I have of Djezzar finding out that I helped you—which he would not appreciate in his current mood."

Mirelle and Daniel looked at one another. Daniel leaned forward and took her hand, holding it to his heart. "America," they whispered in unison.

Three days later they boarded a Portuguese schooner out of the port of Acre. It would take them first to Lisbon, and from there, they would board a ship bound for Boston. Leaning on the railing, heedless of the sea spray washing over them, they stood shoulder to shoulder, arms about one another.

"A new world," Mirelle murmured, as Daniel looked behind, watching Acre grow ever smaller, gazing at the city's fortifications that Napoleon could not breach. "A new life. I wonder what it will turn out to be like?"

Epilogue

August 30
Cairo

Esteemed katib,

You have asked me my thoughts on what is happening now in Cairo, and I can tell you that the city is in a state of utter confusion. For a week ago, unbeknownst even to his faithful followers, the Şāri 'Askar, this Napoleon Bonaparte who bedeviled us with his cannon and befouled our Islamic nation by his rule, sailed away in secret to his own country. I hear from the French scholars at the so-called Institute of Egypt that he has political aspirations that can only be realized if he reaches Paris. As you may know, our law forbids us cursing a single person, unless they are a wrongdoer or oppressor—yet surely this man is both. And so, may he be removed from the mercy of Allah—worse than that, no one can say.

He leaves behind his paramour, the woman they call "Cleopatra," that loose woman he seduced out of the arms of her husband. Zina, we Muslims believe, being that unlawful intercourse between any aside from husband and wife, should be punished by a hundred lashes. But instead, she continues to be rewarded for her sin by being taken up by the new commander, General Kléber. He, it is said, cursed Bonaparte when he discovered how he had abandoned his own troops. Excuse me for repeating the vulgarity of this infidel, but I'm told he said, "That bugger has deserted us with his pants full of shit! When we get back to Europe, we'll rub his face in it!"

So we are still under the thumb of the French, but one assumes it will not be for long, for this Kléber is negotiating with the British seaman who vanquished Bonaparte in Acre, Sir Sidney Smith. Let us pray that we will soon be free of these infidels and that our country will once again be under Muslim rule. It is in Allah's hands, as always, and I have ultimate faith that he will not desert us.

In many ways, the last couple of years resembled that optical illusion that the French named a mirage. The French hoped to find blessed water here in Egypt, groped stubbornly toward it, utterly convinced of their false vision. But they instead were greeted with the harsh reality of acre after acre of arid desert sand.

One more note that may interest you, esteemed katib, as it fascinated me. At Rosetta this past month, a French soldier stumbled across a black basalt slab. I've been told by the French archeologists of the so-called Institute of Egypt that this is a remarkable discovery. For it contains passages in Greek, Egyptian hieroglyphics, and ancient Egyptian script. According to them, it honors Ptolemy V—and most importantly, that all three passages contain the same text. The Frenchmen are incredibly excited, feeling it will help them uncover the secrets of our ancient language. I only wish my friend, Ethan the Jew, were still here to enjoy this momentous find. Surely he has the language acumen to be able to assist in deciphering it. One wonders where he is and if he is still alive. Unlike most infidels, he is worthy of my friendship and I only wish he shall find solace in his grief for his lost family.

I must break off here, for Hasani is calling me to come admire my newborn son. I truly hope these reports have been useful to you, katib. *I will of course continue writing them, along with my chronicle of the French occupation, until we rid ourselves of these worthless French mongrels.*

Peace be upon you and your family with the mercy and blessings of Allah, whom you call Lord.

Abd al-Rahman al-Jabartī

AUTHOR'S NOTE

I had always planned to write a sequel to *Beyond the Ghetto Gates*, chronicling Napoleon's somewhat absurd expedition to Egypt and Israel, continuing Mirelle, Daniel, and Christophe's story. Having been in a long-distance relationship myself early in my twenties, before the advent of email and the Internet, I knew enough about yearning for physical letters from my soon-to-be husband to extrapolate how much worse that must have been for Mirelle and Daniel, separated not only by distance but also by a blockade preventing any communication whatsoever.

As I researched the Egyptian campaign, I became fascinated by Napoleon's attempts to win over the Muslim population of Egypt by claiming to be an adherent of Islam himself. I wanted to portray the Egyptian side of the conflict accurately. Luckily for me, I found *Napoleon in Egypt: Al-Jabartī's Chronicle of the French Occupation, 1798*. Abd al-Rahman al-Jabartī was a real-life Egyptian whose perceptions of the French were invaluable to this novel. I will note that his reports to Haim Farhi, another real-life character, are pure fiction. Far from being an expert in Islam myself, I had *Napoleon's Mirage* read by an Egyptian Muslim reader from Salt and Sage Books, which specializes in sensitivity readings. I am grateful to my sensitivity reader for correcting my inadvertent mistakes as well as my Arabic. Any errors that remain are my own.

The absolute brutality of war in this novel, and Napoleon's myriad mistakes during this campaign, may shock some readers. Writing this book during a certain American president's term, it was impossible not to draw comparisons to Napoleon's insistence that he was infallible. Perhaps the young general learned some important lessons from this expedition; it wouldn't be until encountering winter in Russia that he would repeat errors on a similar scale to those committed in the summertime desert.

I owe the creation of Jacopo the baker to fellow author Claudia Long, who invented him in her blog post, "Dear Madam Mariana, advice for the lovelorn" when Mirelle "wrote" her, wondering why she had not heard from Daniel and what to do about it. My affection for the British Baking Show helped form Jacopo's pastry and bread experiments. I enjoyed this character and do hope he finds the love he deserves outside the pages of this novel.

The big question of the book—namely, did Napoleon really issue a Proclamation to the Jews while in Egypt and Israel, offering support for the Jewish homeland—remains contentious. I experienced the controversy firsthand while attending a virtual panel at the Napoleonic Historical Society. During the Q&A, I revealed what I was writing next, and was astonished at the heat of the two historians who took either side of the question and debated it on the spot. As a writer of fiction, of course, I am free to imagine that Napoleon did send out his proclamation—and hope that some of my fictional solutions to why there is so little evidence of this will satisfy my readers if not the historians.

Of course readers always ask: who is real and who imagined in this work of fiction? The real-life characters include all of Napoleon's officers; his "Cleopatra" and her unfortunate husband; Denon and the other savants; and all the Muslim characters in the novel, including al-Jabartī and the brutal Djezzar. Haim Farhi, with all his disfigure-ments, was also real, as were the British seamen. David and Ezekiel Morpurgo, Francesca Marotti and her daughter Barbara, as noted in *Beyond the Ghetto Gates*, were actual people, but Dolce was not, nor was Mirelle, her mother, or any of the other characters in Ancona. And Daniel, Christophe, and Ethan were all imagined as well.

As for the events of *Napoleon's Mirage*, I used the following books primarily: Paul Strathern's *Napoleon in Egypt*, J. Christopher Herold's *Bonaparte in Egypt*, Gareth Glover's *The Forgotten War Against Napoleon*, Andrew Roberts's *Napoleon*, Abd al-Rahman Al-Jabartī's *Napoleon in Egypt: Al-Jabartī's Chronicle of the French Occupation, 1798*, Nina Burleigh's *Mirage: Napoleon's Scientists and the Unveiling of Egypt*, and Nathan Schur's *Napoleon in the Holy Land*. Naturally, there were many other sources, including David J. Markham's "Napoleon in the Middle East 1798–1799" and his photos of the French Institute of Egypt (posted on Facebook), Allen Z. Hertz's "Jews, Napoleon, and the Ottoman Empire: The 1797–1799 Proclamations to the Jews," Shmuel Moreh's "Napoleon and the French Impact on Egyptian Society in the Eyes of Al-Jabartī," and Michael Waas's "The Wall that Stopped Napoleon: Ẓāhir al-'Umar al-Zaydānī's Wall and the Siege of 1799." All of the newspaper items cited by David Morpurgo were published on the dates noted. Of course, this is far from a comprehensive list of the many sources I consulted.

I sincerely hope the readers who were wondering what was next for Mirelle, Daniel, and Christophe at the end of *Beyond the Ghetto Gates* are now satisfied by this conclusion of their story.

Acknowledgments

I have many people to thank for their contributions to this novel. First and foremost, Vinessa diSousa, who led her amazing Revision workshop as part of The Writers Circle and who edited the full novel. In Vinessa's class I received valuable input from my fellow writers: Christina Axelrod, Mally Becker, Margaret Walsh, Naomi Tsvirko, Tarynne Lopez, and Ariel Lopez. As always, I need to thank Judith Lindbergh, who founded The Writers Circle and accepted me as a partner in the endeavor, giving me "the writers life" that allows me to gain inspiration from all my students and to focus on my own writing.

Other early readers include Alex Cameron and Margaret Rodenberg, whose comments helped reshape parts of the novel. I am also grateful to Claudia Long, whose blog "Dear Madam Mariana, advice for the lovelorn" resulted in the creation of Jacopo the baker.

Of course I must also thank the team at She Writes Press, including Brooke Warner, Lauren Wise, and Julie Metz, among others.

I'm grateful to my final proofreaders, Matthew Kreps and Mally Becker, because I'd gone utterly blind by this last round.

As always, I must thank my husband, Steve, who instantly seeks out and buys the research books I need and who understands that I need hundreds of quiet hours tapping away at the computer without interruption.

And I am grateful to all the readers of *Beyond the Ghetto Gates*, whose reactions to the end of that novel spurred me on to write this one. I hope they will agree that I've given Mirelle and Daniel at least— poor Christophe!—the conclusion they deserved.

About the Author

photo credit: Beth Forester

Michelle Cameron is the author of *Babylon: A Novel of Jewish Captivity* (Wicked Son, 2023); *Beyond the Ghetto Gates,* which was awarded a Silver Medal in Historical Fiction by the Independent Book Publishers, won First Place/Best of Category in the Chanticleer Goethe Awards, and was a Foreword Indies finalist (She Writes Press, 2020); *The Fruit of Her Hands: The Story of Shira of Ashkenaz* (Simon & Schuster's Pocket Books, 2009); and *In the Shadow of the Globe* (Lit Pot Press, 2003), which was named Shakespeare Theatre of NJ's 2003-04 Winter Book Selection and performed at the Stella Adler Studio's Shakespeare Benefit. A director of The Writers Circle, Michelle teaches creative writing to children, teens, and adults in New Jersey and virtually. Residing with her husband in Chatham, NJ, she has two grown sons of whom she is inordinately proud.

Looking for your next great read?

We can help!

Visit www.shewritespress.com/next-read
or scan the QR code below for a list
of our recommended titles.

She Writes Press is an award-winning
independent publishing company founded to
serve women writers everywhere.